JONAH'S LANDING

A NOVEL

KAREN L. KURTZ

Author's Notes: Facts and Fiction in *JONAH'S LANDING* and Acknowledgements can be found at the end of the novel.

Springhouse Press, Canada
ISBN 978-1-0688076-0-2 (paperback)
ISBN 978-1-0688076-1-9 (e-book)

Book design by Laura Boyle
Front cover image credit: Miłosz Guzowski / Alamy Stock Photo

*For Bryan and Karla — wise old souls who have inspired
and taught me from the first moment I held them.*

For Paul, my beloved

CHAPTER ONE

The Grove

They shot Dolly. And the rest of the horses, too. Papa said nothing could be done for them. Men in long white aprons led the horses out of the stables to somewhere out back. Ellie counted the shots. Six. She pressed her fists to her eyes to dry them and stomped into the parlor. "Why didn't you let me say goodbye to Dolly?"

Mama's hands flew up, her fingers taut. "Eleanor, have you listened to anything? *People can die* from this disease! Even the stable hand may have glanders now!" Mama never called Old Martin by his name, even though he'd been taking care of the McAllister family's horses ever since Papa was a boy and maybe even before that.

"Are they going to shoot Old Martin, too?"

"*Eleanor!*" Mama had fire in her eyes now.

"Ellie! That's enough," Papa said. His woolen scarf was still around his neck as he stood with his back toward the fireplace.

Ellie didn't know why she had blurted out such a mean thing. She loved Old Martin and never wanted anything bad to happen to him. Her cheeks reddened with shame.

"Your mother is right," Papa said. "You girls may not go anywhere near the stables until we say so. Do you both understand?"

Ten-year-old Ellie nodded.

"Charlotte?"

Charlie, who was four years older, said, "Of course, I won't." She glared at Ellie like she always did whenever Mama had a conniption, as if it were all Ellie's fault. She went in a huff up the stairs.

"Ellie, go to your room, too," Papa said.

Mama's shoulders were shaking. Papa wrapped his arms around her and said, "We don't know that Martin's caught anything, Genevieve. I suspect it's just grief he's feeling."

Ellie slammed her bedroom door and ran to the south window. She pressed her hand against the cold windowpane, melting a spyhole in the frost. When the black smoke billowed up behind the stables, her head got hot, as if she were burning in the fire with Dolly.

Ellie flopped on her bed. She couldn't help but hear the argument that came through the iron grate in the floor.

"Aaron, what are you going to do about this *horrid* disease?" Mama said.

"The County Health Department is incinerating the carcasses, and they will disinfect the stables before they leave today. We're to let it sit for a month."

"I don't think I can bear another god-forsaken winter here." Mama's voice went a few notes higher. "I'm done living in Chestnut Hill. You said this would only be temporary until you straightened out the debacle your father left behind. That was almost four years ago, Aaron! Here we are still living in your uncle's cottage like paupers with no home. This is not how I want to raise our daughters!"

Papa's voice got louder. "This is hardly a pauper's life! Uncle James has been very generous leasing this home to us. And I think our girls have enjoyed living here."

"Eleanor needs a proper school. Her manners are atrocious for a ten-year-old. And I don't like Charlotte having the stigma of being from the country while she's attending Ogontz."

"Stigma? The Ogontz school *is* in the country! That's one of their selling points. The fresh air and pure water are why they charge so much!"

"I want our daughters to grow up in Rittenhouse Square." Mama was crying again.

"You know attorneys don't make enough income to live there."

"We have more than enough of mine. If you weren't too proud to use it."

Papa always got quiet when Mama brought up her inheritance. His inheritance had disappeared when Grandpa McAllister lost almost everything in his Northern Pacific Railroad investment. Mama always called it a debacle. Papa and Aunt Tess didn't even find out how bad it was until Grandpa died four years ago. They had to sell everything, even the townhouse in Philadelphia where Ellie had lived her first six years. That was when their family moved to the stone house in Chestnut Hill. Papa said he wanted to be free and clear from his father's affairs before they moved again.

Ellie hoped they wouldn't go anywhere. She loved her riding lessons in Chestnut Hill. Old Martin said he never saw a girl take to a horse the way she did. He let her take Dolly on the trail in the woods. Her heart ached as she thought how Chestnut Hill would never be the same without Dolly.

"I'm sorry, Genevieve. I know it's hard on you." Papa's voice was so soft, Ellie had to lean over the end of her bed to hear. "My father's estate will close by spring," he said. "And I've already had Weston make inquiries about some properties we could lease in Philly. I didn't want to bring it up before I heard what he's found."

"Lease! Why would we want to lease another place?"

"It will take some time for us to find a home that I can afford and one which will meet your standards," he said. "I promise you if we take our time, we'll find the right one."

Ellie curled into a ball. Dolly was gone, and now Papa was agreeing to move to Philadelphia. She let herself cry with soundless wails.

* * *

On the sixth of January, three days after Charlie went back to Ogontz, a blizzard blew over the Atlantic coast, dropping almost a foot of snow. The chimney howled and the shutters rattled, one after another. Mama paced and said it would be a week before even a sleigh could get through. Ellie finished her breakfast quietly and asked Papa if she could be excused. He gazed at her for a moment and said, "My girl's been awfully quiet the last few days. Are you feeling well?"

"I'm fine, Papa." But she wasn't. There was a sadness she couldn't explain to anyone. It was as if something inside of her had died with Dolly. She didn't speak to Mama unless she absolutely had to. She didn't even yelp when Mama was yanking the brush too hard through her tangle of auburn curls and pulling them tightly into braids.

"Eleanor, that sour expression will become permanent if you keep this up. A young lady with freckles needs to cultivate a pleasant smile." Mama was always letting Ellie know she had homely features but said it as if she were giving kind advice on how to make up for this flaw. Charlie had natural beauty, and Mama fawned over her. It was clear that she liked Charlie better, but Ellie was Papa's favorite. Everyone knew these things but would never say them aloud.

Ellie was sure Papa liked her freckles and her auburn hair, even if it was always falling out of her braids and curling around her face. He said her hair and eyes perfectly matched his lucky buckeye, which was why sometimes he called her his "little buckeye." Papa was a boy when his father gave him a lucky buckeye nut. When Grandpa McAllister died, Papa drilled a hole in the buckeye and poked a blue ribbon through it so Ellie could wear it as a necklace. "It's something your Grandpa would have wanted you to have," he said.

"But Papa," Ellie said, "Grandpa gave that to *you* for good luck."

"I'm already the luckiest man to have two fine daughters," he said.

Mama never liked the buckeye necklace. She said it wasn't appropriate to wear such a thing out in public, but Papa said, "Really, Genevieve? Does it matter?" And Mama pinched her lips together. Ellie usually tucked it inside her dress whenever they went anywhere so that Mama and Papa wouldn't argue about it. Charlie said the bump under Ellie's dress looked like a pathetic attempt to sprout a breast.

* * *

After two days of wild winds, it was the silence that woke her on the third morning. Ellie stretched out from under her warm duvet toward the window by her bed. She scratched away the frost on the lower pane. As far as she could see, white waves rippled over the fields.

The house was quiet, but she could smell Papa's pipe smoke when she crept by his study. Maggie was in the kitchen humming Scottish tunes as she kneaded and smacked the dough for her bread. In the back hall Ellie pulled on her leggings, galoshes, and winter layers. The outside door to the garden pushed into a soft drift, and she jumped into the deepest part, sinking up to her chest. But then she saw how the storm had whittled a winding path between drifts. In some places, the stubble of grass crunched beneath her feet. When Ellie reached the pasture, she discovered the surface had been whipped into a hard meringue that held her weight as she scrambled and sometimes slid toward the woods. The dry-stone fence marked the edge of their property, where she and Dolly had always turned around. But today something caught her eye at the knoll that rose up out of the Henderson pasture. A raven circled above it and then dropped unexpectedly into the pines on the top. Ellie wasn't supposed to trespass on their neighbor's property, but she had to find out where the raven had gone.

The frozen field was bare in places. Near the knoll, the sun had softened the drifts, and she plunged through the glazed surface several times. She was sweaty when she reached the top of the hill and slid under the low pine branches.

As she stood up inside the grove, words went out of her head. It wasn't like the times when she couldn't remember the right word to use. No words had ever been invented to describe this place.

Only a thin layer of snow had fallen on the soft carpet of pine needles beneath her. She stepped hesitantly toward the center of the trees, where massive trunks had grown to a height beyond what she could see. Streamers of sunlight trickled through the boughs to the stillness around her. Then there was a faint sound of air sifting between the blue-green needles as if whispering to her. It was just an ordinary word—*breathe*.

She breathed.

The very moment she pushed out her white breath, the boughs high above her came to life, sprinkling snow dust on her face. She trembled. The trees had called to her. And *her own breath had moved them.*

Ellie felt something happy bubbling up inside of her. She thought of how people said the church was the "house of God," but she was now sure she had found the place where God really lived. It was a … *sacred* grove. She didn't want to tell anyone else about what had happened here.

All Ellie could think about after that was trees. She asked Papa so many questions that he brought back a tree identification book for her from Philadelphia. The cover had shiny, embossed letters, drawn to look like golden tree roots spelling the title, *The Trees of North-Eastern America.* It fit perfectly in her red satchel that had a strap she wore across her chest whenever she went walking. If she met a new tree, she looked for its page and wrote the date and her own notes in the margin. Papa said it was her book, and she could write in it if she wanted to.

Mama was not convinced that this book was a good thing. "Aaron, you are just encouraging this peculiar ar*bore*al obsession Eleanor has!" Mama made it sound like a terrible disease Ellie had caught.

Ellie didn't return to her sacred grove until a week before their family was scheduled to move to Philadelphia. Something had been bothering her. In bible stories, people brought offerings to God. She wanted to give an offering to her grove before she moved away. Something that would be a true sacrifice. As moving day came closer, she grew more worried that she still didn't know what to give to it. On the first Saturday after school was out in June, Ellie woke up and knew what her gift should be. She felt sad about the sacrifice part. She picked at her breakfast.

"Such a forlorn expression!" Mama felt Ellie's forehead. "You need to smile, Eleanor."

All morning, Ellie imagined other things she could give instead, and she almost changed her mind. But then she realized that nothing less would do. As soon as Mama and Charlie went shopping that afternoon, she packed her red satchel and lifted the strap over her head. Her bag bounced against her hip as she walked slowly to the knoll.

There were wildflowers and fresh green blades poking through the clumps of dried, yellow-white grass on the slope up to the grove. Ellie ducked under the pine branches and felt the sense of awe she remembered from the first time. She didn't wait for the trees to speak to her. She walked to the center of the grove and looked up.

"I–I have to move away … to Philadelphia," she said. Her voice sounded so small that she cleared her throat and spoke louder. "I want to give you a gift to … to commemorate…" Ellie tried to remember the words she had heard on solemn occasions, like when a memorial was dedicated to dead soldiers from the War of the Rebellion, but she couldn't think of how to end it. Instead, she just knelt down and opened the buckle of her satchel. Her hands trembled as she removed a pair of scissors from her bag. Ellie pulled her braids forward and firmly snipped one and then the other. She laid the plaited, auburn bundles on the earth. She couldn't keep her tears from wetting her cheeks as she stared at what she'd done. It was a worthy sacrifice. She reached her hand up to her neck to feel the stubs that were already curling, free from any constraints.

Ellie stood up and prepared herself for the consequences.

* * *

Papa let Ellie fidget for the longest time while he studied her from across his desk. She stared at the scuffs on her shoes until he cleared his throat. When she glanced at him the crease between his eyebrows had deepened, and his forehead had the little dent he got when he felt sad instead of angry. "Ellie, why would you do such a thing to your mother?"

Ellie was confused by his question. "I didn't do it because of Mama." She knew he was waiting for some kind of explanation. "It–it was just something I had to do. I can't say why."

"You don't *know* why, or you *won't say* why. Which is it?"

"I … I have a good reason, Papa. I just can't say it."

He folded his fingers and studied her again, but this time she looked at him.

"All right, Ellie," he said at last. "There's been enough excitement tonight. I think it's best you stay in your room. I'll ask Maggie to bring a plate up for dinner."

* * *

Mama had a headache that kept her in bed the next day. No one went to church.

Charlie combed Ellie's hair in front of the standing mirror and couldn't keep from laughing. "You are such an idiot. Mama's never going to get over this one."

At least it felt like Charlie was getting back to normal. She had gone off to a boarding school in September and had come back looking grown up and wanting to be called "Charlotte," which Ellie ignored. It had seemed like all Charlie wanted to do was to draw sketches for her and Mama's dresses from the fashion ads Aunt Lucie had sent from Paris.

Later, Charlie slipped a cartoon she had drawn under Ellie's bedroom door. It was a girl with hair sticking out all over. *Fuzz head* was all it said. There were times when Ellie loved her older sister.

After lunch dishes were put away, Maggie had Ellie lean over the sink while she poured warm water over her head. Then she spread a picnic cloth on the kitchen floor and had her sit in the middle on a high stool. She draped a kitchen towel over Ellie's shoulders and began snipping away at the jagged ends of hair. Finally, she stepped back, and had Ellie twist around on the stool in every direction. "I confess I missed my calling as a barber!" Maggie said and laughed. "You know, Ellie, you're quite a pretty lass!"

Ellie hopped down and hugged her, sinking into Maggie's fleshy arms and the soft mounds of her body.

That night before bed, Ellie stood at the mirror. She shook her hair and watched the curls bounce and fall over her eye. The lightness of it, the looseness! Mama had woven those tight braids every day for as long as she could remember. If strands popped out of the braids, Mama always pursed her lips and tsked, as if the curls were being deliberately unruly and defiant toward her. Ellie scowled. She thought about what Papa had said. It hadn't occurred to her to cut off her braids to spite Mama, but it would have made a worthy sacrifice, too. Somehow, she felt ugly inside just knowing that.

CHAPTER TWO

The Outing

July 1893

It was the first time in all ten years of her life that Ellie had been west of Pennsylvania. The Pullman sleeper on the Western Express to Cleveland had fancy chandeliers hanging high above the thick-carpeted aisle. Draperies were drawn between the sections, forming private compartments. It reminded Ellie of the blanket houses she and Charlie used to make under their dining table on rainy days. Their family's berth had a bed that pulled down from the ceiling for Ellie and Charlie to share. The seat cushions on two sofas below them slid together to make a bed for Mama. Papa said his legs were too long, and he'd rather sleep in an armchair in the drawing room. No one was allowed to use the toilet in the washroom until the train moved out of the city. It flushed right onto the tracks, and cool air came up when the toilet flap opened.

After Charlie fell asleep, Ellie listened to the snoring and coughing from people in the other curtained sections. She could hardly breathe in this small space, and her heart began to pound. Then she discovered the train had a heartbeat of its own that calmed her if she closed her eyes and listened to its clackety thump. She heard the locomotive's long-short-long whistle-moan, which slithered over her and had a way of pulling her with it. Ellie let it carry her out of the tiny berth. She floated above the train and imagined Dolly galloping out of the steam clouds that spiraled from the engine's stack.

* * *

Early in the morning their train stopped thirty minutes in Pittsburgh. When they returned from the dining car, their beds and curtains had been tucked away. The sleeping car was transformed into a parlor. Papa spent most of the morning in the smoking room, where he could read his newspaper in peace. Charlie entertained Mama with stories about Ogontz while they held their embroidery hoops and sewed. They were on the other velvet sofa facing Ellie's, where she sat with her legs tucked under her and her body turned so she could lean against the cool glass of the window.

Ellie watched the steep slopes of the Alleghenies melt into the rolling foothills of Eastern Ohio. She kept thinking about how she would be riding Mr. Ferris's big wheel at the 1893 Chicago World's Fair in a few days. The *Philadelphia Inquirer* said the wheel could hold two thousand people at the same time. Mama had told her to stop nattering on about the wheel and how many people it could hold, or else Ellie wouldn't be one of them. At least Mama didn't act cross about her haircut anymore, except whenever Ellie forgot to wear a wide ribbon to hold her curls back from her face.

On their way to Chicago, they would be stopping in Canton, Ohio to visit Isaac Taylor's family. He and Papa were boyhood friends. The Taylors used to have two daughters but Pansy, who was Ellie's age, got sick and died three years ago, when she was seven. Mama said *no one* was to ask the Taylors questions about her. Their older girl, Opal, was fourteen like Charlie, and they had already been writing letters to each other even though they hadn't ever met.

At Cleveland they boarded a smaller train that took them to the Canton station. Ellie pulled her buckeye necklace out from the bodice of her dress and hoped that Mama wouldn't notice. She especially wanted to wear it here because Ohioans were called "buckeyes." The steam valves were still hissing when they stepped onto the platform. Papa called out, "Isaac, how good to see you!" He strode forward to shake hands with a tall, slender man who laughed and thumped him on the shoulder. Mr. Taylor's dark mustache was full like Papa's but had streaks of gray.

Mr. Taylor removed his hat when he bowed to Mama, and her gloved hand floated gracefully up to his lips. Then he bowed his head toward Charlie and said, "Opal is looking forward to meeting you, Charlotte." When it was Ellie's turn, he said, "What a fine buckeye you have, Eleanor! You must have known Ohio is called the buckeye state!"

"Yes! And that's all because William Henry Harrison gave Ohio Buckeye nuts as souvenirs when he was campaigning for president!"

He laughed. "You have learned your history well, young lady!"

She decided she liked him.

* * *

Mrs. Taylor waved from the verandah as their carriage approached the portico. She had a pleasant face and reddish-gold hair pulled up into a bun like Mama's, but loose strands caught the sunlight and seemed to glow around her head. A tall girl with sandy hair hurried down the stairs to open the carriage door. Opal and Charlie hugged the minute they met each other and started talking as if they had been in the middle of a conversation. Mrs. Taylor touched Ellie's curls and said, "What beautiful hair you have! It becomes you." Ellie couldn't help but smirk, but Mama acted as if she didn't see it.

Ellie noticed right away that informalities were allowed here. Mrs. Taylor even suggested that the adults use their given names. "Please call me Flora," she said to Mama.

Ellie glanced up, but Mama didn't even raise her eyebrow and replied, "Then you must call me Genevieve." Sometimes Mama was surprising.

They were shown to their guest rooms, where their trunks had been delivered by way of the back stairs. "You must be exhausted," Mrs. Taylor said and suggested they "settle in" a bit before dinner. When she opened the door to Ellie's room, the afternoon sunlight illuminated splashes of yellow and purple pansies all through the room. The bedspread and even the pillowslips were embroidered with that flower.

Ellies' eyes grew wide. "Pansies."

"Yes, this was her room," Mrs. Taylor said.

"Oh! I meant the flowers, not your daughter."

"Eleanor." Mama's voice had a frown in it.

"I'm sorry. I–I didn't mean to say that."

Mrs. Taylor smiled. "It's all right. You may talk about Pansy. She would have been ten like you, and I think you would have been fast friends. She was spirited, like you."

Ellie didn't step into Pansy's room yet. There was something she needed to know. "Did she … die here?"

"*Eleanor!*"

Ellie looked up at Mama, who was clearly appalled.

But Mrs. Taylor acted as if it were the most normal question. "No, we were in Pennsylvania when Pansy died. She caught cholera when we were visiting Isaac's mother. She had the best of care there, but she slipped away after only a few days." Mrs. Taylor's eyes watered, and she dabbed them with her fingers. "We've kept her room the way it was, decorated with her name-flower, as you can see."

Ellie stepped into the room and spun around to take in all the pansies. "How wonderful to be named for a flower."

* * *

Charlie and Opal ran up to their room after dinner. Ellie followed the adults to the parlor. Papa and Mr. Taylor seemed like two brothers talking about when they were boys. They exchanged real laughs that made their bellies bounce, not the kind that grown-ups usually make when they are trying to be polite. Ellie always thought those polite laughs sounded like the nickering a horse makes when he's been harnessed too long and would rather be running free.

Mr. Taylor said, "You are all invited to our Canton Outing Club Picnic at Congress Lake tomorrow."

"I know that lake!" Ellie said. "It was the stop where our water tank for the engine was filled."

"Good observation, Ellie. Trains take on water there twice a day. We'll catch the ten o'clock train from Canton in the morning and then come home on the late-afternoon train."

"That sounds splendid," said Papa, who liked adventures more than Mama did.

Ellie saw Mama's shoulders rise a little, and her hand flew up to her cheek. "My goodness, how does one spend an entire day at a lake?"

"Oh, it's delightful, Genevieve!" Mrs. Taylor said. "The railroad company has built cottages, a new hotel, and they have a dance pavilion that extends out over the lake. There are amusements—a carousel, a bowling alley, and lovely trails in the woods. I believe they have in mind to create a luxury resort such as those up on Lake Erie. And it's a perfectly respectable place now for families."

"Yes, the Temperance Society saw to that more than a decade ago," Mr. Taylor said. He didn't seem happy about that. "Those zealous dogmatists pressured the resort to ban alcohol and beer altogether."

Mrs. Taylor nodded. "But Congress Lake was a rowdy place in the early eighties. The dances were well attended, but they often ended in saloon brawls. Now the resort caters to family excursions, Sunday School picnics, and community events. Thousands of people come to some events."

"We'll have a lovely day, I'm sure," Mama said. Her hand fluttered over her mouth to cover a yawn.

Mrs. Taylor shooed everyone upstairs to get a good night's rest. "I'll be right across the hallway, Ellie. If you need anything in the night, just call me. You may leave the lamp on low," she added.

Ellie was glad for the light. She reached her hand down along the side of the bed to her red leather satchel on the floor. She loosened the two buckles and lifted a large book into bed with her.

Her favorite tree was on page 234, the Ohio buckeye. She loved that this tree was also known as the Fetid Buckeye because its bark had "a disagreeable odor," a fact that conjured up all kinds of possibilities! Like when Mama said young ladies shouldn't talk about farts, Ellie and Charlie always said instead, "Am I detecting a *fetid buckeye* nearby?" Papa thought it was funny, too.

Ellie pulled the book under the linens and held it close, enjoying the coolness of the leather seeping through her nightgown. An idea was percolating in her head.

* * *

The first light flickered through the pansy curtains, which were snapping like petticoats on a clothesline. Ellie rolled over and breathed in the cool Ohio breeze. It smelled different from Pennsylvania's air. Her book was sticking out from under her pillow, and it reminded her of the plan that had come into her mind just before she'd fallen asleep. The room was barely bright enough to see inside her trunk. She pulled out her favorite pinafore with an ivory and green leaf pattern all over it.

Two travel dresses ago, Mama had asked the seamstress for a print that would hide all the smudges Eleanor attracted, and the woman had brought out an ivory and green floral pattern. She assured Mama that mishaps would disappear. Ellie had believed the dress would make *herself* disappear when she wore it, which had pleased her very much. When she outgrew that dress, she asked Mama to have another one made with the same fabric. This year, when Ellie chose a similar print as the previous two, Mama's eyebrow went up, and she shook her head as if she'd never understand her youngest daughter's mind. It was Ellie's private joke now to wear her favorite travel dress whenever she planned to do some sleuthing.

She dropped her book back into her satchel and pulled the strap over her head. Next, she slipped her buckeye necklace over her head for good luck. She was ready for a whole day at the lake.

* * *

At breakfast, Mr. Taylor said, "Ellie, you can brag at school that you had a picnic with the governor of Ohio, William McKinley!"

"He's coming to our picnic?"

"He lives in Canton and belongs to our club. In fact, he's the one who came up with idea for the Canton Outing Club."

"I wasn't aware of that," Papa said.

"Well, you could say the club was formed in order to purchase the resort at the lake."

"Isaac and I disagree about this whole deal," Mrs. Taylor said.

Ellie looked back and forth between the Taylors, wondering if they argued like her parents did.

"It's just business," he said. "The railroad got in over their heads and had to sell the resort few years back. Charlie Sliker bought it and turned it into a fine resort. He's ready to sell it now, and a group of us plan to buy it."

"That sounds reasonable," Papa said.

"It's the part about the water rights I question," Mrs. Taylor said.

"We do have plans to make it a private resort someday," said Mr. Taylor. "The problem is the United States government owns the lake, which means the public has a right to use it," he said.

Papa nodded. "Of course."

"McKinley struck a deal with the federal government to turn the ownership of Congress Lake over to the State of Ohio last December. Next spring, the State of Ohio will sell the lake to our Canton Outing Club!" Mr. Taylor grinned. "It's the slickest maneuver I've ever seen."

Papa wrinkled his forehead. "I've not heard of water rights of a public lake being sold off like that."

"McKinley's pretty proud of getting that clause into the fine print of the land titles. Once we buy the rest of the farms, we'll own not only the water, but also the hotel, the cottages, the dance pavilion, the big icehouse, and every foot of shoreline, too.

Papa whistled. "I'll wager that won't go over well with the locals."

"Once they figure out what they've lost, I don't suppose we'll be too popular. If McKinley runs for president in '96, the local folks will come around then."

"It feels like a shifty deal to me," Mrs. Taylor said.

Papa nodded. "I tend to agree with Flora."

Mr. Taylor crossed his arms and frowned. "Will McKinley says it's all legal. I'll concede it's a little self-serving, but what business venture isn't? The club will provide stable ownership, improve the property, and preserve it in perpetuity for future generations."

Papa raised his eyebrows. "The future generations of a select few families. Not for the thousands of people who have been enjoying the lake."

It got quiet for a moment, and then Papa smiled, "Isaac, I look forward to seeing this resort. It's kind of you to invite us."

* * *

The ten o'clock train from Canton rolled to a stop on the spur by the Spelman icehouse. It jolted sharply as their passenger car was disconnected from the train. A ferry took the passengers for a short ride out on the water and landed by the dance pavilion. The pavilion was two stories high, with a wide verandah and wooden railings wrapping around it on each level. The building was magically balanced on the tops of log poles that stood on end in the lake. Lively music drifted out from its windows. It reminded Ellie of the way melodies floated in from the riverboats in Philadelphia.

"Our club always hires a band," Mrs. Taylor said. "After lunch the adults will go to the pavilion. Opal and Charlotte are old enough join us, but children under twelve will have games and eat ice cream over in that clearing."

Ellie imagined that would be fun, but her secret plan would be so much better. Mrs. Taylor took her to one of the blue-checkered picnic cloths spread on the ground and introduced three other girls to her. Four lunches tied up in gingham napkins were piled in the center of the cloth. Ellie saw that Charlie and Opal were seated with older kids at a picnic table. The adults moved toward an open white canopy with a blue, scalloped edge along the roof. Beneath it, a long table with fluttering white linens had been set for them.

Ellie was polite and pretended to be interested as the other girls gabbled on about schoolmates and places known only to them. They all stopped eating to watch a commotion where Charlie and Opal were sitting. A boy who wasn't part of the Outing Club had walked over and was flirting with the older girls. They giggled at everything he said. He had copper-red hair and a bucketful of freckles that had spilled down over his face and arms. There was something about him that Ellie didn't like, especially when he picked up a stone and took aim at a squirrel that had run down the side of a tree. The stone bounced off the tree and the squirrel disappeared, unharmed. Then a family walked by, and the red-haired boy mocked them in a sing-song voice, "Hey look! It's the Dunkers! Who'd ya *dunk* today?"

Ellie had seen Dunkers before in Germantown, which was near Chestnut Hill. Papa said they belonged to a German church that baptized grownups in Wissahickon Creek. This family was dressed just like them. The man and woman both wore dark, plain clothes. He had a bushy beard, but no mustache and he wore a black, flat-brimmed hat. The collar of his coat stood up around his neck. His wife had a small cape that made a triangle shape over her bodice, and she wore an apron that was black like her skirt. A white cloth bonnet was tied under her chin.

Ellie thought the Dunker man would reprimand the red-headed kid for being impudent. But he just smiled as if he hadn't noticed and kept walking.

A little boy lagged behind his parents. He wore a black, flat-brimmed hat like his father. He had an odd way of walking that made him rock side-to-side. She knew it wasn't polite to stare, but she couldn't help it. The big redheaded kid started to mimic how the little boy walked. "Nice hat, Dunker," he said as he snatched it off the boy's head and pulled it low over his own head. Ellie's palms got sweaty.

Just then an older Dunker boy came running from behind. He flew sideways through the air and knocked the redheaded kid to the ground. He punched him in the face and grabbed the little boy's hat off the bully's head. As he stood up, he kicked the mean kid right in the crotch! Ellie had never seen anything like it. The redheaded kid lay there moaning until the two Dunker boys were a long way down the path, walking casually as if nothing had happened. Ellie laughed along with the others.

The redheaded boy got back on his feet. His face was pulled ugly, and he stomped off in the opposite direction from where the Dunker family had gone. Ellie almost felt sorry for him, even though she thought he had gotten exactly what he deserved.

Ellie got up on her knees to look in the direction the Dunker boys had gone and saw them climb the hill just beyond the dance pavilion where a group of Dunker families were gathered.

After lunch, a woman with a pea whistle in the corner of her mouth herded the children to a clearing. Ellie stopped to adjust the buckle on her shoe so that the other girls wouldn't notice she had stayed behind. Then she drifted farther away from the clearing toward the woods. The whistle blew, and children with flour sacks pulled up to their armpits bounced like popping corn toward the finish line, which was a rope with red handkerchiefs tied along it. Ellie lowered her head and walked toward the forest trail.

CHAPTER THREE

Dunker Boy

Hartville, Ohio, April 1893

Thirteen-year-old Cade pressed his full weight on the spade until it broke through the stubborn sod. His sister, Mandy, needed the soil worked up fine so she could transplant a rose bush behind Ma's grave. When he heaved the heavy clods of grass into the back of the wagon, Sander jerked against the harness. "Easy, boy." Cade laid his hand on the dappled rump of the old gelding. "Almost done."

He stared at the name chiseled into the headstone. *Hannah Elizabeth Bauer. 1835–1880.* He had been nine months old when his Ma died. Pa's name had always been at the top of the stone. *Ezra Samuel Bauer, 1832–*

When he was little, Cade had asked his sister why they hadn't finished writing Pa's numbers on the stone. Mandy said they couldn't finish it until Pa died. It had made him feel like there was a devilish thing in the grave waiting to reach up and pull Pa under. Waiting to finish the job. He'd always wished that thing hadn't waited so long.

Mandy and his older brothers didn't understand why he got so mad at Pa. They didn't seem to know their father like he did. Maybe Pa's foot hadn't kicked them like it did him whenever he passed by the chair. Maybe they hadn't gotten the strap or been yelled at all the time. *Are you thick in the head? When are you gonna learn, boy? You want something to cry about?*

The others were all grown up, having kids of their own by the time Cade was born, and when they told stories about their childhood, it seemed like someone else had been their father, not Pa. Mandy said Ma knew how to put her foot down, and Pa didn't get away with his tantrums back then.

He didn't drink from his jug back then either. It seemed like none of them knew the vile words that spewed out of him when he got ploughed at night. Always the same thing. That Ma had never recovered after Cade's birth. That she'd still be here if he hadn't been born, and that Pa wished he'd never set sights on his good-for-nothing-son-of-a-bitch son. Cade yelled back once, "Are you calling my ma a bitch?" And he got whipped something awful that time. Pa never remembered it the next morning. Cade had been too ashamed to tell anybody, because maybe what Pa said was true.

He used to believe what Pa said when he was drunk. But then he'd found out the truth. Doc Williams had hired him to help break in a filly for Mrs. Williams, which meant Cade got to ride while Doc led the filly around on a lead rope. And he always got some walking-around money for his pocket at the end, even though he would have helped Doc for nothing.

Cade asked Doc a question that had been a bellyache for a long time before it had words. *Was it my fault that Ma died?*

Doc stopped walking the filly and looked up at him. "Where'd you get a notion like that?"

"Pa said so."

"*Did* he?" Doc shook his head as if now he'd heard everything. "Cade, sometimes folks can't think straight when they're grieving." He said no, it wasn't Cade's fault that his ma had died. Doc said she'd had scarlet fever when she was little, which left her with a bad heart. It could have happened any time. And she had done well through her pregnancy, given she was almost forty-five when she'd had him. "It was just her time, son," he said. Cade liked the way Doc called him "son."

He also liked it another time when Doc told him, "Cade, you're a country doctor's legacy." At first he wasn't sure what that meant, but it sounded like an important thing. Doc said Cade had been a blue baby. Born dead. But Doc had kept massaging his belly to get his heart going and even blew air into his lungs. "And then you made up your own mind to live!" Doc said with a smile.

He'd always had the feeling that Doc was looking out for him. And Ma, too, even if she was in her grave. Before she died, she had made sure Mandy and Daniel would take him, since Pa was in a state and couldn't have handled a baby. That's what Mandy had said happened.

Mandy's husband, Daniel Holtz, was a German Baptist Brethren. Members of their church were called Dunkers, because they dunked adults in the river or lake for their baptisms. When Mandy married a Dunker, Pa had practically disowned her because of it, she said. Pa couldn't abide their pacifist faith or the way they dressed, all plain and pious. But he did agree to Ma's dying wish about them taking Cade. Mandy said it had made good sense. Her girl, Rachel, was still nursing, so she just put him on the other breast. It was a story that came back to haunt him when he was older. If he cried about anything or wasn't tough enough, Pa would say, "What's the matter with you, Cadey-Boy? Too much Dunker teat?" It was Pa's way of saying he was weak. But what made Cade the angriest was being reminded of how he'd been nursed on his sister's teat. It was embarrassing even to imagine it, even though Mandy said there was nothing to be ashamed of. Pa just laughed and gave him a slap across the head when he got all red-faced and worked up about it. Mandy said Cade should just turn the other cheek instead of getting angry when someone teased him. He'd never been good at that. Especially when Pa made fun of him. Cade got even madder if someone teased his nephew, Petey.

He didn't know why he had always felt like a Collie circling around a lamb if someone got too close to Petey. He remembered feeling that way back when he was four, even before Petey was born. Mandy had let him lay his face against the bulge in her belly. "Be gentle," she said. He felt big and strong when that tiny foot kicked against his cheek through her belly skin. It was the first time he wondered how babies were born. So Mandy took him out to the barn because it was lambing season then. He sat in the hayrack with her and laid his head on her belly, where he could watch through the wooden slats while she explained it to him. The lamb slid out in a puddle of steam and struggled up to reach its mother's teat, and he knew then how *his* baby would be born.

The baby that slid out of Mandy a month later was Petey. There was something about his nephew that always reminded him of that little lamb with wobbly legs, maybe because Petey's legs turned out to be wobbly, too. He had an awkward way of walking on his tiptoes and clomping down his feet. Sometimes Petey would stop dead still and stare, and a little bit of drool would run out the corner of his mouth. Cade thought he heard Doc say they were *Petey*-mal seizures, so he told Petey they gave him magical powers since they were named after him.

Adults didn't say anything, but their eyes followed Petey around to figure out what was wrong with him. Kids were just cruel. Mandy said it was *Cade's* job to watch out for Petey, which he took to mean that if anyone called Petey an idiot or made fun, it was his duty to thump them. Mandy didn't say much about the thumpings, but Daniel made Cade kneel and pray. He said once, "Cade, you're wearing out the knees of your britches atoning for that temper!

* * *

It was back in 1888, the year Cade had turned eight, when everything got turned upside down. It started at the Bauer family Christmas dinner when he forgot to take off his Dunker hat as he went in the door. He knew right away something was stuck in Pa's craw, and that always made him feel jumpy. Usually, when Pa got that sour look it meant he would start criticizing Cade, saying things like he never thought a son of his would be backing down from a fight like some coward. Or dressing like a damn Dunker-boy. No son of *his*, he'd say.

Cade felt him fuming about something, but Pa wasn't saying what it was. After dinner, when the adults were still at the long dining table telling funny stories about when they were growing up on this farm, Cade didn't go outside and play with the other children. Instead, he wanted to stay close to Daniel, who pulled him onto his lap. Pa pushed his chair back and cleared his throat. It took a minute for the room to get quiet. Pa said, "My youngest son here has turned eight now, and I think it's high time he learned how to be a Bauer."

Pa had said that before. Like when Pa wanted Cade to toughen up. To learn to be a Bauer. Daniel sometimes laughed and teased Pa when he said that. "Ezra, Cade is a good *bauer*. He's a good little farmer." And he'd wink at Cade. Daniel liked rubbing it in that Pa's name, *bauer,* meant "farmer" in German. Pa didn't like it one bit when Cade talked Pennsylvania Dutch. In Mandy and Daniel's house, English and German were all mixed, and Cade could never remember which words he wasn't supposed to say when they went to the cottage. Pa always got that disgusted look whenever Cade forgot and spoke Dutch.

Daniel didn't tease Pa about learning to be a Bauer this time. In fact, nobody at the table said anything. Cade saw Pa's mouth was pulled tight, and it was twisted to one side. It scared him.

"I've decided that the boy will live with me now. I'm his father. Cade's old enough to be helping with the barn chores at this farm. He belongs *here.*"

Cade's chest hurt where his heart was pounding against his ribs. He looked up at Daniel, hoping he'd put his foot down about that. But the only thing Daniel said was, "*Ja.* We understand." And that was that.

Cade sobbed and let his tears and snot run all over Mandy's dress that night at home. "Why didn't Daniel say no?"

Mandy hugged him so hard, he almost couldn't breathe. She said Cade had to live with Pa now because Pa was his father.

"But when will you come get me?"

She didn't answer for a long time. She just whispered in his ear that he needed to be a good boy and help Pa. Would he do that for her?

He nodded, but he held on to her for a long time and cried some more. She did, too.

* * *

Mandy and Daniel lived two miles north of Hartville to the east of Congress Lake. Their farm was the only home Cade ever knew. Mandy said he'd been born in the garden cottage on Pa's farm a mile south of Hartville. Ma and

Pa had built the cottage back when they let their oldest son, Garrett, and his family take over the big house and run the farm. Cade didn't remember Ma nor being born there, even though Mandy said it looked exactly as it did back when Ma was alive. To him it was just Pa's cottage, where he always felt nervous about what not to say.

Daniel and Mandy brought him to the cottage on Wednesday after Christmas. Pa came outside and, first thing, he grabbed the black, flat-brimmed hat off Cade's head and tossed it into the back of the wagon. "You'll not be needing that here. The Bauers are *Lutherans!*" Cade was pretty sure Pa never went to church, the way he swore all the time and looked like he just got out of bed whenever Mandy took food to him on Sunday.

Cade bit down on his lip and clenched his fingers around a cloth bag with the clothes Mandy had packed. She gave him a hug and said she'd keep his hat for him on his hook at home. He was glad she said "home" like it was a place he could come back to.

She didn't come to take him home, except for short visits. Even when she saw the bruises on his legs, she didn't take him back home with her. Instead, she said, "What are you doing to set him off, Cade?"

"Just being born sets Pa off," he answered.

And she said, "We need to *pray* for Pa." Which made him mad at God, too. God didn't seem to be in charge as much as Mandy thought.

When he was nine, Cade tried to take charge himself. He stole some coins from Pa's tin box and went to the Hartville Depot instead of school. He wanted a ticket for Out West, he said, but the conductor laughed and said there was hardly enough to get to Cleveland and back. And did his folks know about this? His legs got shaky then. He ran all the way back to Pa's and crawled in the corncrib until dark. Pa welted him good that night for disappearing. Cade kept the coins out of spite and stole some more whenever he had the chance. Someday he'd have enough.

* * *

Cade emptied a bucket of composted sheep manure and worked it into the soil around Ma's grave. It had been four years since he tried to run away. He didn't steal coins from Pa anymore, but whenever he earned some pocket money from Doc, he added it to the box under his bed. Hardly a week went by without imagining how he would get away from Pa someday. He'd leave Hartville for good, and Pa would never find him. He raked the dirt in long, smooth strokes before climbing into the cart. Cade snapped the reins on Sander's rump and drove out between the tombstones. He turned the cart toward Mandy and Daniel Holtz's farm, where he was spending Friday, Saturday, and Easter Sunday.

When Cade was younger and needed to see Mandy more, Pa hardly ever let him, maybe out of meanness. But now that he was thirteen and didn't need her so much, Pa hardly ever said no for Saturday overnight visits. That's when the old bastard drank himself into his darkest hole. When Mandy asked him if Cade could visit two nights because Daniel's family had a reunion, Pa acted like he was put out by it. "Well, the boy never does much around here, so you may as well feed him at your table. I'll have Garrett's boys cover his chores," he said.

"Good luck with *that*." Cade said it low enough that Pa couldn't hear. Garrett's twins were a couple of shit-faced liars. They were fifteen now, two years older than him, and they had more ways of worming out of work than a termite had tunnels. Most of the time, Cade had all *their* chores and his own done by the time they got their asses out to the barn. Mandy asked him once why he kept doing the twins' work for them.

"They'll just lie about feeding the livestock. Why should the animals suffer?" What he didn't say was that he liked to see things done right. He liked to work until all was in order. He liked pitchforks and harnesses to hang straight on the wall. He liked the stalls to be mucked out and fresh bedding spread. He even liked to curry the horses until their hairs lay in straight, sleek furrows. He didn't like hay being pulled out the lazy way from under the stack when it took little effort to climb up and toss it down properly. Cade knew Garrett's boys had figured out long ago that he'd do their work for them if they threatened to make a mess of things.

Pa loved those twins. He was always teasing and roughhousing with them before supper. It had been like that for as long as Cade could remember, and he used to get jealous of it. But after he moved in with Pa, it was a relief to see the old goat snap out of his sour mood for a couple hours each day. Cade usually helped Garrett's wife Clara get things to the table while the boys played with their Pa-paw. She spoiled her boys rotten, but she was kind to Cade, too.

He and Pa ate their evening meal up at the big house with Garrett's family. Clara usually sent leftovers for their next day's lunch. In the morning, it was Cade's job to get fried eggs and smoked ham on the table before he left for school. That was after he had done the milking and the barn chores. It was all Pa could do to scrape himself off the couch after he'd sucked on his brown jug all night.

In the five years he'd lived with Pa, he'd gotten smarter at staying out of the old man's way. Or maybe Pa was slowing down. Cade still got a backhander if he sassed him and the strap if Pa was in a mood. Sometimes Cade got so angry with Pa, he'd get hot ice in his head. It was either burning or freezing. He couldn't tell which. And the only way to melt it was to work like hell splitting wood or hoeing the garden row after row or shoveling snow all the way to the barn. It needed a pounding rhythm, and he couldn't let up until he felt that hot ice running down his neck and soaking into his shirt. The swearing might've helped, too.

When he was at Mandy's, there was no hot ice. Usually, he'd put on his Dunker hat, and the rhythm of his heart would change. Sometimes, Mandy patted his face when he arrived and said, "Relax that jaw, Cade."

He hated getting caught with his chin out. He'd jutted out his jaw so much at Pa that it locked up sometimes and made a loud crack when he'd try to say something. Pa thought it was funny and said, "Overwind your clock today, boy?"

The last time Mandy had patted Cade's face she said, "You'll be needing a razor blade of your own one of these days." He'd smiled at that.

* * *

On Saturday evening after the Holtz family reunion, Cade hurried to the barn to feed the sheep. He scraped the feeding trough below the hayrack with the flat-bladed hoe and then ran like the dickens with the bucket of chop, shaking it into the trough before the ewes barreled in. He'd learned long ago that those wooly ladies would knock him flat if he didn't get his tail out of there. The loud ruckus quieted into belch-y grunts as they shoved each other into an orderly row. Then the lambs bolted out from the shadows, leaping about with their tails wiggling. Cade leaned forward and laid his arms on the hayrack where he sat. He laughed out loud at them butting heads and jumping on each other. It was not so different from the kids in the schoolyard. Orphaned lambs didn't play. They went straight to the row of teats to steal some supper while the ewes tried to kick the little thieves away. There was no love in *that* milk.

After the trough was licked clean, the ewes began calling. It was a different call than before. The mother was calling to her own lamb. And the lamb would echo back. It always took a few minutes with all of them calling at once. But somehow, they sorted it out and found their way to each other. The lambs had a last nip of milk and snuggled in next to their mothers for the night. The barn came to stillness. Only the puffing of breath could be heard. That and the grinding jaws.

"You know you're a natural *bauer*, Cade."

He didn't realize until then that Daniel was standing at the gate, watching him. Cade liked Daniel's meaning. He smiled. "*Danke.*"

* * *

Damn mosquitos. Cade dug his fingers into the wet clay and smeared it around his neck and face where the bites swelled together. That summer he had started sneaking off to Congress Lake on Saturday nights whenever he stayed at Mandy and Daniel's. There was a path from their farm that cut through the woods to Jonah's Landing, which was a clearing by the lake. He elbowed through the grasses by the water line to get closer to the pavilion.

The glittering light, along with the lively rhythms of the band and the laughter, spilled out through the open windows and doorways. Couples holding shimmering glasses stepped outside and stood against the railing of the verandas that wrapped around the pavilion on both levels. The men mopped their brows and struck matches to light their cigarettes, and the women fluttered their fans. They laughed and sipped and swayed with the music, sometimes leaning together long enough to steal a kiss. He could smell the tobacco smoke. Now and then bits of conversations bounced off the glassy surface of the lake and carried intimate words and flirtatious chatter to his mud-covered ears. The sheen of the women's gowns fascinated him, and he loved to watch the light slithering down over their curves. That was something he would never have dared to stare at in daylight.

Desire crept through his body and took him to places in his imagination that made him blush, and he knew he would come back here again to spy. He felt an achy sadness to know that this tantalizing, smoky world of the Congress Lake dance pavilion was so separate from his own. It seemed that he was always on his belly, sneaking peeks into other people's lives, longing to be part of their worlds. He slid into the lake to scrub himself clean and floated to the big rock where he'd left his shoes.

* * *

The moon illuminated Mandy's backyard so brightly that Emma didn't even bark as Cade stripped off his wet clothes and hung them over the side porch swing. He slipped naked through the window of his room behind the kitchen and pulled his nightshirt over his head. He curled under the quilt to warm his body.

Then shame crept into bed with him and began its familiar harangue, berating him for his two-faced life and sinful thoughts and for his awful temper that was just like Pa's. He couldn't sleep until he'd knelt on the floor and prayed for forgiveness. Fervently. He barely heard the living room clock's three hollow chimes that pulled him, finally, out of his self-recrimination. He was shivering as he slid into bed and fell into an exhausted sleep. Mandy woke him for church. She said she let him sleep until seven because of how tired he had been looking on Sundays. It was probably a growth spurt, she said.

CHAPTER FOUR

Baptisms

Cade's decision to join the Dunker church surprised some folks in the congregation. An ordained elder, Noah Longenecker, pulled him aside to talk. He had a full white beard but a smooth face of a man younger than Pa. His clear blue eyes were kind. "You are awfully young to be united with the church, Cade," Elder Longanecker said.

Cade shifted uneasily, wondering if his request for baptism would be denied.

The Elder went on, "But you do seem sincere. I, myself, was baptized when I was but a few years older than you. Did you know they called me the 'boy preacher' when I was elected to the ministry at age twenty-two?" When Cade shook his head, Elder Longanecker said, "Cade, no one else can claim to know what is in *your* heart. And no one knows what God has in mind for you."

Cade was baptized at Jonah's Landing on the fifteenth of July 1893. He didn't tell Pa. Elder Longanecker stood in the lake near Jonah's Landing and stretched his hand toward Cade, who waded in and knelt beside the preacher. Cade sucked in his breath as the cold spring-fed water soaked through his clothes. He felt the warmth of a firm hand on his head while prayers were said. Cade covered his face with his own hands, pinching his nostrils together when the Elder leaned him forward, plunging him under the water three times. He heard the comforting German words invoking the name of the Father, the Son, and the Holy Ghost.

Cade had gone into Congress Lake that day eagerly expecting his baptism would change him. It wasn't that he had thought a dove would descend from Heaven, but as he waded out of the water, he was a little disappointed that he didn't feel any different. Mandy was so happy she dabbed at her eyes with her hanky. Folks from the church were pumping his hand and congratulating him, and Petey was doing a strange little dance and singing, "Cadey got dunked, Cadey got dunked." Cade grabbed the satchel of dry clothes on the ground and stepped behind a bush to peel off his soggy ones. The church said he was an adult man now, but Cade wasn't sure what had changed. Daniel had given him a new black hat, and he was proud to be wearing it.

By the time he got back to the family wagon, Rachel had already gone off with her cousin, Ellen, and Petey started pestering him about going fishing at Jonah's Landing after lunch. They acted like it was an utterly ordinary picnic day at Congress Lake. Mandy and Daniel carried baskets of food and walked on ahead. Petey followed them, zigzagging like he usually did. Cade lingered at the wagon so he could walk by himself like an adult Dunker man.

Out ahead, he noticed a redheaded boy about his own size slip in behind Petey on the gravel walkway and then saw the kid mimicking his nephew's clumsy walk. A group of kids sitting on picnic cloths were laughing at him mocking Petey. Instantly, there was hot ice in Cade's head. He was already running when he saw the bully snatch Petey's hat off and jam it on top of his red hair. The kid was too busy acting as if he had wobbly legs to see what was coming. Cade hurtled himself onto the bully and landed a good punch to his jaw. The kid lay there holding the side of his face. Cade grabbed Petey's hat, and he picked up his own, which had flown off. The kid was giving him hateful looks, and that only made Cade angrier. He kicked his foot hard in the kid's balls and leaned in close to his ear. "Don't you *ever* mess with him again!"

Mandy and Daniel hadn't seen any of it, and Petey stood staring with a bit of drool sliding out the corner of his mouth. Cade gently straightened the hat on Petey's head and then put his finger over his own lips and winked. "Our secret?"

His nine-year-old nephew grinned. "We got 'im, didn't we, Cadey?"

* * *

Daniel Holtz's siblings and their families, who were all pacifist Dunkers, were waiting at the picnic site to honor Cade's baptism. They pounded his back warmly and made a point of inviting him to join the adult men for horseshoes. None of them knew he'd just flattened a redheaded kid in a rage. Nor how much he'd enjoyed doing it. The irony of them welcoming him into the Dunker fold left a flat taste on all his favorite foods Mandy had prepared. Cade had trouble swallowing his lunch. There was a tight spot in his chest where guilt had a way of squeezing his gullet.

After lunch, Petey wouldn't let up about fishing. Cade walked him to the shoreline path. "You go on ahead to the rock. I'll get the poles and bait from the wagon." He watched Petey's black hat bobbing up and down in the tall grasses. Petey was always in his own little world of fantasy, probably playing the Chippewa brave like he always did when they went to their favorite fishing hole at Jonah's Landing.

Cade wasn't in any particular hurry. There was a white tent down the way with a fancy table set up inside it. A white tablecloth, even. City folks, he guessed. They were just standing up from the dining table and stepping outside. A breeze caught a woman's gown. It billowed slightly and glinted in the sunlight. His face grew warm as he thought how he had lain on his belly, spying on such women. His hand reached up to straighten his hat, and he turned abruptly toward the wagon.

He avoided the city folk on his way to Jonah's Landing. The quiet coolness of the forest path was a relief. He needed time alone to think about his choice to become a pacifist. His hair hadn't even dried from his baptism when he'd gone into a rage and knocked a kid down for taking Petey's hat. How could he call himself a Dunker after that?

* * *

Within moments, Ellie was in another world. She looked closely at every tree she met, searching for the one with the hand-shaped, edge-toothed, five-leaflet foliage. At last, she laid her hand reverently on the trunk of a bona fide Ohio buckeye! Ellie ran her fingers lightly over the small, spiky-looking, pale-green fruit pods. She was expecting sharp prickles but found the spikes were soft and spongy. This was exactly the kind of new information she wanted to record in her book, which she pulled from her satchel. She also wrote in the margin, *Congress Lake, Hartville, Ohio. 15 July 1893.*

Then Ellie broke open the young fruit pod, hoping to find a brown nut that matched her hair, but there was only a mushy white pulp inside. Too early. She sniffed the pulp and sighed. It smelled as ordinary as an acorn. Her book said that the *bark* was "ill scented," so she sniffed all around the tree with her nose touching its bark. Nothing.

Her teacher had once said that scientists "must stay curious and not succumb to disappointment." Ellie wasn't about to succumb, but she was beginning to doubt that the author, Mr. Newhall, knew much about Ohio buckeyes. Maybe the "disagreeable odor" was on the inside. She walked around and around the tree, her gaze spiraling slowly upward to its higher limbs, which was where she spotted exactly what she was seeking: a broken branch with loose bark that could easily be peeled back. Ellie quickly dropped her book and pencil back into her satchel and grabbed the lowest branch, hoisting herself up into the buckeye. It was a perfect tree to climb, with alternating limbs that formed a natural stairway to the canopy. At last, she reached the broken branch with its snaggle of bark. Her hands trembled a little as she peeled it back to the green fibers. She lowered her nose into the moist inner fibers and finally found out why the fetid buckeye was so named. There was an odd mix of familiar scents.

Ellie settled herself comfortably in the crook of two limbs, carefully took out her book, and wrote in the margin: *Odor—blackstrap molasses and skunk.* It was all there in her first whiff of the inner bark of the buckeye.

Ellie smiled. She put her book away and relaxed her arm over the limb beside her. The light filtered through every imaginable shade of green. About twelve feet below, she saw a black hat bobbing amongst the tall grasses along the shore. The hat moved toward the clearing, and a small, barefoot boy appeared beneath it. It was the younger Dunker boy. He plopped his black hat on a cattail stalk and crawled on his belly to the edge of a low gray boulder that extended out into the water. His golden hair flopped forward as he leaned over the edge and stretched his hand as far as he could. His fingertips dipped into the water and made tiny ripples that circled their way toward dragonflies hovering over the lake's surface.

Ellie loved being a secret spy in her flowered dress that was well concealed by the leaves. There was a kind of stillness in the rhythmic slap of water against the shoreline, the buckeye leaves whispering all around her, and the chatter of insects, birds, and forest creatures. It was almost like being in her sacred grove of white pines. The boy below her lay very still on the rock, and Ellie wondered if he was listening to the same noisy silence of the forest.

She felt something from the outside breaking into the peace of this clearing, even before she saw the movement in the mound of grasses behind the rock. Two figures were crawling cat-like toward the small boy. With startling speed, they leapt up and pounced on him, scaring Ellie almost as much as if it had been herself lying on that rock. She squeezed her eyes shut, not wanting to take in what was happening. She heard the youngster's shrill screams, but his cries seemed to be swallowed up by the dense undergrowth of the forest. She couldn't hear any birds flapping away in alarm.

A growly voice said, "So what's the little Dunker-boy doing here? You come here to be *baptized*?"

The little boy kept yelling, and Ellie opened her eyes. It was worse to hear the sounds and not be able to make sense of them. The big boys had each grabbed an arm and suspended him above the ground. The boy's legs kicked in the air as he let loose a long, quivering wail. Ellie's own limbs had turned into stone. She could hardly breathe for fear the bullies would look up and find her in the tree. A hot feeling started spreading from the back of her head. Sweat covered her upper lip, and she felt dizzy.

As her eyes came to rest on the tallest boy's face, she recognized the bully's mop of unruly red hair and his freckles. His face was now twisted into a hate-filled scowl.

"The captain thinks this little sinner needs salvation. Isn't that right, Twitch?" he said to the other boy.

"W—wait a minute, Cap," the boy named Twitch said hesitantly. "He's just a little kid." Twitch had pale skin and straight, dark hair that dropped forward enough that Ellie couldn't see his eyes. But she could see that one side of his face did twitch a lot, like he was nervous about what they were doing.

"Dunk the Dunk! Dunk the Dunk!" The redheaded kid chanted it as if it were a wicked kind of nursery rhyme. Ellie saw him jerk his thumb toward the lake, and Twitch obeyed.

As the bullies dragged the boy into the water, the youngster gasped for air, having none left for yelling. The redhead was now talking in a deep, man-like tone. "In the name of the Father," he said mockingly.

Cap laughed as they held the little boy under. When they pulled him up, he coughed out lake water and sucked in air with desperate, squawking sounds.

"And of the Son."

"Cap, stop…" Twitch started to protest, but the redhead scowled at him and pushed the boy down, holding his head under even longer a second time. The little boy's kicking legs went limp, and when they pulled him up, he didn't even cough. The laughter stopped.

Ellie heard Twitch say, "Hey, kid! You all right?"

"Drop him," the redhead commanded.

"B—but, what if…"

"Drop him!"

The command silenced him. Ellie gasped. Twitch let go of the boy and fell in behind the tall redhead, who was already wading to shore. They disappeared into the tall grasses.

Ellie screamed. Her shaky legs found their way to the ground. She yanked the red leather strap over her head and dropped her satchel. She pulled off her shoes and ran in her stockings past the boulder. The weedy plants in the shallow shoreline grabbed at her ankles, and she fell forward into the water, aiming herself to where the boy's yellow hair was floating loosely on the surface. Her arms pulled hard until she bumped into the boy. The lake floor was a little deeper than her tiptoes could reach, but she grabbed his arm and struggled to keep her own head above the water as she swam on her back toward shore. Without warning, someone else's arm reached over her shoulder and pulled the boy from her grip. Ellie's feet dropped to the sandy bottom and she stood up, yelling, "You let him go, you big bully!" Her wet hair had fallen forward and mostly covered her eyes, but her fists found their target, and she pounded him as hard as she could. Each punch made her braver. And angrier about what they had done.

"Stop ... please, stop!" he said.

Ellie swept her hair back from her eyes and glared into the face of a boy taller than her. He was the older Dunker kid she had seen earlier! He lifted the small boy over his shoulder and hefted him to the shore. He laid the child on his belly and began pumping his back in a steady rhythm. Ellie knelt across from him and heard him pleading, *Please, Gott, help!*" Water spurted out of the little boy's mouth onto the grass. The shaky feeling in Ellie's legs went all the way up to her teeth, which started chattering as if she'd been out sledding too long on a winter's day.

"C'mon, Petey! Breathe," the older one said as he rolled the lifeless boy face-up.

The little boy's face was white and his lips were gray-blue. Only the whites of his eyes were showing through the half-opened lids. *Is this how it looks when you die?* Ellie had seen Grandpa McAllister in his casket, but he had looked like he was just taking an afternoon nap. This was different.

The older boy placed his mouth over the blue lips and began blowing air into the child. Ellie could see the little boy's chest lifting and then falling each time the older boy took another breath for himself. There was a gurgle, and water began to dribble out of the small boy's mouth. Then a wave of vomit sloshed onto the grass as the older boy turned the child on his side. She heard the weak, choking sounds as the little boy sucked in air on his own. His eyelids fluttered open.

The older boy's face was contorted as if he were about to scream, but instead he dropped to the ground, sobbing, and wrapped his body around the small child, who lay limp in his arms. Ellie understood the prayer he kept repeating. *"Danke, Gott."*

"Petey, are y–you all right?" His voice was quivery, and his teeth were chattering as much as Ellie's. Shiny mucous was streaming from his nose, and he wiped his wet sleeve across his face.

The little boy breathed with a loud wheezing sound, but at least he was taking in air of his own accord. Ellie saw his head move, but he didn't seem to have enough strength even to look over his shoulder to the older boy lying behind him. "C–Cadey? " The little boy's voice was hoarse.

"I'm here, Petey. You're safe. I'm so sorry. I should have been with you. I'm sorry."

"Mama ... where's Mama?" the little boy sobbed. His eyes were closed, and his breathing had a rasp, but his face had some color now.

"I–I saw where your family had their picnic," Ellie said. "Shall I go get your parents?"

The older boy looked up at her and gave one quick nod. "Yes, that would be good. Ask for Daniel Holtz."

Ellie noticed he was staring at the buckeye that was dangling from a soggy ribbon. Her hand wrapped around it. "It's my lucky buckeye," she said.

His eyebrows wrinkled together for a moment, but he didn't respond. She rose to her feet. Her stocking was torn, and her big toe stuck through it. She stepped into her shoes, wiggling her feet under the buckles. She pulled the strap of her red satchel over her hair that was curling wildly. Then she ran, retracing the trail that had brought her farther from home than she'd ever been before.

CHAPTER FIVE
Buckeye

Ellie burst out of the woods, her satchel bouncing wildly. She stopped. The sack races were over, and the grown-ups had called their children to them. Ellie spotted Charlie, who had her hands on her hips and was looking this way and that. She saw Papa coming down the slope toward them.

Charlie hurried toward her. "You are in so much trouble, Ellie McAllister! What has happened to you?"

"Charlie, I have to find someone! Tell Papa I'm fine, but I have to find the Dunkers!"

"The *Dunkers?*"

* * *

Ellie ran to the place where the Dunker folks had gathered. She thought she recognized the man the red-haired bully had mocked earlier, but she asked to be sure, "Are you Mr. Daniel Holtz?"

"Yes?" he said and wrinkled his forehead. He was sitting on the ground against a tree, watching an older man tossing a horseshoe toward an iron post, when she approached. He cupped his hand over his eyes to block the sun when he looked up at her.

Ellie said, "You need to come help your boys. The little one, Petey, was drowned, but your older boy saved him. They're in the woods."

"Where?" He leapt up from the ground.

She pointed. "The trail behind that white tent. It goes to a big rock."

"Jonah's Landing!" he said. "Mandy! Come quickly!" Then he spoke in German to his wife, whose eyes filled with tears.

"Thank you," she said as her husband ran on ahead. "I didn't hear your name."

"Eleanor. Eleanor McAllister."

"Thank you, Eleanor." She hurried toward the trail after him.

Ellie saw Papa walking quickly toward her. "Ellie, what in God's name has happened?" He scooped her up as if she were a little girl. Ellie didn't care.

"I didn't mean to make trouble, Papa. I only went to find a buckeye tree." He set her on a bench and sat beside her.

"Start from the beginning. Everything."

When she got to the part about the bullies, her tears couldn't be stopped. She felt the terror all over again. It was like her lungs were being squeezed shut, but as she told the part about saving the little boy, her fear loosened its grip a little more.

"I didn't tell Mr. Holtz about the bullies, Papa. One of them was really mean. He was the same kid who mocked the Holtzes when we were having our picnic!"

"I'll watch for them and tell them," Papa said. "Ellie, you were very brave this afternoon. I'm proud of you."

"But Papa, I didn't help Petey when they were hurting him. I–I was too scared. I just stayed in the tree. And I don't know what I would have done if his brother hadn't come."

He kissed her forehead. "What happened to Petey is not your fault." He lifted her chin up so that she had to look into his eyes. "Did you hear what

I said, Ellie? *What happened to Petey was not your fault.* You couldn't have done anything better to help him. You did exactly the right thing."

Mama was waiting and rushed forward with an exasperated look. Papa stepped ahead and pulled Mama away to talk. When she came back, she just hugged Ellie and didn't say anything. Ellie wrapped her arms around Mama's slender waist.

"There they are," she heard Papa say. "I'll talk with them." He walked over to the path to wait. He stood with his legs apart and his hands in the pockets of his trousers.

Ellie noticed Mr. Holtz was carrying Petey, who seemed to be sound asleep on his shoulder. Ellie needed to say something to the older boy, who was walking behind his parents, but she waited until they drew closer. The wide brim of his black hat cast a shadow over his face, but she could feel his dark eyes focused on her. When she stepped toward him, he stopped.

"I–I'm glad you came when you did. I wouldn't have known what to do next," she said.

"It might have been too late if you hadn't already pulled Petey to shore. So … um … thank you," he said.

"I'm sorry I punched you. I thought the bullies had come back."

The boy looked at her oddly and didn't say anything for a few moments. "It didn't hurt me," he said.

Ellie smiled a little bit. "How did you know how to blow your breath into him?"

"It's something Doc Williams taught us. He came to our eighth-grade to teach us resuscitation because a kid in our class drowned last year. But I never thought I would need to use it."

Papa called to her. "Eleanor, do you have a pencil and paper in your satchel?"

"Yes, Papa." She quickly pulled them from her red leather bag.

Papa wrote something on the paper and gave it to Mr. Holtz. "This is my law firm's address. I'm licensed in the State of Pennsylvania. But if you need someone to represent you in court, I know a good lawyer in Canton who can help."

Mr. Holtz stared at the paper, and then he looked up at Papa. "We don't use courts, Mr. McAllister. God will deal with those boys in His own way."

"But surely you won't let two hooligans leave your boy for dead and get away with it!"

Mrs. Holtz slipped her hand through her husband's arm. "We thank you for your kindness to us."

Ellie noticed that Mr. Holtz's blue eyes had white smile crinkles in the corners. She liked how he placed both of his hands, one on each side of Papa's hand, to shake it. Then he said something that sounded like it should be said in church. "May the peace of Christ be with you."

Mrs. Holtz leaned down and took Ellie's hand. Her dark hair was pulled straight back and fastened neatly under her white bonnet. She had a kind, pretty face. "Thank you, Eleanor. So much good happened amongst the sorrows this afternoon. Cade told us that you had already pulled Petey to shore when he got there. If it weren't for you, perhaps Petey wouldn't be alive. You were a *godsend* to us."

Ellie shivered. *What did it mean to be a godsend?* She watched the Dunker family walk toward their picnic area. They were almost to the dance pavilion when Cade looked back at her. His hand lifted in a kind of wave, and she raised hers a little, too. Then he turned back to his family. It occurred to her that she would never see him again, but even so, they were connected in a special way. Together, they had done something good amongst the sorrows.

* * *

On the four o'clock train back to Canton, Ellie made an awful discovery. Her buckeye necklace was gone. Mama said Ellie probably lost it in the lake, jumping in like that. Ellie said no, it was still on her chest after Petey started to breathe, which was just before she ran to find the Holtzes. Papa said maybe the ribbon had come loose when she was running. Ellie couldn't keep the tears from drizzling down her cheeks. Mrs. Taylor said she would look for a buckeye nut in the fall and send it to her. Ellie shook her head and said she didn't want *another* one. Which made Mama say, "Eleanor, where are your manners?" Ellie thanked Mrs. Taylor, and nobody talked about her buckeye necklace after that.

Ellie didn't want supper. She just wanted to go to bed. Mrs. Taylor fixed a warm bath for her. Mama said it would be a wonder if she didn't catch her death after running about in wet clothes and hair at the lake. Ellie wondered if she had used up all her buckeye luck that day.

* * *

Ellie tried to pull herself out of an awful dream. She may have yelled. She sat up and sucked in short, rapid, wheezing breaths. Even though she had always survived her asthma attacks before, every time it happened there was a terrifying feeling that she might not.

In the dim lamplight, she saw Mrs. Taylor hurrying toward her. "Ellie, you'll be all right," she said. "Just push the air *out!* As hard as you can. I know you want to suck air in, but it helps if you breathe *out!*"

Ellie obeyed, even though she'd never heard of trying this before. And to her relief, each time she pushed her breath out hard, air filled her lungs quite naturally.

"That's the way." Mrs. Taylor's voice was soothing.

Ellie's chest hurt each time she breathed. A deep, wheezy cough came up.

"Oh, dear! I need to make a plaster for that cough," Mrs. Taylor said and hurried downstairs. When she returned, she rubbed warm lavender oil on Ellie's chest and back. Then a sticky, pungent, flannel cloth was placed over her chest. Mrs. Taylor asked her to "take a deep breath and hold" while a wide strip of bandage was wrapped around Ellie's torso several times. "There!" she said as she tucked the end of the bandage in. "You know, Ellie, I had asthma, too, when I was young. But I outgrew it eventually."

"You did?" Ellie liked the idea one could outgrow asthma. As her tight, ragged breathing became soft, she felt very sleepy again.

* * *

Dr. Hampton had eyebrows that looked more like whiskers sticking out all over. He introduced himself directly to her, and Ellie liked that. His cold stethoscope went up and down her back and chest before he tucked the blanket around her again. "I'm concerned about a rattle in your right lung.

I don't want an infection setting in." He turned to Mama and asked, "How long will you be in town?"

She told him about Chicago. "Shall we cancel our plans?"

"Eleanor should not travel. She needs to stay in bed for the rest of the week, at least."

Mama sighed. "Oh dear. Then Chicago is out of the question. I am so sorry for this imposition, Flora."

Ellie felt shame warming her face. It was all her fault.

Mrs. Taylor said, "Nonsense. It is no imposition at all!"

Dr. Hampton dug into his leather bag and handed Mama some small squares of folded paper packets. "These are powders for her. Dissolve one packet in water each morning and one at night until they are gone. Mrs. Taylor, if you will continue the plasters until the phlegm turns clear, I believe this young lady will feel much better in a week."

* * *

That afternoon, Papa sat on the edge of the bed. "I'm sorry, Ellie. You must be disappointed about not riding the Big Wheel."

"I wanted to go to the fair, but the worst part is that I'm making all of you miss it, too." Ellie's eyes watered. "I'm sorry, Papa."

"Mrs. Taylor had an idea. Isaac has a business trip, but she's invited you to stay here with Opal and her. We would take Charlotte on to Chicago. It would be about two weeks until we pick you up again. What would you think about that?"

"It's fine, Papa." Ellie was relieved to have the guilty feeling lifted off her. "Maybe Opal would like to go with Charlie instead of me?"

"That's a splendid idea! I'll talk to Isaac and Flora." He smiled. "My youngest daughter is becoming very grown up."

Ellie had imagined she would be sad to see Mama, Papa, Charlie, and Opal climb into the carriage bound for the train station the next morning. But she wasn't. She felt grown up, just as Papa had said.

CHAPTER SIX
Hot Ice

All the way home from Congress Lake, something wasn't being talked about. Cade had overheard enough to know that much. After Daniel carried Petey up to bed, Mandy made lemon tea for their nerves. The three of them sat at the table with their fingers folded around their mugs, not saying anything at first. Then questions piled up in Cade's mind as he tried to make sense of things. "What did Mr. McAllister mean when he said we shouldn't let those two hooligans get away with it? And why did you say that we don't use courts? Is this about Petey's accident?"

Daniel raised his eyebrows and looked over at Mandy. She nodded, and he began. "Mr. McAllister said his daughter, Eleanor, happened to be at Jonah's Landing and saw what happened to Petey. It wasn't an accident. Two boys bullied him and left him in the lake."

It wasn't an accident. Cade's head pounded as he tried to take in what those bullies had done. *To Petey.*

"Who were they? Did she say what they looked like?"

Daniel just got silent about that, but Mandy finally said, "She recognized one who had red hair and freckles. He was the only one she got a good look at. We don't know who they were, Cade. Or why they would do such a thing."

Cade's face got sweaty. He knew exactly who and why. He pushed back his chair. "What the hell is wrong with you two? You're not even gonna *try* to find them? They attacked Petey and leave him for dead, and you won't do anything about it because our church doesn't believe in using the courts?"

"I knew it would upset him, Mandy," Daniel said. "You need to calm down, Cade. What those boys did to our Petey was *schreckliche.* Terrible. But *Gott* will take care of this."

Daniel's words came out like smooth glass, and Cade wanted to shatter it. "Was God taking care of things when Petey was attacked? If I'd been there, those bullies wouldn't be walking right now."

"There will be no talk of retaliation in our house. *Any* act of violence is the seed of more violence."

"The seed of more violence?" Cade pounded his fist on the table. "Well, maybe the same could be said about an act of cowardice!"

The back door slammed against the wall as he ran outside. He grabbed the wheelbarrow that was standing on end against the barn. The afternoon heat was stifling, but he hauled load after load of manure out to the pile by the barn. When fresh straw covered the floor of the horse stalls, he emptied the water from the moss-covered barrels in the sheep pen and scrubbed them with a wire brush down to the yellow grain. The late-evening sky bathed the barnyard in purple as he pumped buckets of water from the well and carried them, two at a time, to fill the barrels again.

When his muscles cramped up and got quivery, he ate leftovers from the plate that Mandy had set on the bench. Only a crescent moon and fireflies lit the ground as he pumped the handle of the well a few times and knelt under the running water, letting it soak through to his skull. He reached up to pump the handle again, and this time he gulped the cold, clear water. He pumped it again and felt coolness wash over his eyelids, down his cheeks, and through the fuzz on his chin.

He stood and looked toward the house, where the only light came from a coal oil lantern in the kitchen window. He headed back to the barn. Night air came through the opened doors at the end of the loft, along with the pale light of the sky. He crawled up the stack of sweet-smelling hay that had been cut two weeks before. His clothes reeked of an odor he recognized: the smell of hot ice, melted.

Daniel's words about violence being the seed of more violence had nagged at him, and now that he was emptied out, there was room to think about it. Violence was in his blood. For as long as he could remember, he'd been using his fists whenever he got mad. It had never occurred to him to handle the redheaded bully in any other way. Knocking the kid flat hadn't been enough for him. He had to kick him in the balls, too.

Cade's cheeks burned with shame. He knew he wasn't any kind of a pacifist. What was worse, he'd acted like the person he loathed most. What if he was becoming just like Pa? He let his tears flow, as if they could wash away the guilt.

* * *

When Cade came back inside the house the following morning, the washtub was sitting in his room and a large pot of water was steaming on the stove. He thanked Mandy.

All she said was, "We'll be leaving for church in an hour."

He didn't say any more either. He carried the hot water to the tub and added some fresh to cool it off a bit. Salt coated his skin and had even caked on the seams of his clothes. He lathered up his body with the washrag and rinsed himself clean. He was about to towel himself dry but instead plopped down in the tub of dirty water with his legs draped over the side. The heat relaxed him a little.

He looked over to his bed, where his suit was all laid out with his black hat beside it. Mandy had altered one of Daniel's suits for him. It had the high, rounded collar the German Baptist Brethren men wore. Yesterday morning he couldn't wait to wear his suit to church and sit with the other men. Today, he felt like some kind of a flimflam Dunker. And he didn't know how to set it right.

He was still sitting in the tub when Mandy knocked and opened the door.

"Cade! What are you doing? Daniel's waiting outside in the buggy."

"I'm not going."

"The elders are giving special recognition to new members today. You're expected. So stop sulking and get out of that tub!"

"I said I'm not going! I don't belong with the Dunkers. I never should have got baptized."

She gave him a look that could have withered a fig tree. "I don't know *what's* gotten into you, Cade. And *what* am I supposed to tell everybody?" When he looked away, she slammed the door. He heard her stomping all the way out the back door.

For a moment, he wanted to scramble into his suit and hurry after her and tell her that he'd try to be a Dunker after all. He hated it when Mandy got mad at him, but at the same time he liked knowing she also had a temper. He shivered in the cold water, which now had a gray film on the surface, and pushed himself up over the edge of the tub. He wrapped the flannel towel around his waist and stared at the clothes hanging on the wall peg. The ones he wore at Pa's. He put them on. It was funny how clothes say who you are without you ever saying a word. The ones he wore at Mandy's didn't seem all that different from any other trousers or shirts, but there was a look about them that Pa despised. *Damndunkerclothes*, Pa called them, as if it was one word. He opened the dresser drawer and pulled out all *those* clothes. He stacked them neatly beside his suit at the end of his bed. Petey would grow into them someday.

Cade dumped his bath water on the grass and rinsed the tub at the pump before placing it back on the porch. He grabbed a thick slice of bread from the kitchen to take with him. Emma was asleep on her rug by the hearth. She raised her head momentarily so he could ruffle the fur on her neck. When he dumped his dirty clothes in Mandy's laundry basket, he saw a blue ribbon hanging from his trousers pocket. He pulled out the shiny, chestnut-red buckeye that Eleanor McAllister had worn. When he had picked it up on the trail near Jonah's Landing, he knew it belonged to the strange girl with the wild, curly hair. She had said it was her *lucky* buckeye.

Cade knew he should have given it back to her, but something had made him want to keep it. Dunkers weren't allowed to have lucky charms, and that made it all the more tantalizing. He was ashamed of himself for wanting it, but he slipped it in his satchel anyway and went out the back door. It was three miles back to Pa's.

* * *

The odor in the cottage put him on edge as soon as he opened the back door. Whenever he caught a whiff of that acrid, metallic smell, he knew Pa was slipping into a crazy place. And it wouldn't take much to set him off. Cade caught sight of him passed out on his chair in the other room. He tiptoed on the stairs, avoiding the boards that creaked. His room door hinge always groaned, so he closed it behind himself very slowly with his ear cocked toward the stairwell. He stuffed his satchel under the bed and glanced at the door. The safest place to be when Pa was like that was in the barn. He crawled out his window onto the porch roof and scooted over to the limb of the maple at the far end. He'd figured out this escape route years ago. He felt kind of silly running out to the barn like a scared ninny, but he didn't want to go back inside again either.

The barn was a mess. Hayforks were not put away, and it looked as if the watering troughs hadn't been filled since Friday. His muscles ached from the surge of work he'd done at Mandy's the day before, but he carried buckets of water to fill the troughs. It calmed him some.

It was midafternoon when he felt a chill entering the lower level of the barn. Cade looked up from the forkful of hay he was pitching into the racks, and he knew it wasn't good. Pa's mouth was set crooked, and he started in on a tirade that Cade heard every time he came back from Mandy's. How he was the laziest excuse for a son, running off to be suckled by his sister while everyone else around here was working their ass off. The usual. Cade kept piling hay in the racks. But he stopped and turned around to face him when Pa got down to what was really eating at him. Cade didn't know what he was talking about, but he had a good idea of what was coming. And he didn't want his backside to the old bastard. Pa was going on about how he couldn't stand it *when a son of his lied to him*. The words were spat out like Cade had told the most despicable lie on earth.

Pa was just starting to burn. Sometimes the black muck fields around Hartville would spontaneously combust beneath the surface. The fire smoldered out of sight, and only a whiff of smoke seeped out of the earth. Then flames would suddenly shoot up through the field and a wildfire that was almost impossible to put out would swallow up everything around it. That was how Pa was when he was working himself up.

"I want to hear the truth straight from your mouth!" Pa's eyes had a muck-fire burn now.

Cade shrugged and said, "What?"

Pa's arm swung back, and he slammed the back of his hand across Cade's face. "Are ya gonna keep lying to me? 'Cause I'll beat the truth out of you if I have to." And he struck another blow, knocking Cade backward.

"I don't know what you think I lied about."

Pa barreled his arms full force into Cade's chest and knocked him to the ground. "Keep it up, you little bastard. I'll kill you before I'll have you lying to my face."

Cade felt the weight of Pa's foot on his neck. He could only sputter and gasp.

"So, do you want to start telling me how you became a damn Dunker-boy yesterday?

The baptism. Someone had told Pa. A few seconds before this, he had been scared of Pa, but now he felt an ice-cold rage burning from his head down into his arms. He grabbed Pa's foot that was on his neck and jerked it upward, throwing the old man off balance. Cade made it to his knees and yelled back, "It's none of your damn business what church I join!"

Pa's boot caught Cade in the chin and snapped his head back. He hit hard when he fell. The barn got dark for a second or two, and when he was able to focus again, he saw the motion even before he comprehended what was hap-pening. Pa's two hands had grabbed the pitchfork from the pile of hay, and two arms were moving upward in a large arc that raised the fork in the air. By instinct more than reason, Cade rolled aside as the tines gouged down into the earthen floor where he'd just been. Pa's face was white and pinched into a hor-rible look of pain. The craziness in his eyes went dull then, and he crumpled down to his knees with his fingers still clenched around the handle of the fork.

Cade slowly backed away, keeping his eye on this madman. But Pa didn't move except for his chest, which made wheezing sounds with each breath. Cade reached the doorway and backed outside. He turned and ran. Not to the cottage. Not to Garrett's house. Not even to Mandy's. He jumped over the fence and ran across the field to the woods, where he could melt into the tree line and still have a view of the barn. He shook uncontrollably.

* * *

When Pa came out of the barn, he was staggering as if he'd been the one knocked flat. Pa didn't look in his direction, but Cade hunched down behind the scrub brush and peered through the stalks as if he had. His jaw was aching, and he touched his fingertips to the goose egg popping out on the back of his skull. He didn't want to think about Pa kicking him in the chin, but it came anyway. And what had followed came unbidden, too. He leaned over and vomited into the grass. Cade slid onto the ground and let the sharp pain that ached in his heart seep slowly into the earth. It wasn't until mosquitoes were keening in his ear that he realized it was dark, and he'd been lifeless for hours.

* * *

Cade's stomach pulled him back into life. He was starved. He tried to stand, but his head spun, and he landed on his knees. The ache in his jaw brought back the awful details of what had happened in the barn. *Pa had gone mad.* Cade looked across the field, half expecting a shadowy figure to emerge from the dark shape of the cottage. But there was nothing. Pa was likely passed out on the chair with his finger hooked in the loop of his brown jug.

Cade kept his eye on the cottage as he crept back through the garden to where the stone springhouse was built into the hill. He opened the door. There was just enough moonlight reflecting off the whitewashed walls of the room to make out the row of crocks half-submerged in the cold water and the cloth-covered bowls on the stone shelves above. He raided it like a bear out of hibernation, gulping the cream in the large crock, licking fingers that had gouged into the small crock of butter, slurping up leftover stew from a lidded bowl, and devouring a bowl of berries. When his humanity finally caught up with his stomach, he wiped his sleeve across his mouth and thought about how in the morning his sister-in-law, Clara, would stand here with her hands on her hips and wonder.

He stepped outside into the damp air and stared at the cottage. He sure as hell wasn't going to spend another night in there with that madman. But he couldn't live like a Dunker at Mandy's. There was the box of coins hidden under his bed he'd been saving for the day he would leave this hellhole for good. A sense of certainty came over him. That day had come.

His thoughts sped up as he hoisted himself up on the branches of the maple tree and tiptoed across the roof. As he neared the window, his legs started shaking so badly, he had to sit down. He leaned his back against the dormer and looked up at the sky. There was something comforting about the constancy of stars and the sky clock. When he was ten, he'd read an astronomy book that told how to tell time using two stars in the Big Dipper, and he'd gotten quite good at it. He looked up now and found the Big Dipper. He did all the calculations in his head and noted it was a little past midnight. Knowing the time brought him back to this place. Cade stood up and eased himself into his room. He moved quickly, dodging the creaky floorboards, his ears cocked.

He tossed things into his cloth satchel: a change of clothes, his coins, and a small tinderbox with the flint and steel in it. He put the folding knife Doc had given him into his pocket. He had never thought about parting with the books his ma had left behind. Over the years he'd moved them all to a shelf he'd built right by his bed. He knew he couldn't take them with him. He rolled up a light wool blanket and stuffed it in the bag. The only other thing he needed was the small iron pan he always took when he camped. It was hanging on the wall in the kitchen.

There were no sounds coming from the stairwell, so he began his descent, staying close to the wall where the floorboards were firm. His hand slid into his pocket, and he wrapped his fingers around his knife just in case. A cross-breeze from the windows let him know he was near the bottom, and his eyes strained in the dark to find an even darker form of Pa in his chair. He wasn't sure what he saw there. He paused to listen for the ragged breathing Pa usually made. The silence was unnerving. His feet stepped onto the solid floor at the bottom of the stairs, and he turned left toward the kitchen entrance. He just wanted to grab the skillet and run out the back. Pa would never catch up, even if he did get awake.

Cade nearly made it to the door when he went sprawling. He found himself lying with his cloth bag wedged beneath him on top of a massive object on the hallway floor. As his mind pieced it together, he realized the object was Pa! Passed out. He scrambled off the old man, and his palm landed on Pa's hand. The hand that had gripped a pitchfork the last time he'd seen it. He jerked back from it and scooted against the wall, shielding himself with his bag in front of his chest.

Pa didn't move. Cade suddenly couldn't get enough air. He was trying to make sense of something else he had noticed. Gradually, he realized what it had been. Pa's hand had been cold. *Dead cold.*

Cade sucked in air loudly now, unable to catch his breath. Unable to move. *Pa is dead.* The window shade that Pa always pulled down begrudged a sliver of moonlight beneath it, and now Cade could make out the form of the body sprawled out beside him. He had no idea what to do. He didn't want to answer any questions about what had happened before Pa fell over dead. He just wanted out.

Cade got to his feet and flattened himself against the wall, still holding his bag like a shield. He prayed that he wouldn't brush against that cold hand again. When he reached the door, he bolted like a skittish colt in a lightning storm. The door slammed behind him, and he ran.

A swath of stars pointed a direction that his feet followed in a mechanical, mindless rhythm. He ran full-out to the far side of the pasture, hopped the zigzag rail fence, and kept running down the dirt road. Away from the cottage. Away from the farm. Just away from. He let his feet take him where they wanted. When he found himself staring at Mandy's back porch, he realized he wanted to be inside this house more than anything. He laid his shoes against the porch wall and lifted the window sash. He crawled through to *his* room and sank into his bed, too numb even to cry.

* * *

"Cade?"

A dark, foreboding dream had hold of him, reluctant to release him from its realm, but he heard his sister call again. He lifted his head and squinted in the daylight. "Wha–what?"

She was standing in the doorway. "I didn't know you were here."

He rolled over. "It was late. I didn't want to wake you."

"What happened to your chin?" She came to the side of his bed and leaned over him. "Cade, you've got an awful bruise there."

"I fell. In the barn." He didn't know why he was lying about it.

"Oh, dear. I'm out of comfrey root for the witch hazel poultice. I'll pick some up while I'm in town." She closed the door behind her.

Cade sat up and dropped his legs over the side of the bed. Maybe it had just been a nightmare. But there was his satchel on the floor. His sore jaw brought vivid images of what had happened in the barn. He remembered raiding the springhouse and packing his bag. His breathing sped up, and his chest hurt as he remembered the rest of it. It was the thought of Pa's cold hand that made him gasp for air. *Pa is dead.*

How could he admit to Mandy that he'd left Pa dead on the cottage floor? How could he tell anyone that the last thing his Pa had done in life was to try to kill him? Sweat beaded on his face, and he smelled an odor on himself. An acrid, crazy smell.

He pulled off his shirt and headed out the back door, grabbing the lye soap from the shelf on the porch as he went by. At the pump, he worked up a lather between his hands and rubbed it vigorously over his chest and arms. He tossed his trousers aside, and standing in his drawers, he pumped a cold stream over his legs before scrubbing them hard with the chunk of soap. At last, he laid the soap down and let the cold water carry away the lather and the stench. When he returned to his room, he stripped and sat naked in the patch of sunlight on the floor, pulling his knees up to meet his forehead.

* * *

Cade was alone eating breakfast when his eldest brother walked in the back door without knocking. Garrett and Pa never knocked. It was like they owned everyone else in the family.

"I got something bad to tell you." Garrett's face twisted up, and his eyes got wet.

Cade tensed up for what was coming.

"Pa's dead. I–I found him lying on the kitchen floor." The words spurted out like they'd been dislodged from a broken field-tile, followed by a gush of emotion.

Cade felt a chill spreading through his body. It was true then. He'd almost convinced himself that it had been some cruel joke Pa was playing. That Pa was home sitting in his chair, having a good laugh.

Garrett was all broken up, and Cade started to reach out to steady him but then thought better of it. His brother wasn't one for touch unless there was a fist involved. Garrett had snot running down his upper lip, and he blew noisily into his handkerchief. "I don't know how it could happen. Two weeks ago, Pa was plowing the corn hisself. We were going to head over to Bixler's this morning to help with thrashing, but he didn't show. And I went looking. The basket of leftovers that Clara gave him was on the floor beside him, so it must have happened right after he left our place."

Cade was relieved not to have been the last one to see Pa alive.

His brother scowled. "Where were *you* when Pa needed you? Of all nights for you to up and run off to your sister's. He told us how you snuck around and joined up with the damn Dunkers. And then you shit-faced lied about it."

"I didn't lie. I just didn't tell him."

"Did you ever think of what that would do to Pa, Cade? I never seen him so worked up. Reckon that's what killed him!" Garrett turned away as his shoulders shook. "Well. You can live with *that* on your conscience, Dunker-boy."

Cade wanted to cram his fist into Garrett's pompous, snot-covered face. He wanted to scream how that old bastard had tried to drive a pitchfork into his heart. Maybe *that's* what Pa couldn't live with. Or maybe God had finally got fed up with Pa spreading misery around like manure. Cade's shoulders drew up tight and his fists clenched, but he couldn't move. His feet were held fast, and no words came out at all. He kept thinking about that cold hand of Pa's. He didn't want to end up like that, crumpled on a hallway floor, bitter and hollowed out.

His brother sniffed and straightened his back. He headed toward the door without looking at Cade. "Tell your sister. Family meeting at the farm. At two."

Mandy took it hard. She pulled Cade to her and spilled tears on his ear and down his neck.

"Did you see Pa yesterday when you went home? Did he say anything about not feeling well?"

He didn't know how to answer that, and it must have shown.

"Cade? What happened?"

"Pa was … upset that I'd gotten baptized."

"You had a fight with him?"

"I didn't even know he knew about it. Until he came at me."

She stood back and stared at the bruise on his chin and then locked eyes with him until he had to look down. "Cade? *Did Pa do that?*"

He didn't answer. But she hugged him tightly again.

"I'm so sorry, Cade. I haven't kept you safe. He wasn't like that when the rest of us were growing up."

She looked so grieved that he couldn't tell her all of it. What Pa had done felt like a shame on their family, and Cade felt the poison from it seeping into his own veins.

* * *

The weight of the coffin dug into Cade's shoulder, but he didn't let it show. He was carrying Pa to his grave, no matter what Garrett thought. His brother had tried to convince the others that he was too young to be a pall-bearer. That was bullshit. He was as strong as any of the men in the family. He *needed* to carry Pa to his grave. It was feeling the weight of Pa inside the box that made it real.

The earth was gouged with a fresh hole beside where Ma was laid. Cade stared at the coral bells he had weeded in the spring, now with their roots exposed to the air. He thought they'd never get Pa in the ground. All the others wanted to hang on to his dead carcass and go on about what a wonderful father he'd been. The pastor prayed, but Cade didn't close his eyes. He and God hadn't been on speaking terms lately.

At last, it was time to lower Pa into the grave. It helped to throw dirt on the coffin and watch it disappear into the bowels of the earth, a phrase he'd read once and had saved for this special occasion. He kept thinking of Pa down in the earth's bowels. And then squeezing through the devil's ass into Hell, which was surely where he was headed.

A drizzle started coming down almost as soon as they tossed dirt on the casket. Cade stayed behind and watched the grave diggers fill in the hole. Mandy tried to get him to come inside their buggy, but he shook his shoulder loose from her grip. She didn't say anything then. They all left, and he stood like a sentry in the rain, making sure the old bastard didn't get out.

CHAPTER SEVEN

Claybourne Oaks

By the end of the first week the asthma had disappeared, but Mrs. Taylor had Dr. Hampton check to be certain. He said, "Your lungs are clear, young lady."

Ellie didn't know why adults needed doctors to say what was perfectly obvious to her.

Mrs. Taylor looked relieved. "I wasn't sure. I was going to cancel my plans to stay at our cottage next week, but now I'm wondering if it would be good for Ellie to spend a few days there. What do you think?"

"By all means," he said. "Country air will do her good!"

That evening Mrs. Taylor told Ellie more about their cottage, which was called Claybourne Oaks and had been in Mrs. Taylor's family for half a century. It was part-farm and part-swamp, she said. Ellie had always wanted to visit a real farm. She wasn't so sure about a swamp.

A train took them to the Hartville Depot, and Harvey the liveryman took them the rest of the way. When their carriage turned onto a lane between two pin oak trees, Ellie saw a red barn with a foundation of stone on the hillside behind the house. She stretched her head out of the window to look at the sheep eating dandelions along the lane. A dog ran from the porch and barked at their carriage wheels, which set the chickens in the yard squawking and flapping. A woman waved from the garden and walked toward the driveway to greet them. Mrs. Taylor waved back.

"Is that Tilda?" Ellie asked. Mrs. Taylor had told her about Tilda and Hank Jeffreys, the caretakers for the farm part of Claybourne Oaks.

"Yes," she said and then called out to Tilda, "Where are the children?"

Tilda had a wide, toothy smile and silvery streaks running through her dark hair. "Hank's folks are keeping them until next Wednesday. They always take them for a spell when I'm deep in canning season. Bless them."

Mrs. Taylor introduced Ellie.

Tilda smiled warmly. "You're welcome down here anytime, Ellie. I might put you to work gathering eggs, though." She winked.

"I'd like that." Ellie smiled happily and looked over at Flora, who was nodding.

"Your larder's full, and I opened up your windows after the rain," Tilda said.

"You take such good care of us when we come. Thank you, Tilda." Flora reached out her hand, and they grasped each other's fingertips for a moment.

The carriage continued along a gravel lane, which wound through a stand of trees and opened into a clearing. It was as if Ellie had just dropped into the illustration from a storybook. There was a two-story stone cottage with an apple tree in the yard. Ellie spotted a bench swing on the porch. Trees covered the hillside behind the cottage. A stream wound, snake-like, out of the woods and down the hill to a flat marsh below the cottage. Mrs. Taylor said that was the swamp. Ellie had expected a smelly green pond with dead tree stumps like she had seen once in Philadelphia, but this swamp looked alive. There were bushes and cattails and big willow trees with birds flying about.

Mrs. Taylor said her parents had bought this hundred-acre farm, but they hadn't been the least bit interested in farming. Her father was an entomologist who studied insects. Her mother was an artist who painted wildflowers for botanical books. They had liked this land because of the woods and the swamp, where all kinds of wonderful specimens could be found. So that was where they built their cottage. Mrs. Taylor said every summer she and her brother were allowed to run free at Claybourne Oaks. "They were the happiest summers of my life," she said.

Ellie liked the idea that this was a place to run free.

* * *

The arched stone wall of the springhouse had a door that opened right into the hillside near the stream. Grasses and wildflowers grew over the top so that when you were up on the hill you wouldn't even know you were standing on its roof.

Ellie loved her job of being the pack-horse between the springhouse and the kitchen. The door swung into a cool, damp room with whitewashed walls like the horse stable at their country house where she used to live. Sounds didn't come into this room, even with the small window above the door. It felt like she had stepped inside a mountain. There was a rectangular pool of water. Jars and crocks, some with lids and some with cheesecloth tied over the tops, sat in the water. Bowls of plums and berries were lined up on a stone ledge, and on the floor was a basket of peaches. Mrs. Taylor always gave Ellie a list of what was needed for their meals.

The fields surrounding the swamp were flat muck-lands with the blackest dirt she had ever seen. Ellie didn't know it was possible to get so dirty while playing. Mrs. Taylor had given her Opal's hand-me-down "cottage dresses" for play so that her Philadelphia clothes would not be ruined beyond hope.

Sometimes Mrs. Taylor would stop her at the door and point to the basin of water she'd brought out to the porch. "Oh, my! Down to your petticoat, young lady," she'd say. The blackened dress was left in the big washtub, and Ellie would scrub her hands and face with castile soap in the small basin. Mrs. Taylor just laughed and shook her head. "If Genevieve could see you now."

Most mornings, the two of them went walking in the meadow and through the woods, Mrs. Taylor with her foraging basket and Ellie with her red satchel. Mrs. Taylor showed Ellie things like how to harvest roots from the spindly sassafras saplings growing everywhere under the mother trees. The roots were best in the early spring when the sap was running, she said. Ellie learned how to scrape the bark with her fingernail to release the fragrance of the sassafras. There was a tall glass jar of dried roots in the pantry that they sometimes boiled in water to make the red tea. Ellie wrote notes about it in the margin on page eighteen of her tree book. She added: *Claybourne Oaks. Hartville, Ohio. 26 July 1893.* Last of all, she slipped a mitten-shaped leaf from the tree between the pages and placed her book back in her satchel.

One morning, rain was pounding on the roof of the cottage and blurring the windows so much that she could hardly see the woods. She sighed and slumped into the rocker by the stove.

Mrs. Taylor said, "I know just the thing to do on a rainy day like this!"

"What?"

"I won't tell you until we get there." Mrs. Taylor dug through the closet and brought out Opal's corduroy leggings. Ellie put them on and tucked her skirt inside them, as she was told. Then she tried on Opal's overshoes, but they had to stuff paper in the toes to make them fit.

They sloshed side by side down the muddy lane under a big, black umbrella, with Mrs. Taylor gathering her long skirt up with her other hand. Ellie noticed that mud splashed on her skirt anyway, but it didn't seem to matter much to her. Mama wouldn't have liked that one bit! They went past the farmhouse and up the bank to the large double doors of the red barn. Mrs. Taylor let Ellie lift the wooden handle to release the latch on a small side door. The scent of sweet clover from the mow greeted her. The darkened interior was dimly lit by shafts of daylight cutting through the cracks between the wallboards. Gradually, her eyes saw through the dark. It was the highest and widest ceiling she'd ever seen, except maybe at the train station in Philadelphia, where more than a dozen trains could park side by side.

They climbed into the wide hayloft, where Mrs. Taylor unhooked a heavy rope from the wall. "This is why we've come here. It's been here since I was a small girl."

The rope floated slowly toward Ellie, and she noticed it was as thick as her arm. She caught it and let her eyes follow it up to where it was suspended from a rafter beam in the center of the loft. There was a large knot tied at the bottom end, which hung waist-high.

"Hop up on the knot, Ellie. I'll swing you."

Ellie straddled the huge knot, which made quite a nice seat, and Mrs. Taylor gave her a push. Her hair, which had gotten wildly curly in the damp morning air, flew back from her eyes, and she grinned. It was the most wonderful swing.

"I think you are ready for the big challenge."

"The big challenge?"

"Follow me." Mrs. Taylor hooked the rope under her arm and walked to a large, square post that had a ladder attached to the side. Up she went, and Ellie followed. When they reached the wide crossbeam, Mrs. Taylor showed her how to scoot out on the beam, letting her legs dangle over the edge.

"I—I think I'm kind of dizzy."

"We'll just sit until you feel perfectly settled. It is a wide beam, and it's no different than sitting up in a treehouse."

That made sense, and Ellie felt her heart settling. She loved being up in trees.

"When we were children, we'd swing from this very beam we're sitting on. You don't have to do it, Ellie, but I can tell you it is something you'll remember all of your life!"

Ellie was astonished by the thought of flying across the span of this barn. It both thrilled her and scared her at the same time. "But how far does it go?"

"You will swing over to just above that mound of hay. Right before the rope swings back, you will feel a little pause."

Ellie nodded. She knew about that moment of stillness at the farthest point a swing goes.

"When that happens, you can let go and drop down into the mountain of hay. It is wonderfully soft to land in. Opal still likes to swing from up here whenever she comes to the farm. Pansy did, too, when she was young."

Ellie swallowed a few times. Her mouth was dried out, and her heart was pounding again. She slipped the knot between her legs. After a few deep breaths, her curiosity won out. She let herself slide off the beam, squealing as she swooped down. Giggles erupted as she flew upward to the other side, her toes brushing the edge of the hay mountain. She let go of the rope at that very moment before it changed directions, and she sank into the soft hay. She laughed so hard, it made her belly bounce. Ellie scrambled down from the haystack, grabbed the rope, and ran toward the ladder again.

"Well done, Ellie! You are a real farm girl now!"

There was something about those words that soaked into Ellie's skin and made her feel happy all over. It was the best compliment anyone had ever given her.

* * *

The rooster over at Tilda's woke Ellie every morning. Usually, she'd scoot to the other end of her bed, where the air with its smells and sounds drifted through the screened window. She liked to watch the morning fog lift and listen to Claybourne Oaks waking up. This morning she wanted to be out in it.

The boards on the front porch felt damp under her bare feet, and she shivered a little in her summer nightgown. Steam was rising out of the swamp, and this morning she could hear the bleat of the ewes as plainly as if they were in front of her. She'd never seen it for herself, but Mrs. Taylor had told her how the ewes always followed each other in a line, the oldest one first.

"How do they know who's oldest?" Ellie had asked.

"They just know." Mrs. Taylor had told her how the cowbells clanged when Flossie and Della were finished being milked and were on their way to the pasture. Which meant Hank was carrying a bucket of warm milk from the barn into Tilda's kitchen now. Ellie let the sounds make images in her head. She liked that there was an order to the day one could count on.

The door opened behind her. Mrs. Taylor was in her nightgown, too, with her gray woolen shawl wrapped around her shoulders. "Here. Come and get warm," she said as she sat on the porch swing and held half of her shawl open. Ellie snuggled in.

"I wish we didn't have to leave. I'll miss Claybourne Oaks."

"Yes, this land is a magical place that lays claim to those who understand her. She will always welcome you back, Ellie."

Ellie felt a tingle in her chest at the thought, as if her heart smiled just then. They sat saying nothing at all until the sun had cut through the mist.

When Mrs. Taylor went inside to make breakfast, Ellie stepped into the grass and let the dew soak between her toes. She thought about the idea that there was magic in this farm. She was sure it was true, not only because Mrs. Taylor had told her so, but because she could feel it. She walked a short distance into the woods. The sunlight through the trees shifted this way and that, casting leafy shadows on the ground and Ellie alike so that her body seemed to blend into the path beneath her. She felt a pleasant vibration that came up through her bare feet from the earth. Perhaps Claybourne Oaks *had* laid claim to her.

The odd thought came to her that she was *home.*

CHAPTER EIGHT
Quarantine

Ellie raised her head and peeled back the damp hair stuck to her cheek. It was so hot in the upper berth she and her sister shared on the overnight express to Philadelphia. When Charlie coughed, Mama opened the heavy curtain, and cooler air came in. Then she heard Mama gasp and say, "Aaron! She's burning up!"

Charlie was so sick that Papa had the driver take them directly from the train station to Dr. Sturgis's home near Rittenhouse Square. The doctor came out to the carriage to look in Charlie's throat. Her tonsils had the gray coating, he said, and her neck was already starting to swell. Ellie didn't know what that meant, but Mama started to cry, and Papa's face was pale. The adults stepped away from the carriage to talk while Ellie stared at Charlie, who was lying on her side across the seat. She was breathing noisily through her mouth, her eyes barely open.

Papa opened the door and helped Mama climb in.

Dr. Sturgis said, "I'll report it to the health officer. Your house will be flagged sometime today." He gave Mama a booklet to read and bottles of disinfectant to dilute in water. "You all must wash with it and disinfect everything Charlotte touches." He said it was important that every handkerchief that Charlotte used was burned right away and that disinfectant was poured on her bowel movements and urine before disposing of it. Ellie wrinkled up her nose when he said that. He gave Mama cloth "wrappers" to wear over her clothes whenever she was in the sick room, and she had to wash the one she wore in disinfectant every night.

"What did he mean that our house will be flagged?" Ellie asked. Her chest felt jittery.

"We will be quarantined," Papa said. "A flag will be put on our door to let people know that no one can come in. It means our family can't go out of the house for at least a month. Charlotte has diphtheria, and it is very contagious. There are strict laws that forbid us from letting anyone else be exposed to the germs."

"What about Maggie?" Ellie wanted their cook to be there. Maggie always knew what to do.

"She can't stay with us, Ellie. Mama will take care of Charlie, and I can cook and take care of you."

"Papa, you don't know how to cook."

"Says who? I learned some things in the army. The only thing is, I might have to build a campfire on the kitchen floor."

Ellie laughed. When Papa joked, it put things back to normal.

Mama started reading aloud from the booklet, and everything got serious again. Ellie could hear the worry in her voice.

"The sick room should be on the top floor with lots of light and air," Mama said. "And it says we must burn everything in it when the quarantine is lifted. Maybe we should burn everything in the house when this is over!" Her voice got shaky, and her shoulders shook. "How could this happen to *us*? We'll be treated like lepers!"

"We'll get through this, Genevieve. No one is exempt from diphtheria. Even in Rittenhouse Square. Our friends know that."

The guest room at the far end of the upstairs hall became the sick room, and Ellie wasn't allowed near it. She was glad. It seemed like Charlie was locked in a prison cell, and Mama was the warden who came out sometimes but not very often. A wooden bucket of disinfectant water sat outside the door. When Mama came out, she always removed her wrapper and reached back inside to hang it on the coat tree by the sick room door. Then she knelt by the bucket and washed her hands over and over.

When Ellie walked toward her, Mama said, "Don't touch me. I'm covered in germs." Ellie concentrated hard to see them, but all she could see was Mama. Later, when the door to their bathing room was open a bit, she stood outside watching Mama in the copper tub scrubbing her arms with a washrag until it seemed they would bleed if she didn't stop. Mama was sobbing, so quietly that no one would have known unless they looked in.

Two nights later, Ellie woke with a croupy cough. Papa came quickly and lifted the lamp close so he could see down her throat.

"Looks like you'll be moving into the sick room with Charlie," was all he said.

"No, Papa. Please don't make me go in there."

Dr. Sturgis had said nobody was allowed to hug someone who had diphtheria, but Papa didn't seem to care about that now. When she cried, he lifted her up for a big hug and pulled out his good handkerchief to wipe her nose on. She laid her head on his shoulder, and he held her for a long time. Then he carried her down the hall to where Charlie was sleeping in the big bed and Mama was sleeping on the sofa.

"We have another patient," Papa whispered.

Mama just sighed and pulled back the covers on the bed. Charlie was sleeping and didn't even stir.

Ellie's head and throat hurt worse than any other time she'd been sick. Even her bones ached almost too much to move them. Mama always seemed to be nearby, sometimes with a spoonful of bitter medicine or salty broth that Dr. Sturgis said they had to sip. Both liquids burned her throat. Mama fed her by hand for several days when Ellie was too weak and dizzy to sit up. Her fever brought scary dreams, and sometimes she was burning in a firepit with Dolly, but when she cried out, Mama was there stroking her hair and laying cool, wet rags on her forehead.

One day she realized she felt a little better and her throat didn't hurt so much. Mama said it was the middle of August now. Charlie was sitting in the armchair all wrapped up in a blanket, her blonde hair shining in the sunlight. She grinned at Ellie and said, "Hey, fuzz head."

"Charlie-horse," Ellie said back. A warm breeze came in from the window when Papa opened the door. He stood in the hallway with Maggie's big apron over his suit.

"Did someone order my popular McAllister Stew?" he asked. Mama held the sick mugs out through the door for him to pour in the stew.

Ellie took a sip. "It just tastes like the same old broth, Papa."

"Not if you imagine the vegetables and beef in it."

He was right. It did taste better then.

Ellie's fever broke two days after Charlie's, and both could stay awake long enough to play card games with Mama. Charlie drew cartoons of everything that happened to her and Opal at the Chicago World's Fair. And she drew a good picture of what it was like at the top of the Ferris wheel. Ellie missed Papa, but it was the best time she could ever remember having with Mama. And Charlie was becoming more like a friend than an older sister.

One afternoon, Dr. Sturgis came into the sick room. He inspected their throats and pressed on their necks. He listened to their lungs and said he had good news. The quarantine was over, he said, and he signed their certificates they all had to carry with them when they went out in public. Dr. Sturgis instructed Papa and Mama on how to disinfect the house. How everything in the room needed to be burned and every inch of this room scrubbed. He said bricks should be placed in a tub of water and a tin pan with three pounds of sulphur laid on the bricks. Papa was to light the sulphur and seal the door for twenty-four hours. The fumes leaked into the rest of the house and smelled like rotten eggs. Ellie could see why that would kill those germs.

The night the quarantine was lifted, Mama and Papa asked Charlie and Ellie to come into the parlor. They said they had some sad news to tell. A telegram had come from Isaac Taylor a couple of weeks before. Opal had caught diphtheria, too. Papa said the older girls must have caught it at the World's Fair in Chicago. The doctors had not been able to save Opal, Papa said. At first Ellie did not understand what he was saying, but his face looked so sad, and Charlie was crying. She realized then that Opal had died. She didn't know how she was supposed to feel. She had never known a child who died, especially someone who had been alive like her and Charlie just a few weeks before. It seemed like she should feel sad, like Charlie, but too many things were happening inside her head, and it started to ache. A terrible ache. She squeezed her head between her hands and moaned.

Papa held his arms open to her and she sat on his lap. She laid her head against his heart, listening to its slow beat, but she still felt shaky inside. *Opal died of diphtheria.* The same diphtheria that she and Charlie had. They could have died, too. Her skin got clammy thinking about it, and she shivered.

Mama wrapped her arm around Charlie, and they went upstairs. Ellie kept imagining Opal inside a coffin under the earth. She took a big breath. And another one. Every time the image came to her, she felt like she could hardly breathe. She cried then.

Papa probably thought she was sad. But really, she was just scared of dying.

CHAPTER NINE

Broom Man

Hartville, May 1895

A small poster on the board at the general store caught Cade's eye. The dance pavilion at Congress Lake was opening for the season next Saturday. The Spring Fling, they called it. He thought about the last two summers, when he had crawled on his belly and spied on the dancers from the shoreline. A pleasurable ripple swept through him.

His next thought surprised him. He was fifteen now, and he could almost imagine himself being bold as anything, walking into that pavilion along with all the others. His head went giddy at the thought.

On Saturday, Cade said he was turning in early and closed his door. Then, after the family had gone to bed, he climbed out of his bedroom window wearing his best shirt. At the lake, he fell in behind a small group in fancy suits and dresses walking on the gravel path toward the dance pavilion. He could hear the band playing lively music, and a woman was humming along. Cade looked down and suddenly felt embarrassed. Even his *best* shirt looked out of place in this crowd. As he neared the pavilion, his legs got shaky, and he thought about hiding again in the grasses along the shore. Instead, he spied a maintenance cart parked next to the walk. He stopped there as naturally as he could and pretended to organize it. It held wooden crates, buckets, brooms, rakes, and all kinds of tools.

A train over by the icehouse had dropped off dozens of folks. He noticed that even though he wasn't blocking their path, the line flared out when it went around him as if he were an invisible rock in their stream. It seemed that no one wanted to make eye contact with a broom man. His heart settled down and gave him a chance to collect himself again.

A ticket-taker was seated in front of a small bridge connecting the shoreline to the dance pavilion. A cigarette hanging out the side of his mouth bounced as he bantered with the fellows and smiled at the ladies. Cade watched how easily people paid for their tickets and were allowed to pass, but he couldn't find the courage to step in line himself. When the sound of shattering glass echoed from the upper verandah, he saw his opportunity. He grabbed a broom and dustpan from the cart and hurried to the gate. His pulse was pounding, but he told himself it only takes a big smile and a little lie to get past a gatekeeper. "I'm supposed to clean up the glass," he said and smiled at the man.

"Sure, kid," the guy said and jerked his head toward the pavilion. Cade thanked him and hurried up the steps. He spotted the broken glass that had been dropped and went right to it, sweeping it into the dustpan. He stepped into the smoky, glittery dance hall and stared at the bodies moving and touching in ways he hadn't even imagined from the mud.

"You're working here?" The stuffy young man who asked was wearing a black jacket and bow tie. Cade guessed he was a waiter who'd been legitimately hired to work at the pavilion.

"I was told to clean up when there are spills. I'm new at this. Mind telling me where to dump this?" The lies were getting easier. Guilt didn't stick to an oiled tongue.

The fellow relaxed and pointed to a dustbin nearby. "It's about time they hired someone to help with that. We usually have to clean up after everyone goes home. I'm Thaddeus, by the way."

"Cade." At least that was the truth.

And just like that, he created a job for himself at the pavilion. Unpaid, but no one else knew that. They all must have thought someone else had hired him. He came back the next week and worked from the minute he entered the pavilion.

In fact, every Saturday night he showed up for work. "Hi Cade," they greeted him as if he'd always been one of them. It was a lie he almost believed himself. The dance pavilion served lemonade. He watched when the large punch bowls were getting low and carried gallon jugs from the kitchen on the floor below.

There was plenty to do. He swept floors, mopped spills on the tables, and chipped ice from the blocks wrapped in burlap. Along with a couple of other guys, he hauled tubs of glasses and plates to the dishwashing room. Karl, the adult in charge of keeping thirsty dancers paying for their lemonade, sometimes flipped a few coins to him at the end of the night. "Good job tonight, Cade." Karl was from Cleveland, where he'd once worked as a bartender at a big hotel on Lake Erie. He said he learned the science of mixing fancy drinks and tending bar there, but he couldn't be around alcohol anymore. Cade nodded and thought of Pa.

"How much are they paying you, Bauer?" Karl asked as they were cleaning up one night.

The question caught Cade off guard, and he fidgeted uncomfortably. He liked Karl, though, and for whatever reason, he found himself confessing everything. Cade was stricken by what he'd revealed. Then Karl began laughing so hard that he used his apron to wipe his eyes. "You mean you've been working your ass off for free all this time?"

When he put it that way, it was a little embarrassing. Cade blushed and nodded.

"Well, we're going to have to do something about that."

Cade was never quite sure how he got on the payroll, but at the end of each Saturday thereafter, he collected pay, like everyone else. It was cash to put in his pocket, if he wanted to, but he saved it instead. Someday he would buy shoes that didn't have manure in the creases. Then a proper suit and tie. And maybe some talcum. That smelled like city.

It was a summer in which he was learning some things about himself. He discovered that he had a certain charm and a wit that made people laugh. He found out that cigarettes didn't make you cough after you smoked a few and that lemonade spiked with rum tasted good at the end of a long night of cleaning up. He'd always hated it when Pa guzzled from that brown jug. Cade had the notion that inebriants made a person meaner, and he hadn't wanted any part of it. What he hadn't known about liquor until he tried it was that flirting with the girls came easier.

Mercy Mae, who must have been almost twenty, worked in the kitchen. She had a toothy smile and always looked like she had dabbed her cheeks and lips with a little beet juice. She laughed boisterously at the guys' jokes and cozied up to them in a way that almost looked innocent.

"You're a quiet one, aren't you?" she said to him one night as he leaned over the wooden railing on the lower verandah with a cigarette in his hand. It was the darkest corner of the pavilion off the kitchen entrance, where the staff took breaks now and then.

Cade felt her breast slide against his arm briefly as she came too close, and he blushed. "Just saving my thoughts for the right occasion." He sucked on the cigarette and got a little dizzy from the smoke and the attention.

"Is this the right occasion?"

"Could be." He gave her a big smile that she must have thought was an invitation.

Mercy reached up and touched the curls at the back of his neck. "I've been wanting to do that." She laughed and leaned forward against the railing so that her dress pulled tightly around her curves. "I just love naturally curly hair on a gentleman."

I'll bet you do, Cade thought, but he didn't say it aloud. He could hardly breathe. Heat was spreading through his body like a grass fire gone wild. He flipped his cigarette into the water and turned around so that his back was leaning against the wooden rail. Mercy inched over close enough that the sweet odor of her perspiration, which had blended with cooking smells and god only knew what, filled his nostrils and set his head spinning. Of all the times he'd imagined something like this happening, it hardly seemed proper now. He'd been taught to treat ladies with respect, and what he was feeling was hardly that. It occurred to him that a gentleman would step away from this intoxicating situation and get control of himself. He tried to make himself do just that.

Mercy Mae stretched her face up toward his and puckered her lips. They were a magnet bending his iron will. He lowered his head and kissed her hard, pulling her against him.

"Oh my!" She giggled, fanning her face with her hand. "You just said volumes." And she came back for more.

Cade felt a tidal wave building inside him, and he didn't care in that moment where he was.

"Mr. Bauer, may I speak with you?" The deep voice boomed out over the verandah.

Both Mercy and Cade jumped and untangled their startled bodies. She ducked under his arm and made a quicksilver disappearance through the kitchen door. Cade couldn't make out who was standing in the shadows near him until he heard the laughter.

"Artie Hanson! You scared the shit out of me!"

"You're lucky it wasn't the boss. It's a good thing I took a break, Bauer. You're in way over your head with that girl."

"What makes you think that?" Cade gave him a mock offended look.

"Hell, I don't know. You and Mercy were halfway horizontal when I came out here. Maybe that was the first clue. What are you *thinking*, messing with her?"

"Hey, I was just having a smoke, and next thing I knew she was fluffing my curls."

"I'll bet she was. You know what the joke is over at the bowling alley? Someone says, 'Have Mercy' and the other guy says, 'Already have.' They say she's always looking for fresh game. And you're about as fresh as they come."

"Am I detecting a little envy?" Cade grinned, tucking in his shirt that had somehow pulled up out of his trousers, and pushed past his friend. "Let's get back to work." He smiled at the thought of his first kiss. *Have Mercy.*

His friendship with Artie had started the first night they cleaned tables together, and they discovered they both had an irreverent sense of humor. They liked to joke about couples who were oblivious to others and who were absorbed in earnest conversation. He and Artie filled in their own version of what was being said. "Oh, Wilbur," Cade would say in falsetto, and Artie would reply in a deep voice, "Yes, Fanny?" It was always a Wilbur and Fanny routine.

Some Saturdays, Artie worked as a pin boy in the bowling house, but when there was a large dinner group in the lower level of the pavilion, he helped clean up. Cade always thought Artie had sort of a startled look, but it was just that his blue eyes were magnified by the spectacles clamped to his nose. His dark, straight hair was parted neatly down the middle, unlike Cade's, which grew more like an untended garden, ends popping up whenever the weather turned humid.

Every Saturday night at the pavilion, Cade was a sea sponge soaking it all in. He watched everything. He memorized the dance steps and practiced them in his room at home while the band played the latest tunes in his head. He watched couples and how they behaved with each other.

And although he didn't tell anyone else, he was always watching for the redheaded kid to show his face again at Congress Lake. The kid had disappeared. It had been more than two years since the day Petey nearly drowned. Mandy and Daniel never mentioned it at home, but he didn't expect them to. Dunkers had a way of stretching time around an objectionable thing and pretending it never happened. They called it forgiveness. *You need to forgive your Pa and put it behind you*, they said. *You need to forget what those bullies did to Petey and move on.* Cade couldn't. But he noticed that he wasn't thinking about what happened at Jonah's Landing so much anymore.

* * *

Emma's bark jolted Cade out of a dead man's doze. Then he heard the family's carriage rattling down the lane. He scrambled out of bed and yanked off the shirt he was still wearing from when he'd climbed in the window at 3:00 a.m. He pulled another from his chest of drawers and buttoned it while he glanced in the mirror. *Shit.* A crease ran diagonally across his cheek. He splashed water on his face and hurried to the rocker before they reached the door. He was absorbed in a book and looked up casually when Petey ran through the door and pounced on him. Cade laughed and wrestled with him on the floor.

"Cade? Why didn't you come to church with us?" Petey said when his giggles had subsided.

"I had my own church service right here at home." He was glad Petey didn't demand an answer that made sense. He'd reached an unspoken understanding with Mandy and Daniel. They seemed to accept that he did not want to attend Dunker services on Sunday mornings, but he was sure they'd never approve of his surreptitious life at Congress Lake on Saturday night.

When lunch dishes were put away, Mandy said she wanted to talk to him. Alone. He followed her to his room, and she shut the door. She sat straight-backed on the chair, and he sat uneasily on the edge of his bed.

"Cade, you're old enough to decide what is right for you. You've been through a lot, and we understand that you need to sort out your relationship with God and the church in your own way."

He nodded, not sure where she was headed.

She seemed to be searching for words, but not for long. "Cade, I know about your job at the dance pavilion. Hartville is a small community. And I know that you climb through the window before dawn. And I can smell the tobacco smoke on your clothes. This room reeks of it."

He blushed and didn't know what to say.

There was a long moment where neither one of them spoke, which was the way he and Mandy usually talked, but this time it was awkward. She said, "I remember what it was like at your age, Cade. And I wasn't a Dunker girl back then. I think maybe it's time we go shopping in Canton and get you some proper clothes for going out. But there is one thing I will ask of you."

He looked up and saw that there was no judgment in her eyes.

"When you come home at night, please hang your clothes on the porch to air them out. Agreed?"

"Yep."

She got up, kissed him on the forehead, and left him sitting there stunned. He was grateful for Mandy's blessing, if he could call it that. But it was also like the wind had died and left his sailboat sitting dead in the water. There was something about sneaking out through the window into a forbidden world that had thrilled him. Some of the allure of the dance pavilion was gone.

CHAPTER TEN

Artie

When Artie showed up at Fritch's Pond Sunday afternoon with one cheek puffed out and blue around the edges, neither of them said anything about it. Cade figured they'd get around to it when the time was right. He had brought a tin of worms he'd dug up from the edge of the manure pile. Plenty for both of them, he said. Artie had brought molasses cookies his Grandma Hanson had baked for the two of them. Seemed like a fair trade.

Cade knew Artie was living with his grandparents in Mishler now. His mother had died last year. He'd never talked about his father, though. "What does your pa do?" Cade asked as they made their way through the stand of trees to where they could cast their lines just at the edge of the lily pads.

"He throws pots."

"At you?" Cade laughed.

"No, I meant on the wheel. He's a potter. But he's thrown a few at me, too. He's a mean bastard when he's drunk."

When Artie said it like that, as if it was nothing for him to be ashamed of, some part of Cade relaxed. He'd never let himself get too close to people his own age. There'd been too many secrets about Pa that he didn't want anyone else to know. But Artie's father seemed have been cut from the same cloth as Pa. "My pa was like that before he died," he heard himself confess.

"I'll bet your pa never threatened to kill you, though," Artie said.

"You'd lose that bet." Out of the corner of his eye, he saw Artie's head pop up and look over at him. Cade surprised himself by blurting out something he'd never told anyone. "He always blamed me for ruining his life. And he tried to kill me with a pitchfork the night he died." His eyes watered up unexpectedly, probably trying to dilute the truth.

"Bloody hell. I thought I was the only one. My dad nearly strangled me the night he lost his job at the pottery works. He blamed me for it."

"Why?"

"I had … some problems with the factory owner's son, Lyle Fletcher. And then Lyle got my dad fired. That's how the son of a bitch was. If you ever went against him, he got revenge one way or another.

Cade whistled. "That's a big grudge. What had you done to him?"

"I told Lyle I wasn't going to be his whipping boy anymore. He just laughed and said if I didn't obey him, my dad wouldn't have a job. He actually said that. *Obey him.* I said go to hell. And then two days later my dad was blamed for breaking a machine at the factory. I'm sure Lyle broke it himself."

"Bastard!"

"My dad went into a rage when I told him Lyle had probably staged it. I've never seen him so mad at me."

"At *you?* It was Lyle that did it."

"Dad said that every day he had to do what those son-of-a-bitch Fletchers told him to do, so why did I think I was special? Dad said he was ruined now, all because I wouldn't toe the mark. He beat the shit out of me. Would have killed me if my mom hadn't come in. That's when Mom and I left home for good. We moved down to Grandma and Gramps' place."

"That took courage to stand up to Lyle Fletcher. Your mom must have been proud."

"Yeah, but she never knew all of it."

"Like what?"

"You don't want to know. The good thing was that Lyle's family shipped him off to some military school in another state. That was the year my mom died. The last thing she did was to get our names changed from Whitacre to her maiden name, Hanson. She told the judge she was dying and didn't want the name of a man who beat us to be on her tombstone. Gramps offered my dad money to sign off on papers for them to adopt me. He took it, and I became Artie Hanson."

"What did your mom die of?"

"Lead poisoning. From the glazes. Women do all the dipping at the factory. Lots of them die from it. Mom got palsy in her hands at first. Then she just got weaker. It's dangerous work."

"I'm sorry, Artie. It must have been awful. Where's your dad living?"

"Up in Mogadore still. He staggered down to Mishler this morning after he'd been drinking all night. He's done that a few times. Yelling at me from the yard, but this morning he pushed his way in and gave me a shiner. Gramps came in with his rifle pointed right at him, and my dad sobered up fast."

"That's awful, Artie." Cade shivered. They'd come to their favorite spot and set about baiting their hooks in silence. Cade wanted to talk about something other than drunken fathers. Then he remembered. "I almost forgot to tell you. Mandy wants you to come for supper next Thursday. Said it's about time they meet you."

Artie grinned. "I'd like that."

* * *

Cade greeted Artie at the door. There was a surprised expression on his friend's face when Mandy came from the kitchen in her white bonnet to introduce herself.

After she disappeared again, Cade said, "I didn't tell you my sister's a Dunker."

"Yeah, I didn't see that one coming."

"I was a Dunker, too, for a while."

"No. Really?" Artie had an incredulous look that maybe would have slid into a hoot if he'd been less polite.

By the time Rachel, who was sixteen, came down the stairs with her hair neatly tucked under her prayer bonnet, Artie seemed to have regained his composure. She was wearing an attractive, embroidered white blouse with a pale blue skirt. She had Mandy's good looks, and Cade noticed that Artie lit up when they were introduced.

"My nephew Petey is out in the barn, finishing chores with Daniel," Cade said.

Mandy was packing up the picnic baskets. She asked Rachel to fetch butter up from the springhouse. "How about you boys head down to the creek to check the fire? The coals should be ready for the corn by the time we get there. Oh, and set these jugs of mint tea in the wagon before you go."

"Guests are never pampered here," Cade said.

Artie grinned. "Makes me feel right at home."

The flames had died down, and the thick bark had turned to gray ash with vermillion heat shimmering through the cracks. It was perfect for roasting corn by the time the wagon rolled down the lane. Rachel and Petey were riding on the back. Daniel tied the mare to the hitching post and greeted Artie with a handshake. Rachel was all smiles and more interested in talking to Artie than helping Petey lift the wet burlap bag of corn to the ground.

Cade went back to help his nephew drag it to the fire. "Hey, Petey. I have a friend who wants to meet you."

Petey grinned. "I know who." He'd been going on for three days about how Artie was coming for a picnic. When their guest walked over to meet him, Petey's legs got tangled in the corn sack, and he landed in a heap on the ground. As Artie reached down to help him, Petey's eyes glazed over, and a little drool ran out the corner of his mouth. His seizure lasted only a few seconds, which was the way it usually happened for Petey. But then he squeezed his eyes shut and began to sob.

The color drained out of Artie's face, and he stepped back from Petey.

Cade leaned down and rubbed his nephew's shoulder. "Hey, Petey, are you okay? Artie's here, and he'd like to meet you."

Mandy hurried over and knelt beside him. He flung his arms around her neck. Petey had always been small for his age, but he looked even younger clinging to Mandy. He sobbed as she picked him up and carried him to the seat of the wagon.

Daniel talked briefly to Mandy before he walked toward the fire, where the older boys and Rachel were watching. "I'm sorry, Artie, we think we may need to take Petey back to the house. You three go ahead and get the picnic going. I'll be back in a bit to join you."

They heard Petey wailing the whole way down the lane.

"I don't know what was wrong with him, Artie. My nephew has petite mal seizures that usually last only a few seconds, and then he's fine." Cade was trying to make it all seem normal enough, but he could see that his friend was shaken.

"He hasn't cried like that since he was a little kid," Rachel added. There was an awkward silence that followed.

Artie stared into the fire. His face was still pale. "I guess I didn't … I'm sorry. I wasn't expecting…"

"No, I'm sorry," Cade said. "I should have warned you that Petey is a little different from other kids. You'll get to know him the next time you come." Cade took the long iron tongs and began lifting the corn out of the coals into a kettle. Some of the charred husks fell away from the yellow kernels, and his mouth watered.

Rachel stepped into Mandy's role of spreading out the picnic cloths and organizing the supper dishes. When Daniel returned, he asked Artie about what fish were biting at Fritch's Pond and how he liked living in Mishler. Artie was polite but didn't say much the whole meal. The sunset sky cast just enough light that lanterns weren't needed to load the wagon. The kids piled in the back, their legs dangling. Cade noticed that Rachel sat beside Artie, who scooted closer to her so that there was room for Cade on the other side of him. She looked pleased.

Mandy came to the porch and said Petey was sleeping, and wouldn't Artie like to come in for some tea? He said he needed to get back home and declined a ride in the buckboard that Cade offered. He needed to run off that big meal, he said. He thanked Daniel and Mandy for their hospitality.

Rachel offered to walk him to the road. Cade grinned and said, "Okay, I guess I'll unload the wagon by myself. See you later, Artie."

When the dishes were washed and put away Mandy poured mint tea in Cade's mug. "Artie seems nice.

"Yeah, but he sure got quiet. He's not usually like that."

"Perhaps he was not used to young children. I don't know what got into Petey. Maybe he's coming down with something. We'll have Artie over again sometime under better circumstances."

* * *

Artie didn't show up at the dance pavilion. Cade decided to run up to Mishler Sunday afternoon. He took a shortcut to Congress Lake and followed the train tracks two miles northwest to the Mishler Station. Artie's grandparents lived three blocks from the depot.

Mrs. Hanson welcomed him in. "Artie's been under the weather the last few days. No fever, but he hasn't eaten enough to keep a bird alive." She pointed Cade toward the cookie jar. "I just made a fresh batch of the molasses ones you like. Help yourself. I'll tell him you're here." She went upstairs.

Soon, heavy footsteps descended the stairs and Artie appeared around the corner. Dark circles accentuated the puffiness around his eyes, which were magnified by his thick lenses.

"You look like hell, Artie. You all right?"

"Yep." He looked at his shoes and cleared his throat a couple of times. "Cade? We need to talk. But not here." Artie glanced up toward the floor above them, where his grandma was.

"Sure. You want to walk over to Congress Lake?"

Artie gave a shrug. He was silent the whole way, staring ahead with his jaw clenched. Cade just walked. Sometimes when they fished, they both liked the silence. That part didn't feel odd, but the look on Artie's face did.

There were people all over the place at Congress Lake, so Cade led the way down the east trail to Jonah's Landing, where they could talk. When they reached the clearing, he couldn't stand the suspense any longer. "For God's sake, Artie, what's up?"

Artie coughed, and his hand gestured as if he had said something, but he hadn't. Finally, he said, "You know how I told you Lyle Fletcher got my dad fired from his job at the pottery factory?

"Yeah. After you stood up to Lyle. And then he got sent off to military school."

"There's more I have to tell you."

"Okay."

"You told me I had courage, standing up to Lyle. But I was a white-livered shit before that. I went along with him. Until it was too late. I didn't know it was Petey. Not until last Thursday."

Artie was half crying, and Cade was confused by it.

"I hate myself for what we did. And I've been trying to figure out how to tell you."

"Artie, what are you talking about?"

"I came back to help him, Cade. Lyle said to leave him, but I came back. There was a girl and an older kid carrying him out. Now I realize it was you. God! I'm sorry. I never knew it would go so far." Artie was sobbing. "Honest. I never meant to drown him."

The words ricocheted in Cade's head like a bullet on a cavern wall. "Lyle Fletcher's the red-haired bastard who tried to drown Petey? And it was *you* with him?" His fists clenched as he realized what had been right in front of his eyes all along. "You *lied* to me!" A tidal wave of rage rose. He punched Artie in the jaw, sending his spectacles flying. Then he hit him hard in the gut, knocking him off-balance. And when Artie fell to the ground, Cade kicked him and pounced on him and hit him again. Artie made no effort to defend himself. He only stared. Cade raised his fist to deliver another blow and stopped midair. The flatness in Artie's face was as if life had gone out of him, and it was impossible to strike him again. His fist melted. A groan came up from Cade's belly as he crumpled onto the grass. Waves of grief washed over him and carried him out to sea.

* * *

He had lost sense of time, but the low-lying clouds were still tinged with pink where the sun had set. Cade lifted his head slowly and looked around. Artie was gone. He dropped his forehead on his arm and tried to make sense of what had happened. The fact was that his best friend had done an unforgivable thing, and there was no other way to look at it. He curled his knees into his chest and tried to shut out the images of Artie and Lyle Fletcher attacking Petey. Artie's face pushed its way into his thoughts. His lifeless face, waiting for Cade's fist. The tears came again, and he pounded his swollen knuckles into the earth.

When he awakened, the sky had turned indigo-black. The fire in him had died down. Dampness from the ground had seeped through his clothes.

There was a shard of pain from his heart that had gouged its way up to his head. He'd never admitted his own blame for what had happened to Petey. The redheaded kid had made fun of his nephew, but Cade had gone into a rage about it. And that had set in motion a terrible chain of reactions. It had been his own hot temper that ended up almost costing Petey's life. Earlier this afternoon, he'd been so angry with Artie, he could have killed him. He despised the violent blood in his own veins. The same that had run through Pa. He saw Pa's face all twisted in anger, the beatings, the pitchfork coming toward his chest. He could even smell Pa's madness now. It filled his nostrils. But it wasn't Pa's. It was his own madness he was smelling. The rage he had felt when he was beating Artie was the same vile madness he couldn't forgive in Pa. It was what he had always feared would happen. He was just like Pa.

He was struck still.

He didn't know how he could live with this family curse. The truth was that he didn't want to live with it anymore. It was a cancer that was taking over. He'd cut it out of his body if he could.

Cade pulled himself into a seated position and sat hugging his thighs to his chest, listening to the constant slosh of warm water against the rock. A soothing sound. He slowly stood and unbuttoned his shirt, dropping it to the ground. Then the rest of his clothes fell in a pile at his feet. He walked naked into the lake.

He stretched out just below the surface, where it was still warm. Then he dove down into the chilly darkness, where he brushed against the spongy, moss bed of the lake. He felt the bubbles of his breath bouncing against his face and the hairs on his head swishing in his wake. The stench of madness began to dissolve. He felt himself come to calmness, and he floated peacefully, indistinguishable from the water that cradled him.

Cade heard a voice then. It was Doc Williams saying, "You're a country doctor's legacy, son." Images passed through his mind. A woman. He recognized her as his mother, Hannah. She was looking at a baby that lay lifeless and blue in Doc's hands. He saw the old doctor leaning down, breathing his own breath into its mouth and nose. The image faded into blackness, and Cade became aware that his lungs were exploding in a way he hadn't experienced before. His arms were flailing. They thrashed and pulled against the weight of the water. He broke through the surface at last and took his first breath.

CHAPTER ELEVEN

In Step

Ogontz School for Young Ladies, May, 1897

Something had been gnawing at Ellie all week. She could never catch the varmint, but it had left its signs. Like holes in her concentration and untidy little nests of clothes, books, and papers strewn about their dormitory room at Ogontz School for Young Ladies.

Norah stepped over Ellie's geometry book and assignments. "You know Miss Eastman will be doing room inspection on Monday?"

"I'll clean it up! I don't need to be told!" Ellie's face reddened. She knew Norah hadn't deserved that. "I—I'm sorry, Norah. This German paper is driving me crazy. I can't figure out what I want to say."

Norah's face softened. "I know you've been stewing about it for days. Look, I have time before my fencing lesson. Maybe I can help you sort out your ideas. I don't know German, but you can tell me about it in English."

"That would be wonderful!" Ellie grabbed a fresh piece of paper from her desk and found a sharp pencil in her drawer. "I always write it in English first."

Norah Miles had been her roommate and best friend ever since they had started boarding at Ogontz the year before as eighth graders. Ellie had skipped the sixth grade because she had done so well on her examinations. It had made no difference to Norah that Ellie was a year younger. Their classmates had anointed them "the instigators." They were famous for their impromptu skits performed on the stage of the entertainment room at the top of the tower. Ellie did the funniest impersonations of faculty members or fellow students, which tended to give her the credit for their humor. And the blame if the parody crossed the line.

Their friendship had a serious side, too. Ellie could talk to Norah about anything. They would lie awake long after the bell rang for lights-out, discussing philosophy or what President McKinley was going to do about the insurrection in Cuba. Or whatever was on their hearts.

Ellie stuffed a pillow between herself and the headboard of her bed and tucked her feet under her blanket. "Fräulein Klock gave us maxims from German philosophers. We're to choose one of them and write about how it applies to modern times. I've been thinking about Friedrich Schiller's use of the term *jahrhundert.*"

"*Jahrhundert*? What's that?" Norah pulled the coverlet from her own bed around her shoulders and flopped across the foot end of Ellie's bed.

"*Jahrhundert* literally means 'one hundred years,' but Schiller uses it to refer to 'our particular time in history.' Kind of like our social backdrop. He said that we belong to a specific time in history—like us belonging to the culture of the nineteenth century. He warns that we shouldn't let ourselves become its creature.

"Why were you drawn to that?"

"What jumped out at me is that we have a choice! We don't have to *let* ourselves become creatures of our times. It made me think about how Mama always throws up her hands and says, 'What choice does a woman have?' But then my Aunt Tess says the problem is that too many women *believe* they don't have a choice, when they *do.*"

"Your aunt may be right, but I tend to agree with your mother," Norah replied. "I worry about what will happen after we graduate. I think Ogontz has spoiled us with all these choices we have here. We choose whatever sport we want to do, any art and music classes we want, and we are free to speak whatever is on our minds. It's not like that out in the world."

Ellie wrinkled up her nose. "Yes, but men take these things for granted. Don't you think it's about time women have choices, too?"

"I know we're overdue. Miss Adams lectured just last week about how we're the 'renaissance generation for women.' But I wonder if society is ready for that."

"When will it be unless we do something about it ourselves? Schiller wrote this a hundred years ago."

"Ellie, I doubt that an eighteenth-century philosopher was writing this for women."

"Maybe not. But I think modern women need to hear it. Schiller also said we shouldn't trust what society praises. And it's true! Society praises women when they act like they are less than men. We've become creatures of our times by going along with these silly beliefs about ourselves instead of challenging them. We'll be graduating in 1900! That's only three years from now. It's a perfect time for us to question women's roles in our culture!"

"Ellie McAllister, you little suffragette! I like where you are headed with this. The point you are making is that we're colluding with society's opinion of women whenever we accept its praise for being proper little ladies."

"Exactly. One of the quotes we may use for our essay is about praise. It's from Goethe: 'To praise a man is to put oneself on a level with him.' I think I can use that, but I haven't figured out how it fits in with Schiller's thoughts."

"You might get away with paraphrasing the maxim to fit what you want it to say. That's what I do when it doesn't quite say what I want. Acknowledge the maxim, but then start talking about how it affects you, and you can twist it around and stretch it to your liking."

"Norah, you're brilliant. I could come from the perspective of the person receiving the praise. Like what I was just saying about women. What if I said, 'To *accept* praise is to put oneself on a level with it?'"

"I think you are on to something, Ell."

Ellie grinned. "Did I tell you before? You're the best."

"I know." Norah laughed and stood up. "I have to run.

As her roommate stepped into the hallway, Ellie was already back at her desk, sinking into her writing. The outer world was fading from existence.

* * *

Ellie vaguely heard a tapping penetrating the inner sanctum of her desk and looked up. She glanced at the desk clock with porcelain flowers around the face. Mama had brought it back from Paris. An hour had gone by, and all she had to show for it was a mound of crumpled papers on the floor. She sighed. When the sound came a second time, she recognized it as a knock on her door. A young girl, one of the primary students who attended the day school at Ogontz, was looking up at her with a concerned wrinkle on her forehead. Ellie recognized the little girl, though she couldn't recall her name.

"Miss McAllister? I–I'm supposed to ask if you are coming to Walking Down the Stairs," she said. "Miss Eastman sent me to ask."

"Oh! I forgot! I'll be there. Well, as soon as I can! Thank you, Miss…"

"Kendall."

"Oh, yes. Sally Kendall, right?"

The little girl bobbed her head, happy to be recognized by one of the high school girls.

Ellie ran to her closet and hurried into her evening dress. She gathered her hair as best she could into a somewhat neat bun. She licked the spot on her finger where there was a stubborn ink stain, but it remained. As she hurried toward the grand staircase, she could hear the principal's voice on the landing.

Miss Eastman always assigned older girls to work with groups of younger students from the Primary Department. They were supposed to model for the young girls the proper way to descend the stairs. Walking down the stairs with perfect posture was regarded by some as the crowning achievement of young ladies of Ogontz. Sometimes they had to balance books on their heads as they descended the grand, winding staircase to the main hall. Today, the Primaries were rehearsing for the last day of school, when their parents would be standing in the hall below, waiting for the girls to descend the staircase.

Miss Eastman was telling them she wanted to see serene and graceful young ladies. "Whether it is your last day of school, the evening of your debut, or even your wedding day, a young lady's entrance requires the same poise and attention to posture. Miss Gates will now demonstrate how that is done."

Of course! It would have to be Angel Gates. Ellie's cheeks reddened. Angel was the image of perfection with her jeweled comb accenting her sculpted blonde hair. Students were supposed to have simple, plain gowns for evening attire, but Angel managed to have a pale, ivory gown peppered with delicate blue-green flowers on the bodice. A matching satin ribbon encircled her tiny waist and was gathered into a long bow at the back.

Angel rolled her blue eyes up toward Ellie and gave a patronizing smirk before smiling sweetly at Miss Eastman. Angel positioned a nosegay of flowers, just so, at her waist, lifted her chin, and stepped forward into the curved balcony, which extended out from the landing. She paused there and smiled down over the carved balustrades to the imagined crowd of parents below. Angel was clearly in her element, every movement choreographed. Something about it reminded Ellie of the times she had watched Mama transform into a queen when guests came to dinner.

If loathing had been permitted amongst the young ladies of Ogontz, it could have well described the feeling Ellie had for Miss Angel Gates. She was quite certain the sentiment was mutual. Ellie wondered if she and Norah were the only ones who saw through that fluttering, blue-eyed façade. Angel made a big show of being sweet to everyone, but she could also put on the "Rittenhouse airs," an attitude of entitlement that seemed to be directly proportional to a family's wealth.

It was especially confounding to Ellie how Angel did the same physical activities as all the girls at Ogontz but without getting a smudge on her clothes or one curl out of place. Whenever Ellie rode a horse, did calisthenics, marched in the girls' battalion, or played tennis, she was a magnet for horsehair and mud. And then Angel would be there, giving her a disapproving look as if Ellie were ten years old and getting reprimands from Mama.

"Beautifully done, Miss Gates. Young ladies, *that* was a model you should emulate!"

The praise Miss Eastman had just lavished on Angel sent a jolt through Ellie, striking her to the core like a flash of lightning. "Oh!" she heard herself blurt out.

Miss Eastman turned and peered at Ellie over her round spectacles. "Miss McAllister, I see you were able to join us. You were not ill, I hope?" The principal wore the same expression as when she was about to deliver a sermonette on behavior. But there was a pleasant curve to her mouth, the inscrutable mask of an Ogontz woman.

"Miss Eastman, I'm sorry I'm late. I–I was working on a composition, and I lost track of time."

"I see. If you have pressing schoolwork, perhaps Miss Gates will not mind carrying on alone?" She turned to Angel. "Would that be agreeable?" Angel nodded sweetly to Miss Eastman.

Ellie felt crimson heat spreading to her ears. "Yes, ma'am." She turned and fled down the hall to her room.

Tears pooled as she paced back and forth between her bed and her desk. Ellie didn't know if she was infuriated or frustrated or what she was feeling. She could still feel the tingling down her arms and legs from the bolt of lightning that had struck her on the stairs. When she saw her pen lying on her desk, she knew she needed to write. Words spilled onto her paper.

> *Goethe once wrote the maxim, "To praise a man is to put oneself on a level with him." I would like to discuss this maxim from the perspective of the one receiving the praise. Perhaps, for this purpose, I may paraphrase Herr Goethe's maxim and say: To accept praise is to put oneself on a level with the praise. Sometimes, receiving praise has a positive effect of lifting oneself to higher ground. How many of us have been inspired by praise from our parents and teachers? It is natural to want to live up to the expectations of those who see good qualities in us.*
>
> *But what effect does it have on a woman to accept praise for being less than what she is capable of being? Our society praises women for behaviors, which on the surface appear genteel and pleasant, but which diminish our potentialities.*

Women are praised as 'good wives' and 'model women' when they behave as if they have nothing more important to do than to be charming, graceful hostesses. A girl is trained from childhood to mold herself into society's model woman. Even at our school, girls are praised for walking gracefully down the stairs as if it were amongst the highest achievements to which they can aspire. Praise, perhaps even more than criticism, leaves a lasting impression on a young girl's mind. It slips into her thinking in seemingly innocuous ways and shapes how she regards herself as she grows up. Women are praised for deferring to men in the political arena and in nearly every position of authority. Even in their own homes.

What becomes of a woman who accepts this kind of praise from a society that wants her to be less than she can be? All too often, she sinks to the level our society expects of her, modeling all the limitations for which she is praised.

A century ago, Herr Schiller warned that even though one belongs to a particular jahrhundert, one mustn't become its creature. As we approach the threshold of a new century, Herr Schiller's challenge has never been more relevant for a woman. My mother, who is very much a creature of her times, used to say, "What choice does a woman have?"

I feel that we have myriad choices before us. We only need to choose.

Ellie stopped and stared at what she had written. She had felt this battle going on inside of her for as long as she could remember. Ogontz had given girls a taste of what it was to be renaissance women. But Ogontz was also a finishing school, which guaranteed patrons that their daughters would emerge as proper young ladies, fit for society and ready for marriage.

Ellie could feel the renaissance woman bubbling up, straining the rigid seams of the behavior she'd been taught. She'd once read that if new wine were poured into an old wine skin, it would burst. And right now, she felt as if she were about to explode.

* * *

On Thursday, Ellie stopped by Miss Bennett's office. The door was ajar, and she could see her favorite teacher reading by the window. Jack was at her feet with his head on his paws. He sat up when Ellie knocked, and his smile was as broad as Miss Bennett's when she looked up from her book.

"Shall I take Jack for a walk today? Perhaps you'd like to walk, too? It's beautiful out."

"How kind of you to ask. Fresh air is just what we both need!" The little terrier apparently agreed. His whole body wiggled with anticipation.

Miss Bennett, who was maybe the most beloved teacher and one of the principals at Ogontz, had confirmed the rumors that she had a serious kidney ailment called Bright's disease. Ellie found a medical text in the Philadelphia library and was heart-broken about the dismal prognosis for this disease. She felt anxious about death lurking anywhere close to people she loved. Life was a fragile thing. Miss Bennett never let on to anyone that her illness was progressing, but her prolonged absences from teaching to convalesce in Hot Springs, North Carolina, said otherwise.

At least once a week, Ellie offered to walk Jack, but when the weather was pleasant, her teacher often joined them. Miss Bennett always drew two apples from her fruit bowl to take with them. One was for her horse, Maude, and the other for Ellie's horse, Daisy, who lived in the stall next to Maude. Their conversation usually revolved around what had been interesting in classes that day. Ellie was mindful of their pace. Sometimes Miss Bennett made it all the way to the stable, as planned. Sometimes they would walk only to the garden and sit on the bench by the fountain.

"I read with interest the German composition you wrote for Fräulein Klock," Miss Bennett said as they sat and watched the fountain make rainbows in the sunlight.

"You did?" Ellie glanced at her teacher's face to gauge her opinion of the composition. Miss Bennett's lower lip always protruded when she had something serious to say.

"Yes, we both found it interesting. You have a fine mind, Eleanor."

"Thank you." Ellie swallowed. She wasn't sure what Miss Bennett would say about the content of her essay.

"I know it is sometimes difficult for young ladies to appreciate all the formalities such as Walking Down the Stairs. You make a good argument that perhaps we subdue young ladies too much. But Ogontz has a long tradition of offering something rare to its students. Something not offered anywhere else on this continent, to my knowledge. Do you know what that is?"

"No."

"That 'something' is a well-rounded education. We have always tried to teach our girls a healthy balance of mental acuity, physical culture, spiritual fidelity, and artistic expression. How else will a young lady discover latent talents within herself? Do you understand what I am saying?"

"I think so."

Miss Bennett stood to walk some more, and Jack bounced happily to her side. "You know, Eleanor, I remember your mother, Genevieve, quite well. She was a spirited young lady and very talented in art."

"My sister inherited all of Mama's talent for art."

"Did you know that you've inherited something special from your mother as well?"

"I have?"

"Yes," she said. "It is that high-spirited part of your mother. Your mother carried herself with grace and beauty by the time she graduated, and I'm guessing that is how she has comported herself in her adult life. When I read your essay, I recalled that your mother had a fiery spirit as well. And sometimes she even had to be reprimanded about her behavior. Did you know that?"

Ellie shook her head. Her eyes filled with tears to hear it, though. It was hard to imagine that Mama had ever gotten into trouble for misbehaving! Ellie had spent her childhood in trouble for being rambunctious and "high-spirited," and she'd always felt she was a disappointment to Mama.

Miss Bennett stopped speaking and gazed thoughtfully at Ellie. "I am delighted to see that same fiery spirit in your essay. I can tell that your writing comes from an authentic place inside you. Your pen wields power, Eleanor, and I'm imagining that you will find a way to use it for good. Not everyone takes away the same things from Ogontz. Miss Eastman and I hope that our school is a protected space where young ladies can explore to their utmost the gifts God gave them."

"Thank you, Miss Bennett." She was trying to take in all that her teacher had said.

Mama's stories of the school were so different from Ellie's. Back then the school was in the heart of Philadelphia and was called the Chestnut Street Female Seminary. Mama always called it "Sixteen-Fifteen," which was the address. Miss Bennett set high academic standards back then, just like now, but Miss Eastman had introduced the idea that girls needed physical culture. She wanted a country property where the girls could have a gymnasium for calisthenics, a natatorium for learning to swim, and open spaces for playing all kinds of team sports, climbing trees, and horseback riding. She said girls needed fresh country air and healthy spring water.

In 1883, the year Ellie was born, the school rented the famous country estate of Mr. Jay Cooke, eight miles north of Philadelphia. He had called his estate Ogontz in honor of the Wyandotte Chief Ogontz who'd befriended him when he was a boy. Mr. Cooke charged the Chestnut Street Seminary very reasonable rent and generously spent tens of thousands of dollars to have the frescos restored and additional buildings built on the estate to accommodate the school. The school's name was changed to the Ogontz School for Young Ladies with Miss Eastman and Miss Bennett as the main principals. Within a decade it became one of the most sought-after boarding schools in America for affluent families.

Mama said there was a big controversy about having a girls' battalion, another of Miss Eastman's ideas. Parents were appalled. The military drill was common in the best boys' schools but had never been done in a girls' school before. Miss Eastman argued that a military drill was the most expedient way to develop poise, balance, discipline, coordination, and sharp minds. Who wouldn't want those qualities for their daughters? In time, she persuaded them to her point of view. Ellie was grateful for that!

Major Landon, an army man, came two days a week to train the girls properly. People came in droves to watch them perform at the end of the school year. The drill competition was a spectacular event in which four companies competed in maneuvers, ending with a full-dress parade in daz-zling red and gold uniforms with their wooden "rifles." People said it was the highlight of the school year.

* * *

On Saturday, rain was dripping from the wide brim of her battalion hat. Ellie didn't mind. The sound of feet hitting the wet ground in unison was soothing. Marching in the battalion brought order to her mind. Something inside of her automatically responded to the commands of her captain. It kept her in step with Company B but at the same time set her mind free to think.

"…two, three, four, *right flank … march.*"

While she marched, Ellie wondered what Mama had done with her own fiery spirit. Whenever Ellie held that spirit in, she felt like exploding. Did Mama feel that way, too? Ellie recalled a time when she had overheard her parents arguing. Mama had slammed a door and could be heard sobbing dramatically. And then Papa had yelled, which was something he hardly ever did. "You always resort to hysterics when you don't get your way!"

"*About face … march*, two, three…"

Ellie thought about the number of times she'd seen Mama storm out of the room and throw tantrums. Was that the same fiery spirit that Miss Bennett had noticed in Mama years ago? Were grown women naturally prone to being hysterical? Or was it something that society encouraged women to do? Or maybe it was what happened when women didn't find a way to express their fiery spirit properly.

"*Left flank … march*, two, three, four…"

The last time Ellie had been about to explode, she had sat down and written her essay. And Miss Bennett said there was fiery spirit in her writing. *It wields power*, she said.

It occurred to Ellie that it was a *choice* Mama had made to use her spirit in a hysterical way. Ellie made a resolution right then: she decided she was not going to behave like a hysterical creature of the times. She was going to make choices that were different from Mama's. Ellie thought of how her life was poised at the beginning of a new *jahrhundert.* She could step into womanhood in her own unique way.

"*Company … halt!*"

A fire burned in her belly as she stood at attention.

CHAPTER TWELVE

Many Ellies

Philadelphia, June 1897

As if God had taken pity on her, a letter arrived in the morning post. It was an invitation for Ellie to come to Claybourne Oaks for the summer. Mrs. Taylor said she recalled how much Ellie had enjoyed being there four years ago. Isaac would be leaving for Europe on business for two months, she said, and she'd be delighted for the company. Ellie was relieved. She had been dreading the trip across the Atlantic with Mama and Charlie to visit Aunt Lucie, who lived in Paris.

Ellie had been to Paris once before, but that time Papa had come. He had taken her and Charlie to explore the city, to visit the Louvre and to climb the Eiffel Tower so that Mama could spend time with her only sister. Mama and Lucie liked to shop day after day for the latest fashions and attend frilly parties that Ellie detested. This time Aunt Lucie had a special graduation gift for Charlie: painting lessons for the summer from a real Parisian artist. She wrote to Mama that she couldn't think of anything special for Ellie to do. It was always like that with Aunt Lucie. Charlie was her favorite.

Papa was going to stay home in Philadelphia to work in his law firm and to keep an eye on the renovation of their new house. He said it was probably best that Mama wasn't hovering while the work was being done.

Mama had finally gotten her brownstone on Spruce, which was close enough to Rittenhouse Square that she could bask in its glow. They had been renting a townhouse in Philadelphia until this spring, when they found a home Papa could afford. Mama had hoped for something more like the Hockleys' place on 21st Street with its exotic floral design on the tympanum over the entrance. Mr. Hockley was a lawyer, too, she said. Papa said it took more than a lawyer's income for that pile. The house Papa bought needed some modernizing, which made it affordable, he said. He agreed that Mama could use her inheritance money to make any changes to it she wanted. She had immediately chosen the architectural firm of Mr. Frank Furness, who had designed the Hockley home, and was certain he'd create a home she could be proud of.

As it happened, Papa's sister, Tess, was going to visit a friend in Cleveland and was happy to accompany Ellie on the overnight Western Express. In Cleveland, Ellie would take another train to Canton by herself. Mama fretted that she would be unchaperoned on a train for two hours. Papa said, "For heaven's sake, Genevieve, she's fourteen." It seemed like Ellie was always getting in the middle of her parents' arguments.

* * *

As the Western Express made its way into the Allegheny mountains, Ellie settled into the plush chair in the drawing room of their Pullman car. Aunt Tess pulled her knitting from her bag and peered over her spectacles at Ellie. "I know your father has agreed to this idea of you traveling from Cleveland to Canton alone, Ellie, but there are things a young woman needs to know first."

Ellie crossed her arms.

"My concern is that you have become quite a pretty young woman, and you need to be aware of your effect on the opposite sex. I'm talking about men ogling you. If that happens, you must call on the porter at once. You mustn't tolerate that kind of behavior from men."

"*Auntie Tess!* You're embarrassing me!"

"I'm simply saying you are not the rough-and-tumble papa's girl you used to be. You need to be appropriately guarded now."

Ellie rolled her eyes.

"At the very least, if you are going to travel alone, you need to look older. And there is a way to do that."

"Really?" Ellie unfolded her arms.

"Yes. It's not that difficult. You simply need to stiffen your spine and not let your gaze waver from the eyes of the person to whom you are speaking. At your age, it can effectively add two years. At my age, it can be downright intimidating!"

Ellie's eyes widened at this idea. She could hardly believe it could be so simple to look older.

"Women have more power than you may think, Ellie. It comes from here." Aunt Tess tapped her forehead. "Contrary to what we are taught, women can think as well as men. And, I dare say, even more creatively. Men take the direct route to any destination, but a woman usually has several alternate routes in mind and can shift from one to another as needed. It offers so many more possibilities for us, don't you think?"

Ellie dearly loved Aunt Tess, who said things Mama never would. Mama said Tess was "headstrong," but Papa said he admired that about his sister. When her late husband, Uncle Freddie, was alive, he had always said that Tess could run their business better than he could. Freddie had been born into the textile industry. His family made wool fabric for Union army uniforms during the War of the Rebellion. After the war, Aunt Tess had the idea to buy another factory, which made woolen rugs. They built it into a successful enterprise of their own. When Freddie died, she sold the company to his brothers, and Aunt Tess had her nest egg. Ellie intended to make her own nest egg someday and be headstrong, too.

She was glad her aunt suggested they sit for a while. Ellie dreaded sleeping in that upper berth. The last time she'd slept on a train was when Charlie had come down with diphtheria. And lately an old recurring nightmare had started up again. It was always the same. A dark, sinister figure, who seemed like Death, was after Ellie. She could never quite get away. And just as he caught her she would see his hateful, menacing face. It was the face of the red-haired bully from Congress Lake. The nightmare seemed to stop a couple of years ago. That was, until she decided to return to Ohio.

"You look like something is troubling you. Are you feeling well?" Aunt Tess said.

Ellie forced a smile. "I'm fine. I was just remembering something that happened so long ago, it is silly even to bring it up."

Aunt Tess didn't push her to say more and went back to her knitting.

Ellie watched the twilight fade from the sky, and her mood grew more somber. The mountains trudged along the horizon like black-clothed mourners in a funeral procession. Ellie was now the same age Opal had been when she died. It was hard to trust life when it could be snatched away so young. Ellie shuddered. Sometimes she had the feeling that death was waiting for her. It was as if she'd played a trick on death when she suggested Opal should go to Chicago in her place. Ellie felt guilty about surviving her own bout of diphtheria when Opal didn't. She wondered if Mrs. Taylor blamed her, too.

* * *

After Ellie climbed into her upper berth and the curtain was closed around their compartment, she felt as if a casket were closing in around her. She was suffocating. She sucked in all the air she could, but her lungs needed more. She leaned over the edge of her bed and pulled apart the overlapping seams of the heavy drape. The cool air of the corridor rippled over her sweaty face. She gulped it in, relieved to have her lungs filling again.

"Ellie? What's wrong?" Aunt Tess said.

"I—I can't breathe."

Aunt Tess climbed out of bed and peered into Ellie berth. "Oh, dear. I can see why. It's no bigger than a coffin up there. I read where such small spaces can give a person claustrophobia, and we can't have *that*, can we?"

The porter was summoned to push the upper bed back into the ceiling.

"My Freddie and I used to fit in these beds, and there will be ample room for the two of us."

Ellie gratefully scooted in. She snuggled her own back up against Aunt Tess's, which was warm and comforting. Papa's sister was like him. They both liked giving hugs and letting others in close. Ellie was like that, too. Mama and Charlie always kept a space for good manners to fit in between themselves and others.

* * *

Ellie blew a kiss from the open window to her aunt, who stood on the platform below.

Aunt Tess waved. "Remember to stiffen that spine and look them in the eye!"

The route to Canton was peppered with stops and people brushing past her as the coach filled with passengers. She was disappointed that she had not needed to act older at all. No one had even noticed her. When she stepped off the train, both Mr. and Mrs. Taylor made a fuss about what a grown-up young lady she had become.

"You have your mother's eyes, but you are the spitting image of Aaron!" Mr. Taylor exclaimed as if he could hardly believe it.

"Isaac! What a thing to say! I'm sure this beautiful young woman does not want to be told she looks like her father!" Mrs. Taylor said.

"I don't mind at all!" Ellie laughed and thanked him. "It brings me great pleasure that you see a resemblance to Papa!"

Mr. Taylor took Ellie's hand and said, "Well, I can see that you inherited the grace of your mother." He bowed and kissed her hand lightly, just as he had done to Mama's hand the first time they visited the Taylors. She felt her face flush. She wasn't sure how she felt about being treated like a *lady*.

Mama had instructed Ellie to offer proper condolences at the right moment.

"But how will I know the right moment?" Ellie had asked.

Mama had pursed her lips. "Eleanor, do you *ever* pay attention to what I teach you?"

Now she wished she had. Ellie searched their faces for a cue that it was the right moment to offer her sympathy about Opal, but they were both smiling brightly at her. She noticed that some new lines were etched in their faces, and silvery strands now ran through their hair. Mr. Taylor's beard had turned completely gray. Mama once told her that every sad thought turned into another gray hair.

Mrs. Taylor tucked Ellie's arm through hers. "Isaac leaves for Germany tomorrow, and I've arranged for us to be at Claybourne Oaks the day after. Tilda and Hank Jeffreys are still running the farm. You remember them, don't you?"

"Yes, of course!"

It seemed as if she and Mrs. Taylor picked up right where they'd left off.

* * *

When the Hartville Livery carriage turned into the lane between the old pin oaks, the farm was exactly as she remembered it. She looked over at Mrs. Taylor, who was leaning out the window, looking as eager as Ellie felt. She wasn't like a mother or any other adult Ellie knew. She seemed more like a good friend.

As if reading her mind, Mrs. Taylor turned to her and said, "I wonder if we can figure out something for you to call me other than 'Mrs. Taylor' this summer. I know you've been brought up with proper manners, Ellie, and I don't want to ask something of you that feels untoward. But we're much more casual here in Ohio, you know."

"What shall I call you?"

"Well, my name is Flora."

"Flora?" Hearing herself say it aloud caused a giggle to erupt. She tried to suppress it, but that only made it worse. It was contagious.

Soon Mrs. Taylor was laughing uncontrollably, too, and mopping her brow with her handkerchief. "I don't remember when I've laughed so hard. Ellie, you are the best medicine!"

"Thank you, Flora." Another wave of laughter swept away whatever proprieties had accompanied her to Ohio.

* * *

If there were such a thing as the Ten Commandments of Proper Etiquette, Ellie figured she had broken at least half of them by the end of the first month. It seemed as if she were two girls in one body. Philadelphia Ellie knew Mama's rules but was always wanting to break them. Claybourne Oaks Ellie was learning a different way of being that she'd never imagined before coming here. *That* Ellie loved black earth between her toes and letting her skin turn brown in the sun. She loved picking green beans, shelling peas, and canning tomatoes and cucumbers in jars that sat on the shelf like a colorful still-life arrangement against the white-washed walls. Flora and Tilda invited her to join them for coffee. She was treated as an adult for the first time, and she liked the feeling.

The topic of Opal's death was a skittish deer, retreating into the shadows whenever their conversation came too close. Ellie couldn't find the right moment to say how sorry she was that Opal had caught diphtheria on the trip to Chicago. Then, one morning, as they were sipping coffee, the deer stepped out into the clearing. It started as a conversation about something else.

Flora said, "I've been wondering if you would like to go on an outing to Congress Lake for a few days? I've been wanting to make sketches and capture the hues of the lake for a series of paintings."

"Congress Lake?" Ellie's shoulders jerked slightly as the face of the red-haired bully flashed through her mind. She smiled quickly to cover up the fear that had swept through her. "That would be lovely," she said.

Flora held her mug midair as if she were about to say something but didn't speak for a few moments. "Ellie, we don't need to go. I know you had quite a scare at Jonah's Landing the last time you were there."

Ellie had never told anyone else about her fear. "I–It's kind of embarrassing to be scared of something that happened when I was a little girl. I can hardly even remember what the little Dunker boy looked like, but the bully keeps coming back in the same horrid nightmare. I wake up terrified of him." She took another swallow of her coffee. "Why am I so scared of a bully who never actually hurt *me*?"

"But he did hurt you, Ellie. That bully's violence was an awful thing to witness! One's innocent trust in goodness and safety can be crushed by witnessing something like that. I'm guessing ten-year-old Ellie tried very hard to be brave and act like everything turned out fine. I recall that all of us adults were praising you for helping to save the little boy, but none of us paid attention to the terrified little girl who was all alone up in the buckeye tree."

Flora's words vibrated in Ellie's chest and shook loose tears that had been held back by a steely dam.

Flora moved to Ellie's side and held her. "It is good to let yourself feel it, Ellie. From my experience, it will help your nightmares."

"You've had them, too?" Ellie was surprised.

"Yes, after Opal died. Grief is difficult enough, but because Opal had diphtheria, the county took her body from us and buried her quickly. We were still quarantined and were not allowed to hold a funeral. It was as if Opal disappeared from existence without being honored properly. I didn't realize at first how much that had hurt me. I had terrible dreams in which I knew she had died but someone had misplaced her body. I would search and search for her, but all in vain," Flora said.

"How awful," Ellie said.

"Later, Isaac and I realized we needed a funeral service for her, even if her casket was not there. Only our families came, but once we honored our daughter properly, my nightmares stopped. Since then, I've been able to grieve the loss of Opal, just as any mother would."

"I'm so sorry for your loss." Ellie reached over and laid her hand on Flora's. She thought how her words sounded like a proper condolence from an etiquette book. But they didn't express what she really needed to say. There was a guilty pain in her chest, a splinter that had festered in her conscience from the day she heard Opal had died. Her next words came out unexpectedly. "Flora, I'd give anything if Opal hadn't gone to Chicago in my place. It was *my* idea for her to go, and I've never told you how sorry I am. It isn't fair that Opal died, and I got to live." Her cheeks burned with shame.

Flora looked startled. "Opal's death was *not* your fault, Ellie! Diphtheria is a terrible disease that one can catch anywhere—even at home. I am so thankful that you came through it alive and well. Come here, love."

Ellie sank into her embrace once again and felt a relief she hadn't thought possible.

* * *

After dinner, when the wood burner was lit to take the chill out of evening air, Flora laid her book aside. "I've been thinking about that ten-year-old part of you, Ellie. Perhaps she is still stuck in the nightmare, all alone up in the buckeye tree. In the same way I was stuck in my search for Opal's body. If we go to Congress Lake, maybe you'll want to go back to Jonah's Landing and coax her down from the tree."

Ellie liked the idea of talking to her ten-year-old self. She wondered how many Ellies there could be.

* * *

From the window of their second-floor room in the Congress Lake Hotel, Ellie glanced out to see where Flora was headed. The boy who had brought their luggage up was now following her down the walkway carrying an easel and art kit. Ellie turned back toward the mirror, striking several poses and wondering if her new bathing was too modern for Ohio. Aunt Tess had taken her shopping for the latest summer fashions in Philadelphia before her trip. Ellie tried to explain about the black muck at Claybourne Oaks and life on the farm, but Aunt Tess would hear none of it.

"A young lady needs to be prepared for a proper summer outing," she had said and then peered over her spectacles with genuine concern. "They do know what a proper outing is, do they not?"

Shopping with her aunt was lots more fun than with Mama. Aunt Tess loved bright colors and didn't care a whit if pink clashed with Ellie's auburn hair. "Nonsense! You can wear whatever color suits your fancy!" she had said. Ellie had chosen a silky apricot pink bathing suit with a flowered sailor's collar and tie. The short sleeves and bloomers had matching flowered cuffs. The soft bodice was cinched at the waist with a flowered belt. The clerk had said it was perfectly fine for girls to be bare-legged on the beach in these modern times. However, one could purchase apricot-pink stockings and slippers with straps that laced just above the ankles. Aunt Tess had insisted on buying all the accessories. Ellie decided to leave her stockings folded in her trunk. She wrapped herself in a long beach robe and set off for the lake.

She didn't take the direct route, walking instead by the clearing where the Canton Outing Club had had their picnic lunch four years ago. The dance pavilion was where she remembered it, still balancing on hundreds of log poles sticking up from the water, and the shoreline looked the same. She studied the tree line for the trail that had taken her to the Ohio buckeye tree, but it wasn't there. Had she imagined it?

Ellie approached Flora, who was standing by her easel with one hand on her hip and the other shading her eyes as she looked out over the lake. Her leather kit lay open, as a physician's bag would, but this one was stocked with pencils, thin sticks of charcoal, brushes, empty bottles, cotton cloths, and small cakes of dark paint that only needed to be stroked with a wet brush to make vibrant colors. The large tapestry bag next to the kit gaped open, and Ellie could see a sketchbook, various weights of heavy paper, and a thin lap board.

"Oh! I didn't hear you come down."

"You were deep in thought," Ellie replied. "I'll go over to that rock under the tree and read."

Flora looked at the book in Ellie's hand. "*Little Women?*"

"Yes, I'm trying to write a playscript from this book for our fall contest at Ogontz. If it's chosen for the spring play, I'll get to direct it. But I think I'd rather act than direct. I'd love to be Jo March."

"Hmm. You'd be good for that part." Flora's attention was already pulled back to her canvas, so Ellie slipped away quietly. She spread her robe on a flat boulder at the edge of the shore and dangled her bare feet in the cool water.

Near the pavilion at the water's edge, men were pulling up cattails and hauling basket loads to a waiting horse and wagon. She heard the tap-tapping of a mason shaping flat stones for a new walkway and the rhythmic shoveling of the crew preparing a bed on which to lay the stones. The lapping of the water against her boulder reminded her of a little yellow-haired boy lying on a boulder like this. He was dangling his hand in the water. She seemed to see him from above. "From the buckeye," Ellie whispered. Then the image was gone.

CHAPTER THIRTEEN

Luck

Doc William's stable burned to the ground on a Sunday from a grass-fire that had gotten out of control. The story swept through school on Monday about as fast. A couple of mares were lost, someone who lived in town said. Cade left school before his math class started and ran to Doc's place. The rumor wasn't true. The stable had burned down, all right, but the mares were safe.

"I was going to drive out to your place this afternoon to ask a favor," Doc said. "My horses are skittish. They need to be worked with before it becomes a habit. I was wondering if you'd be interested in doing that in your spare time?"

"Of course! We're done with planting, so I'm pretty sure I can come after chores."

That evening, Cade climbed over the fence into Doc's riding corral, situated a distance from the charred timbers that were smoldering as tamely as a campfire at dawn. The four mares were huddled as far away from the smoke as they could get with their ears pulled back and nostrils flared. The whites of Jenny's eyes flashed as she reared her head. Cade reached into the cloth pouch hanging at his side, where he had eight carrots from Mandy's root cellar. He extended a carrot in one hand and held a currycomb in the other so that they could see it. And he told them exactly what he was going to do.

Willow came over first and munched on the carrot while he held the currycomb to her nostrils. "That's a brave girl, Willow. I'm going to just brush you very gently, and you can let me know if you have any burns or bruises." He started with her neck and moved the brush in a slow, circular pattern, ending with a long stroke to smooth her hair in place. The mare was jumpy at first, but before long she was leaning in to Cade's movements, and her eyelids relaxed. He brushed and examined every inch of her before moving on to the other mares. Doc watched from the gate, where he rested his chin on his arms.

"You've got a special way with animals, son. I've noticed they respond to your touch and voice."

"Thanks." Cade kept his eyes on the mare he was brushing. "Princess has a few singes on her hair from the cinders, but she doesn't seem to have any burns on her hide. That'll grow out, won't it, girl? And you'll be beautiful as ever." He patted her rump and made his rounds again with the last four carrots. Willow nickered and tossed her head playfully as she snatched the treat from his hand. "Sometimes it's as if they are talking with me, like you and I are talking right now." He laughed. "I suppose that brings my sanity into question."

Doc didn't laugh. "Have you ever thought of studying veterinary medicine? Your sister tells me you're at the top of your graduating class."

Cade's jaw jutted out, and his brow furrowed. "The Bauers aren't lucky enough to get that kind of education. I imagine I'll be signing on to a steamer up on the lakes or maybe a factory out east. I aim to get out of Hartville one way or another." He hadn't told anyone he'd been planning to leave. It was a nagging fear that if he stayed in this town, he'd end up like his oldest brother. He already could see a mean, bitter old man growing inside of Garrett. The Bauer blood ran through both their veins, and it seemed like the only chance Cade had was to get away while he could and hope the Devil wasn't looking.

Doc shook his head. "Luck isn't something that drops down like manna from Heaven, Cade. Did I ever tell you the definition of luck?"

Cade looked up to see if the old man was going to tell a joke, but he looked serious.

"Luck is what you have when preparation and opportunity meet," Doc said.

Cade was trying to take it in.

Doc continued. "I know a professor at an excellent veterinary college in Philadelphia. Leonard Pearson. A brilliant young man. He studied in Berlin and brought back important research on bovine tuberculin tests. His research is putting the U of Penn's Department of Veterinary Medicine on the map. I hear he's to be the next dean there. I would be happy to write to him about the possibility of you sitting entrance examinations, if you're interested."

"Entrance examinations?" Cade was confused. For once, he couldn't keep up with Doc.

"It wouldn't be easy, son. You would need to study hard, perhaps for a year, to prepare for them. But I believe you can do it. You'd make a fine vet, Cade."

In that moment, it seemed as if Doc had struck a match and held it to the dry tinder in Cade's mind.

* * *

The idea of becoming a veterinarian shook him to the core. He was trembly all the next day trying to imagine something so audacious. *Doctor* Bauer. *Dr. Cade Bauer.* The obstacles were too numerous to count. Even if he studied for a year, like Doc said, what books would he study? Why would a university let someone like him in? And how would he ever pay for a college education? He'd worked hard all his life on the family farm, but that was expected of any boy. Nobody got paid for pitching in. He only had the pocket change he'd saved from the odd jobs at Doc's place and from working as a broom boy at the lake. He still had the coins he stole from Pa when he was little. When he faced the facts, hopelessness swirled around him, and he was right back loading freight on Lake Erie. He didn't see how he could escape that fate.

* * *

"Cade, are you feeling well? You've hardly touched your supper." Mandy was sitting across from him, looking concerned. The others had already left the table without him noticing.

"I'm okay. I was thinking about something Doc told me yesterday. He has this notion I should study to be a veterinarian. He said I'd have to prepare for a year and then take entrance examinations for the University of Pennsylvania. Crazy, isn't it?"

"Is that what you want to do?"

"That's not the point, Mandy. Of course, I'd love to work with animals! But how would I ever pay for a fancy vet school education? People like us don't have that kind of money."

"What if you got a job after graduation and studied for a year, like Doc said? Who knows what luck may come your way?"

"Hah. Doc was talking about luck. He said luck is what we call it when preparation and opportunity meet."

"Sounds like he was saying that it's *your* job to prepare. He's a wise old man." She got up to wash dishes and tossed a towel to him to dry. They worked quietly side by side.

The next day, Cade stopped by Doc Williams's place to say he'd decided to give it a try.

Doc laughed and pumped his hand with an enthusiasm that Cade hadn't gotten around to feeling yet. "I was sure you'd come around to it. In fact, last night I composed a letter of inquiry to Dr. Pearson. I happen to know that the first year of veterinarian training at U of Penn has an almost identical curriculum to the first year of medical school. And that's where I can help you prepare!"

Cade sucked in a gulp of air and realized he hadn't breathed deeply in months.

* * *

The week before he graduated in the Class of '97, Doc and Mrs. Williams surprised him. They said a shipment of first-year veterinary textbooks from the University of Pennsylvania had arrived on their doorstep. "Think of these as a high school graduation gift from us."

Cade felt his throat constrict. "I–I can hardly… I mean, how can I thank you enough for this?" His eyes blurred, and the gratitude he felt couldn't find words.

Doc said quietly, "The look on your face is ample thanks, son."

Cade leafed through the one on top, *Text-book of Normal Histology* by Piersol. He couldn't imagine how to begin preparing for his exam. "Any advice on where to start?"

"You'll practically need to memorize the physics textbook by Gage to get through the exam. Then I'd focus on histology, which will give you the basic structure of living tissue," Doc said. "The others can wait. A fellow can get overwhelmed looking at the whole mountain range that lies ahead. For now, just focus on climbing the first summit."

That night Cade spread his textbooks around him on the floor of his room. Physics, chemistry, *materia medica*, pharmacy, zoology, anatomy, applied botany, and histology. He touched each one reverently and vowed he'd memorize them all if he had to. He was a starved man anticipating the feast.

He rubbed the spot just under his ribs where a knot always tightened when he worried. He knew he could study for the exams, but how in the hell would he pay for college? He'd been checking the wall at the Hartville depot every day for summer employment notices. There were scraps of paper tacked up by local farmers who wanted *temporary* hands during threshing or hay season. Drifters and drunkards passing through town jumped at those jobs, not expecting much more in exchange than meals and a blanket in the hay loft. A new sign had appeared the previous week, posted by the Congress Lake Club Company. It said: *Recruiting Men for Summer Grounds-keeping and Maintenance. Apply at the Congress Lake Hotel.* He'd not been to Congress Lake in a long time, but he turned in an application, hoping this would be his luck.

* * *

Varner Boyle was helping out at the post office when Cade picked up his letter. He shouldn't have opened it there, since Varn was sniffing for gossip.

"I couldn't help but notice your mail was from *the club*."

Cade ignored that remark but couldn't hide his delight when he read the first line. It instructed him to report to Mr. Hawkins at the service entrance of the hotel on Monday, the seventh of June, at seven o'clock in the morning.

Varn noticed. "What business do you have with the *club* that's making you so durned pleased?"

Cade figured he might as well tell him, since everyone in town would know by next week anyway. "Well, it seems I'm going to be working for them this summer." He hadn't expected to have to defend himself so soon.

"Why are you getting yourself mixed up with them uppity Canton folk? They're up to no good, buying that land around the lake and the hotel and all. It's only a matter of time until a gate goes up and folks like us are going to be locked out."

"Varn, I heard you bragging that when McKinley became president, he and his Canton Outing Club were going to put Hartville on the map."

"That was before I heard they changed their name to the Congress Lake Club *Company*. Company means *business*. They're making it a business to turn our lake into a private resort. It's outright thievery!"

"Well, that's just a rumor. This summer I'm gonna be working maintenance up there. You show me where else to get a steady *paying* job around here, and I'll reconsider."

"Tell you what. You keep an eye on them buggers and let us know what you hear. You can be our *inside* man, right?"

"Okay, Varn. I'll keep my ear to the tracks."

* * *

Cade had read from his physics textbook late into the night, and it lay upside down on his chest when he awakened Monday morning. It was much later than he'd intended for his first day of work. He gulped his coffee and grabbed the lunch Mandy had packed for him. His pace, usually a trot, required a canter, and that got him to the back door of the hotel at Congress Lake a few minutes before seven. A group of older men around Garrett's age stood talking. He didn't recognize any of them. He pulled out his handkerchief to mop his forehead and neck as he slipped behind the group as far away from the door as he could manage. Whenever he was in a new situation, he liked to stand at the back so he could get the lay of the land.

When he looked up, he was as startled as the other young man appeared to be. Cade's heart pounded erratically, and his face reddened. Artie's eyes bugged out behind his glasses, and color drained from his cheeks. They stood staring wordlessly at each other. It was the first they'd run into each other since the day, two years before, when he had beaten the hell out of Artie. His remorse from that fit of anger had pretty much cancelled out Artie's sins. It wasn't exactly forgiveness, like the Dunkers preached. It was more like Cade had kept a safe distance from Congress Lake and anything that reminded him of that incident, the way a wolf stays back from a campfire. At some point the fire had died out, and Cade thought he could put it behind him. But seeing Artie brought up Cade's shame. The stench of it was like plowin' the earth where an old outhouse used to be.

"Hey." Artie broke the silence. But barely.

"Hey."

"Guess you applied for the ground crew, too."

"Yep." Cade looked at the ground and shifted his weight from one foot to another. It felt like the need to apologize was a weight he'd been carrying around for some time but hadn't known it. The words came out stutter-y. "I–I, uh, should have talked to you before now. Look, I'm sorry for what hap—"

"No, Cade. You don't owe me an apology. God knows I had it coming."

"I've done things I'm ashamed of, too, Artie. What I did to you … pounding on you like that was … it was just wrong. I know it took guts for you to own up to what you did. You could have walked away from it, and I wouldn't have known."

"No. I had to tell you."

There was a long silence.

Artie spoke first. "So, can we work together this summer? Because if you have a problem with it, I'll quit today."

He'd asked the question that Cade was wondering himself. "I guess we can try."

The service door of the hotel opened, and a well-groomed man who looked to be in his forties emerged with his watchcase opened in the palm of his hand. He clicked it shut and cleared his throat several times. The group quieted, and Mr. Nigel Hawkins thanked them all for being on time. He had a small but commanding stature. His graying mustache was neatly trimmed and twisted into a slight curl at each tip.

Cade muttered, "Short hair. Either this guy has a penchant for discipline or a case of head lice." Artie stifled a laugh and scratched his head a few times. It seemed they were finding their way back. The wound that had been so raw a couple of years before now seemed to have a healthy scab, at least. Artie wasn't looking at him as if Cade were a madman like Pa. He was grateful for that.

Mr. Hawkins said he'd been hired by the Congress Lake Club Company to oversee the maintenance of their entire property. He seemed proud to have worked with the Olmsteds and mentioned a seaside resort in Massachusetts, as if they would know the place. Hawkins said he intended to bring Congress Lake up to speed as a first-class resort. But it would require a rowing-team effort from each man. "One man serves as a coxswain on a rowing team," he said. "That, gentlemen, is me. I plot the course and will keep my eye on the goal. Some of you are my oarsmen who will keep us on course with your skills and technique. Others of you are the hammers. As you may know, the hammer on a rowing team brings his strength to the crew."

"Not his brain," Artie said loud enough that everyone laughed.

Even the coxswain appeared to be amused. He raised his hand. "I'll wager that every oarsman started out as a hammer."

Cade thought about how he'd been a hammer for Pa and Garrett most of his life. The difference was that this summer his hard work would be fueled by a goal, not by his anger.

Mr. Hawkins described the main projects: removing bulrushes along the shoreline to restore the beach, painting the hotel and cottages, making general repairs, and adding stone walkways to "the resort," as he called it. Cade and Artie, clearly hammers, were both assigned to help the mason in charge of a stone promenade. The sun was high in the morning sky when they began digging the trench for the sand and pea gravel, which would form a foundation beneath the new pathway.

The first week passed quickly. Cade enjoyed the hard work, but there was one thing still troubling him. He had done the math every way possible. Even if he labored every day at Congress Lake this summer and signed on for the ice harvest next February, he'd come up short on funds to start vet school the following year. He saw no other way but to take on a second job, perhaps an evening janitorial job in town. But when would he study for the entrance exam? It was a worry that crept into his bed at night, gnawing at him like rats at a granary.

CHAPTER FOURTEEN

The Parlor

Cade stuck his shovel in the wheelbarrow of dirt and mopped his forehead with his sleeve. "Maybe we should have hired on to a steamer. At least up on Erie there'd be a breeze."

"Yeah, but the view wouldn't be near as good!" Artie wiped the fog off of his spectacles and replaced them without ever taking his eyes away from the lake. "Will you take a gander at those limbs!"

He cranked his head in the direction of Artie's gaze. A girl was sitting on a boulder, reading. Her auburn hair glinted in the sun, and her long, bare legs seemed to go on forever into the cool water. Cade whistled softly. "You got to appreciate those new styles. She can't be from around here."

"Well, I'm gonna meet her if it's the last thing I do," Artie said.

"I'd suggest staying downwind of her, Hanson. Or buy some talcum." He acted nonchalant, but her every movement caught his eye.

"Now she's talking to the lady who's been painting by the lake." Artie was giving a report every few minutes. When the two ladies walked to the hotel, he punched Cade's arm. "They're staying at the hotel! You know what *that* means."

Cade feigned ignorance. "Haven't a clue."

"The girl with the legs will be here tomorrow!"

Cade shrugged with the most nonchalant look he could muster. Then he grinned. "Want to lay bets about who meets her first?

"Ha! I knew you were watching her. You don't have a chance, Bauer!"

When they turned in their timecards at the end of the day, Mr. Hawkins said, "Your foreman will be off tomorrow, but you fellows can report to me. Cade, would you be able to stay a few minutes right now? I'd like to teach you a technique for screen repairs."

"Sure." Cade glanced at Artie, who was grinning. He'd be home eating his Grandma Hanson's cookies before Cade got out the door.

Hawkins continued, "The painters reported a torn window screen in the parlor and several others around back. It isn't hard to replace screens once you understand the principle. Would you grab the caddy from the shelf behind you?"

"This is a beauty. Black walnut, right?" The tool trays Cade had seen before were rough, homemade boxes with a dowel rod handle run through the ends. This one was all sanded down with a custom handhold carved into the wooden divider. The oils from years of use had given it a silky warmth that belonged more to a piece of fine furniture than a toolbox.

"Used to be my father's. He worked in wood."

Cade followed his boss to the hotel parlor, a quiet room for reading when tea wasn't being served there. There was one guest in the parlor curled up in a pale green chair that fanned around her like the shell that gave birth to Venus. It was the young-lady-from-somewhere-else. She was so engrossed in her book that she didn't even notice the two men who had come in, and it gave Cade a moment to stare. Her elbow rested on the velvet arm of the chair with her hand poised in the air, a fountain pen between two fingers. A large journal lay open on her lap. Her auburn hair was pulled up into a cluster of ringlets, but loose strands fell down, hiding her face. Her lavender, flowered dress draped over lovely curves. When she heard them, her chin tilted up such that her face caught the light from the window. Cade noticed a smattering of freckles across her cheeks and nose. He felt himself blush, and he lowered his eyes to avoid having anyone look into his soul in that moment.

"Beg your pardon, ma'am," Mr. Hawkins said. "We'll only be a minute."

"Oh, that's quite all right," she said pleasantly.

As they walked past the velvet chair, Cade glanced at her journal. The page of handwriting had enough words blackened out that you could have played checkers on it. The margins were full of scribbly notes.

"I'll move my things over here," the young woman said as she grabbed up her journal and book to her chest. She seated herself at the library table, where she had a good view of the two men working.

"Thank you, ma'am," Mr. Hawkins said courteously, though he was already focused on the window. "Cade, look at this. See how it's been painted in? Now, watch how I run a blade around the frame before lifting it out. Make sure it's a clean cut to the corner, or you'll lift the paint." He pulled a knife from the tray and set about freeing the screen.

Cade half paid attention to what Mr. Hawkins was showing him. The other half was interested in a woman who appeared at the door of the parlor. "There you are, love," she said and walked over to where the girl was sitting. "Our table will be ready at six. I thought you may want to freshen up before supper."

"Thank you. I completely lost track of time," the girl replied.

"How is your play coming along?"

"Miss Alcott practically writes it for me. I hate killing off some of my favorite passages simply because I can't fit them in!"

"Mmm. Good editing makes the play. I'm sure your script will be excellent. So, shall we meet in the dining room? I need to make some arrangements with Mrs. Sliker first."

"Oh, please go ahead. I'll see you in a bit." The girl gathered her things and was moving toward the door when Cade noticed her fountain pen lying on the floor by the chair. He snatched up the pen and called out to her, "Miss, I believe you dropped this."

She turned and smiled. "Oh! Thank you! I would have been so annoyed with myself if I'd lost that."

"You're welcome."

She gave a quick nod as she took the pen from his hand. "I'm Ellie," she said, straightening her spine and looking him in the eye.

He wasn't expecting an introduction. "Uh … I'm Cade. Cade Bauer." His hand started to extend, but he retracted it in time and jammed it in his pocket. He blushed again.

Ellie smiled. "Pleased to meet you."

"The pleasure is mine."

"Thank you. Well! Good evening to you both!" With that she hurried down the corridor. Cade stood watching, unable to move until she had disappeared up the stairs.

"Mr. Bauer, I believe we're done here, but you may want to follow me down to the repair shop. You may not be able to find your way there." Nigel Hawkins looked amused.

Cade whistled under his breath. "Sorry. Guess I got distracted."

"So I see."

As he walked home that evening, he relived every moment of his encounter with Ellie. His cheeks reddened again, thinking how stupid he must have appeared to her. He'd been dumbstruck and scatter-brained when she'd introduced herself. He would have to do better the next time. There was something about her that felt oddly familiar, but he couldn't think why.

* * *

The chime on the longcase clock echoed up the stairwell. Nine. Ten. Eleven. Ellie had been counting them after Flora fell asleep. Things were stirred up inside of her after meeting Cade Bauer. She imagined how Mama would have been scandalized by it all. *Eleanor, what were you thinking? Introducing yourself to a strange boy and using your given name!* But Mama, this is *Ohio*. It was a good defense, she thought.

And he had blushed. More than once. It had never happened before when she'd met a boy. As she lay thinking about him, it occurred to her that *she* had had an effect on him, and it sent a shiver through her. She felt … pretty. A pleasurable wave swept up through her body and made her heart thump oddly.

* * *

Cade was still awake well past midnight. He couldn't stop thinking of an auburn-haired girl and the hundred different scenarios in which they might meet again. Some of the fantasies were too embarrassing to repeat to anyone, even to Artie, who would be asking all kinds of questions. Artie had a way of prying into Cade's thoughts like a farmer digging into a can of tobacco. He'd barely fallen asleep when it was morning.

In the early light, Cade selected a clean work shirt and spent some time trying to tame his strubbly hair, but it was wasted effort in this humidity. He set his brown felt hat on his head just so and cocked the front rim up slightly. It would have to do.

Mandy squinted as if the sun were in her eyes. "You're bright this morning." She scraped a slice of cornmeal mush from the hot skillet and ladled some tomato gravy on top for him.

"I get to replace screens today in the hotel."

"*Get* to? Am I right in thinking you're enjoying this job?"

"It's hard work, but the people are interesting."

"Any people in particular?"

It seemed like his private thoughts were suspended in a cheesecloth. Mandy only had to see what was dribbling through it to know what was inside. He changed the topic and gulped his breakfast down before she guessed more.

When he arrived at Congress Lake, only the maintenance crew and some early-morning fishermen were up at this hour. Each time he carried screens back and forth from the hotel to the maintenance shed, he hoped for a glimpse of Ellie, but she did not appear.

Mr. Hawkins checked on his progress an hour later. "When you are done with the screens, I'd like you to help Artie groom the east trail."

"Yessir." He and Artie always rolled their eyes when Hawkins asked them to "groom" the trail. It was such a refined way of saying there would be blisters from the scythe by the time they were done. He realized the chances of seeing Ellie were dwindling.

* * *

Artie blurted out some news of his own as soon as Cade joined him on the east trail. "Have I got a scoop for you! Last night when I was leaving work, I overheard Mrs. Sliker call one of the ladies *Mrs. Taylor.* You'll never guess who she was!"

"Who?"

"She was the one painting down at the lake yesterday! You know … the mother of that girl! So, the girl with the legs is Miss *Taylor*!"

"Her name's Ellie," Cade said, straight-faced.

"Wh–at?"

"As a matter of fact, I've already met her." Cade was enjoying this more every minute.

"Damn. *When?*"

"She practically invited me for tea."

"Now I know you're lying."

"Okay, I may have exaggerated about the tea, but I definitely won the bet!" Cade took his time telling Artie about meeting her.

"*Ellie Taylor.*" Artie sighed. "I sure didn't expect you to win that one."

"Neither did I."

* * *

Hawkins let them go home at one. But Cade circled back to Congress Lake in hopes of seeing Ellie again. He walked everywhere he could imagine she might be but didn't find her. A heaviness settled into his chest, that old feeling of being on the outside looking in. Of watching and wanting what was beyond his reach. He thought about the nights he'd spent spying on people at Congress Lake, either on his belly or with a broom in his hand, wondering what it was like to have a life beyond Hartville. He sat down on a board swing suspended from the branches of a maple tree, lifted his feet off the ground, and closed his eyes. It took him back to when he was a small child at this lake. The first time he'd landed a bass had been almost too much for a small boy to handle. Then Daniel's strong arms had reached around from behind him, holding the rod steady and showing him how to wear out the fish by pulling the tip of the rod upward and reeling in the slack as the rod was lowered again. "Wait for him, Cade. Steady. That's *it!* By *Gott!* You got him!" Cade remembered the good smells of Daniel's sweat and of the dank shoreline. And how the bass had flopped and wiggled on the grass beside them. It was his fondest memory of Congress Lake. And of Daniel.

"You like to swing, too, I see."

Cade planted his feet in the ground and jerked to a stop. He turned around to find Ellie standing there.

"Hullo!" Cade stood up and tried to act casual. "Uh … Ellie? Right?"

She laughed. "Yes. And you're Cade Bauer."

His pretense of not remembering her name was transparent, he realized. "Are you enjoying your stay?"

"Yes, it's beautiful here. I was thinking there was a trail over there that used to end at a big rock. I walked there once when I was little. But I can't seem to find it."

"That sounds like Jonah's Landing. You're right. The trailhead isn't in the same place. A windstorm ripped through here a couple of years ago and uprooted so many trees, they had to close that path. Take that far trail over there, and you'll come to a clearing by the water. You'll find a big rock there." He pointed to the east trail and then collected himself enough to recognize an opportunity. "Would you like me to show you?"

"Oh! No, thank you. It's something I need to do on my own."

Cade blushed. He must have been too forward. Why would someone like her want to be seen walking with a groundskeeper? He was embarrassed even to have thought that. He stiffened his back and said, "Well, enjoy your walk. I, uh, need to be getting home. It was nice seeing you again." He bowed slightly and left her standing by the swing.

"Good day," she said as he turned away.

* * *

Ellie's face reddened as she watched Cade climb the hill from where she stood. She must have offended him. She hadn't meant to. No matter how many times she practiced the social exercises in etiquette class, she would never learn. Any time her head was focused on a mission, her manners disappeared, and she always blurted out something stupid. It was a McAllister curse.

She didn't have time to lament it. She needed to find her buckeye tree before she and Flora left that afternoon. Mrs. Sliker had informed guests that the barometer was dropping, and storms were expected by evening. Flora arranged for the livery to come at four thirty to take them back to Claybourne Oaks a day early. Ellie followed the trailhead Cade had pointed out. It opened onto a clearing where a flat boulder jutted out into the lake. It *was* the place.

Ellie touched her fingertips to the bark of her buckeye. She could almost see a young girl sniffing, hoping for a whiff of its fetid odor, hoisting herself up on the low limb and discovering the stair-step branches that disappeared into the canopy. Without thinking, she gathered her skirt between her legs and placed one foot against trunk. She pulled herself up onto the lowest limb. The higher she climbed, the younger she felt. When she found the familiar crook in the tree, she looked down to the boulder. In an instant, a numbing fear gripped her chest. It caught her by surprise, and she wondered if she would even be able to breathe. A nauseous, dizzy feeling swept over her.

Ellie squeezed her eyes shut, desperately trying to hold back the scenes that were exploding in her mind. She saw two older boys creeping toward a small, unsuspecting blond boy. They pounced on him and dragged him screaming from the boulder. She heard taunts and cruel laughter as they forced him into the lake. Ellie was choking with terror. She tried to scream, but no sound would come out.

Somehow, she pulled herself back from the terrifying scene, and for a moment she saw herself as a young girl sitting frozen on that limb. *I can help her*, she thought. As soon as that idea came into her mind, she found herself sitting beside the younger girl.

He doesn't drown, Ellie said to her younger self. *And I'm right here with you*. It seemed that the young girl snuggled in close, and Ellie felt her trembling. She understood how desperately the young girl needed someone to be with her through this. *The bullies are not going to hurt you, and the little boy will be saved.*

The ten-year-old girl relaxed into the shelter of Ellie's arm. They sat together, watching the story play out as it had four years earlier. Ellie felt tears spilling over her cheeks as the feelings and experiences of long ago jostled loose from the bottom of a well and floated to the surface. She wasn't sure how long she sat with her eyes still closed, but when she opened them, she was sitting by herself high in the leafy canopy. She climbed down from the shelter of the buckeye. The buckeye that had kept a young part of herself safely hidden for so many years. She leaned and kissed its bark and then followed the path out of the woods.

CHAPTER FIFTEEN

Threshold

"I laid some clean clothes over the railing. Figured you'd be covered in muck," Mandy called out from the kitchen.

"You figured right." Cade scraped the soles of his shoes against the blade of the bootjack before removing them. He gathered the black mud into a sticky ball between his hands and hurled it at the old fence post, the last soldier standing from a flank that had fallen years ago. It splattered on the wood, and he grinned. He wiped his hands on the grass and slipped his suspenders down over his shoulders before removing his shirt. Next, he lifted the stiff brush from its nail and used short strokes to remove the dried mud from his trousers. He grabbed a chunk of soap from the windowsill on his way to the pump. A few rhythmic thumps to the handle set a steady stream running. He lathered his upper body and leaned under the cold, clear gush.

"Just toss your shirt in the wash tub. I'll soak it later with the others," Mandy said through the screen.

Something savory drifted out to the porch, and his stomach gave an appreciative growl. "It took most the day digging, but I finally found the broken tile. Should be able to finish up tomorrow if the weather holds."

"That's good!" she said. She was dishing up beef stew into bowls. "Would you ring the bell again? Daniel's either ignoring me or he's going deaf."

Cade buttoned his clean shirt and gave the dinner bell rope a strong yank.

Mandy came out on the porch and stood beside him. "Thanks for fixing the field tile, Cade. We've had our hands full with our move coming up."

"Still can't believe you're heading out west. Is this what you want?"

"Daniel's never had his own congregation in the two years he's been ordained. It's what he's always wanted."

"That's not what I asked. Is it what *you* want?"

"With Rachel married now and you heading off one of these days, it seems the right time."

"Garrett had some opinions about it."

Mandy laughed. "I'll bet."

"Yeah, he said something about Daniel 'fooling away the farm and traipsing off to god-knows-where-Kansas to be a Dunker missionary.'"

"He's partly right. It is a missionary pastorate in western Kansas, but Daniel didn't fool away our farm. We got a good price for it."

"That's good. Petey seems excited about going."

"He needs a fresh start."

"Fresh start from what?" Cade hadn't heard Mandy talk about this before.

"Now that he's finally made it through eighth grade, I don't think the Hartville school can offer him much more. The real problem is that people around here never see him as a boy separate from his seizures. So how will they see him as a man?"

There was an edge to her words, and Cade glanced over at her, waiting for her to continue.

"His teacher suggested that we may want to consider committing Petey to an institution when his seizures get worse."

"Worse? What does Doc say?"

"He has always maintained that Petey has the type of epilepsy where his seizures will last only a few seconds. It may never worsen, and there have been some rare cases where people outgrow it. We don't know what God's plan is for Petey, but he will live with us."

Cade winced at the determination in her voice as he thought back to the time when they had let Pa take him away.

She wrapped her arm around his waist and gave him a hug. "I know Daniel appreciates your help getting the farm shaped up before we leave, and he is going to pay you the same rate you would get in a regular job."

"I'm glad to do it. I'm not going to start a new job anyway until I know where I stand with the vet school. If I'm accepted, I'll probably head to Philadelphia and look for work there. Do you think they even received my exam?"

This worry had been gnawing holes in him for weeks. Doc Williams had pulled some strings so Cade could take the entrance exam in Hartville. Mr. Ledbetter had proctored it at the high school and mailed it directly to Dr. Pearson, dean of the veterinary department. The exam had been difficult. It had the usual grammar and orthography section and an essay to write. Cade wasn't worried about that part. The other part was based on *Elements of Physics*, a textbook by Alfred Gage. Cade had spent most of the winter studying physics concepts inside and out. It was a background he needed to master if he was going to study veterinary medicine.

"I think the answer to that question is sitting on the table."

Cade wasn't sure he heard right. Mandy smiled and jerked her head toward the door. He hurried inside and stared at the letter propped up against his water glass.

"It came in today's mail." Mandy had followed him in and was watching from the door.

Cade's mouth went dry. He picked up the envelope and ran his finger over the embossed insignia in the corner. University of Pennsylvania Veterinary Department. His hands were shaking as he tore it open and stared at the letter. He stood motionless for a moment and then used his fist to wipe the moisture brimming on his eyelids.

"Oh, I'm sorry, Cade." Mandy came over to the table and laid her hand on his shoulder. "You can always try again next year."

"No, Mandy." He glanced up with a stunned look. "I'm in!"

* * *

Doc Williams leaned back in his chair and beamed at him. Cade knew he couldn't have pleased anyone more.

"So how are you feeling about starting your university education?"

"I'm a little nervous, to be honest. It … feels like I'm standing on the threshold of the rest of my life. And if I take a step forward, I won't be able to go back."

Doc laughed. "Sounds like you've arrived at the right place."

Cade quietly absorbed this new thought. "I'm thinking I might not wait until September to go to Philadelphia. You may have heard that Mandy and Daniel are moving the first of June, so I thought maybe I'd rent a room in Philly and find work until school starts."

"Splendid plan! You know, just the other day Dorothy mentioned an old friend, Mrs. Danforth, who lives in West Philadelphia near the campus. She's widowed now. She's a dressmaker and has her business in her home. I recall how she used to keep a student who earned his board by doing handyman jobs for her. Would you like me to contact her?"

"Yes. Please do!"

There was no turning back.

* * *

Renting a room proved to be more difficult than it had seemed. Doc Williams reported that he'd gotten a reply from Mrs. Danforth. "She has a room but said she only rents to divinity students now. Apparently, she'd had a medical student once whose character was less than virtuous, need she say more?"

"So, she won't rent the room to me?" Cade's heart sped up. He'd had a feeling it was too good to be true.

"Not so fast. I posted a response arguing that veterinarians are right up there with divinity students in godly virtues. Vets are just tending a different kind of flock, I said. And I told her she wouldn't find a finer fellow than Cade Bauer!"

"You make me blush!"

Doc pulled a letter from his pocket and waved it with a grin. "You have a room in West Philadelphia! Providing you agree to some chores in exchange for your room and board. She mentioned you'd be her gardener's assistant this summer. She has some repairs around the house, which I'm sure you could handle quite well. In the winter, you'll be shoveling coal for the boiler and cleaning snow off her walks. She sometimes needs bolts of fabric to be lifted down from the shelf. She'd like an immediate response."

"Yes, of course! Thank you!" Cade was relieved to hear about the duties expected of him. He knew how to work.

* * *

Once a fair price was struck, farms passed between Dunkers without legal formalities. A Dunker's word was his bond, and a handshake closed the deal. The sale was registered with the Stark County Clerk, according to the law, however. The young couple who bought the farm from Mandy and Daniel were from the East Nimishillen congregation. They had bought many of the Holtzes' household furnishings, the livestock, and most of the farm implements. The new owner had been eager to take over the spring plowing and planting, so Daniel had just worked on bringing the farm buildings up to snuff. Mandy had even planted a garden she wouldn't be harvesting and thought of it as a gift to the young woman who would be making this home her own. Cade had helped Daniel replace roofs on the outbuildings and put the field tile back into good working order. It was a do-unto-others sort of thing.

The week before they moved, Mandy and Daniel called Cade to the kitchen after the others were in bed. Their serious expression unnerved him. He sat down at the table opposite of them and clutched his coffee mug with both hands. He noticed they were clutching their mugs, too. Daniel cleared his throat a couple of times but couldn't find words.

"We wanted to talk with you about something," Mandy prompted.

Daniel nodded. "Your *schwester* and I have been praying about this, and we are in agreement."

Cade was unable to read Daniel's expression and had no idea where this was going.

"*Gott* has blessed us with bounty. Our farm brought a good price. We decided, if you are willing … we want to pay *die kosten*—the tuition—for your first year of veterinary school."

Cade could find no words to respond.

Daniel reached both hands across the table and folded them around Cade's. "Mandy and I both want this for you, Cade. You are … like a *sohn* to us."

Cade met Daniel's intense gaze and held it, as the Brethren did. They silently shook hands and exchanged a quick nod, acknowledging what had just been given and received. That matter settled, Daniel cleared his throat again, and said, "*Das ist gut.*" He stood up and headed out to the barn to check on the livestock before bed.

Cade scrambled out of his chair and held his arms open to Mandy. She allowed herself to be swept up into a hug that lifted her feet off the floor.

"I don't know what to say, Mandy."

"There's more," she said. "I've talked to your brothers. They all want to help with your second year of school."

"I don't understand. Why would they do that for me?"

"Our parents gave every one of them land and plenty of help to start their own farms, Cade. This is the least they can do for their youngest brother."

"Were *you* ever given anything, Mandy?"

"Oh, I got the best gift our parents could have given me."

"What was that?"

"They let me be your *mutti* for the first eight years of your life."

Cade's eyes filled with tears. "*Mutti.*" It had been years since he'd heard that. It was a special name Mandy had allowed Cade to call her. Rachel and Petey had called her *Mutter*, of course. But *Mutti* was his alone to call the person he'd loved most. Some other Dunker kids had called their mothers by that name, but for him it had always meant sister-mother, which had been a doubly special relationship no one else had. When he'd gone to live with Pa, he wasn't allowed Dutch words. Especially the one for Mandy.

Cade hugged her again, but this time he felt like he was eight years old.

* * *

He hadn't anticipated all the rituals involved in saying goodbye. There had been a tearful and celebratory family picnic for all the Bauers and the Holtzes together on Decoration Day. A few days later Mandy, Daniel, and Petey boarded the train to Kansas. Cade was surprised by the ache in his chest and the tears he couldn't hold back when Mandy waved from the passenger coach window. He thought of that other time watching her leave him when he was left standing with Pa.

Doc and Mrs. Williams insisted that Cade stay with them his last two weeks in Hartville. Their children were grown and gone, so rooms were sitting empty, Doc said. "We want you to think of our home as your home whenever you're in town," Mrs. Williams said. She told him to store his keepsakes in the attic room above the stairs and to go ahead and put any books he wasn't taking to Philadelphia on the shelf by his bed. *His* bed. He'd liked the thought of that.

Cade and Artie had their own ritual. They decided to go fishing one last time at Fritch's Pond before he left for Philly. There wasn't anything more that needed saying between them before he left. Cade was grateful that they'd been able to salvage their friendship out of that Lyle Fletcher mess. And maybe it was even better now, since neither one had to hide from the other what he was most ashamed of. That was a rare thing between friends. Something earned.

As they stood on the bank casting their lines into the pond, he was about to suggest they meet back here in three years after he graduated. As if things would pick up again where they left off. It was a comforting thought.

"I've decided to head west." Artie blurted it out like a forced confession.

"You're joking! Where to?"

"San Francisco, I think. But I'll work a while in St. Louis. Uncle Riley, my mom's brother, lives there and says there are lots of jobs." Artie's voice got quiet. "Seemed time to set off on my own. It won't be the same around here after you leave for Philly."

Cade swallowed the emotion that was coming up. The thought of exploring the west tugged at some vagabond part of himself that had always longed to ride the rails. "I'm full of envy, Artie!" He grinned, but there was more than envy filling him. The people and places he'd called home were disappearing. He felt as if his anchor had just pulled loose, and he was a small craft, suddenly adrift.

* * *

The night before he left for Philly, he was packed, and it was well past midnight. He sat back on his heels and studied the small trunk, which lay open on the floor next to his leather bag. It held all his textbooks, and he'd also tucked in a volume of Longfellow poems that were dog-eared from someone else's lifetime. His ma had underlined some passages, and he'd memorized those over the years, hoping to get a sense of the woman he'd never known. There was space in the trunk for one more. He ran his fingers lightly over the well-worn spines on the shelf. They were old friends who had been with him every night of his childhood, letting him know there was a world beyond Pa's farm. His hand came to rest on a newer one. It had been a gift from Doc, the last revised edition Walt Whitman had blessed the world with before he died. Cade liked the fact that the old philosopher had kept revising these poems right up until the end of his life, as if saying there was no "way of thinking" that couldn't be changed. He pulled the book from the shelf. *Mr. Whitman, I know you don't like cities, but I'm gonna need you with me.* He placed *Leaves of Grass* reverently on top of the others and pressed the lid shut. The trunk would take no more passengers.

CHAPTER SIXTEEN

Walnut Street

The wheels creaked as they bit into the rails. Cade sat stiffly, unable to settle back into the padded seat. His fingers pressed into the felt rim of his hat, which he bounced on his knee. In four hours, he'd be in Pittsburgh and board the overnight express to Philly.

An hour short of the Pennsylvania line, the brakes screeched, and the train convulsed to a stop. A half hour later, the porter announced that men were working to shore up a washed-out rail bed ahead. The second hour passed, leaching all hope that he'd make his connection in Pittsburgh. He'd once watched a cat in Pa's barn toying with a mouse, letting it think it would get away and then pouncing on it again. God was like that.

* * *

"I reckon you'll be camping here tonight, son," the ticket master at the Pittsburgh station said. "Best I can do is get you on the eight o'clock in the morning. You'll be in Philadelphia by tomorrow night."

Cade's brow wrinkled as he glanced at the benches along the walls and noticed the air inside the depot was stale with tobacco smoke and body odors.

The ticket master leaned toward the round opening in his window. "It's warm tonight. You'll probably find the platform bench outside more to your liking. And you may want to catch that vendor by the door before he packs up for the night. He'll have some bread and cheese left. Fruit, if you're lucky."

Cade nodded. "Thanks for your help, sir." His stomach was even more appreciative.

The evening trains spat out folks who seemed to belong to this city. The constant noise of the rail yard eased his loneliness. Eventually, he grew accustomed to the sounds and slouched sideways over his luggage. The loud dongs from a clock inside the station echoed out through the iron bars above the platform bench. He was mostly asleep, but something in him had to count all the chimes. All eleven.

* * *

The day express to Philly wound through the Alleghenies. Photographs in books had not done justice to Pennsylvania. Farms were tucked into the valleys and on the forested slopes. Cade was fascinated by the contoured fields with sheep and cattle grazing on the steep terrain.

The sun was low as the train made its way through the outskirts of Philadelphia along the Schuylkill River that divided the city in two. He'd read everything he could about the city, but it was Doc's voice in his head telling him what he was seeing. All the trains had to stop and then back up across the bridge all the way to the center of the city on a two-story brick viaduct the locals called the "Chinese Wall." Doc said there was a time when engines were detached on the west side of the river and teams of oxen pulled the train across the bridge into the city.

Cade's eye was drawn to the way the last rays of sunset cast red shadows on the manmade cliff-walls of the city canyon they were moving through. At last, they eased into the cavernous Broad Street Station with steam billowing as they came to a stop.

Cade stepped from the coach and stopped abruptly, staring at the ceiling where the great arches of the train shed stretched over sixteen tracks. It was an unfathomable span—a world record, he'd read. Another train eased into the track next to him and disgorged its passengers. The Broad Street station had sounds he'd never heard before. There was an echoing blend of human voices and the clatter of crates and luggage being tossed on carts. Then the grinding metal wheels, the groan of steel against steel as trains lurched back into the outer world in a gush of steam. He stood for many minutes sorting out these first sounds of the city.

The evening sky had already darkened by the time Cade made his way to the street level. The Pennsylvania Railroad Station was a dozen stories high. The station was built right over 15th Street, and carriages were driving through it! In the other direction he could see the Chinese Wall stretching into the dark distance, with lighted city streets disappearing beneath the arches at every block. He could hear the trains moving high above him on this elevated railbed. How many millions of hand-laid bricks?

Cade set his bags down when he spotted the new city hall. His jaw went slack. Electric lights were aimed on the massive structure. And halfway to the heavens stood the portly figure of William Penn looking off into the distance.

A voice interrupted his wonder. "It's the tallest building in the world. Seventy feet taller than the Great Pyramid of Egypt."

Cade realized his mouth was hanging open, and he blushed. The man by the curb was a driver of one the horse-drawn hansoms lined up outside of the train station.

"Your first time in the city?"

Cade grinned. "Is it that obvious?"

"First-timers do have a certain look. Welcome to Philadelphia. You need a cab?"

Cade recalled Doc saying Philadelphians called these carriages cabs. "Uh, yes. To Walnut Street?"

Cade heaved his trunk of books and the leather bag that held everything else onto the floor of the carriage before climbing in. He leaned out of the open window of the cab to study the electric trolleys stopped in the middle of the street for passengers to climb aboard. Bicycles and horse-drawn carriages wove in and out, flowing effortlessly amongst them. And the lights.

The Philadelphia map in his mind was a grid that had been laid out in the seventeenth century by William Penn. Cade had studied it for months and had expected to know precisely where he was when he arrived here. But his eye kept taking detours from the carriage's route, disorienting him completely.

How could he have imagined the neighborhoods here? Rows of houses connected to each other as if they formed one long building with a dozen front doors. Other houses had two separate halves, with each painted a different color but joined under one roof. There were homes that sat almost to the edge of the street. Some had barely enough space for a cat to pass between one and the next. Then there was a castle-like mansion with mature trees surrounding it.

Soon after the carriage crossed the river and entered West Philadelphia, it stopped in front of a low wall draped in ivy on Walnut Street. The three-story stone house was set back thirty feet in the middle of a flowery garden. There was a bright, incandescent lamp on a stone pillar, which stood like a sentry at the walkway. Cade thanked the driver and paid him an extra coin, as Doc had suggested.

Lights from inside illuminated the stained-glass flowers in the panel above the entrance door. The large window to the right had curtains that blocked the view to the interior, but a yellow glow silhouetted lettering painted on the glass:

PARISIAN TAILORING FOR LADIES
Mrs. Rose Danforth, Dressmaker

Mrs. Williams had told Cade that city folks rarely used their front entrance. She said he should always look for a side door first. He followed the walkway through a wrought-iron gate at the east end of the house and saw a light above another door. He tapped the brass knocker against the strike plate and waited. In a few minutes, a woman leaned close to the narrow window beside the entrance and frowned as she peered out at him.

She opened the door slightly. "Yes?"

"Mrs. Danforth? Uh, I'm Cade Bauer. Your boarder?" Cade straightened up awkwardly while his landlady eyeballed him from head to toe.

As she opened the door, he saw that she was wearing something that was more trouser than skirt. Her graying hair was swept up into a bun, but strands were flying wildly. She had rolled the sleeves of her white shirt up above her elbows, not unlike a man would do on a hot day in July. A cloth tape measure was draped around her neck, and a large pincushion was attached to her wrist by a small band. Her blue eyes were crystal-clear and had an unnerving way of looking right through him. At the edge of her pursed lips there was a hint of a smile, which belied the initial impression of sternness she'd given when he'd first caught a glimpse of her.

"Well!" she said finally. "I'd given up on you. I understood you were to arrive this morning on the overnight express."

Her one eyebrow was raised, and Cade understood that he would need to prove himself worthy of her hospitality. "My apologies. The train was stopped for track repairs before we reached Pittsburgh, and I missed my connection there. I spent the night in the train station and caught the first one to Philadelphia this morning."

This news softened her face considerably, and he noticed that she was a nice-looking woman. In her fifties, he guessed. "These things happen," she said and smiled briefly. "Pleased to meet you, Mr. Bauer."

She extended her hand toward Cade, and he was surprised by her strong, warm grip. It was the first time he had shaken hands with a woman. He followed her up four stairs into a hallway. There was an alcove with wrought iron hooks for coats and a boot rack below.

"You may wear shoes in the house, but I'll not have you tracking in whatnot from the animals you're doctoring over at the school," she said, looking down at his feet. "They can be cleaned, if need be, at the pump out back and set to dry on that rack."

He nodded. "My sister has no tolerance for animal dung in the house, either."

"You may set your luggage here for a moment, and I'll give you a brief tour." She led the way to a large entrance hall, which was lit by an incandescent chandelier. "My tailoring business occupies the front quarter of the main floor." She nodded toward a half-opened door on the left.

There seemed to be soft coal oil light coming from that room. Cade could see a large oak counter with a bolt of silky fabric and rolls of lace and ribbons scattered on it. An empty dress form with a wooden hoop apparatus that reached to the floor stood against the far wall.

Mrs. Danforth nodded toward the spacious hall beneath the chandelier. "This vestibule is strictly for my use. Most of my clientele and guests use this entrance. *Your* entrance is the side door, and you will always use the back staircase from the kitchen."

Her eyebrow went up again, and his head bobbed up and down. He couldn't help but touch the balusters along the stairs, which spiraled up to the balcony above them. "This black cherry is beautiful. The color is quite deep. How old is it?"

"We had it built ten years ago. Before Mr. Danforth passed away. But it does get sunlight, and perhaps the electric chandelier has helped to darken it." She seemed to look at him with deference now that he'd shown some knowledge about fine woodwork.

Mrs. Danforth headed back toward the side entrance hall. "You may bring your luggage with you upstairs." She continued through a doorway. "You'll eat breakfast here in the kitchen with Mrs. Fox, my cook. However, you're invited to join me in the dining room for supper. Unless I have guests, of course. My housekeeper, Mrs. Ruby, comes weekday mornings. She'll do your laundry on Monday and make your bed up fresh, but your personals won't be ironed until Wednesday. Understood?"

"Yes, ma'am."

Mrs. Danforth continued up the kitchen stairs to the landing on the second floor. "The bathroom is here. Mrs. Ruby will be instructing you about how to clean the bathtub after you use it. We have a more egalitarian arrangement here than in other households. We all help with household chores. And we all pick up after ourselves. I believe I wrote about some of your responsibilities."

"Yes, ma'am. I noticed that each room has a…" Cade paused to search for the word he'd read in a magazine ad. "A radiator."

"My husband wanted the best in heating systems when we renovated this house. Radiant heat has become more common now."

"We just have a wood burner back home."

Mrs. Danforth was opening another door. "This is the water closet. You are familiar with a flush system for the commode, are you not?"

Cade's bewildered look gave his answer to the contrary.

"I see," she said. "Well, it is not difficult. You simply pull that chain." She motioned to him. "Go ahead."

He set his luggage down and stepped into the small room. When he pulled the chain on the tank, which was positioned high on the wall, water gushed and swirled around the toilet bowl and disappeared down the drain. He'd always been fascinated by the ads that described these wonderful contraptions and how they connected to a septic system. It was a wonder.

Mrs. Danforth pointed toward a bank of cupboards and drawers built into the hallway wall. "Linens and towels are stored there." She led him to a door at the end of the hall. "And your room is here. It's above the kitchen, which makes it a bit warm on baking day. You'll appreciate that in the winter. You have a nice view of the back garden from your desk."

A pleasant outdoor scent of trees and flowers spilled into the hall as she swung the door open. She walked to the center of the darkened room with her hand swaying in the air until it touched something. Suddenly, a bright light illuminated the space, and a chain dangling from the ceiling swayed in the air. Cade stood in the doorway and admired the pale gray wainscot that wrapped around the room. The wall above it was the color of rich cream. An oval braided rug centered on oak floorboards echoed the hues of the floral bedspread above it. Gray shutters opened to the inside walls and vibrated slightly in the cross breeze. A moth drawn to the light banged incessantly against the screen behind an oak desk and chair. Cade noticed a small oil lamp on the night table by the bed.

Mrs. Danforth said, "My husband was in the electricity business and had an affinity for every electrical invention he met. He wanted a twentieth century home. I would have preferred to wait for the millennium to arrive first. Inventions need a few years to iron out the wrinkles. I still use kerosene for reading and sewing. It's what I grew up using."

Cade nodded. "I *do* know how to use that."

Mrs. Danforth opened a door to a long, spacious closet. A bank of drawers was built into the wall next to six cedar compartments. One of the cubicles had two woolen blankets, folded neatly. There was a fan-shaped window near the ceiling. "You'll find ample storage for your luggage and clothes in here."

Cade obediently set his leather bag and small trunk on the floor. He had never had his own closet before.

Mrs. Danforth seemed to be finished with her tour, and she walked toward the doorway. "You may rearrange the furniture to your liking. This is your home while you are here. Do you find it suitable, Mr. Bauer?"

"I'm … ecstatic." The word that came out surprised him, but it was honest. He couldn't remember feeling this excited about anything before. "And please call me Cade."

His landlady's face brightened into a warm smile. "Goodnight, Cade," she said as she closed his door behind her.

It was then that he noticed the oak shelf cabinet near his desk. He lifted it and carried it across his room to the empty wall space by his bed. When he opened his little trunk, he was delighted by the familiar smell that wafted out. Having his books on the shelf made it feel like home.

CHAPTER SEVENTEEN
Compost

He was the indentured damned. Cade stared at the calendar. Until his classes started on the first day of October, he belonged to Mr. Pescadore, the gardener. Cade didn't mind the hard work. He already had the necessary sinew and callouses for that. What he did mind was being naked prey to the old vulture. Pescadore was always circling over him, waiting for any chance to swoop down and rip more flesh off his bones. "No. No. No, boy! You doingitallawronga! The roots haffatobreathe! You holda the plant like so! *Capisci*?" Sometimes the old man would shake his head and mumble. Cade didn't need to know Italian to catch his drift.

This morning, Mr. Pescadore pointed to the mound of horse manure that had been aging since last fall and said it was time to work it into the rhododendrons and azaleas. *Not* the roses. Cade had to listen, again, to the chicken shit lecture he'd received his first week on the job. There were two distinct piles of manure by the shed: chicken and horse. God forbid that you put horse manure on the roses. "It *kills* them! *Capisci*?"

But before Cade could start spreading the horse manure on the rhododendrons, the dried stalks of the spring perennials had to be trimmed and tied off all along the east border of the house. He did like learning about horticulture and proper gardening. The old gardener seemed to know what he was talking about.

Mr. Pescadore had slowly lowered himself to the ground with the help of a rake to support his weight. "I show you," he said. Cade saw pain shoot across his face as he shifted his weight to his knees. There was a correct procedure for putting spring flowers to sleep and for working the soil without disturbing the root system of the fall mums that bloomed next to them.

Cade was intent on completing the south border before the gardener returned from lunch. There were only a few more feet to go beneath the screened windows of Mrs. Danforth's shop. The noon sun was intense, and he rested his back against the house under the little bit of shade the sill provided. He didn't realize until that moment that he was overhearing a private conversation from inside Mrs. Danforth's shop, as if he were thirteen again, eavesdropping from the tall grass along Congress Lake. He pulled his legs in close to his body.

A woman was speaking. "Angel has been begging me for one before she goes back to Ogontz this fall, but I've heard they can do terrible damage to a young girl's delicate bones."

Mrs. Danforth replied, "Yes, I personally do not condone the way some use them to contort their waists into small sizes. It isn't healthy. But a *properly fitted* corset offers support for the natural alignment of the spine. My corsets are tailored to the individual so that even an active, young woman who plays tennis, like Angel, will be comfortable wearing it. Mrs. Gates, may I show you this one so that you may put your worries to rest?"

"Yes, of course."

"Here you can see my design has a slender panel of elastic, such as the kind used in stockings and surgical corsets. It gives a flexibility that allows for freedom of movement. But I've also kept the traditional satin coutil over the whalebone stays in the front to give a lovely line to the figure."

"It's beautiful!" a girl's voice exclaimed. "Look at the velvet trim and the adorable ferns embroidered on it!"

"Thank you!" Mrs. Danforth said. "And that shade of robin's egg just matches your eyes."

"Mother, I love it!"

"It is quite sweet, Angel. I do like the idea of the elastic panel. I don't remember anything this fancy when we were young."

Mrs. Danforth laughed and said, "It adds a little mystery to a woman—this hidden layer of beauty, don't you think? Shall I take Miss Gates's measurements?

"If it's what you want, Angel."

"Yes! The other girls will swoon when they see it."

"If you'll just slip out of your dress, I can get a better measurement."

Cade thought of the time when he and other young boys had peeked through a fence at Mrs. Hickenbaum's sizeable corset hanging on her clothesline. That singular garment had given rise to all sorts of guilty pleasures of his adolescence. Even now, listening in secret to the conversation above him aroused more than his curiosity. He couldn't bear eavesdropping while this young lady was being measured. He scooted away from his hiding place and crawled on his hands and knees toward the backyard as fast as he could scramble. Cade reached the corner of the house on all fours, and he practically collided with a pair of legs that were planted firmly on the garden walk.

"Mr. Pescadore!" Cade's breath froze in his chest. He had no idea how long the gardener had been standing there, so there was no use pretending. It seemed as if the old man knew every embarrassing thought in Cade's head.

Mr. Pescadore's voice was uncharacteristically soft. "That bed can wait," he said, waving his hand toward the border under Mrs. Danforth's shop. "You can work on the compost now." With that, he headed toward the back garden and began clipping the grape vine that had woven through the fence. Cade filled the wheelbarrow with horse manure and pushed it toward the front veranda.

He was turning the compost into the soil around the rhododendrons when Miss Angel Gates and her mother emerged from the house. Mrs. Gates swept by him as if acknowledging a garden boy were beneath her dignity. The lovely young woman who followed, however, glanced at him with a momentary startled expression and then a second time with restored composure. She lowered her long eyelashes and gave a hint of a smile in his direction. Cade's heart fluttered at this slight attention, and he blushed for the second time. She did indeed have robin's-egg-blue eyes, and her soft, oat-colored hair fell over her shoulders from beneath a fashionable feathered hat. Miss Gates *was* an angel if he'd ever seen one. It was her eyes he remembered that night when he lay awake thinking about her. And the garment that matched them.

He woke at four when the early-morning vendors rattled along Walnut Street. They were the city's roosters. Usually, he went back to sleep again, but this morning thoughts of Angel and the corset filled his head. He didn't have a plan when he got out of bed and pulled on his clothes. He only knew he was on his belly again at Congress Lake. He just had to see the robin's-egg-blue corset. He tiptoed barefoot through the hallway lit by moonlight to the kitchen stairs. Halfway down, terror seized him unexpectedly, and sweat beaded up on his face. He gasped for air, feeling as if he could not suck enough oxygen into his lungs. He sat on the step, trying desperately to avoid the images that came anyway. Of falling in the dark. Of landing on a body. And Pa's cold hand. He hugged his arms around himself and rocked, crying as quietly as he could. The memories finally faded. Cade wiped his eyes and went to the kitchen. He lit a flame under the kettle and threw coffee beans in the grinder. He was sitting at the table waiting for the brew to steep properly when Mrs. Danforth came in.

"Do you have enough in there for me, too?"

"Sure." He reached for another cup and saucer from the shelf.

"Is everything going all right for you?"

Mrs. Danforth had a concerned look, and he guessed that his eyes were still red from crying. "I thought I might be catching a cold," he lied. "Nothing a strong cup of coffee won't cure." He poured the dark liquid into both of their cups.

She sipped. "Mmm, I see what you mean. Quite good, though! Listen, since we're both up early, I am wondering if you have time to come to my shop. I've been looking for the right time to train you, but Mr. Pescadore has been keeping you busy. Is that going well?"

"He's particular! But he's a walking encyclopedia on horticulture. I like learning it."

"He says you're picking it up quite well."

"He *did*?" Cade was incredulous. He'd never heard that from the old man's lips.

"He does have textbook knowledge. He was a respected horticulturist at Fairmount Park. Years ago, we consulted with him on a variety of rhododendron he was developing there. He helped us with a garden design. He was experimenting with combinations of perennials that work together to control pests. He retired from Fairmount the year Mr. Danforth died. I don't know whether he took pity on me or if he just enjoyed our project, but he offered to do gardening for me if he could have free rein to experiment with new varieties. He's been in charge ever since, and I am happy to pay him well for the beauty he creates. He is a good-hearted man."

Cade was a little embarrassed about his resentment toward Mr. Pescadore. He shifted in his chair, hoping it didn't show. "Uh, what did you mean about training me?" He could hardly believe Mrs. Danforth had invited him into her shop.

"I'll want you to learn all the labels and uses of the fabrics in the textile room. You need to know because there are proper procedures for handling them. My business picks up in August, and I'll need you to lift bolts up and down quite often. I want to be able to tell you what I need for the day and to have you know exactly which fabric to bring out without me showing you each time. The same goes for putting the fabrics away in their proper place. Is that something you feel you can do?"

"Yes. I'd be glad to do that."

When the lamp was lit in the tailoring shop, his eyes darted about. Several silky garments of different styles were displayed on leather dress forms here and there. But then his eyes came to rest on one in particular. It was glistening upon a dark torso balanced on a single pole that rose from a four-pronged metal base. The turquoise-blue corset had a brownish-gray, velvet trim along the top edge that flared wide over the brown leather bosom. Lacy beige ferns curved gracefully down over the blue satin to a tapered waist.

"You have a good eye, Mr. Bauer. That's one of my best designs."

Cade blushed and stammered. "Y–your sign in the window said "dress-maker." I–I didn't realize…"

"I apprenticed as a corsetiere in Paris years ago. But I primarily design dresses. My mother and her mother were both dressmakers and designers of all sorts of women's apparel in Paris. It's in my blood."

She opened a door to what he assumed was a closet and pulled the chain for the light. He was surprised to see a space the size of a small bedroom. Deep wooden shelves built out from three walls held bolts of fabrics. The room was filled with colors and textures that quenched some craving inside of him. It reminded him of being a young boy when he accompanied Mandy into the mercantile to buy cloth. The fourth wall had sewing notions, ornate buttons, a rainbow of threads, cotton embroidery floss, and fancy ribbons and lace. Wooden pegs held skirt hoops and an array of tailoring tools he could not name.

"Before you handle fabric, you must wash your hands." She indicated a sink in the corner of the room. "Even if you think your hands are clean, you must assume that they need to be washed. The oils from one's skin will leave a mark on some of these fabrics. I always wash my hands as well." She demonstrated how to lather up with soap before rinsing and how to carefully towel each finger dry, since water damages some fabrics.

Cade followed suit.

Mrs. Danforth's expression softened into a smile as she pulled a bolt halfway out from the shelf. It was a delicate, lavender floral cloth that rustled slightly as she bunched it between her fingers. "I'll start by telling you the story of this fabric I purchased in France…"

Cade's interest in what she was telling him was genuine. He was eager for every word.

* * *

Most of the flowerbeds had been put to rest by the end of October. The tender dahlia bulbs had been dug up and dried for storage, the stalks of other perennials had been cut back to exactly six inches, and the correct manure had been worked into the soil around them.

They finished up the last of the garden work on a Saturday afternoon in early November. Cade scrubbed and oiled every garden tool they had used that summer and saw to it that each hung straight from its hook. Mr. Pescadore watched him from the garden shed door and nodded approvingly. "You're a good gardener, Cade," he said as he extended his hand.

Cade wrapped both of his hands around Mr. Pescadore's. "I—I appreciate all that you've taught me, Sir. Thank you."

"*Prego*. We work next spring?"

Cade grinned. "*Sì!*"

He watched Mr. Pescadore step around the fresh manure piles outside of the back gate. If there was anything he'd learned from this cantankerous and kind old man, it was this: all shit becomes compost eventually.

CHAPTER EIGHTEEN
Awakened Eye

5 November 1898

Dear Doc and Mrs. Williams,

I hope my letter finds you both well. My apologies for this delinquent response to your last letter. School started on the first of October, and I'm finally catching up on correspondence.

My day at the veterinary compound starts when the free two-hour clinic opens at eight. There's always a lineup of folks with horses and dogs, which the second-year juniors treat. The third-year seniors staff the veterinary hospital. We have around fifty patients in residence — horses, large farm animals, and currently one zebra from the Philadelphia Zoo! Last year students treated 3,500 patients. The first-year freshmen get to assist wherever we're needed, (which includes mucking stalls, hauling water, holding nervous critters steady, etc.)

A little before ten I run a few blocks to Medical Hall, hoping the barn odors air out on the way. Freshmen join the regular medical students (and we do hear deprecating jokes about us "farmers"). Every evening I'm back at the vet compound for dissecting lab. Oh, and we all take turns doing ambulance duty, transporting sick and lame patients.

Herr Enge says I have a knack for shoeing! He's a master farrier from Germany who was brought here to teach us. Freshmen only get to work on dead hoof specimens, but next year, I'll shoe live horses in the clinic! If I don't make it as a vet, maybe I could be a farrier. (That is, if Mrs. Danforth doesn't turn me into a tailor first! She sends her greetings.)

With fondness,
Cade

* * *

The week before Thanksgiving, a note on fancy stationery came by post from Doc and Mrs. Williams. It was in her handwriting:

Dear Cade,
It was wonderful to receive your letter describing your first month of school! We send good wishes for continued new discoveries. You may not know it for yourself yet, but we both remember how wet Philadelphia winters are. We have arranged for a package to be delivered to Mrs. Danforth's home. The Farmer's Almanac predicts early snows this year, and we wanted you to be prepared. We hope they live up to what the advertisement claims!

Affectionately yours,
Dr. & Mrs. Williams

Cade was mystified, but not for long. A pair of heavy "Klondike" rubber boots from the Geo. Watkinson Co. was delivered to the door. Apparently, the Yukon gold rush had found its way into the 1898 retail market.

A following week on Thanksgiving Day, a blizzard blew in. It turned out that the advertisement was true. As heavy as those boots were, they were "worth their weight in gold." Cade spent most of the four-day recess wearing them as he shoveled waist-high drifts from the courtyard of the veterinary compound at the university. All the guys pitched in so that their free clinic and veterinary hospital could stay open to the public. They could have been farm boys from Ohio threshing oats together or pitching hay from a fresh-mown field. All backs were bent to the same task. And when the juniors and seniors ganged up on the freshman in a snow fight, Cade and the other first-years sent a barrage of snowballs at them as if the Rebels were coming at them over the Angle wall at Gettysburg. It was the first time the freshman had stood together on level ground, where privilege and wealth held no sway.

One fellow thumped his hand on Cade's back. "We're all going over to Houston Hall later. Maybe play billiards. You want to come?"

"Thanks, Tom, but I can't. I've got walks to shovel at home."

"Ease up, man. You're working your ass off." Tom grinned.

"You got that right." Cade laughed, but he thought about it all the way back to Mrs. Danforth's. He wasn't sure he was capable of relaxing. He had a constant worry in his gut that if he ever slowed down, even for a moment, he'd lose this one chance he had to make something of himself. It wasn't like that for Tom and the other guys. They were at ease with university life. They lived on campus in the Quads. They all met over at Houston Hall on Saturday afternoons to swim, bowl, or play billiards. And it seemed as if they'd always known they would pursue a university education. If vet school didn't work out, they'd be lawyers or businessmen instead.

The *idea* of a university education had taken Cade by surprise, but once he knew he wanted to be a vet, he had a singular goal. Hard work seemed like the only thing he could count on to make it happen.

* * *

On a Friday morning the week after the blizzard, Cade rounded the corner onto Pine Street. The usual line of men with hats pulled low and collars pulled up waited with their animals outside the gate for the free clinic to open. Farrier services were not free, but the rates were so reasonable that a steady stream of horses needing shoes or hoof care came through the clinic. It gave the upperclassmen ample practice.

Cade cut through the side door to the inner courtyard and stomped the snow from his boots before entering the farriery. The circle around one of the forges opened to let him in. The heat was seductive on winter mornings, pulling students and instructors into a bedfellow familiarity before the day started. Cade leaned against a rough-hewn block that had an anvil mounted on top. Above him, suspended from the joists were huge bellows with their weights and counterweights dangling from them. Wooden panels with rows of standard horseshoes were mounted on the brick walls between the eight forges spaced around the room.

Dr. Adams cleared his throat. "A mare will be coming by ambulance this morning. I was told she has a nasty laceration on her thigh from a sharp edge of metal cladding. It happened last week, but because of the snow they couldn't get her here. The wound has been festering. It will be a good opportunity for the first-years to learn how to debride and suture this type of wound properly. We'll postpone the dissection demonstration until eleven. The ambulance should be here by nine thirty. Mr. Bauer, would you take the mare directly to Veterinary Hall and get her calmed down?"

"Yes, sir," Cade said.

A murmur went around the circle. The time for camaraderie around the fire had ended.

Dr. Adams motioned Cade over to him for a private word. "I'm going to allow you to assess what kind of restraint and anesthesia is needed for this surgery."

"Yes, sir."

* * *

The mare's head flared up when Cade approached. There was fear and pain in her eyes. He stood in front of her and let her get his scent. "Easy, girl," he said. Her muscles twitched beneath her hide when he laid his hand against her shoulder and stroked her neck. The jagged gash in her left thigh had yellow ooze at the edges. He talked to her softly until her head relaxed, and then he led her into the open room where Dr. Adams would hold the demonstration.

Cade noticed a particularly tense, heated spot on her shoulder where he let his hand rest for a minute. The thought came to him that she was trying to move her pain away from the injury through her muscles into the palm of his hand. He closed his eyes and dug his fingers into an odd, sludge-y mass of energy that seemed to move from the mare's body through his fingers. Without analyzing it, he gave a few quick strokes and felt the mass dissipate into the air. Cade opened his eyes and stared at his empty hand, confused by what had just happened. The mare nickered a little. When he straightened up, Cade realized that Dr. Adams was standing in the door, watching.

"You seem to have made a good connection with our patient, Mr. Bauer. What have you decided for the preparation?"

Some other freshmen were coming into the hall and gathering around to listen. Cade's mind was sifting through constraints he'd observed before. Major surgery required fully casting the horse with leather hobbles to prevent kicking and biting. Sometimes a horse was forced down on a large mound of clean hay and given an anesthesia such as chloroform or ether. But this mare had a flesh wound.

"I don't think ice or an ether spray will numb the wound enough for debriding. Maybe a subcutaneous injection of cocaine at the wound site is better. Say ten percent?"

"A syringe of cocaine is good," Dr. Adams said. "But I'll go with fifteen percent. What about constraints?"

Cade knew a simple rope hobble on one or more legs was expected. But the method Daniel had taught him when he was a kid seemed kinder to the mare. "I think I can keep her calm just using the local anesthesia."

"Of course, you'll not be the one getting kicked," Dr. Adams said with a slight smile, and the guys all laughed. "You realize there's an infection in that wound? I'll need to debride it first and then perhaps suture layers of tissue."

"I'll stand close to her face and pay attention to her movements. If she wants to rear up, I'll pull her head downward. If she's engaging her posterior legs to kick, I'll lift her head. I'll keep countering whatever way she moves. I think she trusts me."

"Well, Mr. Bauer, I'm going to choose to trust you. *And* the cocaine."

Everyone laughed. Dr. Adams showed them how to debride the wound and gave very clear instructions about suture techniques that would leave minimal scarring. Cade steadied the mare, who stood perfectly still. He thought about the surge of energy he had felt from her earlier. It seemed that the mare was showing him another level of treating injuries, as if she were communicating what she needed from him, telling him about her pain and how best to approach the wound. It informed him in a new way and felt significant to everything he was learning in the veterinary program. What if each animal had an innate understanding of what it needed to heal? And what if his job as a veterinarian was first to listen to the animal's wisdom before he did anything that came from textbooks?

* * *

Five nights a week after supper, the first- and second-year students reported to the dissection lab from seven to nine thirty. The specimens were laid on flat iron wagons that served as portable dissecting tables. Upright posts bolted onto the wagon's bed were used to tether the legs in any position required to allow access to internal organs. The lab had ample daylight from the windows on both sides of the room, but in the evenings overhead gaslights illuminated the tables. Cade preferred the evening labs, when everyone spoke in subdued voices and concentrated on their work under the intense lights.

Cade's freshman class had only a horse's leg on their dissecting tables. When they had started this unit, the anatomy professor, Dr. Harger, had said, "Gentlemen, if I had to pick the most important dissection study for practical veterinary work, it would be this one. We'll spend the rest of this semester dissecting and sketching the foot from the lower end of the cannon bone to the hoof."

There had been some laughter around the room at the thought of spending so much time on such a small area of a horse's anatomy, but by the midterm, somewhere between the phalangeal bones and articular ligaments,

Cade realized this single leg had taught him more about a horse than he'd thought possible.

Cade finished his sketch of the lateral sesamoid ligaments and held it next to the drawing in Lungwitz's textbook. He had to admit it was good. The book, which had just been translated into English by Dr. Adams, had been written for horseshoeing students, but it had such accurate detail of the anatomy of a horse's leg that it was used in the dissection lab as well. Cade liked the style of the illustrations and had practiced copying them at home to learn how to draw. He was pleased how he'd picked up that style.

Dr. Harger stopped by Cade's cart and picked up the drawing. "Your sketching skills are good, Mr. Bauer. These illustrations are very attractive."

"Thank you, sir."

"The problem is that you are drawing what you *think* you see, not what is there," he said. "Sketching will be of no use to you until your eye can really see what is in front of you. Put your pencil down and study the specimen. Your eye has not awakened yet." Dr. Harger had said it kindly enough, and he patted Cade's shoulder before he moved on to the next table.

Cade's face reddened. From the start of this unit, he'd been fascinated by the articulations of the foot and the intricate ligaments that bound bones together with layers of muscle and tendon. His drawing showed every detail accurately. What more did Harger want?

Cade ripped the drawing from his lab journal and crumpled it as he sat heavily on the stool. He stared at the leg splayed open in front of him for the longest time. At first it seemed no different from before, but then he noticed some striations of the tissue. These ligaments and bones had worked in tandem with the muscles and tendons to create a powerful movement in this horse. He wasn't sure when he had picked up his pencil. He didn't want to take his eyes from the leg lest he lose his connection to what was starting to come to life. He let his hand just draw what he felt. It seemed that blood was flowing through the tissue, and just for an instant, he could see the fluid gait of the horse that had used this leg. He glanced at his drawing. It wasn't bad. He was surprised by the sense of movement in the sketch. It reflected more than a clinical image of the tissue. The dead leg had come to life in his journal.

When Cade finished his drawing, he sat back and realized the other students had packed their things and left for the night. Dr. Harger was leaning against the wall, watching him.

"Beautiful work, Mr. Bauer. *That's* what I mean by an awakened eye."

CHAPTER NINETEEN
Fête Accompli

"Cade? Is that you?" Mrs. Danforth called from her tailoring shop.

"Yep, I have the afternoon off," he called back. "Our biology instructor is away."

"Oh, good. Would you mind coming back down in five minutes? I need some bolts brought out before my next client arrives."

Cade hurried upstairs and changed into something clean.

Mrs. Danforth was in her upholstered armchair, concentrating on her needlework draped over her lap. Her lips were clamped around several pins. "Give me a minute. Those rolls can be put away," she said without looking up. A mug of coffee, no longer steaming, sat nearly full on the lamp table beside her.

Cade could identify most of the bolts by now. Mrs. Danforth was always teaching him the attributes of these fabrics and their uses in her garment design. He knew she preferred poplin that had a warp thread of silk, which gave the fabric its soft luster, and a weft thread of worsted wool, which together were perfect for decorative needlework. He knew horsehair inter-facing was used in the stand of a jacket collar and that a special padding stitch held the shape so that the soft top layer of fabric simply needed to drape itself over the understructure. He was surprised by his enjoyment of knowing the details. Precision in anything pleased him. Cade cleaned his hands before he lifted several rolls of fabric from the cutting table and hoist-ed them up over his shoulder.

He placed the tweed in the deep, cedar-lined cupboard where all the wool fabrics and yarns were protected from the mandibles of moths. He closed the doors and turned the ornate key, which stayed in the lock.

Next to the wool cupboard stood a cabinet with small drawers for alpha-betized card files for each client. Mrs. Danforth kept swatches of fabrics from the garments she had designed for them along with their "natural color chart." The outer shop had a bay window, where she'd seat her clients in good daylight and hold various swatches to their chins until she found just the right hue to compliment a woman's natural skin tones, hair, and the flecks of many colors in the iris.

"Let me see," Mrs. Danforth said finally as she laid aside the piece she had been sewing. "I'll need the two palest silks in the heliotrope palette and the chartreuse satin coutil today."

Cade gathered the light red-violet shades of silk and pivoted to where the corset fabrics were stacked. As he reached for a bolt of pale green, his eyes lingered briefly on the robin's-egg blue, his favorite.

"Please bring the white batiste from the top shelf, too. Silk, not cot-ton." She peered over her spectacles as he carried them to the long oak is-land where she cut out her garments. "Good. And I'm nearly out of muslin. Would you please bring down a large roll from storage upstairs?"

"Sure thing."

"Thank you, Cade. When you come back with that, I may need a few more fabrics brought out. I'm designing several garments for my client's European trip."

* * *

By the time Cade returned with the muslin, he heard voices from the shop. He hesitated in the hall, wondering if he should interrupt now that her client had arrived.

"Oh, there you are," Mrs. Danforth said as she opened the door to the hallway. "Come in. Mrs. Gates, may I introduce Mr. Cade Bauer. Miss Angel Gates, Mr. Cade Bauer. Mr. Bauer is studying veterinary medicine at the university, and he boards here. He's a wonderful help to me!"

Cade laid the muslin on the counter, and then he must have bowed and said something proper enough, though he couldn't be sure what came out. Mrs. Gates smiled and seemed to perk up with interest when she heard he was studying at the university. Cade was absorbed in her daughter's robin's-egg-blue eyes, which were widening with recognition of him. Miss Gates smiled and said something kind in return, but he could only hear his heart pounding loudly in his ears. He didn't know if he was blushing or blanching. Mrs. Danforth saved him in that moment.

"Cade, would you bring the chartreuse-colored sateen with the turquoise blue stripe, please? And I think the white eyelet, too."

Cade fled to the fabric room and took a deep breath to calm himself. He heard Mrs. Danforth say, "I'm thinking of a lovely sateen stripe for her travel dress. And she'll need seaside and tea dresses, of course. Something soft and flowing will be popular this year. I'm thinking of a lacy bodice and layers of ruffles at the flare of the skirt. When are you leaving for Europe?"

"After the Ogontz school year is over. Not until the second week of June," Angel said.

Mrs. Gates added, "I want Mrs. Danforth to have enough time to ensure a unique design for you. You need to shine, dear, especially with your debut approaching."

Cade pulled the bolts from the shelf and carried them to the island.

"Thank you, Cade. If you'll install the muslin on the upright, then that will be all." She turned back to Mrs. Gates and continued. "Now, this I would trim with Battenberg lace and accent with tiny blue satin rosettes. I want to keep bringing that shade into her gowns in subtle ways to coordinate the wardrobe. It will accentuate her lovely eyes and enliven the overall effect."

Cade understood that he was dismissed, and he intended to leave quietly, but Angel Gates had slipped over to where he was standing.

"Are you really studying to be a veterinarian?"

"Yes. I'm just in my first year, though." Cade felt his heart rate speed up again. She came no higher than his chin, he noticed.

"Daddy has thoroughbreds, and Dr. Gifford is our veterinarian. Do you know him?"

"Yes, of course. He's a guest lecturer at our school. I've heard him speak several times."

"Angel, come over here, please, and listen to what Mrs. Danforth has in mind for you." Mrs. Gates gave Cade a stern look as if he had dragged her daughter over to talk.

Angel lingered a moment longer. "It is nice to have met you, Mr. Bauer."

"The pleasure is mine, Miss Gates." Cade bowed to the young lady, who smiled brightly and fluttered her long eyelashes before she turned to join her mother. Cade made his exit, his hands sweating profusely.

* * *

He wasn't surprised that Dr. Gifford was connected to Angel Gates's family. Mrs. Gates and Gifford had the same accent that back home would have been dismissed as "uppity." In Philadelphia it indicated status and placed a person in a certain neighborhood of affluence. Cade had heard guys say that Gifford wasn't a true blueblood, but he'd bumped elbows with that circle often enough that some of it rubbed off. Gifford's private clinic catered to wealthy patrons who could afford the prices he charged.

Dr. Gifford donated generously to the veterinary department, and he regularly volunteered to supervise students at the free clinic. Some said he had an ulterior motive for donating his time. They said he was keeping his eye on promising students he could hire cheaply for his private clinic after they graduated. It was implied that he'd help them seed their own practices from the wealthy clientele, but that rarely happened. Some graduates were still slaving away for Gifford years later.

Cade didn't like the man. Gifford's lectures always set the group on a competitive edge. He'd toss out a rapid series of questions like slop to the hogs, and Cade watched while the second-year-juniors shoved their way to the trough. He knew why they were grubbing for his approval. Every spring, Gifford offered a summer practicum to one of the top second-year students. It was well known that if you made the "Gifford list" at the end of your junior year, you were almost assured of being offered a position in his clinic when you graduated.

Cade figured he was the only student who didn't aspire to do a practicum with this veterinarian. He'd learned back at Congress Lake that fawning over the wealthy had never gotten him anywhere. When it came down to what he really wanted, like getting into vet school, it was his own hard work that got him there. And he figured Gifford would never understand that. The doctor was brilliant, though. He knew his horses, and Cade always paid attention to the meat of his lectures.

* * *

The flowers that had opened to the warmth of May were all but drowning in the downpour. Cade looked out through his trolley window at the blurry dabs of color from gardens along the route. When the trolley came to his stop, he pulled the collar of his jacket up over his neck and dashed to the side entrance at Mrs. Danforth's. He scraped his boots across the wrought iron blade by the door and placed them on the lower rack beside Mrs. Fox's galoshes. He laid his hat on the upper shelf to dry. The odors from the small animal hospital, where his biology lab class had spent the afternoon, wafted up from his damp wool jacket. He greeted Mrs. Fox, who said, "Phew! Cade, you reek to high heaven!" She always let him know.

"I'm on my way up to change," he apologized.

Mrs. Danforth stuck her head out from her sewing room and called, "Cade? Would you come to my shop for a few minutes before supper?"

"Sure thing," he called back. He hurried up to his room and gathered up some dry clothes before heading to the bathing room. He would have lingered in a hot bath if there had been time, but this afternoon he lathered himself quickly with a washrag dipped in the basin. He leaned over the tub and held his head under the faucet before scrubbing his hair with a bar of castile. He'd never bathed this much when he was growing up, but Mrs. Fox would probably refuse to feed him if he didn't.

Mrs. Danforth asked Cade to lift bolts of pale blue charmeuse and matching organdy up onto the high shelf in the fabric room. "Did you see your letter on the hall table?"

Cade paused in the hallway to open it. When he saw the lettering embossed on the flap of the envelope, he knew it was the invitation for the "Fête Accompli," a veterinary department banquet held in Houston Hall during the last week of school. It was a fancy affair held every June primarily to honor seniors. Awards were given to some students in each class. Cade had heard that formal dinner attire was appropriate. That meant a black bow tie and a fitted tailcoat or dinner jacket. He'd noticed gentlemen who stepped from cabs for an evening in the city wearing such finery. He had gleaned what he could about formal attire from magazine advertisements, and he understood that the plain wool suit hanging in his own closet would be an oddity at the banquet.

"Bad news?" Mrs. Danforth said.

Cade looked up from his letter. "No. There's a banquet for the veterinary department at the end of the year."

"You look as if you're not too excited about it."

"To be honest, I think I'll feel out of place. Most of the guys in my school come from different backgrounds than I do."

"Are you concerned about the proper etiquette for a formal dinner?"

"No, it's not that. I can keep my eyes open and follow along. But the fellows at the university have the proper attire for such occasions. I don't."

"Mmm. I see."

Cade was quiet during supper. When he excused himself from the table, he glanced out the window. "At least the rain has let up. I should be able to make it back to the dissection lab without getting soaked."

"During dinner I was thinking about your banquet. My late husband, Mr. Danforth, was quite an elegant dresser. European styles and staying at the forefront of fashion in Philadelphia was an interest we shared. He's been gone nearly ten years, but men's styles haven't changed all that much. I have a cedar closet in my guest suite upstairs that is filled with his clothes. You are not so different from him in build, Cade. I would be delighted to alter one of his formal evening suits for you. I know there is a brocade waistcoat, many shirts with links, white ties, black ties, gloves. There are silk top hats, of course, but he also had a fine bowler, which is more the style now. If it fits properly. The trouser legs have widened a bit, but I think we can find something that will be suitable for your dinner. He may even have worn your shoe size!"

Cade had never seen Mrs. Danforth as animated by anything as she was at this moment. He could tell that she was genuinely happy for him to have her husband's clothes.

"Oh dear," she said. "Perhaps you do not feel comfortable wearing clothes of someone who has passed on. I may have gotten carried away with the idea. Forgive me if…"

"No. It would not bother me at all. I'm just without words to express my gratitude for your generous offer. I never dreamt that I would have anything like that to wear." He felt emotion rising up from his chest and fought to keep his eyes dry. "You are very kind, Mrs. Danforth. Thank you. I accept."

Mrs. Danforth smiled broadly. "Come to my shop at seven tomorrow morning. I'll measure you and show you some possibilities for your banquet attire. This will be such fun!"

When Cade stepped out into the evening air, the clouds had lifted and a chilly spring breeze carried fresh, dry air into the city. The streets of West Philadelphia were filled with folks strolling, stopping to chat with their neighbors. He tipped his hat quite often and pretended it was a finely milled bowler.

CHAPTER TWENTY

Naughty-Naughts

It was a coveted status to be one of "the old girls." They always made their first appearance in their caps and gowns at the annual Halloween party. Ellie shivered in the chilly evening air and listened to the warm laughter from inside the gymnasium. This moment was the beginning of the end of her life at Ogontz. She stepped into the column of white-gowned girls and adjusted the rosy-lavender tassel on her cap. As if apparitions in the moonlight, they moved solemnly toward the entrance, humming their class song, music they'd borrowed from "Say You Love Me, Sue." The festivities quieted to whispers as the Class of 1900 formed a semicircle at the front of the room.

Ellie and her classmates sang the witty lyrics they'd written, starting with the chorus: *Naughty-naught they call us, / Far from naught are we, / We're the best of all the rest, / We will close the century;/ Though we are completing / Work at Ogontz sought, / Ever dear will Ogontz be / To the class of naughty naught.* Ellie grinned when the roomful of students and faculty cheered. She and her classmates would reenact this cap-and-gown ritual many times throughout their last year at Ogontz. The final time they would have diplomas in their hands.

Ellie felt pulled in two directions. She wanted to enjoy her senior year, with all its pomp and its shenanigans. But she also had to prepare for Radcliffe's entrance examinations offered just two weeks after she graduated. There were several parts to the examination, which would be proctored in Philadelphia over the entire last week of June. They were identical to the Harvard exams for men. It had become more complicated when the two principals at Ogontz asked her to meet with them.

Miss Eastman invited her join them in the small sitting area overlooking the perennial garden. "Miss Bennett and I were discussing your academic aptitude, Eleanor. We both feel you are quite capable of taking the advanced-level examinations for Radcliffe. They do permit first-year students to be examined for a second-year status, upon request."

"I read about that, but I hadn't imagined how to do it."

Miss Bennett nodded. "If you are willing to commit to this idea, we could design an individual curriculum to prepare you for the advanced examinations." Her lower lip protruded as she paused. "Much of your schedule would be the same as the other seniors in your class, but you would have private tutoring by members of the faculty in addition to your regular classes."

Miss Eastman said, "Your year would be quite rigorous. Would that interest you?"

Ellie was stunned at the thought of completing a Radcliffe degree in three years instead of four. But the idea had an undertow that pulled her into it. She nodded. "Yes, I think I would like to try."

"Splendid," Miss Eastman said for the second time. "We'll discuss this with the faculty and determine what areas you may need to bolster before June."

* * *

When Norah heard Ellie's plan, she groaned. "Your chances of having fun this year are seriously dwindling!"

"I know. I know." Ellie flung herself across her bed. "Norah, do you real-ize that when we graduate next June, we will have lived together for almost five years? How am I going to get through Radcliffe without you?"

"Well, you could come to Bryn Mawr with me."

Ellie rolled onto her side. "It's not so simple. My parents love the idea of sending me to Radcliffe. Papa always wished he'd gotten into Harvard law school."

Nora laughed. "Well, Radcliffe *is* the 'Harvard Annex.' It's as Harvard as women can get."

"The same professors teach the courses at both schools. It's ridiculous that they do not combine classes for men and women."

"Something else for you suffragettes to work on after women get the vote," Norah said. "Look, I understand why you want to go to there, but do you really want to spend this year studying for the advanced exams?"

"Don't worry. I'm not going to throw away our senior year!" Ellie hoped what she was saying was true.

* * *

Ellie stopped by the Wing Room, which had been renovated into a private sitting room for Frances Bennett. Her teacher had returned that fall after a long convalescence in Maine and had brought a new Collie with her. Fritz seemed pensive at first about having one hundred young women living with him but was warming up to the attention everyone gave him. He was per-mitted to sniff Ellie's hand, and she stroked his head before he settled back by Miss Bennett's feet.

The tea service was waiting on the low table by the window. Miss Bennett poured tea and said, "I've been meaning to ask. How has your mother been this summer?" Her eyebrows drew together with concern as she waited for Ellie's hesitant reply.

"Dr. Turban told Papa there has been no change. Mama tries to make it sound lovely, as if she's on a vacation. Her room faces south with a big window wall where she can see the snow-capped mountains. She said ravens land on the balcony outside. Papa told me all the patients at the sanatorium must lie perfectly still several hours a day on deck chairs outdoors to soak up sunlight and fresh air, even in the middle of winter. Mama jokes that at least her complexion isn't sallow anymore. She's as rosy-cheeked as a Swiss mountaineer, she says."

"At least she has kept a sense of humor. She is in Davos, isn't she?"

"Yes. The pure air there is supposed to help. She still gets exhausted easily. I think she slept most of last year! Dr. Turban said it could take five years before she can come home."

"Tuberculosis has a very slow cure. But at least there are some who have returned to a normal life after a long convalescence. We will all pray for that, however long it takes. It must be hard on you to have her so far away."

Ellie nodded. "Everyone in my family lives in a different place now. The last time we were all together was the week after Charlotte graduated in '97. We had no idea at the time."

Miss Bennett murmured sympathetic words but then let their conversation go silent for a few minutes, which Ellie appreciated. In '97, Charlie had traveled to Paris with Mama. The painting lessons Aunt Lucie had arranged for Charlie changed everything. The art instructor thought Charlie had enough talent to get into the prestigious École des Beaux-Arts now that they were accepting women. But he said she would need to work hard to create a portfolio for her application. Papa gave his permission for her to live with Aunt Lucie and study art. Charlie had stayed in Paris ever since.

A year ago last spring, Mama and her friend, Bea, had visited Charlie. They had planned to stay only two months, but then in August Mama caught tuberculosis. Papa went over as soon as he found out and got her into Dr. Turban's sanatorium in Switzerland. There was nothing more Papa could do there, and he had a law firm to run in Philadelphia. So he came home, and Aunt Tess moved in to help manage their Spruce Street house while Mama was convalescing.

"May I pour you more tea, Eleanor?"

"Yes, please.

"Eleanor, I want to let you to know that when the weather turns cold, I will need to spend a few months in Hot Springs, North Carolina. I have every intention of being back in time for your graduation in the spring. I know it is unlikely that your mother will be able to attend, but we will do our best to celebrate the event for her."

* * *

Papa boarded a steamer for Europe two days after Christmas. Aunt Tess was invited to visit friends in Atlanta to welcome in the new year. Ellie returned to Ogontz, where three other girls and a few teachers had stayed behind for the holidays. She spent the rest of her week quietly studying for her June exams. The new century arrived uneventfully. It was dreadfully quiet. Posted letters did not come to Ellie very often. She liked to turn them over in her hands, feel their thickness, and guess what was inside. She also lingered over the handwriting on the envelope before opening. Norah said it drove her mad watching Ellie play with her unopened mail.

Ellie lifted the envelope to her nose and detected a faint scent of roses that had survived the overseas journey. There was a familiar rose stamped into the blue sealing wax on the back. Her sister's letter was thick, which meant there were sketches inside. Maybe a watercolor of people in Paris or one of Charlie's hilarious cartoons with captions. Ellie had a stack of them in a hatbox, which she pulled out from under her bed whenever she missed her sister.

Ellie slipped her silver letter opener under the flap and broke the seal. Along with the letter was a drawing that made Ellie suck in her breath. It was a very good sketch of a naked woman reclining on draped cloth. Ellie could hardly take her eyes from the woman's sagging breasts and belly. Ellie had seen lots of nudes in the baroque paintings they studied in art. Miss Eastman had shown their art history class lantern slides of European masterpieces. But the woman Charlie had drawn didn't look anything like those. This woman seemed more real, as if any moment she could come to life and yawn.

The letter explained that Aunt Lucie, who had always championed women artists, was livid that they were not allowed to attend life-painting classes in the art schools. So she decided to finance a private salon where women could paint from a live model. Charlie said that Aunt Lucy was hiring models whose bodies looked nothing like the women men painted. *She wants us to paint real women. We even had a pregnant woman pose for us! Aunt Lucie says that these different bodies will teach us to draw how women ARE, not how men think we should be. Don't say anything when you write to Mama. She'd be so angry at Aunt Lucie and probably tell Papa to make me come home!*

She also said Aunt Lucie had introduced her to Mary Cassatt at an exhibition. *I love Cassatt's work, even though her latest pieces seem to be drifting away from Impressionism.* Charlie's letters were always about art.

* * *

Warm April breezes brought Frances Bennett back to Ogontz. She announced that for health reasons she would retire after the graduation ceremonies in June, and Miss Eastman would be the sole principal for the Ogontz School for Young Ladies.

Miss Eastman was past sixty years of age, but she had the vitality of a much younger woman. She also had a formidable presence when she needed one. There was no doubt in anyone's mind that she expected rules to be followed. Mama said that was why parents felt comfortable surrendering their daughters into her guardianship for the school year. Ellie had mixed feelings about her.

She felt uneasy when a note was handed to her during her afternoon elocution class.

> *Dear Miss McAllister,*
> *Would you kindly report to my office after your classes today?*
> *Faithfully yours,*
> *Sylvia J. Eastman*

Ellie's shoulders hunched up a little as she walked toward the principal's office. She wasn't aware of any infractions she had committed lately, but Miss Eastman's note left her with a guilty feeling, as if she had.

"Thank you for coming, Eleanor. I received a telephone call from your father this morning."

Ellie's heart jolted. Girls at Ogontz were allowed to receive telegrams and letters, which were carefully screened by the principals. But telephone calls were generally prohibited, except for emergencies.

"Is anything wrong with Mama?" Ellie's face must have registered the dread she felt, because Miss Eastman's expression changed to sudden concern.

"Oh my, no. I didn't mean to alarm you. I had a pleasant conversation with Mr. McAllister concerning your filly we are boarding here at Ogontz."

Ellie breathed. "He called about Daisy?"

"He's arranged for his veterinarian to check on Daisy's parturition."

"Her parturition?"

"Yes. Her foaling. Your father said it will likely happen before the school year ends. He also said you had expressed to him that you wanted to be present for the birth, if possible. I'm not inclined to expose a young lady to such an indelicate event. Are you certain you want to do that, Eleanor?"

"I think it would be wonderful to see a birth."

"Well, your father has given his permission, so I will consent to this, on one condition. You are permitted to be absent from class if the birth seems imminent during the day. However, if it occurs at night, you will not be permitted to attend. It is out of the question that you would be at the stable after curfew. Your father has agreed to this stipulation."

"Yes, ma'am."

"I'll inform our stable hand to keep me abreast of your horse's progress."

* * *

Now that Daisy had completed the eleventh month of gestation, Ellie had been making several trips to the stable each day. Friday after her last class, she ran directly to the stable.

"Hello, Daisy, my girl!" She tossed her bag of books on the bench and reached for the currycomb hanging on the post. Daisy had been moved to a spacious enclosure for the final stage of pregnancy. She opened the gate and gazed at Daisy's low-hanging belly, trying to imagine how a long-legged foal could possibly fit into such a compact space. She brushed the horse's sorrel coat until it glistened.

The sound of wheels on gravel drew her attention to a carriage, which had stopped outside of the stable. When the veterinarian stepped inside, Ellie recognized him as one of her father's friends who used to come to their home for dinner parties.

Ellie opened the gate with the currycomb still strapped over her hand and bits of straw clinging to the hem of her dress. For a moment she imagined her mother's disapproving sigh and automatically pulled herself into her straight-backed posture. "Dr. Gifford. I'm Eleanor McAllister."

He stopped and smiled broadly. "Well, of course! It has been a few years since I've seen you. Haven't you grown up! You're the image of your mother."

"Thank you."

"I see you are keeping your mare comfortable."

"I still think of her as a filly, but maybe she's too old to be called that."

"Strictly speaking, she's a mare *after* she gives birth. I think we can call her that now that she is in foal."

"I hope to be here for the foaling. Papa has given me permission to watch."

"Has he really?" Dr. Gifford looked amused. "If you don't mind a bit of blood and a lot of bodily fluids, I suppose it would be interesting to see."

"When do you expect it will happen?"

"Ah. Well. There are several signs that let us know Daisy's stage of foaling. I'm not sure your parents would want me to go into detail, though."

"Papa won't mind. He likes me to know the facts. And I need to know what to expect if I'm going to watch the foaling."

"You make a sound case. I think perhaps you could follow in your father's footsteps and study law." He laughed as he said this. "You'll not get me into trouble with your folks, then?"

"Of course not! I won't say a word." She laughed too. "So how do you know what stage of foaling she is in?" Ellie pulled her notebook and a pencil from her bag.

Dr. Gifford was behind Daisy. "Stand here, Eleanor. Do you notice these hollows on either side of your mare's tail? This means that the muscles through her hips are loosening so that the birth canal will be flexible enough to expand and allow the foal to pass through. Have you noticed anything about the size of her belly?"

"I'm not sure, but I thought this week it was getting smaller. Is that possible?"

"Very good. It is. When the foal starts to shift into its birthing position, the belly appears to shrink." He lifted Daisy's tail. "Here's a good sign that she will likely go into labor within the next forty-eight hours. This swelling and loosening around the birth canal happens not long before she foals. The walls of this canal will need to stretch several times its normal size during birth."

Ellie was scribbling in her notebook. She hoped she would be able to translate it into legible notes later.

"You can see how her udder has been filling with milk for the foal. But what is likely a very new development is this waxy substance on the end of the teats. We may even see milk leaking by tomorrow. You can watch for that when you come to visit her."

"How will I know if she goes into labor?"

"In the first stage, Daisy will likely seem restless and act like she doesn't want to have anything to do with you. She'll paw the floor and switch her tail as if she is being ornery. You may see her kick at her abdomen. It means she is starting to feel the contractions. She may lie down and get up several times, which actually helps the foal move into proper position. I'll instruct the stable manager to call me from the telephone at the school. I told your father I would have someone from my clinic stay here around the clock after your mare reaches that stage. Because it is her first foal, we want to keep an eye on her."

Ellie touched her fingers to the hollow in her horse's hip and moved her hand along Daisy's belly. She felt the hard mass that was at this minute positioning itself. With her other hand she wiped away the tears that had unexpectedly welled up. She was losing the filly she loved. She didn't know who Daisy was becoming now that she was turning into a mare. Into the mother of this little intruder. Would Daisy even want to spend time with her anymore?

"Now, don't worry, Eleanor. Daisy will be fine."

"I know." She wouldn't have been able to explain to anyone what she was feeling.

CHAPTER TWENTY-ONE
Perceptions

Cade bounced his heel on the floor as he sat in the straight-backed wooden chair outside Dr. Leonard Pearson's office. At the end of the second year of training, a committee of professors and the dean, Dr. Pearson, met with students individually to determine their readiness to proceed with the last year of training. Some did not make it past this review. If the student was found deficient in any area, he could be asked to repeat his second year or to leave the training altogether. Cade knew his academic record was good the last two years, but after his big blunder with the racehorse a week ago, he'd been mired in a swampland of doubt about his future as a vet. Hopefully the committee hadn't heard about that.

"Good morning, Mr. Bauer."

Cade looked up, and the blood drained from his face. "Dr. Gifford." He gave a nod as the veterinarian swept past him and joined the others in the room. The door closed, and Cade's heart sank. *Well, they'll know about it now.*

Officially, Dr. Gifford was just an honorary faculty member, but his volunteer work for the clinic was respected enough that he often was called in to consult in the year-end student evaluations. Cade had never gotten along with Gifford in his first year, and it seemed that in his second year the negative feeling between them had gotten worse.

For some reason, the veterinarian always came down hard on him, usually for trivial things that would have been overlooked if another student had done it. On one hand, the vet had an impressive knowledge of horses, and Cade was eager to learn everything he could from him. But he never had liked the way Gifford seemed to want students crowding around him like birds in the park, vying for his crumbs. The other guys got all caught up in trying to win his stingy approval. Cade didn't play that game. He could tell it got under the doctor's skin. Invariably, Gifford singled him out. "Mr. Bauer? Perhaps you would like to enlighten us on the subject?" Cade often did have something intelligent to say on the topic.

Last week, things had gone wrong. The worst was that he could have just kept his mouth shut, and no one would have known. Maybe it was what Gifford had been getting at all along. Maybe Cade wasn't cut out to be a vet.

Every year in May, Dr. Gifford arranged for the second-year vet students to visit River Bend Stables, where thoroughbred racehorses were trained. He wanted to show them how a racehorse differed from the working horses they usually treated in the university's free clinic. Pennsylvania frowned on horse racing in general, but that didn't deter affluent Philadelphians from racing their steeds across state lines in New York and Maryland. Dr. Gifford had found his niche treating these horses, and to hear him talk, he did very well by it.

When Cade and the others arrived at River Bend Stables, the sun was barely breaking through the chilly morning fog. White fences demarcating the pastures and various training areas cut through the mist. A white Dutch door on the main stable swung open, and a young man walked a beautiful bay to the paddock, where the students were gathered. Its dark coat caught bits of sunlight and glistened reddish-brown against the black mane, tail, and legs.

Gifford said, "Gentlemen, this handsome stallion is Gold Pepper."

Cade noticed the horse's intelligent eyes seemed to open wider at the mention of his name. The black edges of his ears were turning this way and that as if gathering information about the group of young men admiring him. Gold Pepper had a spirited presence.

Dr. Gifford backed away from Gold Pepper to where Cade and the others were standing and said, "Gentlemen, study the conformation of this horse and imprint it in your minds. This is the *Gold Pepper standard of excellence.*" Gifford smiled and added, "The owners have high hopes for him!"

The way he said it, Cade wondered if Gifford himself had shares in this horse.

"Often you will need to quickly assess the overall balance of a horse," Gifford was saying. "Use your geometry, gentlemen. Imagine extending the angle of the shoulder and the angle of the hip. The intersection should be directly above the middle of the back."

The trainer then trotted the spirited stallion out fifty yards and back. Gifford's attention, however, had turned to regaling his audience with stories of the horse's fine pedigree. Gold Pepper was sired by Fourteen Karats, he said.

"For those of you who don't keep up, Fourteen Karats is no stranger to the winner's circle up in Manhattan. He has sired many champions over the years."

Cade was only half listening to Gifford. He wasn't sure what he had noticed as the horse trotted away from him. He intuited it more than he saw it. It was as though there was the slightest movement out of rhythm. Something was off-balance.

Dr. Gifford asked the stable hand to hold Gold Pepper steady while each student was given the opportunity to step in closely and examine the musculature. When it was Cade's turn, he ran his hands over Gold Pepper's sleek flank and down the horse's left hind leg. He felt Gold Pepper's body tense up slightly as he traced the taut suspensory ligament to where it branched and wrapped around the pastern bone. Cade closed his eyes. It was as though he could clearly see the intricate bones, muscles, ligaments, and tendons of a leg flayed open on the dissection cart. His finger followed first one branch of the ligament and then the other. He couldn't detect swelling, but there was the slightest bit of heat on one side. Cade laid his cheek against the gaskin muscle above the horse's hock and said, "He needs to take a break from his workouts. This leg is strained."

The class grew quiet, waiting for Gifford's response.

"I didn't realize you had expertise in training racehorses, Mr. Bauer. Would you care to give your justification for that recommendation?"

"I–I can't see swelling, and I'm not even sure if I can feel it the way you usually do when there is a sprain. But when he trotted, there was something not quite in alignment. I wasn't sure what I saw. Maybe a slight pronation in this leg. When I ran my finger down the suspensory ligament, on the inside branch there was a bit of heat. Maybe it's my imagination, but I think it feels slightly softer than the other side."

Dr. Gifford motioned for Cade to step back, and he stooped to examine the leg. The veterinarian stood up and gave no indication one way or another whether he agreed with Cade.

"Mr. Bauer, you have only completed your second year of training, so I wouldn't expect you to understand all the nuances of examinations. But let's say the owner hires you to examine his horse. You have one chance to get it correct. Based on what you have hypothesized about this horse, what would you say to the owner?"

"I'd first ask him if he knows of any strain the horse has had lately. For example, maybe he's been training on a hard surface. Or perhaps he's had an inexperienced rider who's been too severe with the bit and the horse is compensating by tensing up."

Dr. Gifford had no discernible expression on his face. "And what would your prognosis be for Gold Pepper as a contender at the racetrack?"

"I'm afraid I wouldn't place any bets on this horse. He's got a beautiful build for racing, as you said, but from what I've read, if there is a suspensory ligament problem, it is not going to go away. That ligament will give out in the last furlong because that is when the stress is the greatest. Perhaps the owner will want to wait and see if anything develops. I–I think I would prepare him for the possibility that the horse should be gelded and a different kind of life found for him."

"That's quite a severe message to deliver. You understand that such a prognosis will not make you popular with your client? And the ramifications are potentially devastating to this animal's career in racing?"

The reality of Dr. Gifford's words settled in Cade's bones like a damp day in winter. It was the first time he realized the gravity of the diagnoses and prognoses he would be giving when he became a veterinarian himself. What if he had been all wrong? What if he had imagined all this? Maybe Gold Pepper was a sound racehorse after all.

Dr. Gifford had asked the class what they thought about Cade's diagnosis. No one else had noticed anything amiss. The veterinarian simply said that class time was over and they were free to go. His mood had clearly soured. As the young men walked to the train stop together, they were oddly polite to Cade. There was a fraternal code about not kicking a fellow who had just suffered total humiliation.

Cade had felt miserable for the week after. And now he was waiting for his year-end review. He wondered if he had made a terrible mistake in coming to Philadelphia. And if he wasn't meant to be a veterinarian, what would he do with his life?

The door opened, and Dr. Pearson extended his hand to Cade. "Good morning, Mr. Bauer. Please come in."

Cade was embarrassed to have such clammy hands, but he did his best to return a firm handshake to each of the gentlemen around the table. They greeted him kindly, and that didn't put him at ease. He sat in the empty chair, waiting for their questions to begin. There were general inquiries about his ongoing projects in the dissection lab, his hours to date for the pharmacy and morning clinic. He discussed his most challenging clinical case. Cade became more comfortable as he fielded questions about his academic performance.

Dr. Pearson finally spoke. "Mr. Bauer, we've reviewed your record over the last two years. You have commendable academic scores, and your facility in the lab work is excellent."

"Thank you, sir."

"Those are important, of course, but this committee also needs to assess the student's practical application of the theories. Many of your instructors have noted *unconventionality* in your approach to veterinary medicine. They suggest that you tend to rely on your intuition more often than one would expect of a second-year student. Would you care to respond to that?"

Cade swallowed. So Gifford had told them about the River Bend race-horse. What could he say in his own defense? "Yes, sir, I suppose I do use my gut feeling. But I try not to make snap decisions based on intuition alone. I always sift through a mental checklist of what I've read and also what I've learned from my professors and from my lab work. Sometimes when I'm examining an animal, it is almost as if am visualizing the interior of its body. As if I were examining it on the dissection cart, and somehow that helps me to locate where the animal's discomfort or disease is originating. I know that intuition is not a foolproof way of diagnosing. And I'm the first to admit that I have a lot to learn. I've made mistakes, but I hope that you will give me a chance to do better. I want more than anything to continue studying here."

Cade must have sounded pitifully desperate, because the men around the table shifted in their seats and exchanged amused expressions.

"It was not a negative criticism of your work, Mr. Bauer. Your methods seem to be unusually insightful for someone of your level of training. You show exceptional potential. From what I and the others have observed, you have very good instincts about what animals need. We've noticed that you gain their trust quickly, work competently, and integrate your intuition with solid base of knowledge. We expect some mistakes. It is a part of learning." He smiled and extended his hand. "We wish you best of luck on your final exams next week, and if all goes well, we will look forward to inviting you back for your senior year of training."

* * *

Now that Cade had nearly completed his second year in the training program, he was noticing how often he'd thought about teaching here, like Dr. Harger. Simon J.J. Harger had graduated in the first class from the Department of Veterinary Medicine in '87 and soon afterward started teaching anatomy for the school. Cade liked the way he welcomed new ideas from his students and fostered a collaborative spirit. He was not much older than the students, and that was another reason Cade liked him.

"We have time for a question or two. Yes, Mr. Bauer?"

"Dr. Harger, you said cribbing could be an *acquired* neurosis. If it is acquired, wouldn't it be possible to retrain the horse rather than resorting to a myoneurectomy? Our textbook says that cribbing is a habitual response to anxiety. What if we could find a way to understand why the horse is cribbing?"

Cade was thinking of a mare that had been admitted to the veterinary hospital with severe colic and bloating. She had the typical symptoms of cribbing: repeatedly biting on wooden rails with her upper teeth, arching her neck as she pulled back and sucking in snorting gulps of air into her belly. Her top teeth were quite worn down, and she had done a lot of damage to fences, her owner reported.

"You have a good point, Mr. Bauer. There is an ongoing argument against doing resection surgery, but for hundreds of years we've been trying to retrain cribbers. Nothing has been effective. My hypothesis is that the nerve centers controlling the muscular contraction have been permanently damaged by the constant repetition of the cribbing habit. That's what I mean when I say it may be an 'acquired' neurosis. I'm guessing horses are obstinate to retraining because of the lack of will and moral power in the lower animals."

There was a smattering of laughter around the room.

Cade laughed too and said, "Maybe I have a higher opinion of the intelligent will of the horse. We *know* their morality far exceeds that of humans."

Even Dr. Harger had to laugh. "We have a cribbing case in the hospital now, don't we? What's your idea for retraining that mare, Mr. Bauer?"

"Traditional retraining has used harsh methods. Wouldn't that tend to cause more stress on the horse? I mean, if cribbing originates with stress, then why not use a gentle approach to correct this behavior? It would take some time, but I would like to try a different approach before we resort to surgery."

"I'd welcome any new research on the cribbing problem. You need to carefully record your methods. Talk to me after class. I'll help you get started." Dr. Harger scratched his wiry beard, and Cade's hand went to the stubble on his own chin.

There was a knock on the classroom door. Dr. Harger studied the envelope that had just been delivered before he walked toward Cade. "Mr. Bauer, I believe this belongs to you." Then he added, "Gentlemen, class is dismissed."

Cade turned the letter over in his hand and stared at the red wax seal bearing the initials "A.G."

Thaddeus Watson, a senior who had received a letter with the same seal the previous year, said, "Well, well, well! Alexander Gifford has made his choice!"

The other guys crowded around Cade, craning their necks to see for themselves what the letter said. They whistled and thumped him on his back. "Who'd have guessed?" one said.

"Not me!" Cade said. He had landed the coveted summer practicum with Dr. Alexander Gifford. Anyone who had been around the last two years would have said he was the least likely student to receive this invitation from Gifford.

Several guys congratulated him.

"Thanks. I guess," he replied, shaking his head. It was a well-paying job, and Cade knew he could hardly turn it down. But what was he getting himself into?

The letter cordially invited him to accept the summer veterinary practicum at Dr. Gifford's private clinic. He was instructed to report to clinic office for an introductory meeting on Saturday, the twenty-sixth of May, at two o'clock.

* * *

On Saturday, Cade stepped off the trolley and followed the directions on Gifford's invitation. A white fence ran along the road for a quarter mile to where a sign hung from a wrought iron standard at the entrance to the driveway. The black lettering, *Gifford Equine Clinic and Canine Care*, along with silhouettes of a horse and a dog, had been burned into the white placard. The lane opened into a wide space. There were formal riding paddocks, pastures with mazes of wooden fences, outbuildings, and stables, all painted white. A walkway led to the side entrance of a three-story brick home with elegant white pillars and a wide verandah stretching across the front and around the side. Cade stepped inside as the sign on the door instructed. The home had been converted to offices along both sides of the main hallway. Cade could hear dogs barking toward the back of the house.

A young man wearing a white clinical coat stepped out of one of the offices and rounded the oak staircase to the second floor. He paid no attention to Cade, who stood at the counter. A small desk bell sat beside a card that read *Ring bell for service.* Cade obliged, and within moments a door swung open from a library across the hall where a middle-aged woman carrying a stack of black bound books emerged.

"Are you the two o'clock? Mr. Bauer?"

"Yes."

"Dr. Gifford is still helping to set up for the Philadelphia Horse-Show. It starts Monday, you know. He should be back soon. Have a seat out on the verandah. I'll bring you some lemonade."

"Thank you."

Shortly after two, the veterinarian's carriage came through the entrance arch and proceeded around back. Dr. Gifford smiled as he stepped through the door to the verandah and extended his hand warmly to Cade as if nothing were amiss in their relationship.

"Mr. Bauer, welcome to my clinic."

"Thank you for inviting me."

"You are aware I offer this apprenticeship to only one veterinary student each year?

"Yes. I—"

"It's an opportunity for you to learn what it is like to work in a private Philadelphia clinic. And I will see how you do with clientele and the staff. Perhaps if you do well this summer, doors will open to you after you graduate."

Cade decided he might as well be frank. "The invitation was unexpected, sir. After my blunder at River Bend Stables, I'm a bit surprised you want me working here."

Dr. Gifford's eyebrows rose. He studied Cade for a long moment before speaking. "If you are referring to your assessment of Gold Pepper, I'd hardly call that a blunder, young man. You moved a full length ahead of the other contenders that day. I've not seen that kind of nuanced diagnoses and prognoses from a second-year student before. Regarding your analysis of the horse's suspensory ligament, you were spot-on. I hadn't noticed it myself, but of course I could feel the heat in that ligament after you discovered it. Even though the injury was caught early, it casts some doubts on his future as a racehorse.

Cade felt his jaw drop at this news, but he managed to recover quickly. "Did the trainer know of anything that may have caused it?"

"I got to the bottom of it. It turns out that the son of one of the owners of the horse had been taking him out for unauthorized rides around the estate. I'm guessing the injury occurred on some rough terrain, though the boy didn't own up to it. That young fool cost the owners an untold fortune!" Dr. Gifford paused for a moment, and his voice shifted into a softer tone. "I've been hard on you for the last two years, Cade. Do you know why?"

Cade shook his head.

"For one thing, it lets me know your strength. But more importantly, I want my apprentices to understand they know next to nothing about veterinary medicine. From my experience, humility gives one an appetite to learn."

Cade couldn't imagine that Dr. Gifford had ever had a personal experience of humility, but he could see how this principle was at work within his own life.

"I watch how all the students handle horses from the first year of their training. My apprentices need to be able to calm a horse and gain its trust within a minute or so. I suppose I notice the potential in an apprentice about that fast, as well. I've not been wrong yet. Either one has the ability, or one doesn't. It is not something one is taught in school. You have a good instinct about horses."

"Thank you, sir." Nothing was as it had seemed. His own intuition about Gold Pepper had been right on target, but it looked like his perception about everything else had been dead wrong.

Dr. Gifford gave Cade a tour of the private clinic. "I have a particular case I took on as a favor for an old friend. I couldn't say no, but I'm afraid the timing is bad. I'm to be the veterinarian inspector at the Philly Horse-Show, and most of my staff will be needed there. I don't have anyone available to cover this case, but I think you could handle it quite well. It's just a routine foaling. Is this something you feel comfortable doing?"

"Sure!" Cade was eager for this responsibility.

"I took the liberty to discuss this situation with Dr. Pearson. You will be allowed to make up your exams, if necessary. I'm guessing the mare will be in stage one by tomorrow. The only catch is that you will likely need to stay at the stable overnight."

"I've slept on straw before."

Dr. Gifford laughed. "It's a little more civilized than that. There will be a small room with a cot for you at one end of the stable. The school will arrange to have meals brought to you."

"The school?"

"Yes. The mare is at a private girl's school. An old friend of mine boards the mare for his daughter's riding lessons. Ogontz School for Young Ladies."

"Ogontz!" Cade's head went into a spin. Thoughts of Miss Angel Gates flooded his mind.

"Do you know the school?"

"No. I met someone who is a student there. Miss Angel Gates. She mentioned to me that you are their veterinarian."

"Yes, of course. Mr. Gates has two thoroughbreds he races. Mrs. Gifford and I know the family well. Their older daughter graduated from Ogontz with my daughter, Cora. The school is quite an impressive place, but you will be restricted to the stables while you're there. Miss Eastman would never approve of a young man who is not on her staff walking about the grounds."

"Certainly."

"I have time tomorrow to take you to the school. If the mare is in labor, you'll need to be prepared to stay overnight."

"Yes, sir."

"Be at my clinic by one. We'll stop by to introduce you to Miss Eastman."

"Introduce me?"

"If you are going to spend the night on the school grounds, she will insist on meeting you first. As a parent of one of her former students, I appreciate that sort of thing. Everyone knows his place with Miss Eastman, as it should be."

CHAPTER TWENTY-TWO

Ogontz

Cade soaked in the bathtub and lathered his hair on Sunday morning. He tossed his razor kit, a jar of dentifrice, and his toothbrush in his bag. He carefully laid a clean shirt on top of his underwear and tucked in a small bottle of talcum, which he'd purchased in town the year before and which he used only for special occasions.

When he arrived at Gifford's clinic, he was told that a call had just come from Ogontz to let them know that the mare was showing signs of the first stage of labor.

"I called Miss Eastman. She will expect us at two o'clock."

* * *

Two massive block pillars with spherical finials stood at the entrance to the Ogontz School for Young Ladies. Dr. Gifford eased his carriage through the open wrought-iron gates. A firm, crushed-stone driveway wended its way toward a five-story square tower with the four-story mansion proper sprawling behind it.

"What you expected?" Dr. Gifford seemed to enjoy watching Cade comprehend the magnitude of the estate.

Cade shook his head. He had never imagined such a place.

"They accept only a hundred girls. My wife had attended the school when it was still located on Chestnut downtown. Having a family connection was about the only way to get our daughter into Ogontz. They have a fine academic program, but they also emphasize the arts and physical culture. They play sports—baseball, basketball, tennis, fencing, golf. Mrs. Gifford and I still attend the military drill competition at the end of the year.

"They built all this just for a school?"

"No, originally it was the home of Jay Cooke. He's a banker who helped finance the Union army by selling government bonds. He saved the North, some say. Made millions from it and built this estate after the war. Then he went bankrupt in the Panic of '73 and lost the estate. He made another fortune in silver mining and bought it back. But then his wife died. That's when Cooke rented the estate to the ladies running this school."

Cade thought of his brother Garrett living his whole life in Hartville and not even seeing the point of graduating from high school. What would he think of a school like Ogontz?

Gifford was pointing out the glass walls of the conservatory. "It has living palm trees, tropical flowers, and a fountain in the center."

"Are those hot houses down the hillside?"

"Yes. Half a dozen or so. The girls have fresh vegetables and cut flowers all winter. Cooke has a separate gas plant with a boiler system that heats the whole estate, including a natatorium."

Cade gave a low whistle. He wondered if Queen Victoria had an estate this fine.

"They claim the mansion is fire-proof with iron beam and granite construction. And there was no expense spared in the interior. Plush velvet carpets and the finest plate glass windows." Gifford stopped the carriage by a post. "Miss Eastman asked us to come to the garden entrance of her office. It's at the end of that walkway."

Cade hopped out and attached a strap from the post to horse's halter. His eyes widened as Miss Eastman invited them into a spacious room with a lovely, flowered rug of burgundy, cream, and brown hues that complimented the wallpaper, draperies, the rich luster of the woodwork and desk. She had large bouquets of fresh-cut blooms, some of which he had noticed growing in the garden outside her door. Soft light filtered through the stained-glass flowers in leaded windowpanes.

Dr. Gifford introduced his young assistant to her and praised Cade's abilities to handle the foaling. She looked at Cade with interest and welcomed him to Ogontz. She asked about his studies and wondered which of the sciences had best prepared him for veterinary school.

He replied that physics had been most useful for the entrance exams. "To be honest, I wish I'd had training in art. Our study of anatomy in the dissection lab requires skill in making illustrations."

Miss Eastman became very animated and said she couldn't agree more. "The study of art is essential to any well-rounded education. I'm certain you must find your work with animals a very rewarding endeavor, Mr. Bauer. I wish you all the best in your studies."

Then her attention went fully to Dr. Gifford. While they exchanged pleasantries about his daughter, who lived in New York, Cade had a chance to study Miss Eastman. She was small but at first had appeared taller than she was. He noticed the fine needlework and the quality of the fabric in her dress, which was in a soft gray palette that complimented the color of her hair. He smiled at himself, taking in all the details of her dress design. Mrs. Danforth's tailoring shop had given him a new appreciation for a garment's aesthetic balance. When beauty appeared unexpectedly, it nourished some hungry part of him. He thought of his sister Mandy in her plain Dunker garb and her home utterly devoid of this lavish décor. Did she ever feel starved?

Dr. Gifford and Miss Eastman were having a friendly conversation, but there was a cordial edge to her manner that gave her the upper hand. Cade had the impression that she could intimidate anyone who got on the wrong side of her. He could imagine that she kept up with a hundred young ladies quite handily. Before they took leave, Miss Eastman reiterated the boundaries of his stay, which meant that there would be no reason whatsoever to wander beyond the stable. Cade had no intention of doing so.

As they made their way back to the carriage, Dr. Gifford said in a low voice, "Well, you certainly charmed Miss Eastman. How did you know teaching art is one of her passions?"

"It is?"

"Well done, Mr. Bauer."

They were seated in the carriage when someone called, "Dr. Gifford? Is that you?"

Cade looked up and sucked in his breath. Angel Gates was approaching them.

"Miss Gates, how nice to see you," Dr. Gifford said as he tipped his hat.

"Thank you. It's lovely to see you. All the girls are talking about the foal that will be born here. Miss Eastman mentioned you would be coming. So I watched for you." She tipped her head to the side and smiled at Cade. "Oh! Mr. Bauer. I thought I recognized you from a distance. Are you a veterinarian now?"

"Hello, Miss Gates. No. I have another year to go. I'm working for Dr. Gifford this summer."

"Mr. Bauer will be handling the foaling," Dr. Gifford said.

"Oh!" Angel's blue eyes widened. "Miss Eastman said the stable is off-limits to us at half past four today, but perhaps after the foaling, we'll have a chance to chat more, Mr. Bauer."

"I'd like that very much," Cade said. "It's nice to see you."

"It is a pleasure to see you both. I'll tell Father that I spoke to you, Dr. Gifford."

"Please do. And give your parents my regards. Good afternoon."

"Good day!" She spun and lifted her skirt slightly with her right hand as she stepped onto the walkway and floated to the entrance door.

Cade leaned forward, watching her until she disappeared inside.

Dr. Gifford laughed. "Let's not get distracted, Mr. Bauer. You are here for a foaling."

"Yes, sir." Cade glanced at the doctor. His naked feelings for Angel left him blushing, but there was no reprimand in Gifford's voice or in his face. Cade changed the subject as they clipped along the driveway. "Are the buildings ahead also part of the school?"

"Yes. These were added to accommodate the programs offered. The science building to your right has the finest labs you could want. That building over there has the gymnasium. And in front of us are the art and music buildings."

The driveway gently curved, giving Cade a view of the grounds from many angles. "I see gas lights throughout the estate."

"The mansion has been converted to electric lighting now, but outdoors they still use gas."

To Cade's thinking, the estate grew even finer as they wound their way down the driveway past the mansion. There were small ponds in terraced gardens, fountains, a bridge over a stream, and a web of walkways made of the same crushed stone, all glistening in the afternoon sun. The hemlock and spruce mixed with the deciduous trees were beautiful.

"That granite building ahead of us is the coach house. The stable is at the far end."

"It's quite … fancy."

"Were you expecting an Ohio barn? The carriage house and maintenance staff live in the rooms above. There will be a small guest room on the main level for you."

At the stable entrance, Cade hopped out to secure the horse to the hitching post. He grabbed his bag from behind the seat and followed Dr. Gifford. They walked through an entrance hall into a spacious area with horse stalls on both sides. There was a Dutch gate in the far doorway with the top half swung open to a fenced corral, where several horses were standing. A young man who was busy spreading fresh straw in the stalls looked up when they came in.

"Hello, Dr. Gifford. She's been restless, and I thought she was showing all the usual signs of foaling, but now I ain't so sure."

"Thanks, Billy. I appreciated the call. This is Mr. Bauer, my assistant. He will likely be staying the night and tending to the foaling."

Billy eagerly extended his hand to Cade with unmistakable deference. "Mr. Bauer, welcome to the Ogontz stables."

Cade shook Billy's hand. "You can call me…" He was about to introduce himself more casually to the stable hand, but Dr. Gifford interrupted.

"Mr. Bauer. Our mare is in this pen." Cade was puzzled by the frown on the veterinarian's face. When they were alone, Gifford leaned toward Cade and said, "You are representing the Gifford Clinic, Mr. Bauer. You will need to dispense with your usual *in*formalities when working with our clients."

When it was confirmed that Daisy was having contractions and the foal was well positioned for birth, Dr. Gifford took a basin from the corridor wall and dipped it in the water trough nearby. He set it on the bench and rinsed his hands, shaking them a bit before patting them dry with his handkerchief. "It looks fairly straightforward," he said. "I doubt that you'll have much to do other than watch the mare follow her own instincts. You are not obliged to stay any longer than necessary. Check her after the placenta is delivered, and when things are tidied up, you're free to go. Any questions before I leave?"

"No, sir. Of course, I'll keep a record of what happens."

Dr. Gifford smiled. "Excellent. You know the school has a telephone from which you can call my clinic or the veterinary hospital if something unusual comes up."

"Yes. I have the numbers in my bag."

"Well, I believe Daisy is in good hands. I'll leave you to it, then."

They shook hands, and Dr. Gifford left. Cade felt a grin forming of its own accord. He was in charge.

* * *

Billy had a dozen questions about what it was like to be in the vet school, and he was hanging on to every word. The stableman appeared to be a couple of years older, but Cade was surprised how easy it was to take on a superior position while talking with him. Being a representative of the Gifford Clinic carried some clout, to be sure. But there was something else. Billy seemed to make many assumptions about Cade's status in society. There was a respect that felt undeserved. Cade also felt reluctant to dispel the myth. He realized for the first time how his own attitude of deference toward the wealthy helped to prop up the social class system.

Billy said he had the afternoon off, but he'd show Cade to his quarters before he left. The room was the first door inside the hallway. "It's got a cot where you can catch a few winks. If the mare lets you sleep. They said they'd send a tray of food down here around five. It's a little early, but it gets busy up there when the ladies are being served. The rest of us eat up at the kitchen later on."

"That will be fine. Thanks, Billy." Cade opened the squeaky door to a small, darkened room. It was strictly utilitarian, not much more than an enclosed horse stall itself. The spring on the door slammed it shut behind him as he stepped inside. A bit of daylight squeezed through the cracks of the wooden shutters, and as his eyes adjusted to the dark, he made out the whereabouts of the cot in the corner, the washstand and basin and a wooden chair. A kerosene lamp sat on a bed stand.

The shutters opened to a view of a paddock, where a circuit of barrels were set up for riding lessons. Cade reset his hat on his unruly hair and hurried out to Daisy's pen. He let her sniff his scent and began a careful massage of her muscles, noting where there was tension. As he worked his way toward her belly, he felt it tighten up a bit. She turned her head and nipped at him, but he stroked her neck and talked softly. "That was a mild one, Daisy-girl. It's going to get a lot worse, but I'll be right here with you."

She nickered and munched on the carrot he pulled out of his pocket. Mrs. Fox always laid out a couple of carrots for Cade to take to his patients.

He heard the chatter of young ladies nearing the stable, sparrows in a hedgerow. The front door opened, and their tittering turned into whispers. Cade slipped his hand through the currycomb and methodically swept over the mare's flank. He felt his shoulders rounding over like a pimple-faced kid trying to make himself invisible. The whispers came closer and stopped at Daisy's pen. Two lovely blue eyes and an angelic smile appeared over the wooden wall. Her golden hair was pulled back into a soft bun at her neck.

"Miss Gates!" Cade felt his face flush. He stood up and smiled more than he intended.

"Are you settled in, Mr. Bauer?" she said. The other two girls squeezed in close to her and giggled as if there had been an implicit joke that he didn't understand.

"Yes, thank you." Cade took a breath. "Uh, she is in very early stages of foaling, so there is not much required of me at this point. She and I are just getting acquainted."

"That's nice," Angel said. "The stable will be off-limits to us soon, so we thought we'd make a quick visit to see our Daisy. This is so exciting for all of us." The girls giggled again and nodded. "How soon do you think it will be born?"

"It's hard to say. Sometimes it goes longer for the first foal. At the earliest, ten to twelve hours from now."

"Well, perhaps we'll check back in the morning."

"I'll look forward to that." Cade was feeling a bit inebriated by her beauty. He had not noticed that another girl had come into the stable.

"Excuse me," she said to Angel. "I need to hang these blankets where you are standing."

Angel rolled her eyes and pursed her lips so that Cade could see her displeasure at having their conversation interrupted. But she replied sweetly, "Of course," and stepped away.

* * *

Ellie's face was red, and her curls flopped down over her eyes as she struggled to lift a stack of heavy wool blankets up to the top of the fence. She had begged them from Mr. Tyndall, the headmaster of the carriage house staff.

Mr. Tyndall was not amused to be disturbed on his day off. "The blankets have had their spring beating and are already put away," he said. "I don't see how your mare would need them."

Ellie hadn't intended for tears to fill her eyes, but in retrospect she realized it hadn't hurt.

"Well now," he said. "Seeing as how it is her first foal, I suppose it can't hurt to make sure she is comfortable."

"Thank you, Mr. Tyndall. You are so kind."

Ellie had checked on Daisy after breakfast. She had fidgeted nervously all through church and had rushed through her school assignments.

"Here, let me help you with those blankets," Cade said as he stepped forward to pull them up over the fence. All he could see was a mass of sweaty auburn curls behind the pile of blankets.

Ellie gratefully released the load into the strong arms reaching toward her. "Thank you!" she said and stepped back. She swept her hair back from her face and left a streak of dirt across her nose. She was startled to see a familiar face looking back at her, but somehow it was out of place. He seemed to recognize her as well. Then it came to her where she had met him before.

"You were at Congress Lake. It was three years ago when we talked."

"Miss Taylor?" Cade was dumbfounded.

Angel Gates laughed. "Taylor? There must be some mistake. But then how could one tell with that dirt on your nose." Angel and the other girls all laughed at this.

Ellie's hand flew to her nose, but she only managed to smear the dirt even more. Normally she would have a good retort for Angel, but for now she ignored her. Ellie couldn't take her eyes off of Cade.

"I'm sorry. I dropped one the blankets in the mud on the way here and I must have…" Ellie laughed and shrugged. "I know we met at Congress Lake. You're Cade. Mr. Cade Bauer, right?" How many times had she thought about him after she'd visited Flora that summer? He had been the first boy to make her heart flutter oddly.

"Yes. Congress Lake. You're Miss Ellie Taylor. We didn't get to say a proper goodbye. Your mother whisked you off before I came back to work that week."

"My mother? Oh! No, that was Mrs. Taylor, a dear friend who I visited that summer."

Angel Gates stepped forward and leaned in so that she effectively broke the gaze between Cade and Ellie. "Mr. Bauer, it was a pleasure chatting with you. I'm sorry we were interrupted, but I'm sure we'll have an opportunity to continue our conversation in the morning. I'm afraid it's half past the hour, and the stable is off-limits to all of us. We all need to prepare for supper and evening services. Shall we go, ladies?"

Ellie saw right through Angel's weaselly attempt to get her out of the stable, but she was determined not to let Miss Gates get under her skin today. She knew something Angel didn't. Miss Eastman had already given Ellie permission to miss Sunday evening services. And she was allowed to stay at the stable until the curfew bell. She turned to Angel with her most cordial expression and smiled. "Yes, thank you, Miss Gates, for reminding us. Have a good evening, Mr. Bauer." Mama would have been proud.

"I still don't know your name, Miss…"

"McAllister. Eleanor McAllister."

CHAPTER TWENTY-THREE

Foaling

Cade flopped on his cot and pulled the pillow over his head to muffle the groaning that rippled up like a shudder of laughter from his belly. She's *Eleanor McAllister*. He could see her clearly now. The girl with wild, curly hair whose lucky buckeye he'd kept all these years. And her brown eyes! No wonder she had looked familiar when he met her three years ago. Cade's heart was pounding, and a clammy sweat was dampening his shirt. How was this possible? The two of them had been brought together three times now, and under such odd circumstances. He imagined how surprised she'd be when he told her, and almost as quickly he was horrified at the thought of it. He'd come a million miles from that Dunker boy he'd been the day Petey almost drowned. A sophisticated, wealthy young woman like Ellie would never understand his complicated life. The Dunkers were an oddity, even in Hartville. And then there was Pa, with his jug. The beatings. The pitchfork. Cade thought about his own dark temper and the way he'd attacked Artie. Shame was a shadow that appeared whenever his past came into the light. He didn't want Ellie to know any of this.

He stood up and tucked his shirt neatly into his trousers. He needed to be professional. The veterinarian-in-charge. The door to his "stall" swung shut behind him just as a fellow about fifteen years of age came through the stable door holding a covered tray and a coffee pot. "Mr. Bauer? Your supper is here."

"Thanks. You can set it on the bench, uh … your name is?"

"Ralph. I'm supposed to bring you more coffee later tonight. Maybe about ten?"

"Sounds good, Ralph. Thank you. It looks like a long night."

"If there's something else you'd like me to bring down…"

"Perhaps a few apples … if they have some?" It hadn't occurred to Cade before now that he could simply ask for fruit.

"Sure. They always have apples and other fruit, too. Mrs. Cordes made cinnamon buns. I can talk her out of a couple for you." The boy grinned.

"Good man! I'll look forward to that!" Cade shook his hand, and Ralph blushed, apparently pleased by the attention and embarrassed at the same time. The boy made an awkward exit, and Cade caught a glimpse of himself at that age, working at the dance hall.

The Ogontz cook had not underestimated his appetite. It was the kind of stew that could have been simmering in a pot over the fire for days. He dipped his bread in the bowl to sop up the remaining gravy and savored the flavors all over again. A couple of fellows came in and tended to the evening chores. They nodded hello to him but didn't linger. When Cade was alone again, he pulled a blanket down from the fence onto the pile of straw. He stretched his legs out and closed his eyes.

Sleep didn't come. Instead, a familiar worry seeped in. What would he do after graduation? What if he worked for Dr. Gifford a few years? He could learn how to cater to the wealthy and set up a good practice of his own in Philly. No one needed to know about his past.

* * *

Ellie wrapped her cape around her as she hurried down the driveway toward the stable at half past seven. She only wished she could have seen the look on

Angel's face at the evening services. Miss Gates would realize exactly where Ellie had gone.

Something felt surreptitious being unchaperoned after dusk. She'd never been here this late in the evening. The horses' jaws were still grinding away on loose hay in their racks, soothing music to her ears. When she approached the gate to Daisy's pen, she was alarmed to see her horse panting as if they'd just gone for a good gallop.

"Miss McAllister!" a voice said.

Ellie jumped and looked off to the left. Cade was sitting in the corner with his back to the wall, his arms crossed over his chest, but he quickly stood up.

"Is Daisy all right?" Ellie's voice had an anxious edge.

"It's a contraction. She's still in the first stage of labor."

Then Daisy whinnied softly at Ellie, just like she always did. Ellie released the latch on the gate and stepped inside. "There you go, girl. Good girl." She laid her head against Daisy's neck while the horse nuzzled her cape. "Now, what makes you think I have something for you in my pocket?" Ellie smiled and produced a shiny red apple from under her cape. "You know me too well." Daisy bit into the treat and eagerly came back for more.

Cade smiled at the obvious affection between them. "I wasn't expecting you back this evening."

"Didn't Dr. Gifford tell you? I have permission from my father and Miss Eastman to be here when the foal is born."

"Have you ever witnessed a birth?"

"Well, no. But Dr. Gifford explained all the gory details to me, and I have no qualms about it. I want to see it. That is, if it happens before the nine o'clock bell."

"Nine o'clock! Little chance of that. Daisy's contractions are still far apart. This isn't anything we can hurry along." He saw the disappointment on her face and softened his words. "Perhaps the foal will wait until tomorrow morning, after you are up for the day."

Ellie brightened. "I'll keep that good thought. So how long have you been in Philadelphia?"

"I've completed two years of veterinary school at the university. I'll graduate next year. How about you?"

"I graduate this year from Ogontz, and then I'll take my entrance exams for Radcliffe at the end of June. Are you sure Daisy is all right? She's perspiring a lot."

"That's normal. She's working hard to move that foal along the birth canal." Daisy nickered and switched her tail. Cade stood up and brought a bucket of oats mix for her. She ate as if she hadn't been fed in a long while. "That's a good girl. We all like our favorite food when we're hurting, don't we?" Cade patted her back and felt along her belly.

Ellie stroked her fingers through Daisy's mane from the opposite side. "You know, when we met at Congress Lake, I always had the strangest feeling that I knew you from before. It still feels that way. It is almost like I've always known you." She paused. "Is it too forward of me to say that?"

Cade felt his heart pump a bit faster. "Not at all. I suppose it happens to all of us when we're reminded of someone we know."

"But I couldn't think of anyone like you who I knew from before. Anyway, what are the chances of us meeting again here in a stable?"

Cade wanted to change the topic before it went too far. "Has your family always lived in Philadelphia?"

"Yes. But Papa and I are the only ones here at the moment. His law firm handles contracts for the city. My sister Charlie—Charlotte is her real name—lives with my Aunt Lucie in Paris. She's studying art there. My mother…" Ellie took in a breath. "She's recovering from tuberculosis in a sanatorium in Davos, Switzerland.

"I'm sorry to hear that. It must be hard to have her so far away."

"Mama went to visit Charlie last year. That's where she got sick. Sometimes I pretend that she is just visiting Paris." She was quiet for long moment and then asked, "Do you have siblings?"

"Yes, a sister and three brothers. They are all quite a lot older than me. My mother died when I was a baby, and my father died a few years ago. I lived most of my life with my sister's family."

"And where was that?"

Cade shifted his legs. It seemed as if all roads in this conversation led back to Hartville. "Not too far from Congress Lake. Uh, when we met there three years ago, I was working to earn tuition for vet school."

"What made you want to be a veterinarian?"

"I've always loved horses, and I guess I have a knack for handling them. I grew up on a farm, so maybe it came naturally to me. I'm sure it was a very different life from what a city girl like you must have experienced."

"You haven't any idea what I've experienced. Would you be surprised if I told you I've swung on a barn rope and landed in a pile of hay? I've picked vegetables from the garden, and I know how to can them. I've gathered eggs, I've milked a cow, though not very well, and I've even slopped the hogs!"

"What?" He didn't hide his surprise. "Miss McAllister, I *am* impressed!" Cade looked at her with a new respect. "Where on earth did you do all that?"

"Please, just call me Ellie. It was on a farm near Hartville, Ohio. It's called Claybourne Oaks."

"Where Hank Jeffreys lives?" Cade said it before he thought about the questions that would surely follow.

"You know Hank and Tilda?"

"I've never been to his place. But we both worked the ice harvest up at Congress Lake. And we ran into each other now and then in town. Would you care to sit?" He motioned to the blanket that covered the mound of straw where he had been sitting before. He extended his hand politely to assist her as she sat. When she settled her back against the sidewall of the large stall, he sat in the clean straw by the gate and pulled one knee up to rest his elbow on it. "How do you know the Jeffreys?"

"I stayed with Mrs. Taylor at the farm for the summer three years ago. She owns the whole property but only stays in their cottage in the woods during the summer. The Jeffreys are the caretakers of the farm."

"Oh, that was your friend, Mrs. Taylor, who you mentioned this afternoon."

"Her parents were the Claybournes, for whom the farm is named." Ellie began to tell Cade the stories from when she first set eyes on Claybourne Oaks back when she was ten years old. She told him how her hands and face were caked with black muck after she played outdoors. And how she took baths by the kitchen stove. And about picking blackberries and making sassafras tea. She described how it was to wake in the loft with birds chirping at dawn and about the herbs that hung from the ceiling in the pantry.

She surprised herself when she told him about the morning she had walked barefoot in her nightgown into the woods and how she felt a vibration in her body that came from the earth. "It was as if the land had magically laid claim on me. It let me know I would always belong there. I even felt it when I returned there three years ago." She glanced up quickly to gauge his reaction. Cade didn't laugh. His eyes opened wider, she noticed, and he gave a nod.

"Yes, I believe the land does that," he said. They both sat quietly in their own thoughts. Cade noticed how comfortable it was to just sit here in silence with Ellie. He had been touched by the wonder in her voice and every lovely detail of her animated face when she talked about Hartville. He hadn't imagined what farm life must look like through the eyes of a city child. He'd never dreamt that a girl from a wealthy family would appreciate the land so.

Ellie pulled her coat around her and hugged her legs.

"Those are wonderful stories, Ellie. You've given me a new perspective on Hartville. I'm glad the Taylors have that farm. Hank said it belonged to someone from the Canton Outing Club. I'm afraid many folks in my hometown have prejudiced feelings about the club."

"In what way?"

"I suppose they regard the club folks as kind of uppity."

"Some of them are uppity, but the Taylors are not like that at all. The first time I saw Congress Lake, I was at a Canton Outing Club picnic. But I was only ten years old then. That's another long story I'd rather not repeat." Ellie stopped talking.

Cade noticed the change in her expression, and he was sure he already knew that story. "It looks like she is starting another contraction," he said. He hopped up and felt Daisy's belly. "Would you like to feel it?"

"Yes!"

"Well, come over and place your hands right here."

Ellie's eyes widened, and her smile reached from ear to ear as she felt the muscles in Daisy's abdomen tighten. Then, without warning, the mare's hoof kicked up at her, and Ellie gave a little yelp as she stumbled backward.

Cade's arm went protectively to Ellie's shoulder, but he quickly let go. "Oh. Pardon me." It was one of those awkward moments. He didn't know the appropriate etiquette with someone like her. "Did she hurt you? I'm sorry. I should have warned you that could happen."

"Thank you. I wasn't hurt. Dr. Gifford warned me she may do something like that. I won't take it personally, will I, girl?" She stroked her horse's mane, and Daisy quivered.

Cade smiled, relieved that Ellie hadn't seemed to take offense at his unexpected touch.

The bell by the kitchen door up at the mansion began to ring, and Ellie frowned. "Oh, no, that's the first curfew. Miss Eastman said I have to leave now."

"I'm sorry, but I'm guessing Daisy will give birth before morning," Cade said.

Ellie winced. She stroked the mare's velvety chin and kissed her on the forehead. "I'm sorry I won't be with you, Daisy-girl."

Cade watched the darkened hall even after Ellie had disappeared around the corner and after he heard the outside door close behind her. Almost as soon as she had shown up at Daisy's stall that evening, Cade realized her presence was fresh air to the embers in his heart, and he was drawn to this young woman more than ever.

An evening mist was settling over the Ogontz estate. Ellie had intended to go directly to the mansion, but instead she stepped onto the damp grass by the stable where lantern light was shining through the window. She watched Cade as he stared over the gate of Daisy's pen into corridor where she had just been. She wondered what he was thinking. She felt a quiver in her heart. Only this time it didn't confuse her, as it had three years before. She smiled and then ran up the driveway as the final curfew bell began to ring.

* * *

The alcove clock in the corridor outside of her room emitted three hollow notes. She crawled from her bed and stared out the window. There was no moon, but the lights along the driveway pulled her heart toward Daisy. And to Cade.

Her decision was made quickly. Ellie felt her way to the closet and ran her hand along her row of dresses until her fingers recognized the fabric of her woolen travel dress. She pulled it on right over her nightgown. It was dark green and would blend in well with the shadows of the night. Ellie picked up her boots, which she wore for riding, and realized that it would be hopeless to find her stockings in the dark.

She tiptoed to the door and lifted her cape from its hook. Ever so slowly, she eased the door open. The creaking of its hinges came in short spurts, much more loudly than she had remembered. The air from the corridor felt cool against her nose, where nervous moisture had beaded up. She scooted barefoot into the hall. It seemed as if her heart were thumping so loudly that everyone would be awakened by its guilty beat.

She crept down the circular staircase and ran the length of the main hall to the palm court, where the fountain was silent at this early hour. Ellie slid her bare feet into her boots and pushed her way through the door into the crisp, night air.

She darted between shadows and ducked below the shuttered windows of the coach house. From the entrance hall she saw a light glowing at the far end of the stable, in Daisy's pen. She tiptoed to the gate and saw her mare lying on her side in the bright yellow straw that had been piled generously over the floor.

Cade was kneeling nearby. His jacket had been flung in the corner, and the sleeves of his white shirt were rolled up to his elbows. His attention was focused on a bluish, shiny bag protruding from the birth canal below Daisy's outstretched tail. Ellie stared at this odd protrusion. It didn't look anything like a foal to her. She quickly shifted her eyes away, feeling embarrassed and maybe even a little sick. She looked at Cade's face instead, which seemed not at all alarmed by what was happening. In fact, there was a soft smile at the corners of his mouth. She observed things that her undetected presence permitted her to see. The stubble of a beard that had not been shaved. She noticed his eyelashes were quite long, and without his hat, his curly hair stuck out every which way.

Cade reached over and patted Daisy's thigh. "That's the way, girl. You'll get through this," he said gently. From the corner of his eye he saw some-one at the gate. He turned toward the auburn-haired girl watching him and grinned broadly. "You're back. I'm guessing Miss Eastman doesn't know you are here?"

Ellie shook her head. "No. Miss Eastman would not approve."

"You may come on in and have a closer look. Daisy is doing very well. It will be a while until the foal is fully birthed."

"I don't know. I'm feeling a little sick."

Just then Daisy made a sound that was part cough and part moan, blended altogether in an unearthly, groaning noise. Her legs had stiffened, and her belly heaved. Ellie pushed the gate open and started to rush toward her head, but Cade's arm jutted out in front of her.

"No, Ellie. Don't go to her yet. She won't be so aware of you, and she may flail unexpectedly. Daisy is fine. This is what happens in every birth."

Ellie felt shaky and knelt in the straw near Cade. The bluish bag protruded a bit more each time her mare strained and groaned. She saw two tiny white hooves shining through the translucent bag. Soon the shape of a head flattened out over the foal's knees could be seen through the membrane.

As if reading her mind, Cade said, "What you are seeing is the amniotic sac. It is exactly the right color and should break open soon, perhaps when the shoulders are free. See how the hooves are faced down? This means the foal is positioned well, so it is best to let Daisy do this her way."

Daisy's back arched, and she groaned again. Sure enough, the legs and shoulders of the foal were pushed free, and the tip of the sac broke open. Two tiny, wet, dark legs stuck out.

Cade leaned forward and took the torn edges of the sac in his hand. "I'm going to slide this up over the foal's head. There. And now I'm squeezing its nose a bit to clear some of this amniotic fluid. It'll be taking its first breath, and we want it to be a good one."

Ellie gasped when she saw the foal come to life. Its head shook slightly, and there was a raspy cough. Its front legs pushed down into the straw. "It's breathing!" she whispered. "But the back half of it isn't even out yet." What followed was an orchestrated effort between Daisy and her foal. The foal struggled to pull forward, and Daisy continued to push. Suddenly, with a splash, the amniotic sac broke free of the birth canal, and gangly legs kicked and struggled to break out of it. Daisy lay panting on the straw, but she twisted her head back toward her foal now and then. Ellie couldn't help but scoot in to give her mare a hug. Daisy nickered softly.

Cade said, "She has some more work to do. There is a placenta to be birthed yet, and there will be fluids and blood, Ellie. Don't be alarmed. It is natural." He was on his hands and knees now, looking closely at the foal. "It looks like you have a little colt!"

"Daisy, you have a son!" Ellie patted Daisy's neck, but she could hardly take her eyes off the exquisite colt. She thought she could see a reddish color in his hair, but she wasn't certain. The colt braced his front legs and tried to stand up but tumbled into a comical heap instead. Immediately, he tried again to stand, but this time his hind legs buckled under. Ellie had once watched a wet monarch butterfly emerging from its chrysalis. It had struggled so pitifully that she wanted to help it, but Papa said the struggle was necessary. How else would it become strong enough to migrate all the way to the Gulf?

Daisy stretched herself around until her nose barely touched the foal's chin. Her tongue flicked out and licked some of the viscous fluid that soaked the colt, who in turn made sloppy kissing sounds against his mother's lip. Ellie laughed aloud. With a valiant heave, the colt managed to stand on four feet for the first time in his life. His front legs were braced at an odd angle, and his back legs stuck out at an equally odd angle the other way. It reminded Ellie of her rocking horse in their attic. The colt took short, faltering steps forward and collapsed under Daisy's chin. The mare happily licked away at her colt and seemed oblivious to anything else around her. Ellie backed away slowly until she felt the wall of the pen against her. She pulled her cape tightly around herself and slid down onto the soft straw, where she watched as Daisy transformed into a mother.

Cade leaned against the adjoining wall with his legs outstretched. He had seen a mare with her new foal many times in his life, but he had never had the opportunity to quietly watch a lovely young woman like Ellie: everything about her, her disheveled hair, her dark eyes and freckled face, the ruffle of a flowered flannel nightgown sticking out from beneath her dress. Every detail was beautiful. It did feel as though he had known her forever. He saw Ellie's eyes drooping shut. When she started to slowly drop to the side, he got up and placed a folded blanket where her head would land in a minute, and he put his woolen coat over her legs. She curled up like a barn kitten and never even moved when Daisy delivered the placenta, or when the fuzzy colt noisily suckled milk.

Cade worked away at cleaning up the pen and giving Daisy and her foal a postpartum exam. He never noticed that the sky was lightening or that the world was stirring outside.

CHAPTER TWENTY-FOUR

High Wire

"Mornin', sir."

Cade's head snapped upright, and he turned around from where he was leaning against the gate, half dozing on his feet, the way a horse sleeps. Billy, who was pulling his suspenders up over his shoulders while he walked, stopped for a moment to dip a tin cup right into the horse trough. He swished the water around in his mouth and spat it on the ground. Cade guessed it was the most care Billy's teeth got on any given day. He passed his tongue over his own teeth and was glad he had some dentifrice powder in his bag.

Cade was a little slow to realize Billy was heading toward the pen, where Ellie was sound asleep in the straw. Cade could imagine the kind of rumors that would circulate about her through the coach house. Why hadn't he thought to awaken her earlier? He did the only thing he could think of in the moment. "Say, Billy, would you dip a tin for me?"

"Sure thing, sir!"

While Billy returned to the trough to refill the cup, Cade grabbed a blanket from the fence and placed it over Ellie. Her eyes popped open, and he put a finger over his lips. Then he covered her head as well. Ellie's form blended in with the lumps of straw in the pen.

"Will you look at that!" Billy was back with the tin cup of horse water, which Cade only pretended to sip. "Filly or a colt?"

"It's a colt. The mare did well. I think she'll be fine for breeding in the future." Cade didn't want to encourage a long-winded exchange, so he kept a professional demeanor. He deftly positioned himself between Billy and where Ellie lay hidden.

The foal sprang to its feet, and Daisy hoisted herself up, though not so lively. The little colt poked his nose several times into her udder, which drew a reflexive kick from the mare. It seemed to release her milk, however, and he gulped eagerly.

"He's a dandy. You done good, Mr. Bauer."

"Well, the accolades go to Daisy." Cade yawned loudly.

"I suspect you'll be wanting some shut-eye before heading back to the city."

"Perhaps so."

Ellie understood why Cade had hidden her from sight. How would she get out of this mess? It must be morning, and even if Billy didn't see her, she could hardly get back to her room undetected now. She heard Cade step outside of the pen, directing Billy's attention away from her, but she didn't move from her hiding place. She had absolutely no plan for an escape. Ellie lifted the edge of the blanket enough to see her new colt. His fuzzy coat was a dark chestnut. She watched him guzzling his breakfast, and her own belly growled. Billy's voice had faded into the background, and she heard the gate open again.

Cade whispered, "I think it is safe to come out now. I'm sorry. I should have awakened you earlier."

"That's all right. I knew what I was risking when I came down here in the night. I'll take my lumps."

"It's foggy out, so maybe you can still get back undetected. Billy said he had to get the tack room organized for riding lessons today, so I think he's out of sight for a while. Maybe you should run for it."

Ellie sat up and combed her fingers through her tangled hair as best she could. Cade watched her twist it like a strand of rope and tie it into a knot at the nape of her neck.

A voice came out of the darkened area of the stable. "Mr. Bauer?"

Cade straightened his stance. "Yes, I'm Cade Bauer."

A tall, pale-skinned young woman with black hair emerged from the walkway between the stalls. "I'm Norah Miles, Ellie's roommate. She, uh, mentioned you last night. I was hoping to find her here. With her horse."

"Norah?" Ellie popped up from behind the wall.

"Ellie, what are you thinking? Miss Eastman will be furious if she finds out."

"I didn't intend to stay all night. I fell asleep. What time is it?"

"It's quarter past six by now. If we hurry, we can make it back before the rising bell."

"First, you have to see Daisy's colt!" Ellie unlatched the gate.

Norah squealed. "Oh, he's splendid, Ellie. What are you going to name him?"

"Funny you should ask. I was just thinking of a little boy I met when I was child. I think I'll name the colt for him."

"Do tell!" Norah said.

"Petey." Ellie wrinkled her nose. "I know. It sounds kind of odd for a horse, but I like it."

Cade felt gooseflesh rise on his arms, and his heart skipped a beat. To hide his startled response, he turned his head quickly and coughed. He leaned over to pick up his jacket from the straw and appeared to be busy brushing it off.

"I like it!" Norah said. "But we have to get out of here, Ellie." She looked anxiously out the window at the gray mist that had thinned some. "The fog will lift soon. And I don't want to have to tell another lie about why I was out."

"Another lie? Did someone ask?"

"Miss Priss caught me as I was leaving."

"Angel Gates?"

"She asked where I was going at six in the morning. I told her I wanted to capture the morning fog on my new Brownie camera."

"Photographing the fog?" Ellie laughed. "Norah, you're brilliant."

She gave Daisy a hug and patted the rump of her colt, who instinctively kicked up his hind legs. "Goodbye, Petey." She turned to Cade and grinned.

"Thank you, Mr. Bauer. Papa sent a telegram last evening. He's coming to have lunch with me today, and I'd like him to meet you. Will you still be here?"

No one expected him back for exams today, so he had time. "I'll make sure of it," he said. "I think I need to take a nap and clean up a bit. Until later?"

Ellie smiled happily and hurried after her roommate, who was already moving determinedly toward the stable's outer door. Before she turned the corner, she looked back and gave Cade a quick wave. He waved back.

* * *

Ellie and Norah locked arms as if the two of them had simply gone out for a morning walk, and no one who happened to look outside would have thought twice about it.

"Thank you, Norah. I didn't know how I was going to get back to our room without raising eyebrows."

"McAllister, you can't seem to stay out of trouble."

"I know. But what did you think of him?"

"He's a beautiful colt. Do you think he'll be a deep sorrel like Daisy?"

"No, I mean Cade."

"Cade? Hmmm, I see. Well, he's quite lovely, too."

Ellie grinned. Her jittery heart calmed a little when they came to their own corridor, still undetected. Then as they reached their door, Angel stepped from her room across the hall with her hand on her hip. She slowly scrutinized Ellie from head to toe. "Aren't you a sight! I didn't see you leave with Norah. Are you into foggy photography, too?"

"I caught up with her later. We both stopped by the stable to see Daisy's colt. Mr. Bauer said everything went well last night."

At the mention of Cade's name, Angel sniffed. "Well. How lovely." She turned abruptly and disappeared into her lair without another word.

Ellie pushed against her roommate and managed to get their door shut behind them before laughter doubled them both over. "Did you see the look on her face?"

"We finally got her!" Norah wiped her eyes. "McAllister, I think we can graduate now."

When the seven thirty bell rang for morning prayers, Ellie hurried to take the empty seat beside Miss Bennett. She whispered the good news about Daisy.

"That's wonderful, Eleanor." Miss Bennett smiled, but her forehead wrinkled a little as if there was something of a serious nature she wanted to say. She paused and then added, "I'd like to speak with you after breakfast. Would you mind coming to my sitting room?"

The look on her principal's face made Ellie feel uneasy.

* * *

At eight twenty, Ellie knocked on Miss Bennett's door.

"Thank you for coming by, Eleanor. Perhaps you'd join me in the sunroom?" Miss Bennett led the way through the French doors to the pleasant porch adjoining her sitting room. The warm morning breeze carried the scent of lilacs through the screened windows from the garden surrounding it. She motioned to a matching wicker chair across from hers.

Ellie sank into the pastel floral pillow that lined the seat and waited.

"I wanted to ask you about something I observed last night. I was up in the night and came out here to sit for a while."

Ellie felt her cheeks burning as she realized what Miss Bennett was about to say.

"You can imagine my surprise when I happened to see a young woman hurrying down the driveway toward the coach house. I'm wondering if you could tell me more about that?"

Ellie lowered her gaze. "Yes, ma'am. I suppose I could." She swallowed hard. She'd imagined making this sort of speech standing before Miss Eastman. It was even harder sitting here with Miss Bennett and knowing how disappointed she must be. That hurt worse than any punishment she may be facing. When she started to talk, her voice came out thin and much younger than she wanted. "My decision to go to the stable was made quickly when I woke in the middle of the night. I knew Daisy was giving birth, and

I had to be with her. I know that is no excuse. I take full responsibility for what I did. I'm sorry that I've disappointed you, Miss Bennett."

"My disappointment is not the important issue here. Your father gave you an opportunity to experience something as an adult, Eleanor. He made a special effort to work out acceptable parameters with Miss Eastman. Your father trusted that you would respect them. You've let him down."

"Yes, ma'am." What had seemed so clear to her in the middle of the night now felt confusing. She had never intended to let anyone down, especially not Papa.

"Eleanor, I do understand why you went to the stable. I know how much Daisy means to you. But as an adult, you will often be faced with having to sacrifice something you want to do." She paused while Ellie took it in. "You know I will have to discuss this with your father. He informed us that he will be visiting you today at noon, but now I am going to call and request a meeting with him beforehand. I wanted to give you the opportunity to tell me about it first."

"I understand, ma'am. I'm sorry. Would it be possible not to mention this to Miss Eastman?"

"That puts me in a very awkward position. I do not wish to be complicit with your deceit. I will, however, discuss it with your father privately, and we will decide together what to do. He may want to discuss this further with Mr. Bauer and perhaps Dr. Gifford as well."

Ellie was beginning to see that perhaps Cade would be in trouble now for something she had done.

"Mr. Bauer was a gentleman. There was nothing untoward that happened," she said, hoping she didn't sound too defensive. "He was tending to the foaling, just as Papa had wanted."

"I'm glad to hear that, Eleanor. I'll convey that information to your father. Thank you for coming by. I'm aware you have your first class at nine, so I won't keep you."

"Thank you, Miss Bennett." Ellie fled to the hall, wiping tears away. She hoped no one would be angry with Cade. She couldn't bear for him to be in trouble after he'd been so kind to her.

* * *

When the sluggish minutes of her morning classes came mercifully to an end, Ellie made her way to the palm court, where Papa was waiting for her. He looked tired, and she noticed for the first time that his beard had some silver in it. He held out his arms and hugged her warmly. Things always felt better when she was with Papa.

"Your Aunt Tess had Maggie make a picnic lunch for us, and I asked Miss Bennett if we could be excused from the dining room today. She thought it was a good idea, as we may need a chance to talk privately. Is a picnic all right with you?"

"Yes, Papa." The painful knot in her throat earlier now returned.

They set off down the driveway, the picnic basket in Papa's hand.

"Shall we walk to the stable and take a look at the colt on the way?" he asked.

Ellie wondered if her father intended to discuss this whole matter with Cade, so she decided to face it directly. "Papa? I know you are disappointed in me," she started to say. "It was all my fault, and I never intended to hurt you or to get anyone else in trouble."

"Ellie, sometimes adults must have enough discernment and courage to make decisions that do not follow the rules. I understand why Ogontz has rules, and I know they mean well. But you are to an age where you'll be out in life and must make choices for yourself all the time. I don't expect your judgment to suddenly develop the day you graduate. You need to exercise your own judgment a little more each year. Within safe parameters, of course."

"I didn't let you down?"

"I once watched a high-wire artist walk on a line stretched between two tall buildings in Paris. He walked confidently and even did some fancy tricks on that high wire without any net below him. But you can be certain that he practiced for years with a safety net in place. Your teachers and your family are the safety net for you, Ellie. If you happen to fall, we're there to help you get back up again and hopefully in such a way that you want to try again. It seems to me if you have enough opportunities to make decisions, you'll be able to walk with confidence when you graduate and maybe even have a trick or two up your sleeve."

He hugged Ellie close, and she put her arms around him. She loved him so much.

"Thank you, Papa." Everything felt right in her world again. "I named my colt Petey."

"Well, that's a name I've never heard for a horse. But why not?"

"He's beautiful. I don't think he'll be as dark as his sire. He's more sorrel, like Daisy. And I want to introduce Mr. Bauer to you. I met him three years ago at Congress Lake when I spent the summer with the Taylors, and now he's in Philadelphia studying to be a vet. He's working for Dr. Gifford this summer. He's so nice, Papa."

"Well, I look forward to meeting him." Papa looked at her for a long moment with an odd smile.

Ellie blushed. They entered the stable door and made their way to Daisy's pen. Cade was not around. Had he left without saying goodbye? Ellie was dismayed, but she told her father all about the foaling, how seeing the amniotic sac had made her feel sick at first, but then when she saw the two tiny hooves appear, she had wanted to stay.

While they were talking, Cade appeared at the gate in a clean white shirt. He was freshly shaved, with his hair all combed neatly in place. "Hello. You must be Mr. McAllister."

"Oh!" Ellie's eyes widened. "Papa, this is Mr. Cade Bauer. And this is my father, Aaron McAllister."

"It's a pleasure to meet you, sir."

"Dr. Gifford said he's been quite impressed with your work. I appreciate what you did for our mare."

Cade remembered him now that he saw him. He had aged quite a bit in seven years, but there was lively quality in Ellie's father that he recognized from before. "You're welcome, sir. It was fairly routine, but one never knows until the foal appears. It's good to have a safety net in place."

Ellie and her father glanced at each other and laughed. Cade looked confused.

"Ellie and I were just about to go for picnic. If I know Maggie, she packed more than enough for the two of us. Would you care to join us?"

Ellie noticed Cade's face brighten at this suggestion, mirroring her own surprised happiness.

"I'd be delighted," he said.

* * *

Later, when it was time to leave, Papa shook out the picnic cloth while Ellie rearranged the bowls in the basket. Cade asked if he and Papa could have a word privately before they parted. They walked a few steps away, and she overheard Papa say, "I have no objection to the idea, but my daughter will need to decide for herself." Then he called her over to join them. "Ellie, this young man is interested in calling on you. Is that something that meets your approval?"

She could see that Papa was teasing the two of them, so she paused as if she had serious doubts. "May I think it over?"

"Ah, my daughter already knows a trick or two for the high wire." He winked at her.

Cade laughed, enjoying the banter. He turned directly to her and bowed. "Take as long as you need. I am your obedient servant."

Ellie blushed. She had been partly joking when she said she needed to think about it. She had been envious of other girls who already had callers. But now that she had one of her own, it unnerved her.

* * *

"Don't you think it's odd, Norah?" Ellie said in the dark.

"What?"

"That Cade and I ran into each other at Ogontz after meeting at Congress Lake? What are the chances? What do you think it means?"

A pillow from nowhere landed on Ellie's chest. "McAllister, you think too much. Lucky coincidences happen all the time. Now go to sleep."

"Cade asked if he could come calling. Papa said it's up to me."

"You didn't tell me that. Sounds divine. When will he be calling?"

"Cade said he'd write soon, but I told him maybe we should wait until I'm home for the summer."

"Ellie! You told him *not to write*?"

"No, I just said to wait. Since Miss Eastman requires a formal letter of approval from our parents before a boy is allowed to contact us, it seemed like such a bother when we only have two weeks of school left."

A groan came from Norah's side of the room. "Ellie. *What were you thinking?* I know you're smitten with him. Why would you dump cold water on him just when he's warming up to you?"

"I guess I wasn't very encouraging, was I?"

Ellie heard her roommate turning away from her instead of answering. She wanted to explain to Norah what was really bothering her. "It's just that I'm kind of scared about the whole thing. How does a girl know if she's ready for this? I mean, I'm very fond of Cade." Ellie stopped and sucked in her breath. She knew she wasn't being completely honest. The words blurted out of her then. "I think I'm falling alarmingly in love with him." There. She'd said it. And loud enough for even God's deaf ear to hear it. The steady rhythm of her roommate's breath told her no one else had. "Norah?"

Ellie's exhausted body seemed to awaken with this new proclamation. As if it hadn't been known to herself until she had said it aloud. Images of the previous night with Cade filled her mind. The intensity of her feelings for him unnerved her. She shivered recalling how his arm had shot out when Daisy had kicked at her. She could still feel his touch on her shoulder. A ripply feeling rose up through her body and took her breath away. Her mind slipped into a timeless place where fantasies have free rein. The last thing she heard was the hall clock calling her back. Two hollow chimes.

CHAPTER TWENTY-FIVE

Letting Go

Ellie's last exams she would ever take at Ogontz were completed on Wednesday, the thirtieth of May. There was no time to celebrate. She and all the other girls focused on polishing boots and buckles and brushing away lint from their red and gold battalion dress uniforms.

The following day, crowds of visitors arrived at Ogontz after lunch to watch the Competitive Drill Competition, in spite of the intermittent rain that had moved in from the coast. Ellie's eyes skimmed over the faces of visitors until she spotted Papa.

Just as the competition was about to start at two o'clock, there was a sideways-slanted downpour. Papa and the other spectators had umbrellas, but they still got soaked. It was the first time ever the military drill had to be delayed. When the skies cleared at two thirty, the judges wasted no time starting the first event. Each company was allotted just five minutes to execute its manual of arms drill. When it was their turn, Ellie's captain, Lizzy Camp, brought Company B to attention, and the drill was performed flawlessly, their wooden "rifles" snapping in unison. After the setting-up exercises, there was the competition between the "new girls" and the "old girls" and then the final event with all four companies dazzling the crowd.

Major Landon said he'd never been prouder of the battalion's performance. The judges—prestigious colonels from as far away as New Jersey—concurred that "minute points of excellence" had to be considered before they could decide the winner. Spectators cheered. And the Bordentown Military Institute Band, which had been invited to play for this year's drill, started a lively marching tune when Captain Camp was called forward. The coveted flag went to Company B! The sun briefly cut through the gray skies as Ellie and the others posed for their victory photograph.

The last day of school, which was also graduation day, was the following Tuesday. But there were five days in between for all kinds of year-end rituals. Saturday was filled with picnic lunches, farewell gifting, signing yearbooks. Kodak box cameras clicked incessantly. Ellie joined the clusters of girls who draped their arms around each other in silly and serious poses in their dormitory rooms, on the bridge, by the fountains, and even in their favorite treehouses. The baccalaureate service was on Sunday. Monday was the day for final packing up of their rooms for the summer, filling trunks to take home or to store in the luggage room until next fall. Ellie had left space on Monday morning, however, to say a special goodbye.

When she knocked on the door of the Wing Room, she heard Fritz's bark from somewhere inside. "One moment, please," a voice called out. Ellie felt an ache in her throat. It was likely the last time they'd chat.

Miss Bennett looked pale and puffy in her face, an indication that her illness had flared up again. "Eleanor. How kind of you to stop by."

Ellie smiled. "I hope it isn't an inconvenience. I see you are busy packing."

"No, this is a perfect time. I'm ready for a break. Please come in."

The room itself was already devoid of life, having been stripped of Miss Bennett's paintings and warm touches. The plate rail was bare. The pots of African violets were missing. Her oak table remained in its familiar place, but the crocheted lace cloth and cut flowers that had always graced it were gone. Packing boxes bound with string sat on the floor. Fritz whined pitifully from behind the glass doors of Miss Bennett's sun porch.

"You can let him in. He'll be indebted to you for his reprieve. I'm afraid he was quite naughty earlier, and he's been sulking in solitary for the last hour."

Ellie opened the doors, and he rushed in, wiggling and dancing all around her. She knelt down and gave him a hug. Then he ran over to Miss Bennett's side and waited contritely for the head pat to let him know he was forgiven.

"I was just going to have some black tea," she said. "May I pour a cup for you?"

"Yes, thank you," Ellie said. "That would be lovely." She thought about the formalities they were enacting in this moment, when what she really wanted to do was to throw her arms around this dear woman and tell her how much she'd meant these last five years.

The silver teapot with its repoussé flowers still sat in its place on the sideboard. A small kerosene flame glowed at the base, and a bit of steam floated from the spout. Miss Bennett tilted the teapot in its stand to pour the dark liquid into porcelain teacups and placed a flowered plate of sponge cakes on the low table between them. "I've been sorting books. I've given my first editions to the library already, but beside you there is a stack I simply can't take with me. Any of those you may keep if they appeal to you."

Ellie opened one to the title page. "*A Thousand Miles Up the Nile* by Amelia Edwards. This looks interesting."

"I've read it many times over the last twenty years. That novel planted the seed about exploring the Nile River for myself. And now I'm going to do it! One can't ask more from a book than that, don't you agree?"

Ellie nodded. "When will you sail for Egypt?"

"My niece and I leave on the fifteenth of August. That will give us ample time to rest before we board the Thomas Cook steamer on the Nile in October. After our tour, I'll stay on at the resort. Egypt's dry, hot climate will be excellent for my condition."

Miss Bennett's disease wasn't contagious, but her optimism was. Ellie smiled and nodded. "I wanted to give you something small enough to take with you. To remember me." She laid a small box with a white satin ribbon encircling it on the table.

"How kind of you." Miss Bennett held the box in her hand for a moment and gazed at Ellie as if she had more to say. "You know, your thoughtful visits and our walks have been gifts as well. I appreciate them all." She untied the ribbon and lifted the lid. Folded inside was a white silk hanky. Miss Bennett's initials, *F.B.*, were embroidered within a cluster of blue forget-me-nots in the corner. There was delicate tatting around the edges. "Oh, Eleanor. It is beautiful!"

"I didn't make it myself. My needlework isn't nearly fine enough. I did draw the design I wanted for you, and my Aunt Tess arranged to have it made."

"I will take it with me, and you can be certain I will think of you often. Thank you for such a lovely gift."

* * *

On Tuesday, Miss Frances Bennett awarded diplomas for the last time after forty years at the Ogontz School for Young Ladies. Ellie, in her white gown and mortar cap, stepped forward to receive her diploma and a fragrant nosegay of lavender roses and their class flower, lily of the valley, bound with a ripple of lavender ribbons. The seventeen graduates of the Class of 1900 linked arms and sang together: *"Naughty-naughts they call us; Far from naught are we. We're the best, Of all the rest. We'll close the century…"*

* * *

"Something came in the post for you." Aunt Tess peered over her spectacles and tilted her head toward the telephone stand where it lay. "I believe it's from your young gentleman."

Ellie's heart raced. By the time she reached her room, her fingers had left damp spots on the envelope. The letter was written in small, neat penmanship.

Dear Ellie,

I hope that your school year ended well. I've thought often of our conversations and the picnic lunch with your father and you. It was a pleasure to get to know you.

I hope that Daisy and Petey are doing well. Where will they be boarding this summer?

I've completed my exams, to my great relief, but my school year will not end until the thirteenth of June. I'll be working for Dr. Gifford six days a week until late August. However, I will have Sunday afternoons free. I am wondering if I may call on you at your home on Sunday, the seventeenth of June, in the afternoon. If you are favorably inclined, I thought perhaps we may walk to Rittenhouse Square, weather permitting. It would be my honor to spend time with you again.

Your obedient servant,

Cade Bauer

Ellie read it several times before she sat down to respond. If she were honest, she would tell him how nearly every hour of every day, she had thought of him. How she had lain awake at night remembering the stubble on his chin, his smile, and eyes. And his dark curls that went every which way. How she had worried that he would never write yet knew he was respecting her own request to wait. His letter had arrived the very day she'd come home for the summer, which had given her hope that he'd been as eager for that day as she.

Of course, she could not write such things to him. Nor did she want to be as formal as Mama would have wished her to be. He wouldn't recognize that girl. The Ellie he knew had dirt on her nose and told stories about Claybourne Oaks and fell asleep on the straw beneath his woolen jacket.

She positioned a new sheet of stationery at an angle and wrote:

Dear Cade,

I would be pleased to receive you on Sunday, the seventeenth, at two o'clock. A walk to Rittenhouse Square would be delightful. If we have inclement weather, perhaps we could play a board game in the parlor instead. Do you play chess? I'm not very skilled, but Papa keeps trying to teach me.

You asked about Daisy and Petey. He has grown rapidly. His coat is still fuzzy, but it is quite red in the sunlight. The owner at Fairmount Stables, where Papa has them in boarding, said Petey shows promise in his conformation, though it is too early to know how he will develop.

May I congratulate you on completing your exams? I hope that your work with Dr. Gifford this summer will be an interesting and rewarding endeavor.

I look forward to your visit on the seventeenth.
Faithfully Yours,
Ellie McAllister

* * *

At dinner, Ellie announced that Cade would be coming to call the Sunday after next.

"Oh dear," Aunt Tess said. "I won't be able to meet Mr. Bauer properly until I'm back from the Riviera in September."

"I'm sure Ellie and I will manage fine, Tess." Papa winked at Ellie.

"Well, I'll invite him to dinner when I return. I do feel responsible to step into your mother's shoes while she is away."

Ellie was relieved it would just be Cade, Papa, and her this first time a boy called on her. She felt a little guilty thinking it, but she was glad that Mama would not be here fussing over what was proper or not. She wondered if Mama would even approve of a veterinary student coming to call.

That night she slept with Cade's letter under her pillow.

* * *

The fellows at Gifford's clinic had poked fun at Cade about his night at Ogontz. There had been all kinds of innuendo about sneaking young ladies into the stable. A lesser man would have bragged, but he gave no hint that a young woman had, indeed, spent the night in the stall with him. In the weeks since that night, Cade had daydreamed about Ellie constantly. He wondered how he had spent the previous two years leasing out his heart to Angel Gates's robin's-egg-blue eyes and pouty smile without ever looking for something of substance behind them. She was a silly schoolgirl next to Ellie. He could see that now.

Ellie McAllister had walked in with dirt on her nose and her hair all sweaty, but she had just laughed at herself. Her beauty was on the outside and the inside. He liked her tenderness with her horse, her sense of humor, and her honesty. But it was when they were sitting in the straw with Ellie telling stories of Claybourne Oaks that he'd realized he was smitten with her.

Her stories had even made him homesick for Hartville. She'd made it sound like a wonderful place to live. Doc Williams must have thought so too when he left Philadelphia and set down roots there. For a fleeting moment, a fantasy passed through Cade's mind. He wondered what it would be like to move back home after graduation and start a veterinary practice there. He pushed that thought out as quickly as it had come in. He had always told himself if he ever got out, he wouldn't look back. Of course, he would always visit Doc and Mrs. Williams. And his family, who had all pitched in to put him through vet school, lived there. Hartville would always be a place to visit, but Philadelphia was his future now. Of that he was certain. And he had every reason to stay in Philly now that he'd discovered Ellie lived here. Waiting for the day he could see her again had been harder than he'd expected.

* * *

On the seventeenth of June, Cade arrived at the doorstep of a handsome townhouse on Spruce with a bouquet of flowers in hand and a jittery heart beneath his vest. Ellie's father answered the door himself and offered a hearty handshake, which helped to calm Cade's nerves. "It's good to see you again, Cade. Ellie will be down momentarily. Join me in the parlor?"

"Thank you, sir."

Soon Ellie appeared in the doorway wearing a summery green dress with a matching woven hat in her hand. Cade's face lit up when he saw her, and Mr. McAllister excused himself to finish some work in his study. "I'll join you for lemonade when you return."

Cade liked that Ellie didn't wait for him to take charge of their walk. She pointed out the direction they would take. "We'll follow Spruce to Nineteenth Street and turn north toward Rittenhouse Square," she said. It seemed she knew something about everything, and Cade loved to hear her talk, even if he'd already read about what she was telling him.

She told him how Rittenhouse Square had been nothing more than a pasture for the local livestock for the first hundred years, and then it had brickyards all around it until halfway through the nineteenth century. She explained that the wealthy class had gravitated to the square in just the last twenty years or so, and since it was Sunday, they would see people promenading in all their finery. "Mama liked to promenade."

Ellie showed Cade the bronze sculpture, *Lion Crushing a Serpent*, as it was called. "Our art class came here last year when we were studying French artists. Antoine-Louis Barye is famous for his animal sculptures and for making them of bronze instead of marble."

Cade wouldn't have imagined students taking a trip to see a sculpture or even having an *art* class in high school. He glanced up at Ellie's face, which was all animated with appreciation for this exquisite sculpture, and he felt the hair on his neck standing on end as he appreciated how exquisite *she* was.

They made their way to an empty bench in the cool shade. Ellie said, "I'm sorry. I've been talking ever since we left my house. I want to hear about what it was like to grow up on a farm."

"That's fair," Cade said. "I'm not sure I have anything interesting to say." He chose to begin his story after the time when his father had died and after he'd stayed for good with Mandy and Daniel. He talked about Hartville's businesses, about the swampland and the market vegetables and the celery from Hartville that may have made their way to her family's dinner table in Philadelphia.

"You told me before that your parents died, and you grew up with your sister."

"Yes, Mandy and her husband Daniel were like parents to me. My siblings are around the age of your parents, so it didn't seem that odd." He never mentioned that Mandy had married a Dunker or said a word about Rachel and Petey. He told how his oldest brother Garrett's family lived in the big house his parents had built and how they ran the farm now. He didn't mention anything about the temper that had flared between them. He told Ellie all true things, just not everything that was true.

"Oh, and we had a dog named Emma who kept me warm on winter nights."

Ellie's eyebrows shot up. "You mean she slept with you?"

"Yes. She'd start out lying on my feet, but by morning her dog breath was right in my face."

"Noooo!" Ellie squealed. "Mama would have never allowed a dog in the house, let alone in our beds. But I think I would like that."

He told her about the shelves he had built to keep his ma's books by his bed. And how he used to memorize the Longfellow poems on all the pages that were worn and had dog-eared corners. "I figured Ma must have loved those poems best. It always felt like she was showing me something about herself. So I feel as if I got to know my mother after all."

Ellie's eyes got watery when he told her that.

He talked about the fondness and respect he had for Doc Williams, who had brought him into the world and who had been like a father to him. "I'd have never found my way to vet school if it hadn't been for Doc."

"I'm glad there are people like your Doc Williams in the world," Ellie replied.

Cade took a break from talking, and Ellie said nothing for several minutes. Cade again noticed it was comfortable sitting quietly with her. People strolled by, birds glided onto branches, and squirrels ran their circuitous paths up and down the trees.

Ellie spoke first. "I'm a little embarrassed to say this, but I had never thought about how privileged my life has been. Even back when I was at

Claybourne Oaks, I watched Tilda and Hank working hard to make a living off the land, but it always seemed to be a romantic holiday for me. I think I had the fantasy that it was all constructed to entertain me for the summer. I never gave a thought about them working hard every day of the year to survive and to provide a healthy life for their children."

"Your father works hard, too. Isn't that what adults are supposed to do?"

"Papa does work hard, and we have everything we need. But it's not the same thing. Money has never been a serious concern for my parents. Mama came from generations of wealth through her mother's line. Papa's family lost a lot of money. He's fiercely proud about wanting to provide for us in his own right. But Mama insists on using her own money at times to provide us with the things she was accustomed to having. As I said before, I've had a privileged life."

Cade was understanding that they were getting down to the thing he had worried about the most. Ellie was seeing that he came from a different social class, and no matter how hard he tried to fit in, this was something that would always end up coming between them. He was quiet for some time and then spoke quietly about the topic he'd been hoping to avoid. "It's a very different existence in Hartville. Most of the folks I know back home do not have money. But we never felt poor. We are all self-sufficient on our farms. We build our homes with our own hands. We raise the food we put on the table. Our horses pull the plows and farm wagons. When there is a holiday, we hunt wild turkeys for our dinners. The women garden and cook and bake and sew clothing for their families. In the evenings, a woman's hands are always busy quilting, darning socks, knitting scarves, and sweaters for the winter. It is all hard work. But folks there don't know anything different." He stopped and searched Ellie's face for some sign of rejection.

But she nodded and smiled. "I think I would like that life. It seems like a healthy way to grow up. I've never had to work hard the way Tilda did, but when I ate those fresh vegetables and berries, it felt good knowing I had picked them myself. The canning jars full of fruits and vegetables, sitting on the shelves in her cellar, are as beautiful as any work of art. It makes me happy to think about Tilda opening those jars all through the winter for her family."

Cade's eyes widened as he listened to her respectful comments about the life he'd lived growing up. She didn't know the whole story, of course.

The June sun had hardly dropped in the sky two hours later when he thought to glance at his watch. "I'm sorry, Ellie. I lost track of the time," he said. "Your father will be wondering where we are."

Ellie laughed. "If I know Papa, he is engrossed in his work and probably never noticed. But if Aunt Tess were here, we would have some explaining to do."

* * *

Aaron McAllister looked up from his desk and laid his spectacles on his book. He smiled and asked what was new in Rittenhouse Square. They all sat in the parlor and sipped lemonade squeezed from fresh lemons.

When she walked Cade to the door, he asked if he might call again next Sunday.

She nodded happily. "My examinations will begin the following day, but I would love to take a short break that day. Perhaps we could walk to our bench again."

Cade grinned. He liked that they had a bench of their own.

CHAPTER TWENTY-SIX

Changes

As if she were a general planning a battle, Miss Eastman had studied Radcliffe's admissions examination schedule and advised Ellie on which advanced level exams she should attack in June.

"It is possible to be accepted into Radcliffe as a sophomore based on the June exams, but if you miss the mark, you could always present yourself for advanced-level examinations offered in Cambridge in mid-September." Miss Eastman gave Ellie her summer address. "Do let me know as soon as you hear from Radcliffe, Eleanor."

It still seemed strange to have developed this camaraderie with Miss Eastman after all these years of feeling intimidated by her.

Each morning during the last week of June, Ellie reported to the Young Men's Christian Association building on Fifteenth and Chestnut in Philadelphia, where the Radcliffe admissions examinations were being proctored. Papa's office in the city hall was only a five-minute walk from there, and they met for lunch or a walk whenever she had a free hour during the day. Each evening at six, when her exams were finished, Papa was waiting for her outside the door. They walked while she talked about challenging problems she'd solved or Greek passages she'd translated or literary works she'd interpreted that day. Sometimes they walked all the way home before she had untangled the gordian knot in her brain.

The gauntlet of exams came to an end on Saturday evening. Papa surprised her by having Cade join them for dinner at Boothby's on Chestnut. The evening was exactly what she needed to wipe every academic thought from her head. She slept most of Sunday.

* * *

On Monday morning she was awakened by Papa calling her from downstairs.

"Ellie, come. Please." He was standing in the lower hallway with a telegram in his hands, his face pale and stricken.

She panicked. "Papa, what's wrong? Is it Mama?"

His mouth opened, but no words came. He held his arm out, and when she reached the bottom of the stairs, he pulled her in close. "No ... not Genevieve." His voice was barely above a whisper. "It's Isaac Taylor. He's dead."

Ellie dropped her head against her father's chest. She heard his heart pounding hard, like her own.

"It's from Norman Claybourne, Flora's brother," Papa said. "Apparently there was a train accident a week ago. Flora and Isaac were passengers on it."

"Flora ... is she...?"

"It seems she was injured, but she survived."

Ellie took the telegram and read it aloud so that the message could sink in. "*Sad news. Flora & Isaac in train wreck. June 23. Georgia. Bridge collapse. Isaac died in Atlanta hospital today. Bringing Flo to Cleveland. Injured. Details to follow.*"

"They must have been visiting Isaac's sister in Atlanta," Papa said. "She's the only one left in his family. I will need to go to Canton for a week or so to help Flora settle his affairs. Isaac and I agreed that we'd do that for each other if anything ever happened."

Ellie had never thought about the possibility that Papa could die unexpectedly. He sometimes joked about death, saying things like hardly anyone he knew got through life without dying, but she didn't want to think it would happen to him or Mama any time soon. She thought of how Flora had lost her two daughters and now her husband.

"I need to go, too."

"I know, honey. It will mean a lot to her to have you there. I'll get things in order at my office over the next couple of days. By then we should have the details from Norman. We don't even know yet when Flora will be able to travel home."

* * *

Two days later, an envelope with a black border arrived. Papa sat behind his desk to read the letter, also edged in black. He looked up at Ellie. "Norman says they brought Isaac's ashes with them to Cleveland, so there is no rush for a service."

"He was cremated?"

"Isaac wanted that. He even stipulated it in his will. Norman says the ashes will be interred at West Lawn Cemetery in Canton, where their girls are buried. Whenever Flora is up to it.

"Where is she now?"

"She's at the Lutheran hospital in Cleveland. He says she's doing well enough." Papa gave Ellie a pained look. "The doctors say she may not walk again."

Ellie couldn't imagine Flora being unable to walk in her woods at Claybourne Oaks. "When can we leave?"

"Let's plan to catch the overnight express on Friday. I think we should be prepared to stay in Ohio for a while. I'll assist with Isaac's business affairs however long I'm needed. You may want to stay longer."

That evening, when the house came to stillness after a flurry of making lists and packing trunks, Ellie sat down to write a letter to Cade. She was sorry to have to cancel their plan for the following Sunday. It wasn't certain when they would return from Ohio, she said, but she promised to write to him as often as she could. She sealed the envelope, grateful to have told Cade all about the Taylors that night in the stable. At least he would understand why it was so important for her to be with Flora now.

* * *

Saturday afternoon, they stood outside Flora Taylor's room in the Evangelical Lutheran Hospital of Cleveland. Ellie blotted her hands on the skirt of her dress and made a fist to stop her fingers from shaking. She stepped behind Papa, allowing him to greet Flora first.

She was sitting by the window, where the afternoon sun landed on her reddish-gold hair and rosy face. Except for the large iron wheels on either side of her cane-backed chair, Ellie would not have guessed that Flora had been injured.

"Ellie." Flora smiled and stretched out her hand.

Ellie rushed forward and leaned down to hug her tightly. She felt Flora's tears against her cheek, mingling with her own. "Oh, Flora. I'm so sorry."

"Thank you, love. You're here. And that is exactly what I need. Let me look at you!" Flora's hand went to her heart as Ellie stood tall. "Oh my, you're all grown-up. She's looking more like Genevieve, don't you think, Aaron?"

"So I've heard. Thankfully, she isn't looking more like me." Papa winked.

Ellie pulled a chair close. "Are you in any pain?" She glanced down at Flora's legs, which were motionless beneath a blanket tucked neatly around them.

"I have muscle spasms in my back and a nasty laceration on my right leg. Apparently, there is a spinal cord injury, which may not be permanent. Some sensation is starting to come back. Pain is a good thing, I'm told. They want to start therapy next week to manipulate my leg muscles. I'm not able to move them on my own, yet. Dr. Gerhardt said I may not walk again.

"But it's a good sign that you are getting some feeling back, right?"

"That's what I said. He conceded that he is 'cautiously optimistic.' What I need are my own poultices and teas from the herbs hanging in my pantry. That will make a difference."

Ellie was by her side at Isaac's funeral service the following week. There was a bond she felt with Flora, as strong as any blood ties.

* * *

Ellie, Flora in her wheelchair, and a private nurse boarded the Wheeling & Lake Erie train to Hartville in the second week of July. Miss Edwina Wertenberger had been hired to continue Flora's rehabilitation therapy at Claybourne Oaks for the next month. She had come highly recommended by Dr. Gerhardt.

"Are you certain you cannot stay past mid-August?" Flora asked the nurse. "I want complete recovery."

"Progress will not be limited by the time constraints of my stay, Mrs. Taylor. I'm here to teach you tools to be used after I leave in August." Nurse Wertenberger said it crisply. Her face was expressionless and her manner perfunctory, such that one sat with the words but didn't question them. Flora nodded, but Ellie had to think about what that meant. She guessed it was a hopeful prognosis.

"Please call me Flora. And is there a given name you prefer?"

"Miss Eddie will do, ma'am. I'd prefer to call you Mrs. Taylor, as I am hired as your nurse."

"Miss Eddie it is. That will do quite well." Flora smiled pleasantly.

Miss Eddie was a thin woman who looked to be in her thirties, though she could have been younger. Her brown hair was combed tightly into a bun, with a small, starched nursing cap pinned above it. No matter how you looked at her, there was a straight plumbline down to her toes. Her gray dress stretched up her long neck to her chin, where a white ruffle cupped her pale, too-large, oval face. Ellie studied her, trying to think of how she would draw a cartoon version of Miss Eddie for Charlie. What came to mind was the hard-boiled egg she'd been served in the Pullman dining car on the train from Philly. It had perched atop a white paper ruffle on a gray pewter egg stand. Draw a face on the egg, and *voilà*. The resemblance was uncanny.

Hank met them at the Hartville Depot and drove directly to the cottage. When they rounded the bend in the lane, splashes of color from flowerbeds all around the cottage greeted them. Flora's smile faded when she was close enough to see the wooden ramp that now cut through her irises. Another rude scar resulting from the accident, Ellie thought. Even though Flora had known about the ramp Hank built, it seemed to upset her to see it.

"We'll go easy now," Hank said as he lifted her from the carriage seat and placed her gently into her wheelchair. "Flora, I'm working on another ramp at the back door. And I installed railings on the walls, just like your doc said. Things are moved around some from what you're used to. We wanted you to have plenty of space for your chair." When Flora grimaced, he added, "Until you are up on your feet. I'll take the ramps down when you're done with them."

"It's a fine ramp, Hank," Flora said. She reached her hand over and clasped his. "There are no words to express how much I appreciate all that you've done."

"Well, Tilda's been giving the orders. I just do what she tells me." They all laughed, except for Miss Eddie, who was pushing the wheelchair up the inclined walkway to the porch.

Flora leaned forward to open the door and sighed. "I was beginning to wonder if I'd ever see this dear place again."

Miss Eddie continued to push the wheelchair down the hallway. Ellie walked behind. When they came to the living area, the nurse planted her hands on her hips.

Her eyebrows pulled her tight skin up into a wrinkle as her gray eyes moved slowly up to the ceiling beams and came to rest on the balcony area. Flora's easel and the bookcases were visible beyond the balcony's railing. The nurse's mouth gradually dropped open as she squinted at the sunlight coming through a round stained-glass, flowered window at the top of the stairs. "I didn't expect such a fine place when you said it was a cottage."

"Thank you. It's become more of a second home for us. Isaac had indoor plumbing and hot water radiators installed two years ago," Flora said. She rolled the wheelchair for herself down another hallway. "You'll be in the room on the right, Miss Eddie. Ours ... *mine* is on the end."

Ellie stepped into the spacious bathroom, which had formerly been the study. A large white porcelain bathtub sat on four paws in the space where a glass display case with rare insects had been. "Your butterflies have migrated!"

"We donated them to the Academy of Natural Sciences of Philadelphia. My father lectured there many years, and they were quite interested in his Ohio wetlands collection."

"This is very modern!" Ellie said. "But I'm going to miss the baths by the kitchen stove."

"Those were wonderful days," Flora said. "Isaac had been wanting to renovate for years, but I was reluctant to change anything from the way it was when the girls were little." She was quiet for a moment.

Ellie admired the canning jar full of blooms, which sat on a simple oak dressing table by the bathroom sink. A mirror was mounted on the wall behind it. "I like seeing beauty in unexpected places."

"That's Tilda's touch."

"I see your artistic touches, too. The wallpaper in here is lovely!" The commode and the high tank stood against a papered wall that was covered with violets with yellow centers. A coordinated border extended all around the room near the ceiling, and yellow bath towels hung on a rack below.

Miss Eddie whisked Flora off to reorganize dresser drawers and closets. Ellie said she would see to lunch. The icebox and larder were stocked. There was a pot of Tilda's stew on the stove with crusty bread for dipping. Fresh-picked berries and a variety of vegetables from the garden were piled on a flowered ceramic tray by the sink. As Ellie looked over the stores of food, recipes Flora had taught her years ago came to mind.

She opened the pantry door and sniffed the pungent herbs drying on the rack overhead. Flora must have been busy gathering plants in the spring and early summer before the accident. Ellie thought about her friend's vast knowledge of plants and herbal remedies. She promised herself she would take notes this time and become a diligent student of herbs.

After lunch, Flora was exhausted and needed to move from her wheelchair into her bed. Nurse Eddie used the opportunity to show Ellie how to assist. "You need to learn how to do this. For after I'm gone," she said.

Flora's eyes dropped, and Ellie realized the embarrassment she must be feeling. Miss Eddie hadn't seemed to notice. She demonstrated how she widened her stance and bent her knees so that her legs did the heavy lifting. It wasn't as hard as Ellie had imagined. Some movement and strength had come back to Flora's limbs, so she was able to bear a little of her own weight now. Flora had been very motivated to make progress in her physical therapy, since Dr. Gerhardt wanted to see a level of self-sufficiency before he would approve her release from the hospital. She was determined that her wheelchair would be a *temporary* aid, and although she had acquiesced to having railings and ramps built, she also spoke of them as "temporary."

* * *

July passed quickly, and Flora aged before Ellie's eyes. The dull, black, silk mourning dress she wore made her skin look sallow. Her golden-red hair had a silvery sheen now, and her grief seemed to leave dark, hollow sockets where tears often flowed. Flora's temper flared, but only with Miss Eddie, whose expression never changed as she gave firm instructions for their exercise sessions every morning and afternoon.

Using sketches from Miss Eddie's orthopedic textbook, Hank rigged up wooden pulleys from the back-porch beams and railings. Ellie recalled seeing such pulleys in the barn used to lift slings of loose hay from the field wagon up to the loft.

Miss Eddie hung weights from one end of the pulley, which were lifted by Flora's legs pulling from the other end. Ellie thought the pulley system was brilliant, but she kept her enthusiasm to herself, especially when Flora was straining against the weights with her sweat-soaked blouses and tear-filled eyes.

Improvement came steadily, but more slowly than Flora had anticipated. "I'll never be able to walk in the woods again," she lamented. Sometimes, sobs could be heard coming from behind her bedroom door. Whether it was grief or disappointment, Ellie didn't know.

Hank had an idea for building a raised boardwalk over the soggy area that ran through the upper woods. The pond was on the other side of this marsh, which could only be crossed by hopping from one stone to another.

"I won't be able to work on it until after the oats is harvested," he said. "But you just concentrate on building your strength, Flora, and I'll have a bridge for you by fall."

"By fall." Her eyes glistened. "It's my favorite time to sit by the pond."

The promise of the bridge seemed to give Flora renewed vigor in exercising her legs each day. On the second day of August, Flora was able to pull herself to standing and take her first step on her own. It was the same day Ellie received a letter from Radcliffe informing her that she had passed her exams so successfully, she was invited to enroll as a sophomore in September. They celebrated heartily that evening. The Jeffreys family came for dinner, and Tilda even baked pies.

CHAPTER TWENTY-SEVEN

The Letter

Most mornings, Ellie had a lesson on herbs—their attributes, the medicinal uses, and how to preserve them. But first she had to go down the hill to forage for the plants, as Flora had taught her to do the previous time she'd stayed for the summer. She always started in the cluster of trees near the lower swamp, where a minty blanket of pennyroyal grew. She picked a few leaves and lightly brushed them against her skin to repel the mosquitoes. She recalled that it was a good remedy for bellyaches but dangerous if too much was taken.

Ellie gathered the leaves and flowers of boneset, which was good for bronchial catarrhs and the grippe. She was particularly eager to find a patch of white horehound on dry ground along the edge of the field near the swamp. She smiled when she found it. It was just as Flora had described. There were balls of white flowers every couple of inches from the bottom to the top of the ridged stem. A pair of large, fuzzy, wrinkled leaves stuck out from each cluster of flowers. The leaves were the treasure. She and Flora had used the last of the dried horehound leaves to make candy, and Ellie wanted to make another batch of the dark-brown candy squares to take back to Philadelphia. There was nothing better for a winter cough.

One of Ellie's favorite times of the day was when she sat at the writing desk catching the last light of the day. The desk was in an alcove at the far end of the art loft. The window above it opened into the canopy of an apple tree where birds nested, and the passage of time was marked by the fruit growing fatter. Whenever an evening breeze set the apple branches in motion, it gave Ellie the feeling that she was swaying in a little treehouse, too. She had always written in her diary in the evenings, but now she wrote to Cade instead, telling him the events of the day.

* * *

The bottom edge of Ellie's skirt soaked up morning dew from the long grasses in the lane as she walked toward the Jeffreys' farmhouse. It was Tilda's going-to-town day, and Ellie always rode along. She looked up when the youngest two of the Jeffreys children raced around the bend. "Hello, Ellie," they called, and she returned their greeting.

"Auntie Flora's on the porch swing," she said as they ran past.

"We know," one of them called back. Ellie was sure they also knew there would be cookies in the stoneware jar. Flora's spirits always lifted when the children came on Thursdays. The older two, twelve and fourteen, visited sometimes, too. But they were grown-up enough that their chores started at sunup. Childhood was a fleeting thing on a farm.

Tilda was already seated on the wagon, studying a torn piece of paper in her hand. Ellie had noticed how she saved old envelopes and any scrap of paper to use for writing grocery lists. Tilda even wrote her own letters to other people on these scraps. It was a reverence engendered by scarcity. Nothing was wasted in their household.

"Good morning, Ellie. I thought while we're at Keller's, I'd look for a calico backing for the lap quilt I'm piecing for Flora."

"Mmm. She'll love that. I'll go to the post office first and pick up the mail for both of us. I have two letters to post." Ellie climbed up on the bench. Tilda clicked her tongue, and two horses leaned into their harnesses.

Ellie hoped that Postmaster Bryers would be at the counter. But no, it was Varn Boyle again. She braced herself for the way he sniffed into his customers' business as if he were a stray dog tracking down his next meal. She suspected gossip was his main diet.

"Miss McAllister," he announced. He'd asked all about Philadelphia last week.

"Hello, Mr. Boyle. The Jeffreys asked me to pick up their mail along with Mrs. Taylor's and mine."

He disappeared momentarily behind the stack of mailboxes that formed a wall by the counter and brought out a small pile of letters. Then he proceeded to lay them one at a time on the counter, gleaning what he could from the envelopes. "Mrs. Taylor has letters from all over. Folks don't seem to know she's here in Hartville. Most of these go to the Canton office, and they get forwarded up to us. I suppose they're condolences." When Ellie didn't respond, he continued. "Such a tragedy, the mister getting killed in that train wreck and her being left a cripple. How's she faring?"

Ellie bristled at his assumptions about Flora. "She's walking remarkably well. And expecting a full recovery with time."

"You don't say?"

Ellie regretted giving him even that much information. Flora was right. The man could probably extract news from a fence post.

"Here's the one *you're* waiting for," Varn said with his eye fixed on her face as he laid a letter from Cade on the counter.

There was a return address in the corner, so she couldn't pretend she didn't know what he was talking about. "Thank you." She slipped the letter into the pocket of her skirt.

"How's he doing out there in vetri-nary school?"

"Quite well," she said, offering no more than that. "Would you post these two, please?"

"That's practically a parcel you're sending him," Varn said as he read the address.

She didn't take the bait. He told her what she owed him, and she dropped two coins in his hand. "Thank you," she said politely.

His pinched lips let her know he'd felt slighted by her formality.

She thanked him again. "Have a good week, Mr. Boyle."

"Sure thing. Tell Cade that Varn says hello, will you?"

"I will." She smiled politely and closed the door behind her. She looked over the list of items Flora needed as she walked toward Keller's. The letter in her pocket would have to wait until she was back at Claybourne Oaks. She wondered what Cade had written this week.

He usually told stories about his experiences at the Gifford Clinic. He had a self-deprecating sense of humor that made her laugh aloud. She read his letters to Flora, who thought they were quite endearing. Ellie didn't share the personal postscript Cade added to the bottom of his letters. The last time he'd written: *P.S. Last Sunday I walked to Rittenhouse Square and sat on our bench. I brought every letter you've written and read them all again. I miss you, Ellie.*

Ellie's letters were filled with everyday events at Claybourne Oaks. She told him about Flora's good progress in learning to walk again. And how Flora was teaching her to make poultices and a liniment from the herbs Ellie gathered.

When she was finally alone in her room at the cottage, she opened his letter.

> *"Dear Ellie, I have missed you more each week. I look forward to seeing you again."*

Ellie curled up in the soft chair by the window and read about Cade's week. Her heart pounded wildly as she read his last paragraph:

> *"My summer practicum will be completed early, due to Dr. Gifford's travel to a European conference. I've decided to come to Hartville for a month. I will be staying with Doc and Mrs. Williams in town. May I come calling at Claybourne Oaks on Monday, the twentieth of August around two o'clock?*
> *Your obedient servant,*
> *Cade*

Ellie could hardly breathe. Cade was coming to Claybourne Oaks!

* * *

On the seventeenth of August, the new man from the Hartville Livery loaded Miss Eddie's trunk and waited while they said their goodbyes.

Flora was teary. "I don't know how I would have learned to walk again without your help."

"You have made remarkable progress, Flora. Now that you have a pulley rigged up indoors, you can keep up the exercises all winter. You'll have no limp by spring. I guarantee it."

Ellie could see that a genuine friendship had grown between the two women. At least they were on a first-name basis, which wasn't surprising. Claybourne Oaks had that effect on people. The nurse was still "Miss Eddie" to everyone else.

Before she climbed into the carriage, Flora clasped both of her hands. "You'll consider what we discussed?"

"I'll do my best to find someone. You'll hear from me soon." Miss Eddie leaned out of the carriage window and waved before disappearing around the bend.

"That sounded mysterious," Ellie said.

"It's a surprise. But you'll be the first to know when I get the details worked out." Flora smiled as she took Ellie's arm and leaned into her cane. They walked slowly up the ramp. "I think it's time for Hank to remove this wood from my flower beds," she said.

"Patience isn't one of your virtues, is it?" Ellie grinned, and Flora sighed in response.

* * *

On Monday the sun burned through the morning haze and let everyone know it was still summer. Ellie's hair was completely at the mercy of the humidity. She had twisted it into a fashionable style and pinned it in place, but auburn ringlets were popping out all over. "I know he'll be here any minute, and look at this mess!" she said, frowning at her image in the hallway mirror.

"You look perfect, love," Flora said as she pulled the curtain aside at the window.

Ellie leaned in close to the mirror. "I have twice as many freckles, and they've darkened this summer. Mama would be beside herself to see me now."

"There is nothing lovelier than a woman who is connected to the earth, Ellie. I've never seen you more beautiful, and even Genevieve would agree."

"Thank you, Flora. You always say the right thing."

"I believe there is a young man walking up the lane."

"Oh!" Ellie hurried to the door.

There he was, his jacket over his arm, his white shirt glistening in the sun. She could see his suspenders stretched up over his broad shoulders. He stopped, removed his hat, ran his fingers through his curly, dark hair, and replaced it on his head. Then he slipped his jacket on over his shirt and bent to brush something off his trousers. It made Ellie feel a little better to see him fussing over his appearance as well. She had planned to just wait demurely for him on the verandah, but instead she found herself flying down the steps and across the yard to meet up with him. "I thought you would be arriving by carriage."

He would have liked to lift her up and twirl her around, but he tipped his hat instead. "I thought I could get here faster cutting through some farms I know. It's only three miles."

"Welcome to Claybourne Oaks," she said as she swept her hand toward the cottage.

"Thank you." He looked at the old stone house and smiled. "It's just as you described it, only a little larger than I imagined."

As they approached the porch, Ellie said, "Flora Taylor, this is Cade Bauer."

"Mrs. Taylor, it's good to meet you. Ellie has told me wonderful things about you."

"How nice to meet you, Cade. We dispense with titles here. You must call me Flora." She waved her hand toward the swing. "Why don't the two of you sit there? The armchair is better for me." She leaned heavily on the armrest with her left hand while holding on to her cane with her right. She lowered herself slowly and pushed herself back into the chair. "There," she said. "It just takes a bit of concentration to get all my limbs moving together."

Ellie rarely gave thought to Flora's arduous movements anymore. But she noticed how Cade leaned forward, watching closely as if ready to leap to her aid.

"May I interest you in a glass of sassafras sun tea?" Ellie said.

"Yes, please. I've not had sassafras in years!" Cade sat back and allowed the swing to relax into a gentle movement.

Ellie unfolded the padded wool cloth that had been wrapped around chunks of ice, which she spooned into three tall glasses. She poured the red tea slowly over them.

"You still have ice in August!" Cade said. "It must have been a good harvest last year."

"Yes," said Flora. "The pond ice was unusually thick. We filled our ice-house to the brim. And Hank packed with sawdust instead of straw this year. That's helped."

"I saw him on my way in. He and I used to work the ice harvest together up at Congress Lake. He said he hired on a couple of men for cutting corn next week, but he was still short a hand, so I offered to help him out."

"How kind of you," Flora said. "Tilda's been mending the heavy sleeves for the fellows."

Cade nodded. "I remember once when I was a kid, I didn't bother wearing a sleeve. The corn leaves were so sharp, they wore holes in my shirt and left some nasty cuts on my wrists, too. I smartened up after that." He laughed. "It'll be good to do a little field work again. The only thing is that my hands have gone soft in Philly."

"I can make you a poultice for the blisters," Ellie said.

"I'll take you up on that!" Cade grinned. "Hank asked if I'd help finish a boardwalk in the woods this week before we start the corn. Said he'd planned to get to it done after the oats harvest, but rain has put him behind. If that is all right with you, I'd enjoy working on it."

"That would be splendid!" Flora said. She stifled a yawn. "I'm afraid I need to excuse myself to go lie down. I perhaps pushed myself a little too hard in my calisthenics this morning."

"Ellie wrote that you've made wonderful progress," Cade said.

"It's been more challenging than I imagined."

"I wanted to say how sorry I am for your loss of your husband."

"Thank you, Cade. Yes, I miss him terribly. I don't know how I would have managed without Ellie here with me." She smiled and slowly made her way to her feet.

Ellie hopped up to open the door for Flora. When she and Cade were alone, she said, "Would you like to take a walk? I can show you the board-walk Hank's been building."

"Sure!"

They stood, and Ellie slipped her hand through his arm as if it were the most natural thing to do. Cade liked the feel of her hand resting there. They set off on the shady path through the woods.

As they walked, their conversation picked up where their letters had left off. Cade said he recognized the land from her descriptions. He'd walked this path with her many times in his imagination. Ellie showed him where the sassafras grove was and talked of how worried she was about going to Radcliffe in the fall. "What will Flora do without me here to help?" she wondered.

He talked about how Doc and Mrs. Williams had aged in the two years since he'd seen them last. And how he'd detected a new respect in Doc's voice now that they were going to be colleagues and alumni from the same university. "I feel like I've slipped into adulthood when no one was looking," he said. Ellie smiled. Her hand slid down to touch his, and he caught hold of it.

They walked clear to the end of the property and gazed out over the black muck fields beyond. The afternoon sun shone on Ellie's freckled nose as Cade looked down at her. He slipped his arm around her shoulder. Ellie's head leaned against his shoulder, and then she lifted her face to meet his. Their first kiss was as sweet as they both had imagined.

CHAPTER TWENTY-EIGHT

The Gift

"Ellie, you must *not* postpone your first semester at Radcliffe! I appreciate your concern, but I don't want you to think of staying. It is a wonderful achievement to be accepted into that school, and you mustn't pass up the opportunity."

"But I don't want you to be alone here."

"I received some news today." Flora smiled and patted the sofa. "Sit down with me. I have a lot to tell you."

Ellie placed two cups of coffee on the low table and sat with her back against the curved arm of the sofa. She pulled her legs up under her dress. The air coming in through the first-floor screens was chilly and had the dank scent of summer's end.

Flora waved a letter in the air. "Edwina found someone to replace her at the convalescent home. She's agreed to come back here the first of October and stay with me for the winter!"

"Really? That's wonderful. But are you sure you want Miss Eddie here all winter? She's not much of a conversationalist."

"Exactly. We both like our quiet. She reads books, and I like to paint. I learned to appreciate her. She was always gentle with me, even when I was short-tempered. She may be a bit odd, but she's a good person."

Ellie stretched her hand over to squeeze Flora's. "Perhaps I'll bake an apple pie to celebrate."

"Perhaps I'll put on a bright dress for supper. My soul needs color! Isaac would have been the last person to have me wear all this drab black in his honor. And yet I do. I don't know why. I think sometimes I feel confused about how to be a widow, and so I fall back on the rules that society dictates. Perhaps when I get completely moved out of our Canton house, I'll let go of some of these social conventions."

"That's another reason I don't want to leave so soon. I could help you get your house in Canton sorted. You said the new owners want to move in by Thanksgiving."

"Isaac and I had planned to sell our home for some time. We had been sorting things out for our move long before the accident. It was our intent to start living full-time at Claybourne Oaks this summer. He looked forward to it as much as I." Flora looked away. She took the hanky that had been tucked beneath the cuff of her sleeve and blew her nose. She brightened again when she looked up. "I have more to tell you. I've decided to have another cottage built here at the farm."

"Really? Where?"

"Beyond the bend where my father's workshop sits. Isaac and I had an architect draw up the plans to convert it into a guest house. We intended to wait a year or two, but it has occurred to me I need it now. Edwina will stay there as soon as it is ready. The builder will start next week."

"When did you plan all this?"

"While you've been helping with the canning at Tilda's and spending time with Cade, I've had a chance to reflect on things. I need to focus on how I will go forward. Alone. Of course, Ellie, you will always have a room here with me whenever you visit."

"Thank you. That means a great deal to me."

"Now, there is something else I need to discuss with you."

There was a change in Flora's voice, and Ellie sat up, quietly attentive.

"When your father helped me get Isaac's estate settled, I discussed this with him, but I told him to not say anything. I wanted to find the right moment to tell you myself. I've drawn up the papers with my attorney. I've decided to put Claybourne Oaks in your name, too. You'll be heir to this estate when I die."

"I–I don't know what to say. I mean, what about your nephews in Cleveland?"

"No, I want this land to be passed on to another woman. And Claybourne Oaks chose *you* a long time ago, Ellie. Besides, you *are* my family."

The tingly feeling started in her toes and worked its way up through her body until she thought she would burst. She scrambled forward and threw her arms around Flora. "I–I don't know what to say." Ellie sat back, trying to comprehend what this would mean for her.

Flora said, "I've stipulated that you will share ownership with me until I pass. I want to live here in the cottage until the end of my life. At that time, you will have sole ownership. I'm giving you part ownership now so that you can begin to learn about managing the property. The Jeffreys plan to stay for another year or two, but they've been saving up to buy their own farm. You and I can decide together who we hire to replace them."

"Yes, I'd be glad to help." Ellie felt as if her eyebrows had arched into her hairline. It was an astonishing turn of events.

Flora continued. "I don't want to burden you with too many responsibilities. I am quite capable of making the decisions. My parents gave me this land when I was your age, and I've always enjoyed making the decisions about it. I've loved knowing it was my responsibility to be the steward of it. I want you to experience that joy also."

Ellie nodded. "It is … the most wonderful gift I could ever have imagined. I will always do my best to take care of this land, Flora."

"I know you will be a good steward of this farm. I do not intend for you to change the plans you have for your life. It's important that you are launched into your own adulthood, Ellie. Doing what *you* choose. So many possibilities are waiting for you. The Jeffreys will help us find the right caretakers when they leave, so that's not a concern. Claybourne Oaks can be a bit of heaven where you can always come home."

Ellie hardly slept that night. It was a new feeling about herself, one that she wanted to savor. She had a place to call her own. *"My* Claybourne Oaks," she whispered in the dark.

* * *

Cade watched Ellie wiping the counter and smiled. The early evening sun had bathed the walls of the kitchen with a palette that matched the glow of her auburn curls. She reached for the teacups on the counter at the same moment Cade lifted the last two plates to the shelf above her. Her nose came close to his shirt, which had the strong odor of his sweat from the day. He saw her breathe it in and respond to it with a brief, pleasant smile. He liked her odor, too. One could know a lot about a person by their scent. If the smell wasn't right, the relationship had no hope. But with Ellie and him, the smells were right.

"I'll bring in some wood. It's cooled off this evening," he said. He was glad the Taylors had kept the old potbelly when they'd modernized the heating system. There was nothing like it to take the chill out of an autumn evening.

Flora, who was wrapped in a quilt Tilda had made, raised the lamplight and moved her spectacles to the end of her nose to read a letter. Ellie set the tray on the low table and poured chamomile and lavender tea for the three of them. She sat in her usual rocker by the stove. Cade opened the iron door and added a log. He glanced over at Ellie and saw how the light flickered softly on her face. He smiled.

Flora said, "Ellie, do you remember my friends, Louise and Edgar Thompson, who came to the funeral?"

"Yes."

"Isaac and I were on the Congress Lake Club Membership committee with them. They found another couple to take our place, but Louise writes that they would like me to remain on the committee *in absentia.* Until I come out of mourning. I don't know how to respond to that. Honestly, I can't imagine continuing my membership at the club without Isaac. It would be odd to attend activities on my own."

"Did you enjoy being on the committee?" Ellie said.

"Yes, it was interesting. Any time new couples wanted to join the club, they had to submit their application to our committee. Edgar or Isaac always checked the references on the application. If everything was in order, Louise and I would organize a formal tea. Edgar and Isaac engaged the husband in conversation, and we would converse with the wife. It would give us a sense of how well they interacted in a social setting."

Cade laughed. "So you were the etiquette constables? Checking to see if they had good manners?"

"It wasn't about manners, as it were. Our job had more to do with listening between the lines to see if they really were how they presented themselves on the application. It's in the informal moments when you learn about one's character."

"That makes sense," said Cade.

"We've never turned anyone away. Louise writes that a young couple has applied, and they will have their formal tea this Saturday, the fifteenth. They always hold it in the Congress Lake Hotel parlor."

"That's where Cade and I first met!" Ellie looked up at him.

He nodded and then looked away, pretending to check the log again. He felt as if he'd just lied to her. He didn't know why it had been so hard to tell her the truth about the very first time they met, back when Petey almost drowned. He felt embarrassed about that whole Dunker phase of his life. She was attracted to the person he'd *become*, and he didn't want to risk losing that.

Flora sighed. "Louise has been telling me for the last month that I should spend a few days at one of the Congress Lake cottages. She thinks a change of scenery would do me some good. I told her I would consider it. Now she writes that the yellow cottage happens to be available next weekend. And she and Edgar reserved it for me, just in case. That is so like Louise. Taking charge."

"Do you want to do that?"

"It does sound kind of fun. You're also invited to come, Ellie. Louise said they'd arrange for meals to be brought to us so that I wouldn't have to dine in public. They asked to join us for supper Saturday after their tea. What do you think?"

"I'd enjoy seeing the lake again."

"Then we should do it! It will be our last weekend before you return to Philadelphia and Louise is right. A change of scenery would be just the thing."

"Oh good!" Ellie said.

Flora took a sip of her tea. "Cade, why don't you plan to stay with us at the lake? There's a second bedroom in the yellow cottage. We stayed there when Opal was young. The Thompsons will enjoy meeting you."

"That's kind of you." He looked at Ellie. "If that's agreeable with you, Miss McAllister?"

"It would be my pleasure, Mr. Bauer."

"Then I accept! I've been helping Doc with repairs around his place on the weekends. But I could make it to Congress Lake by four thirty that afternoon."

"It's settled then!" Flora said. "Have you been up to the lake while you've been home?"

He shook his head. "One has to be invited by members of the club now."

"Oh, yes, of course. I've not been there since it went private last September. Isaac and I had been aware for several years that the gate would close when the club controlled the shoreline. Tilda mentioned that folks in Hartville are not happy about it. I can understand why it would be upsetting to lose access to such a beautiful place."

Cade nodded. "Ever since Hartville was founded, we've used that lake for fishing, hunting, Sunday picnics, and ice skating in the winter. Some of us were baptized in the lake."

"Oh, were you baptized in Congress Lake?" Ellie said. "I remember the first time I came here at the Outing Club picnic and saw some Dunkers that day. I'm aware that they baptize in rivers and lakes. Do other churches do baptisms that way, also?"

Cade's breath stopped for a moment. He was unnerved to be caught. "I just … I meant it in general terms. That is, some folks around here are Dunkers, and they used Congress Lake for their baptisms." It was a relief when Flora brought the conversation back on track.

"How do the townspeople feel about President McKinley's role in the purchase of Congress Lake?"

"Doc says most people blame Mark Hanna, the senator from Cleveland. They say Hanna pulls all the strings. I think blaming him gives them an excuse to exonerate McKinley. As you know, the president wears a halo in Stark County."

No one said anything then. Only the crackle in the stove could be heard.

Ellie broke the silence. "I was just thinking about the native tribes who were here first. I wonder how *they* felt about losing their land and the lake to the settlers of Hartville. I don't mean to single out Hartville. The same is true in Philadelphia and everywhere the Europeans landed. We drove our stakes in the ground and claimed the land as our own."

"Good point. And we're still doing that," Cade said. "We just went to war with Spain and ended up owning Puerto Rico, Guam, and the Philippines. I read how we annexed the Kingdom of Hawaii against their will because we wanted a navy base in the Pacific. McKinley calls it 'manifest destiny,' but I agree with Grover Cleveland's opinion that it was more like an act of imperialism. What's honorable about that?"

Flora nodded. "I must agree with you, Cade.

Ellie said, "Sometimes when Mr. Cooke visits our school, he tells us stories about Chief Ogontz, who he knew personally back in the olden days when he was growing up in Ohio. He said the Wyandotte and all the other tribes believed that no one can ever *own* the land, because the earth is a living thing. I've thought about that a lot. When I walk in the woods here at Claybourne Oaks, there are times when a tingling sensation comes up through my feet, and it really does feel like the land is a living spirit. Maybe it's true that no one can *own* the land."

"Exactly," said Flora. "That's why I like to think of myself as a steward of Claybourne Oaks, not a landowner. It means that my job, while I'm living on the earth, is to do what is best for the land. And then pass it on to the next steward. It is a big responsibility to choose the next steward."

Cade saw a look pass between the two women. Maybe it was just a smile. He wondered about it but didn't ask.

CHAPTER TWENTY-NINE
Stone Circle

It was dark when Cade let himself in the back door at Doc and Mrs. Williams's place. They'd already retired for the evening, but an envelope had been placed on the knob of his bedroom door. Mrs. Williams had written: *Cade, A young man named Artie Hanson came by this afternoon asking after you. He said he'd check back another time, but I suggested he write the enclosed message, since you are returning to Philadelphia on the eighteenth.*

Artie! There had been only one letter from his friend, and it had arrived in Philadelphia more than a year ago. Artie had told how he'd made it as far as St. Louis and had taken a job at the printing company where his uncle was a lithographer. There had been no return address. Cade had sent a reply to his Grandma Hanson's address in Mishler. He never knew if Artie had gotten it. Cade sat on his bed and opened the envelope.

> *Cade,*
> *I'm home for my Gramps' funeral, which is on Saturday*
> *morning. I stopped by your brother Garrett's place to get*

*your address again, as I lost it. He said you were back
in town, staying with Doc Williams! I understand you're
heading back to Philly on Tuesday. Would you have time
to meet Friday morning? I'll stop by around eight, in hopes
of seeing you.*

   Yours truly,
   Artie

* * *

Cade didn't recognize the silhouette of the young man standing on the Williams's front porch until he saw his face. "Artie Hanson, what are they feeding you out there in St. Louis? I hardly recognize you." Cade reached out to shake his hand and looked up to the fellow who was well over six feet tall now, slender, and well-muscled. Artie's blue eyes still had that surprised look behind the thick lenses, but his cheekbones and jaw had become handsomely angular, and he sported a full mustache.

Artie grinned. "And it looks like Philadelphia agrees with you!"

"Thanks," Cade said. "I thought we'd walk back to Stone Circle. Doc's patients will start showing up here any minute."

"Sure!" Artie stepped back to let Cade lead the way on the narrow path toward the woods. "Bauer, what are the chances you and I would end up in Ohio at the same time?"

"Yeah, I know. But I'm sorry to hear the circumstance that brought you here. Had your Grandpa Hanson been ill?"

"No, just old age. He was ninety-two last week. He always said he'd never reach ninety."

"How's Grandma Hanson doing?"

"She's taking it hard, but at least she's in good health. My uncle's taking her back to St. Louis to live with him and Aunt Mil. We've been sorting out her household things to pack for the freight car. I was glad to get out of there for a while. Last night they locked horns, like they always do. She wants to take a big collection of pottery my mom painted, and Uncle Riley said their house isn't big enough for all that sentimentality. Grandma said she'd find a place of her own then. She wants me to live with her. Actually, I'd like that."

"So, you're planning to stay on there? Which means you're not going to San Francisco?"

Artie laughed. "That was a nice dream for a kid who wanted to break out of Mishler, but I have a good job now in printing and bookbinding. I like St. Louis. And I've met a girl."

"I should have guessed!" Cade stopped and grinned at Artie. "Okay, say more."

"Her name is Betsy Scott. I guess you could say we're getting serious." Artie bounced his eyebrows up and down to emphasize his happiness about this fact and then went on. "Her father has a printing and book-binding company, where I work. That's how I met Betsy. My Uncle Riley does the lithograph illustrations for their books. And I've been apprenticing with him to learn lithography. It turns out I have some of my mother's talent for art."

"That doesn't surprise me." The path widened, and they walked side by side now. "It sounds like you landed in the right place. Arthur Hanson, Lithographer. It has a nice ring."

"Some say there isn't a future in stone because printing companies are converting to rotary presses with aluminum plates. But there is still a strong demand for the old-style print from a limestone surface. I love working with stone. It renders a quality you can't reproduce on metal. Betsy's father has a modern press, but he's kept the old flat-bed model for the clients who want traditional lithography." Artie stopped and took a breath.

Cade liked the fact that some things hadn't changed. Artie could still fill any space with stories. "I'm glad you love your work. I hope I get to meet Betsy sometime."

"How about you? My grandma sent your letter on to me last year, and I could tell you love veterinary school. Have you met any interesting Philly fillies?"

"As a matter of fact, I have. But you already know her."

"What?"

"You remember *Ellie* at Congress Lake that last summer we worked there? As impossible as it seems, we ran into each other in Philadelphia, which is where she lives. We recognized each other and, well, it's been working out."

Artie's mouth dropped open, and he had no quick retort. He shook his head. "Unbelievable. Ellie. It was Ellie Taylor, wasn't it? The girl with the legs. Oh, sorry. Guess I shouldn't say that now."

Cade laughed. "Well, the funny thing is that her name wasn't Taylor at all. It's *McAllister*. Ellie was visiting the Taylors that summer. In fact, she's here again, which is why I came back to Hartville for a few weeks before school starts."

"McAllister. I don't think I know anyone by that name."

Cade didn't say anything for a minute. He thought about the connection Artie and Ellie had, which neither of them would ever realize unless he told them about it. Sometimes love for another overrules the rightness of telling the truth. He cared for them both too much to bring that kind of hurt to either of them.

Instead, he told Artie a condensed version of the night Daisy had birthed her colt at Ogontz and how he and Ellie had watched it happening. There was a time when he would have told Artie all the details of Ellie sneaking into the stable in the middle of the night. But he'd never consider doing that now. He smiled, realizing how protective of her he'd become.

They walked into the clearing in the woods behind Doc's place. The ash-filled pit had a ring of large, smooth, limestone slabs around it where people sat. It gave Stone Circle its name. There were a few good-sized boulders, too. The circle had been there long before Doc bought the property. No one knew who had built it. Some said the Delaware tribe had used it for council meetings.

Doc made it known that any folks could use it for Saturday evening camp-fires so long as they gathered dead wood only and made sure the embers were contained when they left. He said no alcohol, either, as a courtesy to Mrs. Williams, who supported the temperance league. People respected the rules, and from June to October, Stone Circle attracted people from all around. They'd hitch their horse-and-buggies to the fence row near the road and go by foot back to the clearing, where someone would get a fire going. One never knew who would show up. It was understood that there would be singing and maybe a fiddle. Storytelling and poetry were especially welcomed.

Artie chose a stone, and Cade sat on the ground with his back against a boulder. They talked for the best part of an hour about the new directions their lives were taking. They broke into a rendition of "Wilbur and Fanny" when they recalled their first jobs at the dance pavilion. Cade hadn't laughed that hard since he'd been away, he said. It was Artie who brought up the topic of the Fletchers.

"Grandma Hanson saves clippings from the *Akron Beacon*. She has an envelope for articles about the Fletcher Pottery factory. She calls it her 'reprobate file.'"

A short laugh had shot out of the corner of Artie's mouth, but Cade just nodded. "After what they did to your family, that sounds appropriate to me," he said.

"There was an interesting piece in the *Beacon* last spring. Seems that bastard Lyle Fletcher is running the pottery works now."

"You're joking!"

"Apparently, his father dropped dead of a heart attack, and he stepped in as head of the company."

"The reform school must have done him some good."

"Turned out it was a private military school in Indiana he was sent to. Maybe they polished his veneer, but I don't think anything could have changed his character. That kid had pure evil in his heartwood. The article mentioned that he graduated with honors from Culver Military Academy."

"No! That's hard to believe."

"Exactly. I didn't believe it either, so I did a little research. We did some printing work for the University of St. Louis, and well … let's say I *borrowed* their letterhead. I wrote a letter to the Culver academy from the university's school of law. I said Lyle Fletcher had put in his application to attend our college, and we needed the transcript of his diploma exam scores. I enclosed an envelope with my own address on it, adding some credentials behind my name, of course."

"Geez, Artie. I can't believe your nerve. Did they answer?"

"Yes. And it was just as I thought. Apparently, he was enrolled there, but he was kicked out of the academy in April of '97. Seems he had been on probation for altercations with another student, and then he was caught bringing contraband into the school. They suggested that we contact the police department in Fort Wayne, Indiana, if we need more corroboration in the matter."

"You're amazing, Artie."

"So, Lyle steps right in as president of the pottery works. Slick as a greased pig. Nothing sticks to him. Grandma had another clipping about him marrying the daughter of some industrialist from Akron in June. If only they knew. I thought about paying his in-laws a visit."

"And saying what?"

"Tell them what I know! When I think of all the misery he brought down on my family and how they got rich on the slave labor of people like us! My mom might still be alive if their glazes hadn't killed her." Artie's voice was shaking now. "Sometimes I lie awake at night and wonder if I would have the guts to go through with it."

"Telling his in-laws?"

"No. Strangling the life out of someone else."

Cade glanced over at his friend. Artie looked hollow-eyed in that moment. Shattered. Like the rage had eaten away at him from the inside. Cade remembered how that felt. It was hard to know what to say to him. "Honestly, Artie, I don't know what I'd do if I ever came face-to-face with him again. I hated Fletcher for the longest time. All I wanted was to make him suffer. And I didn't have near the reason you have for hating him. But my animosity didn't hurt him. It just turned ugly inside of me. And I ended up taking it out on you."

"Hey, let's not dredge that up again. Listen, I'm sorry I brought up Fletcher's name. This was supposed to be a good meeting."

"It *is* a good meeting, Artie. I was worried we both had changed so much, we wouldn't be able to talk about what's important to us anymore. But it feels like we've picked up right where we left off."

"Yeah, that's a relief to me, too." Artie stopped talking, but it wasn't an awkward kind of silence. They'd learned long ago how to sit in silence together. When Artie spoke again, he smiled. "It's been really good to be with you, Cade. I should probably head back to Mishler."

As they walked back to Doc's house, Cade said, "Would it be all right if I come by your Grandma's place later on to pay my respects?"

"Thanks. That would mean a lot to her. Normally, she would want to bake you some molasses cookies if she knew you were coming."

"I always *was* her favorite."

Artie punched him on the shoulder. "Don't I know!"

"Oh, I meant to tell you that I've been invited to join Ellie and Flora—that's Mrs. Taylor—at Congress Lake Saturday night. We'll be staying in the yellow cottage. One must be *invited* now to get onto the grounds.

"I know. There was an article in the *Beacon* last fall. I couldn't believe it. A couple of days ago I went down to the lake, just to prove I still could. There's a gate at the Hartville entrance, but there are lots of ways in from the north, if one ignores the 'No Trespassing' signs. Nobody said anything."

Cade laughed. "Well, that gives me an idea. Would you like to join Ellie and me Sunday morning? We planned to take a walk by the lake to give Flora some space. She likes to paint in the mornings.

"You mean I'd finally get to meet Ellie in person? You're on."

"Splendid! How about meeting us by the dance pavilion at eleven?"

"Perfect."

Cade noticed a bicycle leaning against the oak tree in Doc's front yard. Artie walked over to it.

"You're a wheelman now?" Cade said.

"I joined the St. Louis Cycling Club. I brought my bike on the train so I can stay in condition while I'm here. We have a tour coming up in two weeks."

Cade grinned. "A lithographer *and* a wheelman. I'm impressed." He extended his hand, and they exchanged a warm shake.

"I'm impressed, too, *Doctor* Bauer."

"Not a doc yet, but give me another year!"

Artie hopped on his cycle and raised his hand as he pedaled away.

Cade watched him weave gracefully around mud holes in the road until he turned the corner at the next block.

CHAPTER THIRTY

Truth

The mustard-colored cottage, which sat on the rise just beyond the Congress Lake Hotel, had a slightly musty smell when they stepped inside. Sunlight cast a prism of colors on the wall behind the kitchen table, where a cut-glass vase of asters and golden helianthus had been placed. A hand-written note lay beside it. Ellie read it aloud: "*We hope you enjoy your stay. The icebox and larder should have the essentials. We'll arrive at 5:45pm, and the hotel will deliver supper at six. We look forward to seeing you. Fondly, Louise and Edgar Thompson.*"

"Louise has thought of everything!" Flora smiled and moved slowly toward a room that opened off a spacious sitting area by a wall of windows. "The cottage is just the way I remembered it. There are two beds in here for us. Cade will have the room by the kitchen."

"Oh, it's lovely!" Ellie said as she entered the front bedroom. A cast iron duck propped open a door to a verandah, and a warm lake breeze came through the screen door. The décor was simple but pleasant. A flowered rug covered most of the painted floorboards, and the beds had blue-checkered quilts. The tan woolen blankets folded on the foot end hinted at the possibility that it would cool off at night.

"I used to paint out here," Flora said as she opened the bedroom's screen door. She sat in one of the wicker chairs on the porch. "Isaac would sit here and read to Opal." Flora was motionless, gazing at the lake glimmering through the trees.

Ellie realized Flora needed some time alone. "I'll go unpack my things and look around," she said softly.

"Thank you, love."

After Ellie's dresses were hung in the wardrobe, she slipped into the small room where Cade would stay. It had a plain blue bedspread and blue gingham curtains. There was no wardrobe, only wooden wall pegs and a three-sided cabinet of shelves in the corner. She first sat on the edge of his bed and then swung her legs up and lay back. The thought of him sleeping under the same roof with only a thin wall between them sent a wave of pleasure through her body. It seemed so intimate, even though Flora's presence made everything perfectly proper.

When she heard Flora opening drawers in the kitchen, Ellie stood quickly, and the bedsprings squeaked loudly. She blushed as she smoothed out the wrinkles on the spread.

Flora gave no indication she'd heard anything. Ellie noticed the dark circles under her eyes and worried that coming to the lake had been too much for her. "Are you feeling well?"

"I'm fine, but I'm afraid I need a nap." She smiled. "I'm continually reminded of the fragility of life."

"Well, don't you worry about hosting dinner tonight. Please allow Cade and me to do that." She was glad to see Flora nod.

* * *

Ellie stepped outside the cottage, grateful to have some time to herself. There was something about Congress Lake that stirred up emotions. Nothing had ever been spoken between her and Cade, but she could tell their feelings for each other had deepened in the last month. She had fallen in love with him. She wasn't sure he felt that way about her. Sometimes it seemed as if he pulled away from her. As if he kept a part of himself hidden from her. But there were things she hadn't told him either.

When she told him she would inherit Claybourne Oaks, he had been happy for her. "That's great that you'll have a place in the country to visit now and then," he'd said. What she didn't tell him was that in her heart she had a dream of living at Claybourne Oaks someday. What would Cade think about her growing more attached to Hartville when all of his dreams for the future were in Philadelphia? It worried her that they could grow apart because of it. He was attracted to the Philadelphia girl she had been. Would he still want the woman she was becoming?

* * *

Cade dressed in the gray tweed jacket and vest Mrs. Danforth had altered for him from her late husband's wardrobe. "It won't be overly formal for Ohio, but you'll still impress your Ellie." Cade noticed Mrs. Danforth was always instructing him about the proper occasion to wear this or that. He understood she was giving him an education about how the upper class dressed. It was a different level of etiquette, which most young men of good breeding had been learning ever since they crawled out of their prams. He'd had no awareness of such things when he was growing up until he'd caught glimpses of it when he worked at Congress Lake.

He placed his bowler on his head and stepped back from the oval mirror. Then he removed his coat and draped it casually over his arm, as he'd seen many of his classmates do at social events. He frowned. He didn't want to become a chameleon, always trying to blend in, pretending he was something other than himself. Beneath the fine clothes that Mrs. Danforth had sewn for the guy in the mirror, there was an ordinary Hartville boy. A Dunker boy. A boy he'd been hiding from Ellie far too long. Their relationship demanded more honesty now. He knew he had to tell Ellie the truth about himself, whatever the cost.

There was something he wanted to take with him to Congress Lake. He recalled it was in the darkened attic room where Mrs. Williams had made space for a crate of Cade's things. He set an oil lamp on the floor and lifted a small wooden chest from the crate. Inside he found what he wanted. He wrapped the blue ribbon around his fingers and tucked the buckeye into the palm of his hand. He hoped it would help him find the right words to tell Ellie the truth.

* * *

Ellie liked Louise and Edgar Thompson. Their affectionate banter brought a levity that had been missing this summer. It was good to see Flora laugh and come to life again.

"Flora, have you given thought to remaining on our membership committee?" Edgar asked.

"Up until this evening, I couldn't imagine participating without Isaac. But being with you both again has been good. So, perhaps."

"Good! We've had more applications for membership from the Akron area now that we announced our plans to build a fine golf course and a proper clubhouse. Isaac always wanted us to expand the membership to Summit County."

"Yes, I remember." Flora said.

"The young couple we interviewed today are exactly what we want in the club," Louise said. "She's from the *Cordell* family in Akron. And her husband owns the big pottery company up in Mogadore. You know the one. The Fletchers."

Cade's body jolted slightly. "*Lyle* Fletcher?" He blurted it out sharply, and heads turned toward him.

"That's the one." Louise said. "Do you know him?"

Cade's heart pumped faster. He didn't know how to answer without saying too much. "Yes. I mean … I don't know a lot about him. I–I bumped into him a few years ago." He felt his face growing hot in the awkward pause that followed. He noticed Ellie's brow wrinkle up into a question mark.

Louise didn't let the topic drop. "I get the feeling you know something we may have missed. What was your impression of Mr. Fletcher, Cade?"

"We were younger. He was … unruly back then."

Edgar chuckled. "Well, I guess the military academy straightened him out."

"Did he tell you he graduated from Culver?"

"Yes. With honors."

"He never graduated. He was thrown out of Culver." Cade couldn't mince words if Fletcher was going lie to these people about his past.

"Is that so? You got this from a reliable source?"

"Yes, sir. I first want to say that I've done things I'm not proud of, too, when I was a kid. But Lyle Fletcher ... well, I personally know that he's done many things that are ... criminal."

"Oh, dear!" said Louise. "They seemed like such a nice couple. Just married. I wonder if his wife knows about this."

"Yes, it is disturbing," Edgar said. "With the Cordell connection, I suppose we didn't look too closely into his background. I appreciate the information."

Louise said, "The Fletchers will be coming back tomorrow for the club luncheon, won't they? Perhaps you should confront him about this, Edgar."

"I'd like to get him talking more about it. Unguarded. If he's lied to us deliberately, we can let him dig the hole deeper. Cade, I wonder if you'd fill me in a little more in the morning. Say nine o'clock. I'll meet you in front of the hotel?"

"Certainly. I'm sorry to dampen the evening with this news."

"It's good you did," Flora said. "The committee needs to know if someone is lying to us. We want to be able to trust other members completely."

* * *

When the Thompsons had left, Cade noticed Flora looked pale and exhausted. "I'm sorry the evening ended the way it did," he said.

"It was a good lesson for us," Flora said. "Isaac always insisted on a thorough background check of applicants." She yawned and added, "I'm sorry to say I'm exhausted. It was a lovely evening. Thank you both for hosting. I couldn't have managed it. You're a good team." Flora smiled. She made her way slowly to the bedroom, limping.

Ellie watched Flora with concern and said quietly, "I think I should go check on her, and maybe get some sleep, too. I'd like to talk in the morning."

"Me, too. I have a lot to tell you."

"I have things to tell you, as well."

Cade pulled her in close, and they kissed.

* * *

Sleep was impossible. Cade flopped face-down, fully clothed, on the top of his bed. He thought about going for a run, maybe to Mishler. He should warn Artie that Lyle Fletcher would be coming here tomorrow. His worlds were colliding, and it felt like an impending disaster. "Dammit," he said, pounding his fist into his bed. Congress Lake was a powerful magnet, and they were all just bits of iron filings, pulled inextricably back to where it had started.

He rolled onto his side to pull the ribbon from his pocket. He turned the brown nut around until its white circular blotch glowed in the moonlight. Was this buckeye behind all the strange coincidences? It seemed to carry a kind of luck. But maybe not the good kind.

There was a soft knock on his door, and he sat upright. He ran his fingers through his hair as he moved quickly to open it. All he could see was her dark silhouette hugging a shawl around her shoulders.

"I heard you through the wall. I thought maybe you couldn't sleep either," she whispered. "May we go somewhere to talk? I don't want to wake Flora."

Cade nodded and reached down to grab his shoes. He carried them in one hand and held her hand in the other as they tiptoed to the back door. The door squeaked a little, and he felt Ellie's grip tighten. "It's all right," he whispered as they stepped outside.

He released her hand only long enough to pull on his shoes. Then he silently guided her down the tree-lined path with his eyes fixed on the half-moon reflecting on the glassy lake. The two of them seemed to be the only ones in the world.

The dance pavilion was dark. He led her across the plank bridge and lifted her enough that she could swing her legs over the chain strung across the pavilion entrance. They climbed the stair to the upper level. A chilly breeze blew over them, and Ellie shivered. Cade recalled how voices from the pavilion verandahs carried along the shoreline, so he spoke in a voice that was no louder than the splash of the water against the shore. "Let's go inside."

Tables and chairs had been stacked to one side, and a wide swath of planked flooring spread across the room. The warmth from the day still lingered in here, and they relaxed against each other. Cade spied a two-seater bench against the wall and swung it around so they could catch the pale light coming in the front window and have a view of the lake.

"I needed to see you," Ellie said. "I could tell you were upset by the mention of that man, Lyle Fletcher. I couldn't stop thinking about it. Are you all right?"

Cade was touched by her concern. He swallowed, knowing the time had come for the whole story. "I'm fine. I'm more upset at myself. There are things that I should have told you long ago, when I first realized our connection." He looked at her puzzled face, but she didn't say anything. "I—I'll understand if you are angry at me for not telling you."

"Now you have me worried," Ellie said finally. "What could possibly make me angry at you?"

He couldn't break away from her gaze. He breathed out a lungful of air that was mostly a sigh. "I think I need to start with the day we first met."

"Here at Congress Lake? In the parlor?"

"No, it was long before that. I didn't realize it myself until you told me your name was McAllister that day at Ogontz. I realized then you were the girl who had this." He pulled the necklace from his pocket and laid it in the palm of her hand.

Ellie stared at it, unable to speak for a moment. "My lucky buckeye! But I lost that."

"Yes, I found it on the trail after my nephew nearly drowned."

"The Dunker boy ... Petey ... was your nephew?" Images swirled in Ellie's head. Voices came back. *Ca-dey* ... she heard the little boy say. Then his mother, Mrs. Holtz... *Cade said if it weren't for your screams, he never would have gotten there in time…* She remembered the older boy's eyes, dark brown with long lashes. And his curly hair wet against his face from the lake. There was a strong family resemblance. She could see that now. "I remember. Petey's older brother was named Cade, too," she said. She was puzzled.

"Ellie?"

The emotional timbre of his voice surprised her, and she reached for his hand.

Cade said. "He was … me."

Ellie felt her breath disappear, and her heart lurch oddly in her chest. "That was you? Why didn't you tell me?"

"I'm sorry, Ellie." Tears came to his eyes. "I didn't expect it to be this hard to tell you. I–I guess I'm ashamed of what I was back then. Maybe I was afraid you wouldn't want to be with me anymore. My background is *so different* than yours. I mean … my sister Mandy married a Dunker and raised me that way, and my father was a drunk who had terrible rages. He was *nothing* like your father…"

Ellie gasped. "Is that what you've been holding back? Cade Bauer. Kiss me. Immediately."

He looked up in surprise. He wondered how this could be happening, but he leaned obediently toward her. The softness of her lips was a balm for some part of him that had never felt it before. Even after they kissed, their foreheads leaned against each other for the longest time. "Ellie, I love you," he said. "More than anything."

"I love you, too," she said. "More than anything."

They sat in silence, Ellie's head resting on his shoulder. Cade let the delicious grace she had given him settle into his body.

She spoke first. "I can't believe you kept this necklace all these years."

He kissed the tip of her nose and grinned. "When you said it was lucky, it turns out it was," he said. "How else can you explain how a Dunker kid ended up here … with you."

"Tell me about your Dunker family. I want to hear everything."

Cade started from his earliest memories of Mandy as the only *mütter* he knew. Of his respect and love for Daniel, who had raised him to be a good *bauer,* as well as any father could. He told her of Rachel, who was married now, living in Indiana. And he talked about Petey's epileptic seizures and how protective he'd felt toward him. "I'd give anyone a good thumping if they ever teased him."

He stopped. Ellie had listened with an animated face and had murmured encouraging words as he told it, laughing with him in all the right places. He'd never imagined that it would be so easy to share what he'd tried to hide from her all this time. It seemed that the story about his Pa should be told at a different time, but he wanted to let Ellie know that he wouldn't hold anything back about his family. "I will tell you more on another day about my life with Pa. For now, I'll just say that he took me back to live with him when I was eight. It was a very bad time in my life. He ... he was a violent man, and he blamed me for losing Ma. He said it was because I was born. Doc told me that wasn't true, but for the longest time I had thought her death was my fault. Pa died of a heart attack the day after Petey almost drowned."

"Oh, Cade. That must have been terrible for you to have your father die right after that awful thing with Petey."

"Pa's death was a blessing. That may sound cruel, but I was free to live with Mandy and Daniel again."

"And what happened with your Dunker faith?"

"I was briefly a member of the Brethren, but I decided I wasn't cut out to be a Dunker, after all. I left the church. Their teachings have stayed with me, though. And I think I'm a better man because of it."

"Were you baptized in the lake?"

"Yes. The same day I met you. It was in the morning. Then something happened that I've never told my family about. It's something I'm deeply ashamed of, but I don't want to keep anything from you, Ellie."

Ellie squeezed his hand, hoping he knew that no judgment was coming from her, whatever this awful thing was that he was about to say.

"Right after I was baptized, my family was heading toward our picnic spot."

"Yes! I remember. On the hill just beyond this pavilion. I can still see Mr. and Mrs. Holtz sitting there when I went to tell them what happened to Petey."

"Yes, Mandy and Daniel had walked on ahead. Petey was always in his own world, lagging behind. I had stayed back at the wagon so that I could walk by myself. Like a grown man. When I went down the path toward our usual picnic spot, I saw a redheaded kid up ahead mimicking Petey, taunting him and grabbing his hat. That's when I lost my temper. I went into a rage."

"I know!" Ellie said. "I saw the whole thing. It was like you came out of nowhere, flying through the air and knocking the mean kid flat. It was wonderful! He got exactly what he deserved! I was right there where it happened! And *it was that same redheaded kid* who tried to drown Petey!"

"Then you also understand why he did it. He was getting back at me. If I hadn't lost my temper, maybe Petey wouldn't have gotten hurt. I've never forgiven myself for that."

"Cade, you cannot take responsibility for what that bully did to your nephew. He had a meanness that didn't need an excuse."

Cade needed more time to allow this thought to find a place to settle inside of him. "I'm sorry you had to witness such a horrible thing, Ellie. But I've always felt grateful that Eleanor McAllister was there when Petey needed help," he said. "I still don't know how you happened to be in the tree."

She smiled. "Let's save that story for another time." Ellie tried to hide a yawn. "Look at the sky. Has it lightened a bit?"

He nodded. "Yep. We've been talking all night again."

Ellie laughed. "Have you noticed we have our best conversations when I sneak out in the middle of the night? At least Miss Eastman isn't around."

"I'm guessing it's around five thirty. Maybe we should head back before others are up and around."

They stood and held each other in a long embrace before walking toward the pavilion door.

"Have you ever wondered what happened to that redheaded bully?" Ellie said. "Was he ever caught?"

Cade hesitated for a moment. "For years I watched and waited for him to show up. He never did."

"Cap," Ellie said. "That was what he was called. I think it was short for Captain. You knew there was another boy with him, didn't you? Cap called him Twitch. I actually felt kind of sorry for that kid. I think he was being bullied, too. He kept trying to stop Cap, but then he'd give in to what that redheaded bully ordered him to do."

Cade could not bring Artie's name into it—even to Ellie. Of all the people affected by Lyle Fletcher, Artie was probably hurt the most.

"Cade? You're kind of quiet."

"I found out who the redheaded bully is, Ellie."

"You did?"

"He's Lyle Fletcher."

CHAPTER THIRTY-ONE

Forever

Ellie was cooking oatmeal and Cade was setting the table when Flora emerged from her room, looking very refreshed. If she suspected they'd been out all night, she didn't let on. While they ate, they took turns telling her the story she hadn't heard. Cade discovered it was easier to talk about growing up in a Dunker family this time. Ellie showed her the buckeye necklace, and Flora recalled her wearing it the first time the McAllister family visited.

"There's one more thing we need to tell you. It's about Lyle Fletcher," Ellie said. "He's the bully. The one who tried to drown Petey."

Without mentioning Artie's name, Cade related what he knew about Lyle's history at Culver.

"This is quite shocking. Edgar needs to know this when you see him this morning, Cade," Flora said. "But I suppose to be fair to the Fletchers, Lyle should be given a chance to tell what has happened to him in the years since."

"Yes. I've been considering the possibility that he's been reformed, though I'd be surprised," Cade said.

Flora looked out the window for a few moments and then said, "If he's contrite about what he did, he may want to apologize. Would an apology from him be reparation enough for what each of you has suffered?"

Ellie squeezed the buckeye in her palm. "I don't know if a simple apology can come anywhere close to setting things right. I've always thought of myself as a kind enough person who would never want to hold a grudge. But I've never had anything this big to forgive."

Cade nodded. "The Dunkers always preached that we should forgive. It was one of the reasons I left the church. I didn't think I could ever forgive what was done to Petey. I was so angry. And I took it out on others. My brother-in-law, Daniel, is a man of peace. He used to say that any act of violence is the seed for more violence. I think I understand what he was saying."

"Can you ever forgive Lyle?" Ellie asked.

"I think I've become a relativist. It's not always as black-and-white as we think. Emerson says there's an optical illusion about everyone we meet. If I wait until I find out what's behind others' actions, I will have more understanding of them. Maybe that's as close to forgiveness as I'll ever come. At any rate, I'm willing to talk to Fletcher and hear him out. Maybe he can tell me why he did that to Petey. Maybe he's sorry for what he did."

The other two were silent. Cade looked up and saw Ellie's tears. She reached her hand to his and held it tightly. "It takes a lot of courage to have a conversation like that with him. Only a man of peace would entertain the possibility that Lyle may be sorry."

"Man of peace. You mean I've got a Dunker boy in me, after all?"

"Would that be so bad?"

Cade smiled. "No, it feels ... right."

* * *

Ellie kept glancing at the clock while she was plaiting Flora's hair into a new style she'd learned at Ogontz. Both women looked up when Cade came in the back door of the cottage.

"What did Edgar say?" Ellie asked.

"We decided I should be the one to try to find out more from Fletcher. I may need your help with it if you are willing."

"You want me to hold him down while you force him to talk?" Ellie smiled.

"No. I need you to be my fiancée for the day."

"Oh, I see," Ellie said. "Is this your idea of a proposal, Mr. Bauer?"

He grinned and looked at her for the longest time. "As tempting as that is, I'm suggesting that today we will just pretend. Edgar Thompson will introduce us to the Fletchers as though we are another couple moving here from Philadelphia and are interested in joining the club. Your job will be to keep Mrs. Fletcher occupied while I get Lyle alone to talk. We thought it would seem more natural than if Edgar interrogates him. If it seems he's changed and apologizes, then no one needs to lose face."

"I can do that," Ellie said.

"And what if he hasn't?" Flora said. There was tension in her voice. "What if Mr. Fletcher has not changed?"

"If you're worried about how *I* would react," Cade said, "I'm not going lose my temper again with Lyle Fletcher. The cost was too high the first time. If he doesn't show any sign of change or remorse, I'll simply inform him that I'll let the Congress Lake Club know, and they can decide whether to accept him as a member. But if Lyle shows a change of heart, Edgar's in favor of giving him a chance. There is no reason for me to deny the Fletchers that."

* * *

It was well past the time they had expected the Fletchers to arrive. Ellie felt her fingertips perspire inside her gloves when she spotted a young couple descending from the road down the walkway. The man reset his straw boater on his head, and that was when she saw the glint of slicked-down red hair. She clutched Cade's arm. "It's them."

Cade saw Ellie biting her lip, and he wished now that he'd never asked her to get involved. "You don't have to do this. I can say that you weren't feeling well and went to lie down."

"No. I need to face him. There's a ten-year-old in me who is counting on me to look him in the eye," she said. "Let's move toward the verandah and wait for Edgar to call us over. It will seem more natural."

Cade nodded and placed his hand over hers, which was still tightly wrapped over his arm. "We're going to be a little late to meet Artie. But I'll hurry it along as much as I can," he said.

"I can excuse myself and go meet Artie if you need more time. From the way you described him, he should be easy to recognize."

"Artie would love the chance to talk to you alone. He's been wanting to do that ever since he saw you reading by the water in your bathing suit," Cade said and winked.

Ellie laughed.

They both heard Edgar's voice behind them. "I'd like you to meet another young couple who may be joining Congress Lake next year. They're from Philadelphia. Mr. Bauer will have a degree as a veterinarian soon, and we're trying to woo him to our area."

Ellie looked directly into the green eyes of a pretty woman. She wore a well-designed garden dress that would have been admired at any Rittenhouse Square party. Ellie knew she should look at Lyle, but she couldn't manage it yet. She noticed that he was tall and well-dressed, from what she could see.

Edgar began to formally introduce them. "Mr. and Mrs. Fletcher, may I introduce Miss McAllister and Mr. Bauer."

Ellie saw Cade's hand stretch forward and grip Lyle's hand. She remained engaged with Mrs. Fletcher, who said, "Please call me Kate, and this is my husband, Lyle."

"I'm Ellie, and my fiancé, Cade." She straightened her back and smiled pleasantly up at Lyle. She didn't let her gaze waver. The bucket of freckles had not changed. Ellie had expected to be struggling with a wave of emotion when she met him, but other than the physical features of red hair and freckles, he bore little resemblance to the boy from seven years ago. His face had none of the meanness of Cap. He was congenial, smiled warmly at her, and said all the right things as they stood together in a small circle and talked.

Cade had braced himself before he turned around to be introduced to Lyle Fletcher. In his fantasies over the years, he'd never imagined that their meeting would be like this. He turned on the charm, knowing it would disarm Fletcher. Cade focused some attention on Kate Fletcher, while Ellie displayed great poise in chatting with Lyle.

When Ellie and Kate struck up a conversation about what was interesting in Philadelphia, he realized this was the moment to get away.

"I understand they want to build a new clubhouse after the golf course is in. Mr. Thompson was saying the best place for it is on at the south end of the lake, off the east trail. I was just about to take a look. Would you like to join me?"

"Certainly," Lyle said.

Cade turned to Ellie. "Honey, you wouldn't mind if Lyle and I leave you ladies for fifteen minutes?"

"Not at all. I want to ask Kate all about Akron." She smiled at Lyle's wife, who also waved the fellows on. "We're not sure where we'd want to live if we move here," Ellie said to her.

Cade cautiously laid some groundwork for the conversation he hoped to have with Lyle. "My family used to come to Congress Lake when I was child," he said. "I've been trying to get my bearings. I recall there was a path that used to lead to a big boulder that jutted out into the water. We fished from there. But the path doesn't seem to be there anymore. Maybe I'm not remembering it correctly."

"Oh, I know the one you mean," Lyle said. "It was there when I was a boy, too. I think when I was away at school, a twister came through and knocked down trees along the old trail. I've not been there since I was a kid, but we're going the right direction.

Cade had noticed a cigarette case sticking up from an inside pocket in Lyle's jacket. It could provide another way to slip through the formalities. "You wouldn't have a smoke on you, would you?"

"Sure." Lyle reached for his silver case.

"I promised my fiancée I'd quit this habit, but I'd kill for a smoke right now."

Lyle laughed and put his case back in his pocket. "You want to wait until we're out of sight, then?" He smirked. "Take this for what it's worth, Cade. Don't give up too many habits for your woman. I mean, who's in charge? Right? You need to get that straight before the wedding."

"Hmm. Thanks. You said you went off to school. Where did you study?"

"I went to Culver Military Academy near South Bend, Indiana."

"I've heard of that school. They used West Point as a model for their program, didn't they?"

"Yes, it's a fine school."

"When did you graduate?"

"Uh. Ninety-seven. No … eight. A lot has happened in the last two years. Kate and I just married. Last year my father passed suddenly, and I had to step into managing the business my family owns."

"I'm sorry for your loss. What's your line of business?"

"We do ceramics manufacturing. All automated lines now. We ship stoneware, china, and decorative pottery out of Lake Erie, all over the world.

"Very impressive. I've heard there is a good vein of clay here."

"Not what it once was, but we do well."

They had reached the trail, and Lyle pulled out two cigarettes, handing one to Cade. "The little lady won't catch you smoking here." They stopped momentarily to light up.

Lyle had said it with sarcasm, but Cade didn't react. "What prompted you and Kate to apply to the club?"

"Kate likes to follow all the society gossip in the *Beacon*. Having our wedding described in detail was the highlight of her life. Of course, she practically wrote the article for them. They are always commenting about what's going on at Congress Lake, so of course she wanted to join. I figure it can't hurt to rub elbows with guys like you." He laughed.

"Guys like me?"

"Sure. University? Philadelphia? I'm trying to figure out why you would want to move to the least interesting place on the planet? You have a classy little gal on your arm. Why here when you could have Philadelphia? You're not running from the law, are you?"

Cade laughed. "Not currently." He was wishing, even more than before, that he'd not brought Ellie into this ruse. Maybe it was going too far. "I haven't mentioned it to anyone at the club, but I grew up in Hartville. I moved to Philadelphia when I went off to university."

"I'll be damned. Here I thought you were one of those high-falutin' city types, going to university and all."

They were coming to Jonah's Landing, which was what Cade had planned.

"I used to bring my nephew fishing at Jonah's Landing," Cade said. "Before the tragedy."

"Tragedy?"

They stood in the clearing where the flat rock extended out into the water. "Mind if we stop here?" He didn't wait for an answer. Cade walked to the edge of the rock. "Brings back memories, doesn't it?"

"I don't recall."

"Oh, you mentioned you knew where this rock was. I figured you had a lot of memories, too. You asked about the tragedy. My nephew, Petey, was just a little boy, blond hair. He was a little odd. He had epilepsy, and you know how kids can be mean." He paused before going on.

"Petey loved this lake. And that day he couldn't wait to go fishing. He ran on ahead while I went back to the wagon to get our fishing tackle. It was a terrible thing. When I got here, he was floating face down in the water, his blond hair floating out from his head."

"That's a tragedy for sure. Do you figure it was an epileptic fit?"

"Well, I would have concluded that, but it turns out there was a witness who saw what really happened. Apparently two boys, around thirteen or fourteen years of age, attacked my nephew. Did I tell you he was a Dunker boy?"

At first Lyle's face went pale, and his orange freckles looked like a bad case of pimples. Then, gradually, a reddish hue started from his neck and worked its way up. He scowled, but he didn't move.

"They tormented Petey, who was screaming his head off. And then those bullies dragged him into the lake, where the one called Cap pretended to baptize my nephew. In the name of the Father. And he held Petey's head under the water until he drowned."

"I don't know why you're telling me your sob story, Mr. Bauer. It has nothing to do with me."

Cade felt a calm wash over him. It was a strange sense of peace that he hadn't expected. He looked steadily into Lyle's eyes. "You know it has every-thing to do with you, Lyle. All I'm asking is why."

Cade saw Lyle's body begin to tense up, and for a moment there was a familiar scent in the air that he couldn't quite place. Then he knew. It was the same smell that Pa had when he went crazy. He didn't know when Lyle made his move, but it came lightning fast. His freckled face had twisted into an ugly mass of hatred. He ploughed into Cade, knocking him flat. Cade heard a loud crack, and then blackness swirled around him.

It may have been seconds or minutes, he wasn't sure. He was aware he was on the ground, but the blackness hadn't left his eyes yet. Cade struggled to sit upright, but he couldn't move. When light started coming back, he realized Lyle's knee was on his chest and strong hands were holding his arms flat to the damp dirt. He could hear the water lapping close to his ear.

"You little bastard, you think you're so smart. You actually think you can take me down?"

"Lyle, I only want to talk. Like two adults. I just want some truth be-tween you and me."

Lyle's face had a coldness that was beyond Pa's crazy. "I'm sorry, Mr. Bauer. I'm afraid there is going to be another tragedy at Jonah's Landing. You and I walked over to see where the clubhouse will be built. Even your little woman heard you say that. I'll tell them that you'll be along soon. That you just wanted to visit your favorite old fishing hole."

Lyle moved his leg, and Cade twisted, shaking free of Fletcher's grip, but his eyes blurred when he moved. Cade felt his body slam to the ground again, this time with his face against the damp earth, and now there was a knee in his back. No matter how he strained, he could not move from where he was.

"You have a nasty gash on your head, Bauer. What a shame that you lost your footing and cracked your head on the rock that way. You must have tried to wash the blood off in the water. That was when you lost conscious-ness. A tragedy. Drowning in the same place where the little Dunker misfit had his seizure. You Bauers are an unlucky lot."

Cade felt his body being lifted and shoved into the shallow water of the lake. He struggled and kicked, but Fletcher had pulled his arms back behind him now, and his face was submerged. He lifted his eyes above the water line briefly, desperately trying to get his nose to the air. Then there was a splitting pain to the back of his head, and he felt the blackness swallowing him.

* * *

Ellie glanced toward the trailhead where Cade and Lyle had disappeared. An uneasy tightness in her chest was growing stronger. She made her apologies to Kate Fletcher, saying a friend of theirs was waiting on her. "When the guys return, tell Cade I went on ahead."

Ellie hurried toward a tall man standing near the dance pavilion. His bicycle was leaned against a tree. "You must be Artie," she said and extended her hand as she'd watched Flora do many times.

His handshake was firm. "Ellie. It is good to finally get to meet you. I didn't have the pleasure a few years ago."

"I'm afraid Cade is going to be late meeting us." Ellie was worried now, and she couldn't hide it.

"Is there something wrong? May I help?"

"I think I need to go find him. He had a meeting with Lyle … someone who gives me a bad feeling. I need to go to Jonah's Landing."

"Did you say Lyle?"

"Yes. Mr. Fletcher…"

"*Lyle Fletcher?*" Artie's expression turned to alarm. "My God, we need to go there! Ellie, I'll take the shortcut along the lake. You take the trail." He ran to the woods, disappearing into the tall grasses and bulrushes by the shore.

Ellie ran toward the trail. She saw Kate Fletcher heading that way, too.

"Hello, Ellie!" Kate called and waved. "Are you looking for our fellows, too?"

Just then Lyle emerged from the woods, walking briskly. He didn't seem to notice Ellie but grabbed his wife's shoulders and kept moving. "We're leaving," he said.

Kate pulled back slightly and said, "Lyle, we have our luncheon." He jerked her arm roughly to keep her in step with him.

"Mr. Fletcher!" Ellie called out in a sharp voice.

Lyle wheeled around. For a moment he revealed the scowl her ten-year-old self recognized. His face turned red."

"Where's Cade?" she demanded, closing the space between them.

He clenched his jaw and gave Ellie a smile. "I had to get back, but he wanted to walk along the shore. Said how he used to come here as a kid. He said to tell you he'd be along soon."

Ellie didn't wait for more. The cold feeling in her stomach terrified her. She kicked off her shoes and ran down the east trail toward Jonah's Landing.

As she rounded the bend, she saw Cade lying there. "No!" she screamed as she ran.

Artie was kneeling over him, pulling Cade's arms over his head and then folding them back on his chest and pressing on them in a steady rhythm. Cade was soaked from his head to halfway down his trousers. His face was so white, his lips dark purple. Ellie began to shake.

Artie was weeping. "I can't get him breathing. I think I'm too late. Oh, God! Come on, buddy, breathe!"

Ellie's mind was racing. Every year in her natatorium class, they had practiced saving a large stuffed doll. "Quick! Go to the other side and push right here on his chest."

Artie moved immediately and continued to pump Cade's chest.

"Not too hard. Two times. That's it. I'll breathe air into him. While I catch my breath, you pump."

Ellie leaned over Cade's lifeless face and sealed her mouth over his. She blew air into his mouth, and she felt her hand on his chest rise slightly. As she lifted her head and sucked fresh air deeply into her own lungs, she thought of the warmth of his kisses and his bright, intelligent eyes. She couldn't bear the thought of life without him. Each time Artie finished two compressions, Ellie blew air into Cade's lungs. She prayed fervently that, somehow, they were not too late.

When she heard a gurgling from inside him, she gasped, "Roll him on his side." Artie's strong arms turned Cade's body. Water drizzled from the corner of his mouth, and then the contents of his stomach started to spill onto the ground. He coughed and gasped while Ellie held his head gently and watched color begin to edge into his neck and cheeks. Cade opened his eyes and stared at her while he wheezed. Then he smiled slightly. It was only then that Ellie sobbed.

Artie took off his spectacles and pulled out his handkerchief to wipe his own eyes. Ellie reached out her hand to Artie, and he held it tightly.

Cade's voice was raspy and weak when he finally spoke. "Ellie. How did you…?"

"Artie found you, Cade. He got you out in time." She stroked his hair and found that blood was oozing from the back. "Dear god, your head is bleeding!" She pulled a hankie from the pocket of her dress and parted his wet curls to find the source. She could see that it was a smaller cut than it had seemed. She pressed the cloth firmly on it. "Cade, how did this happen?"

"I–I think I fell backward … on the rock. Then … Fletcher … held me down.

Artie jumped up. "I'm going to kill that son of a bitch!"

"No!" Cade said. "Artie! Wait."

Artie stopped, but Ellie could see his body was trembling and his face was taut with rage.

"Don't do anything. Promise me." Cade's voice was almost a whisper. "We got him."

"How do you figure that?"

"We finally got him! He thinks no one saw him." Cade closed his eyes and smiled. "*But I did*. And this time … he's going to court."

Cade was shivering, and Artie pulled off his own jacket to wrap over him. Ellie bent forward, throwing her arms around Cade to share whatever warmth she could give him. "We need to get Doc Williams," she said.

"I'll go on my bike." Artie stood.

Cade laid his hand on Artie's shoe. "Promise me, Artie, that you won't do anything."

"I promise. You're right. About everything. I'll stop at the hotel and send help. Doc and I will come back."

"Come to the yellow cottage!" Ellie called after him, and Artie raised his hand in reply.

Cade lifted his head and sat up with Ellie's help.

She kissed his forehead, his eyelids, his cheeks, his nose. "Don't ever leave me like that again," she said. "I couldn't bear it."

"I won't," he said. "I'm yours. Forever."

"Cade Bauer, is this your idea of a proposal?"

"Yes," he said and looked into her eyes for a long moment. "But I'll do a better job of it someday, I promise."

"Well then, I'll hold you to your promise," she said, laying her cheek against the stubble of his.

CHAPTER THIRTY-TWO

Reckoning

Stark County Prosecutor Robert Henry Day appeared to be in his thirties, though his receding hairline gave him a more mature look. His mouth formed a natural smile. Cade imagined that his pleasant countenance could harden into steel in a courtroom. The attorney's eyebrows wrinkled together and formed a furrow while he listened to what had happened at Jonah's Landing. Cade was not able to tell it without feeling a wave of emotion, the undertow sweeping him away. Tears dampened his cheeks, and he had to stop several times to blow his nose. He accepted the glass of water Mr. Day poured. He was grateful Artie was there to finish the story and bring it to the better ending.

Mr. Day stroked his chin. "Mr. Hanson, did you at any time see Lyle Fletcher near Mr. Bauer?"

"No, sir," Artie replied.

The attorney frowned as he wrote some notes. When he looked up, the wrinkle in his forehead deepened. "Unfortunately, Mr. Bauer, there were no eyewitnesses for the attack against you. I'll be blunt. Lyle Fletcher's story may sound plausible in a hearing before a judge. I personally believe what you've both told me, but I doubt that we'd have a strong enough case to indict him."

All that could be heard, then, was the sound of a pen against paper from the stenographer who sat to the side of Day's desk. Cade's hands tightened into fists, and he cleared his throat, but no words came out.

Mr. Day rested his elbows on his desk and leaned his chin against his interlaced fingers as he quietly studied Cade's face. He seemed to have more to say on the matter. "You said you wanted to confront Mr. Fletcher about an old grudge from your childhood?"

Cade shifted in his chair. He'd been deliberately vague about those details. How could he tell what happened to Petey without implicating Artie? "Yes, sir, it was a long time ago."

"Perhaps I should explain," the attorney said. "Sheriff Zaiser sent the constable's report to me because I've been investigating another case that involves Mr. Fletcher. That's why I've asked you to come today."

"I don't understand," Cade said.

"A man who was trying to bring a potter's union to the Fletcher's factory died last March. The victim's family alleges Fletcher was responsible. Some questions recently surfaced about Mr. Fletcher's own father's death last year. We're looking into the possibility of a *pattern* of violence."

Artie cleared his throat. "Sir, if you're wanting to find a pattern of violence, then I can verify Lyle's attack on Cade's nephew seven years ago. I—I'm involved, too."

"Artie, don't," Cade started to say.

"No, I've been wanting to clear the air for years, and I'm willing to take whatever punishment I get, if it will help."

The prosecutor sat up. "Seven years ago? How old were you when this happened?"

"Thirteen, sir."

Mr. Day listened, his eyes alert, while Artie gave the details of the day Petey had nearly died. The attorney looked at Cade. "Did your nephew's parents ever press charges for that incident?"

"No. They're Dunkers."

Mr. Day nodded and said to Artie, "It was a hateful attack on that child. But you were quite young. And since the boy's parents have never pressed charges, there will likely not be any consequences for that incident. You seem to have changed your ways, Mr. Hanson. Can you tell me more about why Lyle Fletcher influenced you, then?"

Artie told him about the pottery factory and how his family's livelihood was at stake if he were to challenge Lyle back then. The prosecutor nodded several times.

"This would give credence to your testimony. Fletcher's attorney will characterize them as 'youthful pranks.' But a jury, perhaps, will not."

"So, we have a case after all?" Artie said.

"Not exactly. I may be able to use your testimony for the other trial. I can't guarantee a judge will allow it, but if the defense calls character witnesses for Mr. Fletcher, that would open the door for us to call character witnesses to the contrary. It may not be the justice you are seeking, but it may be your only chance to bring Mr. Fletcher to some accountability.

Cade swallowed hard. The lump in his throat didn't go away. Maybe it was the only chance to stop Fletcher. "Yes, of course. I'll help in any way I can."

"Good. We'll get sworn affidavits from each of you today." The attorney stood to shake their hands and added, "Mr. Bauer, you said Mr. Fletcher left you for dead. Is it possible that he doesn't know you survived?"

"Quite possible. Only a handful of us know what happened. We agreed not to tell anyone until I talked to an attorney. I was told he withdrew his application for membership to the club the following day."

Attorney Day smiled. "Well, this is good news. I think we can arrange for an article to appear in the Akron paper mentioning a drowning at Congress Lake last Sunday. Something vague—perhaps mentioning the victim is thought to have been from Philadelphia. A guilty man searches the newspapers. He'll see it. It will leave him less guarded. But please understand, first we need to win an indictment against Mr. Fletcher, and then it could be a year or more before the case goes to court."

* * *

Only thirteen young men graduated from the University of Pennsylvania veterinary school on the twelfth of June in 1901. Twice as many had started training three years before. Cade stepped forward to receive his diploma. Cade Bauer, VMD. *Veterinariae Medicinae Doctoris.* He looked toward the audience and grinned at the four people who were applauding him. Doc and Mrs. Williams from Hartville, Ohio, looked as proud as any parents. Ellie and her father were seated next to them.

Mrs. Danforth gave a small dinner party in Cade's honor that evening. After their toasts, Cade stood. "It seems I have a cat's nature, with many lives," he said. "Doc Williams has given me at least two of them. I've been told he breathed life into my body at birth. I don't remember that, personally, but I do know how he breathed life into my dream of becoming a veterinarian. Doc and Mrs. Williams, I deeply appreciate the way you have always looked out for me, how you've opened your home to me. You've always seemed to see a better nature in me than I knew myself, and I want you to know it's made a difference. Thank you."

Mrs. Williams dabbed her eyes. Doc gave a nod, his smile stretching wide.

Cade changed the tenor. "Mrs. Danforth, you've managed to give me an entirely different education than I ever imagined I'd have in Philadelphia. I know I'll never look at gabardine and organza in the same way again!" Everyone laughed. "Your generosity and teachings have opened a door to a life I'd only glimpsed from the outside. Thank you." She lifted her glass toward him.

Cade looked to his left. "Mr. McAllister, you've always shown an interest in whatever I'm doing, and that's had the effect of instilling more confidence in myself. I appreciate your fidelity to your family, your sense of ethics, and your humanity toward all. These are qualities I regard as a model for success in life." Aaron smiled warmly and nodded his thanks.

Cade looked at the young woman sitting beside him, and color came to her cheeks in anticipation of his words. "Ellie, you truly did give me another life last year at Jonah's Landing. Thank you for listening carefully the day they taught resuscitation techniques at Ogontz." The laughter helped to ease the intense feeling that was welling up in his chest. In his head he'd practiced eloquent things to say to Ellie, but the words were simple when they came out. "Thank you for the joy and new life you bring to me each day." Her eyes said she had received what was in his heart. And when he went down on one knee and held a small jeweler's box toward her, the utter surprise on her face delighted him. In that moment, everyone else around the table faded from the world he shared with her. "Ellie, it would be a privilege and my greatest joy to spend the rest of my life with you, if you will have me."

She and Cade had flirted with the *idea* of marriage, and she had imagined this moment many times. But Ellie was startled by how deeply it touched her when it happened. Her certainty was immediate. "With all my heart. Yes." Her fingers trembled as she lifted the hinged lid of the box, and she sucked in her breath when she saw the delicate gold filigree setting that held a round, finely cut emerald. "Oh, Cade! It's exactly what I would have chosen!" From the glow of her expression, he knew it was true.

* * *

A low-slung, full moon illuminated the flat span of white across the lake. Cade pulled his scarf up to his ears and dug his gloved hands into the pockets of his overcoat. Out beyond the point, the lantern lights glowed yellow, and he heard the steady thrum of the ice saws setting up a natural rhythm. He listened to the staccato beat of the spud bars freeing the large sheets of ice that had been scored in a grid pattern. A deep voice began a folk tune, and two dozen men harmonized. Behind him on the shore, the chugging of the steam powered conveyor at Spelman's icehouse added to the music of the ice harvest.

Cade cut across the ice in a different direction. As he neared Jonah's Landing, he could see Artie bent close to the ground, blowing on the tinder that was beginning to glow. The naked trees around the clearing were huddled over him as if waiting for the smoke to warm them.

When Cade saw the boulder jutting out through the ice, sweat broke out on his upper lip. His heart pounded.

"Hey, Cade."

Cade climbed the bank and reached out to shake Artie's hand. "Thanks for getting a fire going."

"Are you all right?" Artie said quietly. "Maybe it wasn't a good idea to meet here."

"I didn't expect it would be this hard coming back to where it happened. I thought if I made myself come here, I wouldn't fall apart on Monday when I testify. But now I'm not so sure."

"Bauer, you'll do fine. It's been easier on me because I've watched the trial all week. Every day, Fletcher struts in with his Cleveland lawyers. Today the defense's character witnesses made him sound like citizen of the year. You should have seen him gloating."

"You're not helping my nerves."

"This is exactly what Attorney Day hoped would happen. Fletcher's arrogance is his worst enemy. He has no idea what's going to hit him when we get in the stand. I've been sitting in the back, and I'm sure he hasn't noticed me. He wouldn't recognize my name on the list of state witnesses. I was 'Artie Whitacre' when we were kids, and he'd already been sent off to military school when my grandparents adopted me. Personally, it will all be worth it to see the look on his face when he realizes who I am. Day says my testimony will open the door to call you to the stand. It's a good plan."

"I haven't told Ellie about you and Lyle."

"Really?"

"It's not my story to tell. But I think I talked her out of coming to the trial. I don't want her to have to be anywhere near Fletcher again."

Artie stared into the fire. "Ellie has a right to know about me. And if she doesn't want to have anything to do with me, then you need to stand by her decision. I'd give anything to undo what Lyle and I did to Petey, but I can't. I've got to face the truth, whatever the cost."

Cade tossed another log onto the fire. They were absorbed in their own thoughts until only embers were left glowing.

* * *

"The state calls Mr. Arthur Hanson to the stand."

Artie's tall, lean body and angular cheekbones bore almost no resemblance to those of the stocky kid with startled eyes he'd been as a kid. He wore a well-tailored suit and walked confidently to the stand. Cade leaned slightly forward to steal a look at Lyle's bored demeanor. Neither Fletcher nor his team of lawyers looked the least bit concerned about this witness, a lithographer from St. Louis.

Prosecutor Day began the questioning. "Mr. Hanson, you were well acquainted with Lyle Fletcher up until you were fourteen years of age. Is that correct?"

There was an immediate objection. "Your Honor, we've already acknowledged that Mr. Fletcher was involved in pranks and indiscretions when he was young. Whatever story this witness recalls about their childhood has little bearing on the respect Mr. Fletcher has earned as a law-abiding citizen and businessman today."

Mr. Day fired back his reply. "Your Honor, it is incumbent on the State to bring forth witnesses who may shed light on different aspects of Mr. Fletcher's character than what the defense has presented. This character witness has details that are highly relevant to the case against Mr. Fletcher in the death of his employee, Jonas Penway."

Judge McCarty nodded. "The defense has brought in character witnesses on behalf of Mr. Fletcher. It is reasonable for the state to call witnesses to the contrary. However, I'm reluctant to allow testimony of behavior from the defendant's childhood."

"Your Honor, Mr. Hanson has pertinent information as to the motive for a heinous act of violence committed by Mr. Fletcher in September of 1900, three months after the death of Mr. Penway. We intend to show there is a deep-seated violent pattern in Mr. Fletcher's personality that is consistent with how he has behaved all his life."

"Objection overruled. You may proceed, Mr. Day."

Cade watched Lyle squirm around in his chair and glance furtively over the crowded courtroom. Cade lowered his head and listened to Artie describe despicable things he and Lyle had done. He told about the day they had tormented the Dunker boy and left him for dead. Prosecutor Day skillfully brought out the story of Artie's parents trapped in deplorable working conditions at Fletcher's factory and Lyle's threats of having Artie's father fired. Which were then carried out after Artie refused to obey him. There were objections, but Judge McCarty allowed every word. The courtroom fell into a brittle silence as Artie finished his story.

Lyle's defense attorney pointed out that their youthful misdeeds had not prevented Artie from becoming a respectable adult, nor did their childhood "pranks" prevent Lyle from becoming a respectable leader in his community. Then he attacked Artie for inventing the whole Dunker boy story because of a grudge toward the Fletcher family. No one had ever pressed charges for such a crime because it never happened. A murmur went through the courtroom.

Mr. Day said, "The state calls Cade Bauer to the stand."

Cade's legs trembled as he stood, but he paused a moment and stared directly at Lyle, whose face blanched at the sight of him. When Lyle turned away, Cade walked calmly to the stand. Attorney Day asked questions that took Cade and everyone in the courtroom through meticulous details of what had happened back in 1893 when Petey had been attacked.

"On that afternoon in 1893, you have testified that you saw Lyle Fletcher, a high school-aged bully, mocking and tormenting your young, nine-year-old nephew—a small child who suffered an affliction from birth." He paused, allowing the jury time to picture it. "Was that the last time you saw Lyle Fletcher?" Prosecutor Day asked.

"No, I saw him again on Sunday, September 16, 1900, at Congress Lake."

The prosecutor posed a series of questions that moved Cade's testimony along to the point in the story when Cade and Lyle walked together to Jonah's Landing. Mr. Day paused again.

"Mr. Bauer, you've said that you carried a lot of anger toward Lyle for many years. But in September of 1900, you told Lyle you simply wanted to talk like two adults about that incident back in 1893. Is that correct?"

"Yes, I felt he deserved a chance to show that he'd changed."

"That attitude seems rather unusual in our world today. A man who you believe had tried to kill your nine-year-old nephew was finally standing before you, and you only wanted to *talk* with him rather than mete out justice? What would motivate you to do that?"

"I suppose it goes back to my earliest upbringing as a Dunker—that is, a German Baptist Brethren. I was taught that the only way to stop violence from being repeated is to talk out your differences. In good faith, until you come to a consensus. It took me a long time to understand that principle, but I think that is what I hoped could happen between Mr. Fletcher and myself."

"Is that what happened on September 16, 1900, when you met him?"

"At first, I thought so. Mr. Fletcher was very congenial. I expected that we'd be able to work things out. When I brought up the attack on Petey, he suddenly became violent. He knocked me to the ground, and my head hit the boulder. I–I was pinned to the ground. He had his knee on my chest, and he held my arms to the ground." Cade felt his throat constricting, and he coughed. "I–I was shocked by the coldness and the hatred in his face and in his words." Cade swallowed, but he could not find words to go on.

"What happened then, Mr. Bauer?"

The defense attorney rose to his feet. "We object, Your Honor! The defendant is not on trial for the alleged attack this witness is describing. The prosecutor's line of questioning has no relevance to…"

"Overruled. Mr. Bauer, please answer the question."

"He said…" Cade felt a cold sweat forming on his upper lip, and his heart began to pound. "May I–I have some water?" His breath came in shallow gulps, and his hands shook as he took the glass from the Deputy Clerk's hand. Cade tried to calm himself, but like any other time this had happened, he had no control over it.

"Take your time," Mr. Day said quietly. "It is a difficult thing to recall these details.

Cade swallowed. "He said it would appear as if I'd lost my footing and had fallen unconscious in the water. He said, 'I'm sorry, Mr. Bauer, but there is going to be another tragedy at Jonah's Landing.'"

"Lyle Fletcher told you there was going to be tragedy at Jonah's Landing?"

Cade's face was wet, and his voice cracked when he spoke. "Yes, he s–said *a tragedy. Drowning in the same place where the little Dunker misfit had his seizure. You Bauers are an unlucky lot.* That is the last thing I heard. He held my head under the water until … until everything went black."

"How is it that you are here today to tell this story?"

"Two of my friends were looking for me and found me in time. They performed resuscitation and revived me."

"You have testified that Lyle Fletcher dragged you into the water and held you there until you drowned. And were it not for your friends finding you, resuscitating you, and bringing you back to life, you would not be here today. Is that how you understand what happened?"

"Objection! The witness cannot know what would have happened if his friends had not come by."

"Your Honor, I would like to enter a medical report by Dr. Williams, who examined Mr. Bauer, confirming the condition of the witness's lungs were consistent with drowning."

Judge McCarty read the affidavit silently. "Objection overruled. The affidavit of Dr. Williams will be entered into court record. You may continue, Mr. Day."

Stark County Prosecutor Day turned back to the witness box and paused, giving Cade a moment longer to breathe.

"Mr. Bauer, I'm going to rephrase the question. In Dr. Williams's affidavit, he recounts his interview with your rescuers. They said when you were pulled from the lake you had..." The attorney held the paper toward the jury box and read from it. "No heartbeat, pale-white skin, blue lips, and eyes rolled back in the sockets. After they performed resuscitation, you regurgitated, and then your speech came back to you. Dr. Williams states here that this description is consistent with a drowning victim who is being resuscitated. And, after noting the results of his own examination, he concludes that 'Mr. Bauer did indeed drown.' Is that also how you understand what happened on September 16, 1900?"

"Yes, sir."

"And your last memory before drowning was Lyle Fletcher telling you he intended to drown you. Is that correct?"

"Yes, sir."

"And Lyle Fletcher then held your head under the water until you could no longer breathe. After which everything went black."

"Yes, sir. That is what happened."

The prosecutor had no further questions. Cade was prepared for a grueling cross-examination, but the defense attorney had only one question. "Was it not possible, Mr. Bauer, that you had simply fallen on the boulder, had a concussion, and then hallucinated the whole thing?"

Cade paused for a long moment. "I suppose it is possible, but my memory of what happened before his attack and after has never wavered."

As Cade stepped down from the witness box, he hoped to look directly into Lyle's eyes, but the redhead was bent down. Instead, what caught his attention was a face in the far corner of the courtroom, behind where Lyle and the defense team sat. It was Ellie.

He felt the tension drain from his jaw when he saw her. He hadn't realized how much he'd needed her here. He also knew she had heard Artie's story.

The defense asked for a recess until the following day. Judge McCarty agreed and said the trial would reconvene Tuesday morning at ten. He pounded his gavel, and the Cleveland lawyers whisked Lyle out of the courtroom.

Cade made his way to Ellie and sat down beside her while the courtroom emptied. "You came."

"I needed to be with you," she said.

"It means so much to me to have you here, Ellie. Thank you. I guess you heard everything about Artie. I'm sorry I didn't tell you, Ellie." He searched her expression for any judgment. It was better to face it than let his anxiety fester.

"Cade, I do understand why you didn't tell me. I know you were being loyal to him. It only makes me love you more."

"It does?"

She nodded toward the other side of the courtroom, where Artie stood, fidgeting with his hat the way he would have when he was a kid. "Artie's concern for you outweighed his own needs today. You can't ask more of a friend than that."

As they walked toward him, Artie blushed and shifted from one foot to the other. Ellie noticed he avoided looking at her. She extended her hand toward him. "It was extraordinary what you did for Cade today, Artie."

His eyes watered, and he squeezed her hand before letting go. "Thank you, Ellie. That means a lot to me."

Prosecutor Day approached them and laid his hand on Cade's shoulder. "It couldn't have gone better, gentlemen. I don't see any need for you to be here for the duration. It will be all about the Penway case now until the end of the trial. I can have my clerk contact you regarding the results.

"I hope your case goes well," Cade said, shaking the attorney's hand. "It won't be necessary to let me know the results. I think today I got everything I needed. Thank you, sir."

CHAPTER THIRTY-THREE

Peace

The damp snowfall of the previous night had frozen to every meadow stalk and to the needles and cones of the evergreens along the forest path. Cade and Ellie had never walked to the pond during the winter.

"I often think about how peaceful it is at Claybourne Oaks," he said. "I'm glad we could spend an afternoon here before heading back."

Ellie was quiet. There was so much she needed to tell him, and she didn't know how it would land on the terrain of their future together. "I've been thinking of moving my horses here after Daisy foals this spring."

"So I guess you've decided to spend the summer in Ohio."

"Yes. The farmhouse needs renovation, and Flora asked if I would oversee the project."

"You'll be busy." Cade couldn't hide the disappointment in his voice.

Ellie swallowed, trying to release the tightness in her throat. "I had hoped to come back to Philadelphia this summer to be near you, but with Hank and Tilda moving in March, this is the time to make some changes at the farm."

"Is everything all right between us? I'm sorry I've been caught up in the Fletcher trial."

"Everything is fine between us." Ellie slipped her arm around his waist. "The thing I haven't told you yet is that I—I've decided to leave Radcliffe at the end of this school year. I will have enough hours of credit to get a teaching certificate."

"Wh–what?" Cade turned to face her. "I thought you loved studying botany there."

"I did. But I'm frustrated with the curricula. My professors seem to focus on economic trends in horticulture and agriculture as a business. No one teaches about medicinal herbs and the vibrations of plants, as I'd hoped."

"Yeah, the medical model in universities has a very rational bias. Science rarely acknowledges anything beyond what can be measured with a ruler."

"Exactly. I want to learn the things women have been passing down for hundreds of years. My *soul* wants to follow that path. I sometimes feel that Radcliffe puts me at odds with what my soul needs."

"You're describing what I've been feeling, Ellie. There are things I know instinctually about veterinary medicine. Things not found in textbooks. Sometimes I feel I'm losing my natural way of healing the more I work for Gifford. He's all about status and catering to an elite clientele. I thought that was what I wanted. You know, to support us after we're married. But I think it's been putting me at odds with what my soul wants."

Ellie took a deep breath. She had always hesitated discussing gossamer dreams, so fragile in their newness that they could shatter from a careless word or glance. She kept those dreams safe inside herself until they could be looked at from every angle. Until she was certain they had enough substance to bear scrutiny from others. But then she thought of the times Cade had shared his vulnerable side and how she had only loved him more because of it. If they were going to grow old together, she had to risk being vulnerable with him and to trust his love for her. She began slowly. "Flora wants to start a school for women to learn about herbal remedies. The new cottage has space for a classroom and a dormitory upstairs where six students can reside from early spring through autumn. They'd help plant and harvest a garden as part of their training. They'll learn to cook garden vegetables with herbs and roots. But the primary focus of our school will be on the medicinal uses of herbs."

"*Our* school?"

Ellie felt her face blush. "Flora asked me if I'd be interested in teaching the rudiments of botany. We'd be combining both academic and practical approaches to herbal medicine." She swallowed. "It–it's something I really want to do, Cade."

He gazed at her. Her auburn curls were spilling out from under her hat, encircling her lovely face that was peppered with matching freckles. Her eyes shining, almost teary. "Ellie, you never cease to surprise me. It's an exciting plan." His hug lifted her feet off the ground. "I just have one question."

"All right." Ellie's back stiffened.

"Is there room on your farm for a veterinary practice?"

She stared at him for a moment to make sure he was not teasing her. "You'll come back to *Hartville* with me?" she whispered.

"I'll go anywhere with you. But I think Hartville and I have finally made our peace." He kissed her. "I have hardly a penny to give you, but I will put every sinew of my body to work for you."

"Well then, I'll hold you to your promise," she said, lingering in the warmth of his embrace. She pulled away and walked a few steps forward to where the land curved into the pond. "For starters, we'll need an arched trellis built right here. The dahlias will be in bloom in early October. I think I'll weave dahlias, asters, and ivy into the trellis, and I'll carry a matching bouquet."

"October, is it? I think I can arrange that."

She grinned. "And in the future, you'll have to build treehouses in these woods—one for each of our children."

"How many treehouses do you have in mind?"

"Oh, lots! And perhaps another one, just for the two of us."

AUTHOR'S NOTES:

Facts and Fiction in *JONAH'S LANDING*

Ellie and Cade, along with their families and friends, are fictional characters living in historical settings with historical figures of the 1890s.

HARTVILLE, OHIO, and CONGRESS LAKE

I chose Hartville as the location for *Jonah's Landing* because this northeast Ohio community was my hometown. Congress Lake is located a mile and a half from my childhood family's farm.

In prehistoric times the land around Congress Lake was inhabited by Indigenous Mound Builders, who left a mound on the western shore of the spring-fed lake. Later Delaware tribes lived in the region for a century before they were driven westward by European American colonists. Hartville was established on the hilly land south of Congress Lake in the early 1800s.

Area newspapers from the 1880s and 1890s indicate Congress Lake was a hub of social activity drawing visitors from Akron, Canton, and Cleveland. The Connotton Valley Railway built resort facilities on the southwest shore of the lake in 1881, and as many as 5,000 people would attend public events such as hot air balloon shows, picnics, dances, athletic competitions, etc.

William McKinley, then governor of Ohio, was instrumental in transferring land and water rights of Congress Lake from federal jurisdiction to the State of Ohio and soon afterward into the hands of a private club he had organized along with businessmen from Canton. The club was poised to purchase the resort and set its sights on perfecting the title for the remaining shoreline, including its water rights. Newspaper articles note the outcry of bitter feelings amongst the locals when the Congress Lake Club closed its gates to the public for good in 1899. McKinley's original group called themselves the Canton Outing Club. The name of their organization evolved: In 1895 an area newspaper refers to the Congress Lake Outing Club; in 1896, they officially call themselves the Congress Lake Club Company; and by the turn of the century, and thereafter they were known as the Congress Lake Club.

The land and trails described in the novel do not represent the actual shoreline and terrain found at Congress Lake. However, the Spelman icehouse, the railroad spur where passenger coaches detached for weekend outings at Congress Lake, the two-story dance pavilion balanced on wooden pilings, and Charles Sliker's Congress Lake Hotel did actually exist. Other characters, who appear as club members or as employees of the Congress Lake resort, are fictional and do not represent actual persons.

The clearing called Jonah's Landing is a fictional site on Congress Lake. The name is evocative of the biblical story of Jonah, who is consumed by a fear of carrying out his destiny. When Jonah runs away, he's swallowed by a whale. After three days in the belly of the whale Jonah is spat out on land, right back where he must face his destiny again. As Joseph Campbell points out, going into the whale's belly is a necessary part of the hero's journey. For Ellie and Cade, Jonah's Landing is where their belly-of-the-whale journey begins. Eventually, both must return to the place where "Jonah landed" and face their fears.

Claybourne Oaks is a fictional estate in Hartville. However, the description of its muck lands, swamp, and woods mingled with fields and pasture lands could describe many farms in Hartville. Ellie's barn rope experience is an homage to the rope swing in my grandfather's barn, where generations of kids flew across the haymow.

Stark County Prosecutor Robert Henry Day was a notable historical figure who later served on the Ohio Supreme Court.

Reference books with insights about 1890s Hartville include: *A History of Hartville Ohio* (1976) by James W. McPherson III; *Introducing Lake Township* (2003) by Elmer S. Yoder; and *The Church of the Brethren in Northeastern Ohio* (1963) by Edgar G. Diehm.

OGONTZ SCHOOL FOR YOUNG LADIES

The Ogontz school, a private boarding school for privileged young women, existed from 1850– 1950. First known as The Chestnut Street Female Seminary in Philadelphia, the school moved a few miles north of the city to Ogontz, the country estate of Civil War financier Jay Cooke, in 1883. Archival documents and memorabilia for the Ogontz School for Young Ladies contain decades of yearbooks and the student-produced monthly magazines, the *Ogontz Mosaic*, which provide valuable insights into their remarkable education. Miss Sylvia Eastman and Miss Frances Bennett were beloved educators and principals who shaped the progressive program, including the military drill for girls and the scholastic excellence of the school.

DUNKERS

In *Jonah's Landing*, Cade Bauer identifies as a Dunker boy while growing up with his sister Mandy and her husband Daniel Holtz. The German Baptist Brethren church members were commonly referred to as "Dunkers," "Tunkers," or "Dunkards" because of their custom of adult baptism by full immersion. Dunker derives from the German word, *tunken*, meaning to immerse, to dip.

Founded in Schwartzenau (in Southwest Germany) in 1708, this Anabaptist group was led by Alexander Mack. They suffered religious persecution until they emigrated to Pennsylvania in two groups in 1719 and 1729. The Dunkers were faithful to the tenets of pacifism and New Testament scriptures. They used the life and teachings of Jesus as the model for their own lives. To become a member of their congregation, an adult knelt in water, traditionally in a river or lake, made a confession of faith, and was immersed three times forward "in the name of the Father, and of the Son, and of the Holy Ghost." Before the twentieth century, Dunker services were conducted in high German, though most members spoke a low German dialect known as Pennsylvania Dutch at home. Their dark, unadorned attire of the 1890s was characteristic of the plain people such as Old Order Mennonites or Amish today.

Dunkers were among the earliest settlers in what would later become Hartville, Ohio. The Nimishillen congregation of German Baptist Brethren was established about five miles south of Congress Lake in 1804. By the early twentieth century, after several schisms in their wider brotherhood, they adopted a new name, the Church of the Brethren, which is the largest denomination to emerge from the early Dunkers.

UNIVERSITY OF PENNSYLVANIA SCHOOL OF VETERINARY MEDICINE

Dr. Alexander Gifford and his elite equine clinic are fictional. All other faculty members mentioned in *Jonah's Landing* were actual historical figures. The curriculum for the veterinary students and the description of the veterinary school compound closely follow historical documents and archival photographs. The Veterinary Department's Fête Accompli banquet at the year's end, however, was a playful bit of fiction.

DR. KARL TURBAN'S SANATORIUM, DAVOS, SWITZERLAND

Alexander Spengler founded the first clinic in Davos, Switzerland for sufferers of consumption (tuberculosis) in the early 1860s. The alpine altitude, cold air and abundant sunshine were thought to be healing elements. Davos took on a festive atmosphere as it attracted other luxury, resort-type healing hotels which were *open* to both healthy and ill patrons. In 1889, Dr. Karl Turban created a unique *closed* tuberculosis sanatorium, which had a strict regimen for patients that became the model for later sanatoria through the 1950s.

ACKNOWLEDGEMENTS

My thanks to Reid Addis, Philadelphian architect, historian, and city guide, who designed a private walking tour of the 1890s Philadelphia Ellie and Cade would have known. His research, knowledge of architecture, and insightful narrative have been so helpful to me.

I appreciate Lillian Hansberry, Library Services Specialist at Penn State Abington, for her warm assistance and informative tour of the collections in the Ogontz Archive Room.

Thank you to the late Steven C. Espenschied, curator for the Lake Township Historical Society, to Ruth Sturgill, trustee for the LTHS, and to Paul Kamerer, who at ninety-three years of age had an exceptional recollection of his lifelong residence in Hartville and of his father's stories of Congress Lake. All three opened windows into Hartville's history.

I wish to thank Allister Thompson, an excellent editor who has smoothed rough edges of *Jonah's Landing* with a meticulous eye for order and punctuation. I appreciate his sensitive ear attuned to my writer's voice. His sound advice has been invaluable.

My thanks to Laura Boyle for her creative cover design and layouts for *Jonah's Landing*.

Thank you to Barbara Kyle, whose insightful questions about my protagonists inspired a few new twists to the story.

Special thanks to writer and friend Barbara Susan Booth for the many years we've met to discuss, inspire, and encourage each other's writing.

Deepest gratitude goes to my husband, Paul Benedetto, who offers valuable insights when I am struggling with a piece, tirelessly edits my rough drafts, reflects back to me the beauty of a particular passage, and celebrates every milestone reached.

Finally, my family's historical records, diaries, and photographs have contributed valuable details for many settings in *Jonah's Landing*.

9 781068 807602